Becoming

Home

Kirsten Hunt Kowalski

Author's Note

This story is a work of biographical fiction. As it is based on the biography of a Home – a character which has no physical voice – I have crafted the events and dialogue in this novel from the stories told to me by the family of which the Home is a member. I have taken significant creative liberties with these stories. While much of this book is based on true events, many of the events and characters are complete fabrications, born solely of my own imagination.

DEDICATION

For my Family.

We are always "Home" when we are together – no matter where we are

PROLOGUE

I hear them arguing. Their voices reverberate through me as they discuss my fate. They have no idea that I am listening or that I *can* listen. There is a lot they don't know about me. There is a lot they don't know about each other. In fact, I know more about their family than all of them put together.

I have been with them since before they were born; and with their parents and grandparents and ancestors – for over a century. I have witnessed their joy, their pain, their stress, their achievements, and their failures. I have heard them talking to each other, to their friends, to themselves – even in their sleep. Even after their deaths. I know their habits, their secrets, and I know their hearts. I know this family better than anyone. I am one of them, whether they realize it or not.

And yet they talk about me like I am not here – like I do not matter.

I am old, and I am tired. My bones ache and groan with the weight of two hundred years of giving everything I have for the

1

people I have sheltered - for this family. I have kept them warm through long, dark New England winters. I have kept them safe through blinding blizzards and howling hurricanes. I have celebrated their births, their graduations, and their weddings. I have held them on their deathbeds and even allowed their souls to linger when they weren't quite ready to leave. I've lost parts of me that they no longer found useful. I have grown for them when they have needed more of me. My entire existence has been centered on being a Home for this family.

So when I hear one of them raise his voice and say: "Jesus Christ you guys, do we really want to kill ourselves trying to keep something none of us really want? It's time to move on. It's *just* a house!" My foundation rattles with anger and frustration and my roof sags with sadness.

I am much more than "just a house" to these people.
I am Family.

I am Home.

Chapter 1

PRESENT DAY

The Freeman siblings are gathered around the pedestal mahogany table in the formal dining room. Alden, Caroline, Thomas, and Anna Freeman have returned to their family home in the small, New England town of Scituate, Massachusetts to discuss what to do about their inheritance – the almost two hundred year old house they are all gathered in. A house that has been in the family for five generations.

The ivory brocade wallpaper that their mother hung over thirty years earlier has begun to yellow and peel at the seams, giving the room a worn, tired look.

Caroline is staring at a corner of the table where a jumble of numbers is permanently engraved into the wood. She is instantly eleven years old again, working on her sixth grade math homework. "Caroline, this table belonged to your grandmother! *Please* use a pad!!" her mother would scold to no avail. That was over forty years ago.

Caroline stares at the decades-old, imprinted math wondering how many other memories lurk in this room, waiting to be rediscovered if she would dare to lift her head and look up. But she is exhausted – too physically and emotionally drained to deal with old memories right now. And sitting in this room, at this table, feeling the past tug at her, demanding her attention, is only making things worse.

She thinks about the math. What is one divided by four? Because finding a solution to that equation is why the siblings have traveled from different corners of the world to be here. How do you split one house between four people? Seems it should be easy - they each get one-fourth of its value. Sell it, distribute the proceeds and, voila! But what happens when you multiply that one house by over one hundred years of family history? And then divide the four by the number of siblings who can't bear to sell. Add in there somewhere the miles that lie between where the house sits and where each of them live and then factor in the exponential value of each sibling's emotional ties. Or lack thereof. The equation just became much more difficult and coming up with the wrong answer could have devastating, long-term consequences. Caroline's head begins to throb.

"Jesus Christ, you guys," her younger brother Thomas, is saying, his voice rising in frustration. "Do we really want to kill ourselves trying to keep something none of us really want? It's time to move on. It's *just* a house!"

Caroline cringes inwardly and traces "2a-4=4" with the tip of her finger. *Why didn't Mom refinish this table after we all grew up and stopped ruining her nice things?* Caroline wonders, shutting out Thomas's rant. She wishes the solution to their current problem were as easy as the solution to the mathematic equation at her fingertips.

Thomas, who was once the smiley, happy-go-lucky sibling who Caroline always suspected was her mother's favorite, has risen from his chair and his six-foot-two-inch frame is pacing the room, creating palpable tension. He is quicker to anger nowadays and Caroline detects the faint smell of stale alcohol on his breath when he passes behind her. Is he drunk or just hung over? Not that it really matters. *Hell, we all have needed a drink or two this week* she thinks. Caroline knows she certainly has. In fact, a hint of a headache has been lingering at the base of her skull all day thanks to the bottle of Pinot Noir she and her sister, Anna, the youngest by seven years, finished off last night as they recounted some of their fondest memories of childhood. They had laughed remembering the time their brothers got into a brawl over a basketball game, which had escalated to the point of Thomas ripping the front door off its hinges and Alden toppling the refrigerator, its contents spilling across the kitchen floor. Those boys had wanted to kill each other that day. Caroline, then fourteen, had barricaded herself and five-year-old Anna in her bedroom to escape their brothers' rampage. Of course, it hadn't been very funny at the time. Their mother had been furious. She had actually cried when she saw that the glass storm door with her father's etched monogram had shattered. Caroline shakes her head slowly in disbelief at all they had put their mother through.

Thank God these walls can't talk, she thinks.

Caroline draws in a breath and forces herself to look at Thomas who is pacing the room, his agitation growing more apparent with every heavy-footed step. Caroline, who spent twenty five years making a living as a lawyer representing companies who developed big shopping centers where people's homes used to stand, understands better than anyone that sometimes change is necessary ("highest and best use" is a term thrown around in her field all the time). But as she listens to the two hundred year old oak floors creak and groan as Thomas paces, she wonders: *Is he right? Is this 'just a house?'*

Caroline glances toward the tiny bedroom just off the dining room – the room where their mother died less than six months ago - the same room that had been their grandmother's before that. Caroline's chest tightens as she remembers sleeping in that room as a little girl with her Nana snoring softly beside her. She closes her eyes and can still hear the soft static and chatter of a.m. talk radio that Nana played all night to chase away the deafening quiet. Caroline always thought that her grandmother's need for constant background noise was odd. Caroline was the opposite – she liked complete quiet. Even the hum of electricity running through the house, which was undetectable to most people, bothered her at times. She was a thinker and she needed the quiet so she could immerse herself deep into her thoughts without distraction. But now it dawns on her that perhaps that's exactly why her grandmother liked the constant noise - because it distracted her from the traffic in her head. Maybe the chatter had helped drown out unpleasant thoughts or angst that would have otherwise stolen her from her slumber?

Caroline stares at the bedroom door, which is now closed and tries to picture her grandparents sleeping there as newlyweds almost one hundred years ago. That room is where their three children were conceived, including Caroline's mother. But they are all gone now. Nana and Papa each died in this house many years ago. Caroline's parents had both died here. The lives of this family were created, lived fully and ended within these walls.

So, then, how can it be "just a house"?

Caroline turns her gaze to Anna, who is crying and shaking her head in response to everything Thomas says. Anna is the youngest of the four and the only one who grew up in the house. The others were older and had been born in rapid succession – Alden, then Caroline eighteen months later, then Thomas two years after that. Anna didn't arrive until seven years later. She was the baby – born in the final years of their father's career in the Navy and the only one who didn't spend her childhood moving from place to place. She had been merely four years old when their family moved to Scituate to stay. As such, her connection to this house was stronger than that of the other siblings. Anna and Thomas have been arguing for over thirty minutes. Never one to refrain from speaking her mind, Anna glares at Thomas.

"Just a house? Are you freaking kidding me, Thomas? This house has been in our family for five generations. FIVE! Just because you decided long ago that were too cool for Scituate doesn't mean that we should just all turn our backs on our heritage, our history, our *home*!"

Thomas stops pacing and sighs impatiently. "Anna, I'm not exactly the only one who left you know. What about Caroline?" he gestures to Caroline who stares at her fingernails. "She picked up and moved to Florida when she was twenty! And Alden moved around in the Navy his entire adult life and ultimately retired in San Diego. He lives thousands of miles away. Do you really think either of them is going to ever live in this house again? In fact, none of us, except you, grew up here. This house is not 'home' to us."

"Hey now, hold on," Alden and Caroline start at the same time. Caroline nods deferentially to Alden. "Let's all just calm down," he says, slowly in his deep voice. "I think we can all agree that this house is special and, while I may not live here anymore, I can still appreciate the history and the sentimental value here. We at least need to explore our options and respect the history of this house."

"And of our family," Caroline whispers. She then clears her throat, adding louder, "This house will always be 'home' - to all of us, whether we still live here or not. Obviously Anna is more emotional about it because she lived here most of her life. We (motioning to Alden, Thomas, and herself) moved a lot as kids and then we all dispersed after high school. So, it may not be quite as meaningful for some of us, but I think we can all recognize the importance of our heritage and what it would mean to just sell the house to some stranger after all these years."

"It would mean we would all have a little money in our pockets instead of bleeding out trying to maintain this shithole," Thomas cuts in.

"Fuck you, Thomas," Anna spats, crying harder. Alden shakes his head in frustration. Caroline sighs and rubs her temples. She knew this wasn't going to be easy. She looks down at the table. Math. Who knew algebra would look so easy one day compared to real life problems?

✝✝✝✝

I have been listening to the conversation between the siblings and absorbing the mixed emotions as they discuss my fate like I'm not even here. But, of course, I am here. I surround them. My floor supports their weight. My roof protects them from the slight drizzle of rain that has begun to fall outside. My walls shelter them and absorb their voices and their energy. I feel each and every one of them. Thomas's impatience radiates through me. Anna's sadness seeps heavily into my walls and makes me sag. Alden's calmness soothes and keeps me strong. The energy from the three of them is palpable and identifiable. It is what I feel from Caroline that leaves me confused. She is bubbling with uncertainty and conflict. She doesn't know what she wants. I can feel that she understands Thomas's perspective and, practically speaking, she knows he is right. But she also empathizes with Anna. And she misses her mother. I see her looking around the room, desperately searching for something - for an answer. She hopes to find it in my rooms. I see that she wants to feel the connection to her past — to those who made me a "Home." For, only when she fully understands the history of our home and the lives lived here can she make a decision about the future. She is struggling to know the people, the relationships, the happiness and the pain. She is begging me to tell her the stories that live within me.

Well, if she wants my story, perhaps it is time to tell it. Let's start at the beginning …

Chapter 2

BIRTH OF A HOUSE

I was born in 1847 in the small, seaside town of Scituate, Massachusetts. A young farmer and carpenter named John Litchfield built me. John was a descendant of Lawrence Litchfield, one of Scituate's first settlers. He inherited several acres of land on "North Hill" from his grandfather. The land sat on high ground, with far off ocean views and dark, rich soil perfect for farming. Young John dug my foundation by hand and secured it with the fieldstone he encountered as he dug. As strapping and strong as young John was, he was no physical match for the large glacier rock that he struck while digging. Most men would have given up with they realized the rock was as big as a house, but, while John lacked machinery and tools to help him crush and remove the rock, he possessed stubborn determination. Rather than allow the giant granite to thwart his plans, he simply built me on top of it. If you visit my cellar today, you will find the giant rock upon which I sit. It is as solid and strong today as it was almost 200 years ago.

John built me small, but he built me with care and skill. He gave me one bedroom, a living area with a fireplace, and a front parlor where he entertained visitors. Steep stairs led from the front door to a spacious attic topped with a pitched roof. In the back, down a hall, he built a kitchen area with another fireplace. A large barn stood tall in the back field and a small out-house sat discreetly beside the barn. I was small and practical. I was a good house.

The years following my birth went by slowly and quietly. John married but he and his wife were not able to have children. During the years that families *were being torn apart by the country's Civil War, John provided food and provisions for the townspeople from the fields surrounding me. By 1902 John was an old man and could no longer farm. His wife had passed away and he moved to Connecticut. John sold the farm and me to Ned Vickery, a local stable owner with vast wealth who was acquiring land all over Scituate. Mr. Vickery already had a home and I was simply investment property for him. Over the next several years, I was rented to various farmers who lived under my roof and farmed my land. Some were single, some had small families. None stayed more than a year or two. During The Great War, I sat empty and alone. I was, in those early years, just a house.*

Black Tuesday and the collapse of the stock market in 1929 changed my fate and set a course that would bring me to life in a way many houses never experience. Mr. Vickery, like most wealthy men at the time, had invested heavily in the stock market and suffered great losses that fateful October day. To make matters worse for the Vickery family, the rise in popularity of the automobile rendered the stable business moot. Nobody had the need for the vast stables Mr. Vickery owned, as Scituate residents began trading in their horses for the faster and fancier automobiles made affordable by Henry Ford. Mr. Vickery quickly fell on hard times and was forced to sell many acres of his land. In the summer of 1930, I was sold, along with fifty acres of land, to a lovely young couple, Frank Williams and his wife, Grace. The Williams', who had not invested heavily in stocks, had remained virtually unaffected by the stock market crash and were quite wealthy. They purchased many acres of land throughout Scituate. Frank and Grace lived in a grand, sprawling home on the same road, just down the hill, and I served as a house for their chauffer, a single man with fondness for whiskey who lived quietly within my walls for several years until he retired and moved away. Mr. Williams hired a new chauffer but the man had a large family and a home of his own nearby. He requested he be paid a salary rather than live in my tiny spaces. So, once again, I stood, empty and lonely on the hill. The fields became overgrown and dust and spider webs decorated my windowsills.

Then, one day in 1935, Grace walked through my front door with a young couple whose eyes sparkled with barely contained excitement, a hint of promise, and an overabundance of love. The young woman Grace called "Evelyn" stepped timidly into my front hall and looked around my rooms, wide-eyed, and with an appreciation I hadn't felt since I was first built. I knew immediately

10

that things were about to change for me. Instead of saying my rooms were "small" she used words like "cozy" and "charming." My wooden floors were not "uneven" or "worn", they were "beautiful" and "had character." My fields weren't a tangle of overgrown weeds; they were "a wonderland for children." Children! When I saw the way her male companion watched her as she explored my halls, I felt his love all the way to my foundation. Before that day, I had been content to be "just a house." But suddenly I knew that I was finally going to be a true home for a future family.

But to understand fully how I became one of them – how I became "Home", you must first get to know my family.

Chapter 3

EVELYN

Evelyn Johanna Larson was born in 1909 to a seed farmer who had immigrated to America from Norway and settled his family in Hanska, Minnesota. Evelyn was the second born of eleven children. Life on the family farm consisted of helping her mother with the cooking, cleaning, caring for her brothers and sisters and helping her father with farm chores from sun-up to sun-down. Evelyn grew up strong and resilient, and quite beautiful with bright green eyes, velvet skin, and blonde hair. She was petite at only five foot one. She was thin but had just enough curves to make the neighboring farm boys stare as they rode by on their tractors on the way to town. She moved with the poise and grace of a dancer. By looking at her, one would not have guessed she worked all day on a farm.

Like most girls in the small town of Hanska in the early 1900's, Evelyn was expected to work on the family farm until she married. Then, she would move to her husband's farm where she would raise her own children in the same manner. But, Evelyn despised farm life. She loved the animals but hated the hard, dirty work of running a farm. Even more, she loathed the life of a farmer's wife. The early mornings, up hours before dawn, the gardening, the milking the cows, the constant cooking and cleaning and washing – none of it appealed to her. She spent her free time daydreaming of escaping to a big city full of enchanting people, the latest fashions, and plenty of excitement!

"Life isn't always what you think it should be and it isn't always exciting," Evelyn's mother would warn. "Sometimes you have to make the best of what the good Lord has given you and learn to love what you have. We are blessed with family, a roof over our heads, food in our bellies, and all the blessings of a life filled with love, family, and good friends."

Evelyn tried to see it her mother's way but she didn't understand why she couldn't live in the city and have all of those things as well. Surely families in the cities had homes with roofs and food and plenty of friends to boot. She was confident they also had love. Evelyn saw the glossy magazines in the local market depicting city women with their colorful dresses adorned with lace, ornate hats on their perfectly coiffed heads, satin gloves, and silk stockings that ended in ankle-strapped heels made of supple leather. Who wouldn't love them? This was what Evelyn wanted; she had longed for a taste of that world since as far back as she could remember.

Dr. Richard Hanson was the only dentist in Hanska. He was short and almost ten years older than Evelyn, but he was kind and not unattractive, with thick dark hair and soulful brown eyes. His family owned the farm just a few miles down the road from the Larson farm. Richard had been one of the only boys in town to leave the farm after high school to attend the university in Michigan. Evelyn, only eight years old when Richard had left home, had been envious and impressed with his decision to go so far away and pursue his dreams in the big city. When Richard returned home during breaks from his studies, Evelyn always tagged along with her parents on their social visits to his parents farm. She would sit and listen, captivated as Richard described his college experiences and life in the city.

After graduating from his undergraduate studies, Richard enrolled in dental school in Chicago. Shortly after Evelyn's graduation from high school, *Doctor* Richard Hanson returned to Minnesota to open his own dental practice just ten miles North of

13

Hanska in the larger town of New Ulm. New Ulm was about as close to a bustling city as they got in Hanska, and, while it certainly was no Chicago, at least there were stores and restaurants and things to do. Evelyn would see Richard when she accompanied her mother to New Ulm to shop for fabric or household items one couldn't find in the small general stores in Hanska. Her mother always made it a point to stop by "that smart Richard Hanson's" office to say hello. Evelyn also saw Richard when he traveled to Hanska on the weekends to visit his parents at the farm. Sometimes, after dinner, he would stop by the Larson farm in his new, silver Ford to invite Evelyn for a drive and an ice cream cone. As their families had been friends as long as she could remember, Evelyn didn't think much of the fact that Dr. Hanson paid her so much attention. She simply enjoyed talking with him and asking him questions about life in the city. Sometimes, after Richard had traveled for a convention or dental conferences, he would surprise Evelyn with a small trinket from his travels – an ornate silver spoon from Minneapolis, or a gold charm from Columbus. Richard was easy to talk to and over the next couple of years the two became quite close.

It came as no surprise to anyone, except Evelyn, when Richard asked Evelyn to marry him shortly after her nineteenth birthday. Evelyn was stunned by the proposal. She had grown to love Richard like family, but she certainly didn't feel a burning passion or even intense emotion for him. There were no butterflies in her stomach when they were together. *And isn't that what you were supposed to feel for someone you were going to marry?* She thought. *Shouldn't there be butterflies, or some sort of fireworks or at least a spark - like in the books and the movies?* Sure, Richard was kind, thoughtful, and reliable and she cared for him deeply. But, for Evelyn, love was supposed to be more than that; at least a bit of passion would be nice. She declined his proposal, gently explaining that she cared for him but that she just wasn't ready for marriage. Evelyn's mother had shaken her head at her daughter and clucked, "You have your head in the clouds, my dear girl. You have always had your head in the clouds, always wanting more. Sometimes you have to see what is in front of you and count your blessings." But the thought of settling for something less than exhilarating left Evelyn feeling like a flower planted in the shade.

Richard was a patient man and, although his feelings were hurt by her refusal, he knew she was young and still had immature notions of love. So he continued courting her, confident that she would soon understand how much he had to offer her.

At the end of 1928, Evelyn enrolled in Martin Luther Normal College in New Ulm to train to be a teacher. She commuted daily in her father's old gray touring car he let her borrow to attend classes. She continued seeing Dr. Hanson during the course of the next year but also went on dates with other boys her own age, almost always set up by friends who wanted to double date. Most of the boys she met were committed to take over their family's farm, like lab mice born and raised for one purpose, happily running through tunnels built for them, leading them to their predetermined destiny. Others were college boys just looking for a good time. They bored Evelyn with their egoist attitudes and heavy drinking. After several unsuccessful dates, Evelyn found herself preferring Dr. Hanson's company.

In October 1929, the stock market collapsed and the country was sent into a panic. Men who were wealthy on Monday were destitute by Tuesday night. In the following months, the economy spiraled downward and Evelyn's friends began losing their jobs or quitting college because their families could no longer afford the tuition. Farmers began losing their land to banks that were foreclosing on everything in sight. Fortunately, Evelyn's father had been conservative and hadn't joined the rush to expand the farm with heavily mortgaged land purchases like many of their neighbors. Nonetheless, it became more difficult to sell their crops and the Larson's, like everyone in Hanska, fell on hard times. Evelyn's older sister, Mabel, moved to Boston with her new husband after the bank took their farm. People were desperate and there was no work in Hanska. Evelyn was forced to quit school and help more on the farm and care for her younger siblings while her parents devoted their time to selling their crops, sometimes having to travel long distances to do so.

Richard, who was one of the only two dentists in New Ulm, was able to remain in business. Despite that many patients had to forgo routine, non-emergent dental care and sometimes he had to accept payment in chickens or other trade, he was getting by. He and Evelyn continued to spend time together, having picnics in the park or just walking past the now-shuttered shops and dark stores in town. One afternoon in April 1932, the sun shone brightly and the air held a hint of spring. Richard again asked Evelyn to be his bride. They had been sitting on a bench under a large oak tree in the town common, watching the birds and squirrels scurry up and down the brick pathway. Richard had taken her hand and looked deep into her green eyes.

"Marry me Evelyn," he pleaded softly. "I've been patient and you are no longer a girl. You are a woman on her way to be a wonderful teacher. And I'm a thirty-two year old dentist without a wife. I have a solid practice and, despite the financial difficulties in the world right now, I can support you. You can finish up your studies. We can have a good life. I love you. Say you will marry me."

Evelyn had stared into Richard's kind brown eyes and knew what she should do. They had become such good friends and she did enjoy his company. If she married Richard, she would be free of the farm. She would have a stable home in a time of so much uncertainty. There was no reason she shouldn't accept Richard's proposal; except that, no matter how much she wanted to be, she simply was not in love with him. Her mother's words rang in her head: "Romantic love is for fairy tales. True, long lasting love is something that grows with time. See what is in front of you and count your blessings." Surely some flowers did just fine without the sun. Evelyn took a deep breath, smiled at Richard and, trying her hardest to sound excited, replied, "Yes. Yes, Dr. Hanson, I will marry you." Richard had been ecstatic, lifting her and spinning her around, kissing her cheeks, her forehead, and her lips. Evelyn had laughed and kissed him back and actually felt happy in that moment. But, after he had driven her home, she went to bed that night and allowed her true feelings to wash over her and she cried herself to sleep, weeping for her permanently shadowed dreams.

Richard wanted to marry right away. But Evelyn was in less of a hurry and talked him into a longer engagement. With Richard's help, she had been able to re-enroll in school and wanted to finish her studies before the wedding. They set a date for September, 1934. The weather would be lovely in Minnesota in September and they planned to be married in the courtyard of the Lutheran chapel at Evelyn's school, with reception to follow at Richard's home. Times were still hard and, while Richard was doing well, money was nonetheless tight for both the Larson's and the Hanson's. It certainly wasn't going to be a high society affair but at least it wouldn't be a farm wedding.

As the months went by, Evelyn continued her studies and she spent most evenings with Richard, dining in his home or walking through the streets of New Ulm, window shopping and making wedding plans. She purchased a lovely ivory, silk/satin wedding gown that was simple but classy and quite pretty, and hung stylishly on her slender frame. They would have white daisies and the local baker, who still owed Richard money for the crowns Richard did for the baker's wife, would make the cake. The details were coming together and Evelyn felt herself resigning to the idea of being Mrs. Doctor Richard Hanson – even getting a bit excited.

In May, just a few weeks before Evelyn was to graduate, Mabel wrote to inform the family that she and her husband had both found work in Boston and were living in a modest apartment in the North End. She invited Evelyn to come and stay with her during July. "We have an extra room and it would be lovely if you would come and join us for the month. Please come! I know how much you have always wanted to be in a city and there really is no city like Boston for the Fourth of July. Come now before you are an old doctor's wife and you don't have time for us common folk!" *Dentist*, Evelyn thought. *Dentist's wife*. But she had laughed at her sister's tactics, especially since her sister ought to know she didn't need to be begged. A whole month in Boston! It was her dream come true. Evelyn's parents agreed to pay for the train fare as a graduation gift. Her mother had been reluctant, already worried that the costs for the wedding would be too high. But Evelyn's father, who had always loved Evelyn's adventurous spirit and travel lust and knew all too well that once she was Mrs. Richard Hanson she would not have such opportunities, had convinced his wife that it would be good for Evelyn to get away and spend time with her sister.

A mere two months later, Evelyn Larson, the farm girl from Minnesota, stood in the center of an elaborate ballroom at the Copley Plaza in Boston, attending the wedding of a young banker friend of Mabel's. The reception was straight out of one of her glossy magazines. The Great Depression had been left at the door, blatantly uninvited to this elaborate party. As she stood in the most beautiful room she had ever seen, wearing an exquisite gown she had borrowed from one of Mabel's friends, and watching people who looked like movie stars drink champagne and dance, she thought to herself, *"This is everything I've ever wanted. How will I ever go back to Hanska after this?"*

In that moment, she had no way of knowing how her life was about to change.

Chapter 4

EDWARD
1934

Edward Lockhart leaned his six foot three, lanky frame on the edge of the sleek, wood-paneled bar in the Oak Room at the Fairmont Copley Plaza Hotel in downtown Boston. A twenty foot high, gilded, coffered ceiling rose high above him and hundreds of crystals dripped from its massive chandeliers. Edward was sure he had never seen anything so breathtaking in all of his twenty-eight years. But his awe had nothing to do with the glitz that surrounded him. He was used to that. Rather, his attention was focused on a fair-haired girl standing in the center of the grand ballroom, just at the edge of the dance floor. She wore a green, low-back gown with tiered ruffles climbing from her heels to her waist. Her blonde hair was pinned in a low bun at the nape of her long, graceful neck with perfectly placed golden waves framing her face. Her large, green eyes glowed, enhanced by the dress, as she looked nervously and shyly at the crowd of posh wedding guests, none of whom she seemed to know. She stood alone and she stood out. She wasn't one of the sophisticated, sleek city girls dressed in ivory, black, or gold elaborate silk gowns, who stood gossiping in tight circles. Rather, this girl was like a colorful wildflower haphazardly growing in the middle of a perfectly manicured landscape. Edward, who had lived in the Boston area all of his life, knew immediately that this girl was not part of the typical Boston scene and he found her refreshing, endearing, and completely irresistible. He had been staring at her for several minutes when his friend, Doug, clapped him on the back, rousing him from his trance. Edward audibly sucked in air, realizing he had been holding his breath.

"Oh boy, really?" Doug laughed as he looked in the direction Edward had been staring. "That one, huh? She's a looker – in a homegrown sort of way. She clearly isn't from around here. She looks lonely - I think I'll go over and ask her to dance."

"Jesus, Doug, the poor girl will faint at the sight of your ugly mug," Edward laughed, shoving his friend gently to the side. "You'd better leave that to me."

As Edward buttoned his dark grey Filene's suit jacket and sauntered across the dance floor toward the girl, he heard Doug chuckle, "Don't scare her away, Lurch." Edward flipped Doug the finger behind his back, reaching the other end of the dance floor in only four strides. He confidently sidled up next to the girl, who was looking down, fiddling with her fingers.

"May I have the pleasure of this dance?" Edward asked, holding his hand out as the girl raised her head, her bright eyes wide with surprise. Nobody at this wedding had so much as said hello since she had arrived.

"Oh! Well, um, I uh…" the girl stammered as her right hand nervously tucked a blond curl behind her ear and her eyes darted up to Edward's and then back down toward the floor. "I'm, uh, here with my sister," she offered awkwardly, silently cursing her nervousness and lack of sophistication.

Edward offered his left elbow to the girl's side and smiled broadly. "Well, when your sister returns from wherever she has gone off to, I will be happy to return you to this very spot – unless of course you think she might like to dance with us. We would certainly make the social pages in the Globe AND the Herald in that case," Edward winked at her and raised his eyebrows.

A giggle escaped the girl before she realized a lady should be shocked by such a suggestion. Composing herself, she raised her eyes with a half-hearted attempt at a scornful expression. But when her eyes met the twinkling blue eyes of the tall, handsome stranger whose arm remained bent toward her, begging her to take it, her face softened and the only response she could muster was to place her right hand through his arm and allow him to lead her to the dance floor.

"I'm Evelyn," the girl said as Edward turned her toward him and placed his right arm around her back and lifted their enjoined hands for a waltz. "Evelyn Larson."

"Pleasure to meet you, Evelyn Larson," Edward breathed into Evelyn's ear as he pulled her closer than she had expected. "I'm Edward Lockhart. My friends call me Eddie. You can call me Mr. Lockhart until you decide that we can be friends."

Evelyn laughed. She appreciated a good sense of humor. And something about this confident, charming man made her feel at ease. He towered over her, leaving her feeling tiny but also safe and protected with his strong arms around her. Her heart began to race and she felt slightly dizzy. She knew right then, deep in her gut, past the fluttery nauseated feeling that had come on suddenly, that she would be calling this man "Eddie" one day.

Edward and Evelyn enjoyed several dances without speaking, losing themselves in the music and the easy rhythm their bodies seemed to instantly share. As the music faded after the third waltz, Evelyn nodded toward a pretty brunette who stood at the edge of the dance floor watching them with an amused smile. "My sister, Mabel, is back," she said.

"Well, I see good looks run in the family," Edward replied, his lips just inches from Evelyn's left ear, sending a shiver down her spine. "I think I actually *will* ask her if she wants to join us – you know, spice up this party a bit!" Edward started toward Mabel. Without thinking, Evelyn grabbed Edward's arm and pulled him back to her, her face blushing bright pink as he spun back, his body bumping against hers.

"Ahhh, I see Miss Larson. You want to keep me all to yourself!" Edward teased, winking down at Evelyn who was now crimson with embarrassment.

"Don't be ridiculous," Evelyn scoffed, trying to hide the trembles caused by the unexpected contact of their bodies. "I'm simply ensuring you don't do anything to tarnish my reputation in this town before it even gets started."

Edward threw his head back and laughed. "Well, Miss Larson, I'm afraid you've picked the wrong dance partner, then. Your reputation is likely already on the line now that you have been seen dancing with the likes of me."

She looked up at him and raised an eyebrow. But before she could ask what he meant, he twirled her around as the band started a jazzy tune. Nothing more was said. They just danced. As they did, Evelyn glanced at her left hand resting on Edward's broad shoulder and felt both guilt and relief that she had decided to leave her engagement ring in her makeup case. She had been nervous about wearing it out in the city. At the time, she had had no idea that what should have worried her were handsome dance partners.

By the end of the night, Edward knew he needed to see Evelyn again. As the wedding band played the last song and guests began dispersing into the Boston night, Edward escorted Evelyn to Mabel, who had been sitting at a table talking with friends and eyeing them curiously while they danced.

"Well, here you are, Miss Larson. As promised, you are safely delivered back to your sister. I guess we won't be making the papers after all," Edward said warmly, gazing down at Evelyn with a look that caused her sister's right eyebrow to raise. After introductions, during which Edward managed to charm Mabel and her friends, Edward turned back to Evelyn.

"May I call on you next week?"

Mabel's head snapped toward Evelyn, her eyebrows raised with curious anticipation. Evelyn cast her eyes guiltily to the side and bit her lip. She had just had such a wonderful time dancing with this man, but she knew she couldn't lead him on. She was only in town for a few weeks. Her life was in Minnesota – with another man!

"Thank you for the dance, Mr. Lockhart," Evelyn said, looking slowly up at the man whose arms she could still feel around her waist even though they now stood apart. Her eyes bore into his, almost pleadingly; filling him with a sudden sadness that simultaneously surprised and confused him. "I had a lovely time, but ..."

"As I said before, my friends call me Eddie," Edward interrupted before she could continue. "So, next week it is?" Edward meant for this to be a statement of fact, rather than the question it became as the words escaped his mouth. Normally confident and certain, something about Evelyn had put Edward off his game. He felt uncharacteristically awkward and unsure. His eyes searched hers expectantly.

But Evelyn looked away, drew a sharp breath and then raised her chin, looking him square in the eye. "No. I am sorry. Thank you for a wonderful evening, *Mr. Lockhart*, but we must leave it at that." She held his gaze, unwavering.

Edward frowned and stared at Evelyn for a moment, confused and hurt. He wanted to ask her again but her eyes made it clear that her decision was final.

"It was very nice to meet you Mr. Lockhart." Mabel gently broke the silence. "Good night, now."

Edward wanted to argue; to make a case for himself. But he knew that would be too much -- too aggressive. He took their hands, one at a time, bringing them to his lips as he said his goodbyes. Then, with one last desperate look at Evelyn, whose eyes were downcast, refusing to look at him, he turned on his heels and walked away.

In the days that followed, Edward could not get Evelyn Larson out of his mind. It was as if she had rooted in him the moment she first took his hand, and, as anybody who had seen them dancing at the wedding could attest, she had bloomed in his arms. So why had she refused his request to call on her again? Had he said something wrong? He went over it in his mind. Edward was confused and frustrated.

After discreetly asking around to his friends who had attended the wedding, Edward learned that Evelyn was visiting from Minnesota, where she lived on her parents' farm. But his friends didn't know anything else about her. He was desperate to find Mabel and contact Evelyn. But she had been adamant that he not call on her. And, although every bone in his body wanted to find her, Edward was a gentleman and wanted to honor her wishes.

Two weeks later, Edward was passing Faneuil Hall on his way to meet friends for a drink, when he saw her. She stood with her back to him, perusing a flower vendor cart on the sidewalk. She was wearing a pale blue dress and a tilted brimmed hat that partially obscured her face. But Edward knew in an instant that it was Evelyn. Again, he was struck by her natural, effortless beauty that outshone all of the colorful flowers on the vendor's cart. Edward weaved through the crowded street until he stood directly behind her. He breathed in her perfume – the same scent that she had worn at the wedding – and marveled at how it filled the air around her, dispelling the acrid exhaust and dank smells of the busy city streets. Just as Edward reached out his hand to tap her shoulder, Evelyn, who had been paying for a small bunch of white daisies, thanked the vendor and turned abruptly, smashing into Edward and crushing the fresh-cut flowers between them.

"OH!" cried Evelyn, surprised to find a person standing so close to her. "I'm… I'm so sorry! I did not see you there. Are you okay? Oh gosh, my flowers!" she stammered as she attempted to straighten three stems that had bent in half in the collision.

"Please, allow me…" Edward said, calmly putting his left hand on the small of her back and signaling with his right hand for the florist to give him a new bunch of daisies.

Shocked at the audacity of a strange man to touch her so intimately, Evelyn jerked her head up. Just as she opened her mouth to instruct him to remove his hand, her eyes took in the long neck, strong jaw and tall, lean physique that had dominated her dreams since that night at the wedding. Her mouth gaped open but no words came out. She was frozen, unable to move or look away. She just stood, staring at Edward as he paid the vendor, flashed a big smile as he thanked her, and then turned toward Evelyn with the new flowers in his hand.

"Well, hello again, *farm girl.*" Edward said smiling down at Evelyn who was still staring at him, mouth gaping.

Evelyn cringed. She was both shocked and embarrassed that this sophisticated city boy knew she lived on a farm. She was sure she had not mentioned this when they had danced. She snapped her mouth closed, eyes briefly flashing with anger then turning sad as she glanced away.

"I am not a farm girl," Evelyn stated defiantly as she plucked Edward's hand from around her waist and dropped it like a hot potato.

"Pardon me," Edward replied, a smug smirk playing on his lips. "I was told you live on a farm. In Minnesota. And I'm pretty sure you are a girl. Does that not make you a 'farm girl?'" he teased.

Evelyn ignored the question, annoyed that he was teasing her. "How did you find me?" she asked. "And why are you investigating me? Are you stalking me?" Evelyn wondered what else he had found out about her. "Surely you have better things to do than investigate me and follow me around. Or perhaps you don't?" She raised one eyebrow at Edward who was still looking at her, his face full of mischief.

Edward let out a loud, bursting laugh that caused passer-bys to curiously glance their way. "I assure you, young *farm girl* that I am not stalking you. I was simply passing through on my way to meet a friend when I saw you buying flowers and I thought it would be polite to say hello. After all, it was not long ago that I held you in my arms for an entire evening," Edward said, raising his voice on the last words just enough so that others in proximity heard.

Evelyn's mouth flew open and she audibly sucked in her breath, her eyes flashing with indignation. Her face turned crimson as she saw a woman look in her direction with eyebrows raised. But Evelyn recovered quickly and she composed herself. She raised her chin, looked down her long eyelashes at Edward and replied, in an equally loud voice, "Well, Sir, we *were* dancing. And if you had been better at it, you would not have had to hang onto me so tightly to keep yourself from tripping over your two left feet."

The nearby woman chuckled and winked at young Evelyn before turning away. Edward threw his head back and laughed a deep, full laugh. Then he bent toward Evelyn, encircling her waist with his arm. An electric current shot up Evelyn's spine as Edward pulled her close and whispered in her ear, "Touché my dear. I see you are as quick-witted as you are beautiful. Come have a drink with me."

This time, it wasn't a question. He knew she wouldn't refuse. Evelyn's legs, so weak she was afraid she would fall if he let her go, seemed to take on a life of their own as she stepped in sync with Edward. Edward turned them both and headed off down the street, arm still firmly around her waist.

Edward led Evelyn to a small, Italian café where he ordered two Irish whiskeys from a bartender who knew Edward by name. He then pulled out a chair for Evelyn at a small table by the windows, with a checkered tablecloth and a faded yellow rose in a vase. There, the two spent the afternoon, watching the city go by, chatting comfortably, sparring wits and laughing like children. It was one of the most glorious days Evelyn had ever had. But she knew it couldn't last.

Over the course of the next week, Edward called on Evelyn almost daily. He showed her every nook and cranny of the city he called home. Evelyn drank it in, loving the sights, the smells, the fashion, and the pure energy she felt radiating in the streets and shops. She told him of her life in Minnesota, leaving out her engagement. She had started to tell him on a few occasions but something always seemed to interrupt her. But if she was being honest, she would have admitted that she was having so much fun seeing the city with someone who knew it so intimately that she deliberately found excuses not to tell him. She knew that if she told him the truth he would walk away. She felt as if she was betraying Richard, but then reasoned with herself that she and Edward were just friends.

Each day that Edward came to call, Mabel looked at Evelyn and whispered, "Have you told him yet?" reminding Evelyn that she was wading in dangerous waters. "We are just having fun," Evelyn would say, dismissively. "It isn't like that." But she was not very convincing - to Mabel or to herself. Nonetheless, she allowed Edward to play tour guide and she accompanied him all over the bustling city. She learned all about the little-big town called Boston. She drank in its history, felt the pulse of the busy streets and heard the secrets whispered by the old, brick buildings and cobblestone streets. She filled her lungs with the salty air from the Back Bay, thick and humid with summer heat. She tasted the lobster, the fried clams, the Irish Whiskey, and the cannolis on Hanover Street. And she watched how Edward enjoyed all these things with her, with an appreciation and passion for the city that was contagious and exhilarating.

By the end of July, Edward was fully and completely in love. He had known he was drawn to Evelyn the moment he saw her, but the intensity of his feelings by the last week of July took him by surprise. He hadn't kissed her or touched her romantically at all. In fact he had not so much as held her hand. He had wanted to on many occasions, but each time he made a move in that direction, Evelyn seemed to move away or distract him with something else. But he had felt the electricity when their fingers brushed as he handed her a drink or when she slipped her arm through his as they walked down steep stairwells of old buildings.

As the last week of Evelyn's Boston trip drew near, Evelyn found herself becoming melancholy. Even though she had been away from home - away from Richard - for an entire month, she was not ready to go back. With each passing day she realized that it wasn't just the city she would miss. Her sadness was rooted in the feelings she had developed for the charming Mr. Lockhart. How had this happened? She had been so careful to keep him at arms length. She had remained in physical control – never standing too close or holding on too long when he embraced her in greeting. But it had been almost impossible not to gaze into his deep blue eyes longer than necessary as they talked in dark corner tables at city cafés. Despite her physical restraint, Evelyn had underestimated the power of raw emotion. Despite her efforts, Evelyn realized she had not been able to keep from falling deeply in love. And she could tell he felt the same for her. But she knew she couldn't be his. She would be going home soon to Minnesota. There were things there that he did not know about – the kind of things that couldn't be ignored much longer.

What a mess she had made! Evelyn knew she had to tell him her secret. "I can still fix this," she cried to her sister one night after returning to Mabel's apartment after a glorious afternoon with Edward.

"You love him!" Mabel had exclaimed as Evelyn floated through the front door, a dreamy look in her eyes.

Mabel had stayed out of Evelyn's social life all summer, not asking any questions or making a single comment, even when Edward began calling on Evelyn daily. But she had seen the way Edward looked at Evelyn. She had known the moment she saw them dancing in that ballroom that things were about to change for her younger sister. Now, several weeks later, it was no surprise to Mabel to see Evelyn in a state of desperate confusion and self doubt.

"I will tell him the truth about me. Oh, how he will hate me!" Evelyn said, pacing around the small kitchen. "Maybe that's for the best – that way he can just forget he ever met me."

Mabel only nodded -- her forehead knit into a worried frown -- and sipped her tea. She knew it wouldn't be that easy.

The next morning, Evelyn telephoned Edward and asked him to come over for tea. She didn't want to have this conversation in public. Edward arrived promptly at ten thirty and Evelyn ushered him into the small parlor of Mabel's brownstone. When he was properly seated in a burgundy leather chair with a cup of tea on the sofa table, Evelyn sat down across from him in a floral, wing-backed chair, her own tea held carefully in her lap. She looked at Edward, meeting his gaze. He was watching her with a curious, amused expression. He looked relaxed and happy. Her heart fluttered and she cringed inwardly. He had no idea what was coming. Evelyn took a deep breath.

"Edward, there is something we need to talk about," Evelyn began. Edward continued to gaze at her, one corner of his full mouth turned slightly up in a lopsided grin that normally made her want to kiss him but today only made her nervous.

"You know I must return home at the end of the week." Evelyn continued. "And…"

"And you have decided you can't live without me so you are going to return to Minnesota to tell your parents you are leaving and then pack your things and come right back!" Edward said, cutting her off and smiling wide.

Evelyn, unable to resist his sarcasm, responded, "Yes, you got me. Your charms and good looks have cast such a spell on me that I am planning to throw caution to the wind, leave the only home I have ever known and move a thousand miles away to a place where I have no job, no parents, and no place to live. You are just THAT irresistible!" Evelyn laughed at herself. The fact that he was joking about such things was a good sign that he might not be expecting anything more than friendship after all. And while that thought sent a sharp pain of disappointment through her heart, she was also quite relieved. But then Edward's next words exploded through her, destroying any momentary sense of relief she felt.

"Oh, rest assured, I would never want a beautiful young farm girl to move to a big, scary city like Boston all alone. You will, of course, marry me!"

Evelyn froze, her teacup half way to her lips. Her eyes were all that moved as they frantically searched Edward's eyes for the lightheartedness that was there just seconds ago. But Edward's expression had turned soft and serious and his mouth no longer held a smirk but a genuine, nervous smile. This was not a joke. He was actually asking her to marry him. They had only known each other for three weeks! This was absurd! Of course she could not marry him! She had to tell him the truth, now. But as Edward's words sunk in, Evelyn felt a weight she hadn't even realized she was carrying being lifted from her shoulders and a strange current, electric with hope and love, swept through her body. It exploded in her gut, her chest, and caused ringing in her head. She propelled upward from her chair, dropping her teacup, which crashed, full of liquid, to the oak planked floor. She stood before Edward, wide-eyed, her head telling her she must tell him her secret and send him home. But, as she looked down at the man who had filled her soul with a happiness she had always dreamed existed, she realized, in her heart, that her world had tilted on its axis and that nothing would ever be the same. This man – his love – gave her butterflies. *And* fireworks. She squeezed her eyes shut tightly and took a leap of faith – a leap of love.

"Yes," Evelyn's lips whispered, her eyebrows knitting together in a confused frown as the word escaped her mouth, which was now under the spell of her heart and betrayed her brain. But as her brain caught up, Evelyn's forehead softened and her mouth smiled and she said more confidently and loudly, "Yes, *Eddie*! I will marry you!"

Edward laughed out loud, picked up his teacup and threw it to the floor beside hers as he stood. "What was that for?" Evelyn asked, wincing as the delicate porcelain shattered over the floor. *Was he angry? Did he already know? Had this all been a test or a sick game he was playing?* Panicked thoughts swirled in her head.

But Edward's eyes were shining with happiness as he replied, "Well, I guess I'm as shocked by your acceptance as you were by my question. And you finally called me Eddie!" He reached for her and pulled her to him and kissed her for the first time, long and hard.

When they finally came up for air, Evelyn laid her head on Edward's shoulder and whispered, "There is just one small problem," She turned her big, green eyes up to him as he pulled away slightly and looked down at her curiously.

"What problem could there be? You've just made me the happiest man in Boston!"

Evelyn cringed inwardly, closed her eyes to shield herself from the reaction she feared most and replied, "What are we going to do about my fiancé in Minnesota?"

Evelyn felt Edward take a sharp breath in. He paused, silent for what seemed like an eternity. *This is it. He now knows what kind of girl I am – one who leaves her fiancé for the summer and then agrees to marry another man she barely knows. Who wants to marry a girl who would do such a thing?*

She felt Edward's hand cup her cheek and she opened her eyes. Edward's deep blue eyes bore into hers. "Well, you are certainly full of surprises for a little farm girl, aren't you?" Then, with one finger, he tilted her chin to his mouth and kissed her again, this time soft and slow.

✝✝✝✝

Evelyn had returned to Minnesota and gently broke the news to Richard, who had been greatly disappointed, but Evelyn could tell not completely heartbroken. She then packed her belongings and moved everything to Mabel's Boston brownstone. Evelyn and Edward immediately began planning their wedding, which would take place in Scituate, a small fishing community just south of Boston, where Edward's Uncle and Aunt, Frank and Grace Williams, lived. They had a grand home, with a large yard that would be perfect for a June wedding in New England. And just up the street, on North Hill, Frank and Grace owned a small farmhouse that had been sitting empty. They had agreed to rent it to the young newlyweds. Evelyn had initially cringed at the idea of moving to a farmhouse, but Edward had talked her into taking a day trip to the quaint seaside town to look at it. "It will be a much better place to raise a family," Edward had said.

And that is how it came to be that the lovely young couple walked through my front door and toured my rooms and talked about children. While they, of course, had no inkling of what was to come, I knew instantly that they were Home.

Chapter 5

THE LOCKHARTS
1935

The wedding of Edward Lockhart and Evelyn Larson was the social event of the year on the South Shore. Everyone who was anyone, from Scituate to Boston, was invited. Frank and Grace Williams enjoyed a high social status and the event was publicized in all the papers and many of Boston's elite attended. Evelyn looked simply elegant (and nothing like a farm girl), dressed in a sleek silk and satin gown, cut on the bias, skimming her lovely slim figure. The fashionable gown pooled into a circular train at her feet. A long rear train fell from a cropped jacket top, with tiny covered silk buttons up the back. A floor length veil was fastened to a halo of silk florets, set in a crown atop Evelyn's golden curls. Evelyn was the epitome of high fashion. Grace had the yard professionally landscaped for the event. A Grecian portico, entwined with purple, fragrant wisteria vines stood in the back yard and provided a fairy-tale like setting for the nuptials. The guests were seated on the expansive, lush green lawn in folding white chairs tied with gauze and purple wisteria blossoms. Frank and Grace's dear friend, Howard Johnson who was becoming a big name in the hospitality business, did the catering. It was a glorious summer day.

Up on North Hill, while the wedding celebration lasted into the late evening, construction workers were finishing the final touches on my makeover. After Evelyn and Edward had toured my rooms that first time with Grace they had agreed that I would be the perfect place to start their life together. Edward was like a son to Grace, who had no children of her own, and she had offered the young couple a very generous rental rate. But first, Grace had decided the young couple needed a little more room in which to grow. As such, Frank arranged for a new kitchen to be added to the rear of the house with a back hall and a stairwell to the cellar. A small, enclosed sunroom with a wall of windows was built on my south side. An extension was also added to the living room. These changes allowed for the old kitchen to become a formal dining room. These changes would accommodate what Grace hoped would be a growing family.

In the months before the wedding, Evelyn and Edward had come to visit several times during the construction, sometimes sneaking in at night when all was dark and quiet. One such evening, only two weeks before the wedding, Edward had laid a blanket on the floor of the newly constructed kitchen and had pulled Evelyn down beside him. The full moon had shone so brightly through the windows that they could see clearly without a single candle or flashlight.

"This is where you will cook meals for our family, like a good wife," Edward had said, stroking Evelyn's hair. Evelyn lay on her back, with her head in Edward's lap, looking up at the man who would soon be her husband. She still couldn't believe how much her life had changed over the course of the last year.

"Oh, I will, huh?" Why can't you be the one to make the meals?" Evelyn had retorted, smiling. "Besides, how do you know if I even know how to cook?"

"Well, first of all you are a farm girl, so I am sure you were taught to cook quite well. As to your other question, I am the man and I have to go to work every day. You are the woman and that is your role as my wife. And you will do it - with gratitude," Edward said, faking an authoritative tone.

Evelyn snorted. "What if I want the role as breadwinner?" she asked. "Then I can dress all up in business suits and go to a big, important job in the city and you can stay in your farm house and cook the meals you seem to want so badly."

Edward laughed mischievously and said "Well, let's see if you qualify for a man's job." He snaked his arm around Evelyn's waist, lifting her skirt inch by inch until his palm was flat against the cheek of her bottom, her thin, silk panties the only thing separating flesh from flesh. Evelyn sucked in her breath and froze, every inch of her body suddenly alert and tingling.

"Nope. Definitely not a man," Edward whispered, his voice thick with desire. Evelyn stared up at him with flushed cheeks and wide, hungry eyes. Edward removed his hand from under her skirt and lifted her body until her mouth met his. Evelyn arched her back as she allowed Edward to kiss her long and deep. Her body filled with an electricity that both paralyzed her and left her skin begging for more. Edward's hands slowly traveled down her side and stomach. He let his fingertips tease her spine and ribcage. Her skin, jealous of itself, begged his fingers to include the areas that had yet to be touched by a man. The moonlight shining through the leaded glass window above the new kitchen sink bathed them in a soft glow so that they could look into each other's eyes as their bodies came together. Evelyn had been raised a good Christian girl but there was not one doubt in her head or her heart that this was anything but God's plan.

✝✝✝✝

Edward and Evelyn had lain on that blanket in the kitchen for a long time that evening, the shadows from clouds, passing over the moon, blocking the light and then revealing each of them to the other again and again. When, exhausted and happy, they had finally gathered their blanket, smoothed their clothing and left me alone with the night, I knew that the pitter patter of little feet would break in my newly refinished wood floors much sooner than expected.

Sure enough, on February 9, 1936, only eight months after the wedding, Evelyn lay in my back bedroom, drenched with sweat, her extended belly heaving. A midwife worked busily by her side, coaching Evelyn on how to perform a miracle that Evelyn had witnessed several times on the farm, but had never performed herself. As Evelyn moaned and cried out in pain, I struggled with whether the events happening in my small bedroom were a good thing. I had no experience with such matters and wasn't sure if this is how it was supposed to go. Everyone seemed joyous and excited, but clearly Evelyn was in agony. And Edward paced endlessly, nervous and agitated. Suddenly, a bright light that the humans couldn't see filled the room and I felt a warm energy I had never felt before. It was fresh and new but had a familiarity that I recognized as part Evelyn and part Edward. A colorful aura then swirled like a kaleidoscope, faster and faster until finally exploding. A raspy cry filled the room as a perfect little boy made his entry into the world. William Frederick Lockhart was born four weeks "early."

We were officially a family!

Chapter 6

PRESENT DAY

Caroline sits at the old wooden bar and looks at her younger brother over her double vodka with soda. The discussion in the dining room had reached a point where it was no longer productive. Anna had become frustrated and emotional and stomped to her room saying she needed some time alone. Alden had said he was tired and had gone to bed. Caroline, also frustrated, but mostly sad, needed a drink and had asked Thomas to join her at Jamie's Pub, a local bar where Caroline and Anna had both worked as teenagers. Caroline wanted to talk with Thomas alone. They had always been very close and understood each other quite well. Caroline knew Thomas wasn't as cold-hearted about the house as he seemed to be and she wondered where his apathetic attitude was coming from.

Thomas lives in Denver with his wife, Mindy, and their two teenaged children. He spent two years in college in New Hampshire before moving to Atlanta when he was twenty, where he had worked as a police officer for several years. After marrying Mindy, an Atlanta native, Thomas went back to college where he earned his MBA and began working for an international medical device company. He and Mindy had two babies within eighteen months. A few years later, Thomas was promoted and the young family moved to Denver. Thomas collects and restores old motorcycles in his downtime and he loves to ride. He sometimes disappears for weeks at a time on trips with his biker friends.

Caroline had originally chalked Thomas' obsession with motorcycles up to a mid life crisis, but lately she has wondered if there was more to it; that perhaps he is restless. Caroline certainly understands how difficult it is for someone who grew up moving to a new town every two years to feel like he belonged anywhere. Caroline has struggled with this very thing her entire life – always feeling the pull to leave where she was, to start fresh, to make a change. It has taken her years of therapy and some close calls with terrible decisions to realize her inability to feel satisfied was simply a result of her upbringing and not because her life was truly missing something. Thomas isn't the type to ask for help or go to therapy. She worries he might still be searching for something – something that he already has but just doesn't recognize.

Thomas had been such a softy as a kid, despite his rebellious nature. When Caroline's beloved kitten had been hit and killed by a police car speeding down North Hill, Thomas had been the one to comfort her. He had even hand dug a tiny grave in the back yard and built a homemade wooden cross that he painted and stuck in the dirt. Over forty years later, the cross was still there. Sure, Thomas had moved away and had no desire to live in Scituate again but Caroline found it hard to believe that he could simply turn his back on the family history and just discard all of the memories the house held by selling it to strangers. But maybe she didn't know her brother as well as she thought she did.

Two locals sit at the far end of the bar, loudly discussing the fate of the Patriots and whether there would ever be a quarterback as successful as Tom Brady. The dinner crowd has thinned and the waitress who has the closing shift is sitting at a table by the window with a group of friends who are laughing boisterously, empty glasses and beer bottles crowded on the table. Other than some new carpeting, updated televisions, and that the joint is now smoke-free, not much has changed at Jamie's Pub in the thirty-plus years since Caroline had worked there. Back then, Jamie's, also known as the Gannett Grill, had been owned by Jamie, a local legend with a big belly and a bigger personality. Jamie had died years ago but his son and daughter had taken over the business and kept the restaurant running – staying true to the small town pub feel where regulars came every day to eat, drink, and feel a part of the community. That's how Scituate folks operated - parents passed down businesses and homes to their kids who kept their roots firmly planted. Not much changed. But changes were happening just a mile away up on North Hill. Mom and Dad had passed and, unless the siblings could come up with a plan, it was looking like, for the first time in one hundred years, the old Lockhart house would be put up for sale. Caroline sadly wonders how her family, which had such deep ties to this community, had become so uprooted.

Caroline watches Thomas drain his Jack Daniels on the rocks and signal the bartender for another. "So, how do you think that went today?" she asks, needing a way to bring up the topic more so than actually wanting him to give her an answer she already knew. Thomas just shakes his head and stares down into his empty rocks glass.

"Look, CeeCee," Thomas starts, using the childhood nickname he had given her as a kid. "I'm not trying to be an asshole here, ya know. I just don't see how it makes sense to try to hold onto a house that we are never going to use. The costs of maintaining a two hundred year old house are going to be huge. It needs a lot of work. I rarely ever come to Scituate so I know *I'll* never use it. For me, it just doesn't make sense. I can take my share and do something else that will actually benefit my family."

Well maybe if you made more of an effort to come home every now and then and show your kids where your roots are, your family might actually enjoy coming here, Caroline immediately thinks. She bites her lip to keep from saying what she knows will start an argument. Calming her initial, emotional response, Caroline replies, "Hey, I know. I get it. This isn't where you want to spend your time. I don't know why you are so anti-Scituate but whatever, that's your decision. And I do agree that the maintenance costs would be an issue. But Mom and Dad left money to do some renovations and we could fix things up and rent out half of the house to a full-time tenant while keeping the other half for us. Or maybe we could do vacation rentals. It could be income property for all of us."

"Think about all that would entail, Cee," Thomas says. "We would have to manage two houses from a distance, with nobody here to oversee things, unless Anna decides to stay in town; in which case she will probably want to live in the house, which will defeat the purpose. It's a recipe for stress and conflict and I don't really need more of that in my life right now."

So, she was right – something is going on with him. "Is everything okay little brother? What's with all the stress? You don't seem like yourself."

Thomas sighs and shakes his head, then throws back the rest of his drink and orders a third. "I don't know, Cee," he says after the bartender has delivered the whiskey and walks away again. "I'm just kinda pissed off that Mom and Dad left us in this position, ya know? I mean, I feel like I can't win here. If I don't agree to keep the house, I'm an uncaring asshole who flushes 100 years of family history down the toilet. But to keep it will just be a lot of headache that I really don't want to deal with. And, to be honest, I could really use the money. This promotion isn't exactly what I thought it would be and I'm fed up with the corporate grind. I'd give anything to quit and start investing in real estate, maybe flipping some houses. The money from this inheritance could really help me out getting started."

So that's what his impatience to sell is about, Caroline thinks. She isn't exactly surprised. While he was clearly very good at his job, Caroline never could get used to her creative, free-spirited brother as the suit-wearing corporate type.

"Wow, Tom. That's great! Are you planning to stay in Colorado and flip houses there?"

"I guess so. Where else am I gonna go?"

"Well, this is your hometown. Would you consider coming back here? This is where your roots are and you obviously aren't afraid of cold weather and snow."

Thomas snorts and gives a quick and decisive shake of his head. "Nice try, but no way, sis. The weather here is way worse than anything in Colorado. And, you are wrong, this is not my hometown. Just because our ancestors lived here doesn't make this my home any more than anywhere else we have lived. I didn't grow up here. We were all over the place. Frankly, I'm surprised you feel such a tie to this town. You lived here for five years and then ran to Florida as soon as you were old enough to leave."

"But we did kind of grow up here – we lived here in between all of our moves. This was always considered our home," Caroline replies.

"Well, I never felt like I belonged here," Thomas says. "And I resent that I am being made to feel like a dickhead because I'm not all gung ho about maintaining ties here now that Mom is gone. She was the only reason I ever came to visit. Without her here, I have no desire or need to be here. Mom knew that."

Caroline can sense that Thomas is becoming agitated. She watches as he downs the remainder of his drink and she sighs. "Okay. Hey, it's okay," she says softly. "I totally get everything you are saying. Nobody thinks you are a dickhead. We will figure this out. I promise."

Caroline realizes that Thomas' mind is made up. He wants to sell the house and he is simply not going to see it any other way. Caroline takes a long drink of her vodka. If she is being honest, she doesn't necessarily disagree with him. She knows deep down that what she is proposing would be difficult and not all that realistic for any of them. Even Anna, the only one of them who still lives in town, has said for years that she isn't going to stay in Scituate permanently, although she still has made no firm plans to leave. Alden lives in San Diego with his wife, Julia, and they have no plans to leave. Caroline lives between her boat and her condo in Florida. Caroline feels a dull ache in her chest as she contemplates the reality of their lives. They are not a family with roots anywhere. They are scattered, thousands of miles from each other, the oldest three with no real concept of what it is like to have a true place to call Home. How can they be expected to fight for a legacy that they have never been truly intimate with? They are Nomads – Navy Brats – each with roots that have been yanked up over and over until they are no longer able to take hold and grow in any one place. But yet, they all know this is different. They do have some roots here - deep ones, that even Thomas can't just rip up.

Thomas stares sadly into another whiskey, so Caroline drains her drink and orders another. Caroline likes having her baby brother to herself and she isn't ready to go home. She squeezes an overripe lime into the clear liquid, stirs it with her finger and lifts her glass. "Well, we clearly aren't going to solve this tonight. Let's toast to us being together for a change. And to Mom. I know you are mad at her but she loved us and she always knew how to keep things interesting!"

Thomas snorts and nods his head toward the bar top. "That she did!" he sighs as he clinks his glass against Caroline's. "Here's to us and to Mom!" Thomas smirks and looks sideways at his older sister. "You do know that I was always her favorite, right?"

Caroline laughs through her nose and rolls her tear-filled eyes. "Oh I know it little brother," she says. "Why are the worst ones always the favorite?" Caroline winks and squeezes her brother's hand tightly with her left hand. She drinks a toast with the other.

The next morning, Caroline wakes to the smell of frying bacon. The delicious smell triggers a low rumble in her empty belly. She realizes she never had dinner last night. A dull ache has settled firmly at the base of her skull. She sits up slowly and sips tepid water from the cup by her bed. She looks around the little room with the pink floral wallpaper. This had been her grandmother's bedroom. She can almost hear the tinny sound of talk radio, although this room hasn't had a clock radio in decades. During her teens, Alden had this room, Then Nana had moved back into the room when Caroline was a senior in high school. Nana had died in the next room, in Caroline's mother's arms. And more than forty five years later, Caroline's own mother had died right in this room. It was weird to think about.

Caroline is sure she can still feel the presence of both women in the house. As she tries to imagine a new owner – a stranger – coming into the house and tearing down wallpaper, likely even removing walls, Caroline's eyes fill with tears. She squeezes her eyes shut and pulls a deep breath in through her nose the way her yoga instructor taught her. She tries to meditate but the smell of bacon fills her nostrils, hijacking her thoughts as her stomach grumbles a plea for nourishment. Caroline sighs and presses her thumbs to her eyes. She stands and wraps her cotton robe around her achy body and pads silently toward the kitchen.

Alden is at the stove, sizzling bacon in one pan and a pile of scrambled eggs in another. "Good morning, CeeCee," Alden says, smiling as Caroline shuffles in, her left hand gently massaging the back of her neck. He hands her a steaming cup of black coffee and, as her eyes meet his, he raises his eyebrows. "Late night at Jamie's, I see. The bacon grease will fix that."

Caroline loves being in her big brother's presence. His six foot four frame fills the cozy kitchen. Somehow just being near him is comforting. Alden is a big man but not fat by any means. His salt and pepper hair is still thick as a rug. His hazel eyes, the same color as their mother's but with a little pie slice of brown in the left one, tease her as she takes the coffee.

"Not *too* late," Caroline replies. Her voice is much more hoarse than she anticipates, which surprises her and makes her laugh. "Okay, whatever. I drank too much. It was a tough day." Caroline slides the tarnished metal latch on the antique cabinet that hangs on the wall over the kitchen table and reaches for some Advil. Alden chuckles as she shakes two large gel caps into her palm.

"Some food will help. Sit down. I've got eggs, pancakes, and bacon, coming right up."

"Thanks, Alden. You are a good man," Caroline sighs, sinking into one of the high-back ladder chairs.

"So, how was Thomas last night?" Alden asks after he sets a plate with one egg, one pancake and three strips of bacon in front of this younger sister. "He is pretty adamant that he doesn't want to keep the house, huh?"

Caroline nibbles on a piece of bacon, marveling at how good a single food item can taste. "Yeah, too bad Mom and Dad didn't leave us all a bunch of Harley's instead," Caroline says between bites. "He would have no complaints then!"

Alden laughs. "Can you see Mom on a Harley?"

Caroline laughs and shakes her head. Their mother had despised motorcycles. *"Those God-awful things should be outlawed,"* she used to tell Thomas every time she learned of one of his bike trips. Alden looks at Caroline grimly. "You know, sis, Thomas has some valid concerns. This house is old and hasn't been well maintained – at least not the original house," he says, gesturing around the old, worn out kitchen. "It really will be a lot of expense even getting it up to rentable condition. There is probably lead paint everywhere."

Caroline stares into her plate, her now-full stomach dropping in despair. She nods, slowly. "I know, Bro. I get it. I really do." Caroline's voice cracks with emotion. "But this is our Home," she whispers, her eyes filling with tears.

Alden nods sadly. "But it's not anymore. None of us live here. None of us want to live here again. At least not full time. And I don't really need, or want, a vacation house in Scituate. Thomas doesn't either. Even if we agree to keep it as investment property, I'm afraid such an "investment" would actually be a money pit and be much more hassle than it's worth. Maintenance aside, the taxes in this area are outrageous. And you know how Massachusetts' laws are regarding landlord liability and tenant's rights. It is virtually impossible to evict someone – even if they refuse to pay rent." A tear slides down Caroline's nose and drops onto her now-cold eggs. She can't lift her eyes to meet her brother's. She doesn't disagree. "We will always have our memories and they will live in our hearts forever," Alden continues. "The house isn't our family. It's just a house - a structure. Sticks and bricks."

"Maybe you're right."

I have been listening to them quietly but Alden's words suddenly fill me with anger. If only Alden knew how much of their souls were with me he would take back those last few sentences. I became much more than "sticks and bricks" decades ago. My heart breaks a little in that moment and I shudder.

Caroline jolts, startled. "What was that?"

"What?" Alden asks, looking around. "I didn't hear anything."

"You didn't feel that?" Caroline asks, wide-eyed. Alden shakes his head, looking at his sister with concern. "Huh. Weird," Caroline says cautiously, "I thought I felt something – like the ground moving or something."

Alden laughs. "That's called a hangover, sis. The spins." He pats her shoulder and stands to get more coffee.

But Caroline knows it isn't just the after effects too much vodka. *What are you trying to tell me?* Caroline thinks as her eyes roam over the old kitchen. Her gaze is immediately drawn to a long crack that runs along the wall between the kitchen and the dining room. It has been there as long as Caroline can remember. Even though wallpaper has adorned the walls for decades, the crack still shows through, like a raised scar pushing forward to tell its painful story.

"Alden," Caroline says, fingering the spot where the wallpaper protruded, "do you know how this crack happened and why Dad didn't fix it before hanging the wallpaper?"

Alden looks over and shakes his head, "Who knows? Probably Mom got impatient and just threw the wallpaper up thinking she could cover it. It's probably due to some structural issue. This wall was the original exterior wall. Who knows what kinds of problems are hidden in these old walls, which is one more reason why we need to think about selling."

✞✞✞✞

Alden is partially right. My old walls do hold a long history of "problems" – just not the kind he is concerned with. I am a good house. There is nothing wrong with my structure or my bones. It's my heart that has been broken. Yes, I have a heart. I earned my heart. I acquired it after years of living with the members of this family, who loved each other so fiercely that their love radiated from them and rooted in my walls and grew slowly until one day I realized that I, too, felt love for each of them. And just like them, my heart has burst with happiness at times but has also been broken. I have the scars to prove it. They are the scars born of a family that has lived fully within my walls. I have absorbed their joy, their love, their pain, their loss, and their heartbreak. These scars run deep. The particular crack Caroline is asking about is actually several scars that have run together over the years. It started with my first wound – my first taste of what loss and pain felt like. And it was far too big to swallow.

44

Chapter 7

THE DARKEST DAY
1943

Life for Edward and Evelyn in their new home in Scituate was fairly smooth and easy in the early days. Two years after Williams' birth, Evelyn gave birth to a beautiful, golden-haired baby girl they named Katherine. Edward immediately nicknamed her Queenie. "She looks like royalty", he would say, as he held her tiny body in his strong arms. When Katherine was three, Evelyn began working as a kindergarten teacher in the quaint neighboring town of Cohasset. Even when the United States entered World War II, our lives continued peacefully in our small New England town. Edward, unable to serve in the military due to health issues, worked at the Hunt-Spillar Corporation in Boston, manufacturing metal for the war effort. For the first time since I was built, I was full of life, happiness, and loving energy. I was thrilled to be a part of this young family. Life was good on our little hill. Then, one beautiful day in June 1943, a darkness descended that would change all of us, forever.

The sun rose early that morning, as it always did that time of year. By five thirty, streaks of pink and gold stretched across the sky, like ticker-tape celebrating the glorious spring day. Up on

North Hill, we could hear the waves a couple of miles away, crashing against the granite ledge where Minot's Light stood firmly, surrounded by the deep blue ocean. The birds in the fragrant lilac bush that grew along the northern side of my walls, chirped excitedly as the sun warmed them and dried the dew from their wings.

Evelyn was already up, moving swiftly around the kitchen, preparing breakfast for her little family. Edward was preparing to head to work in Boston and he liked to get an early start, as the drive was not always easy. Katherine and William were still sleeping. School had let out for the summer just the day before and Evelyn was letting the children enjoy a little extra sleep – an indulgence that they wouldn't get too much of this summer as they both were to attend camp, participate in summer recreation day school, and suffer through swimming lessons each morning on Peggotty Beach. Evelyn shivered a bit just thinking of their little bodies submerged in the icy Atlantic too early in the day for the sun to warm them. She thought it was ridiculous to try to teach children to swim in water that froze their limbs numb. And with the waves, strong current, and sea creatures, Evelyn was certain they would all drown the very first day. But Edward, who was a die-hard New Englander and believed that a person's character was defined by their grit, had insisted that they would be fine. "It's good for them" he had scoffed when Evelyn expressed concern. "It will thicken their skin and make 'em tougher. I learned to swim in that sea and no cold water, wave, shark, or jellyfish got the best of me. They can do it." Evelyn had acquiesced and told the lifeguards the kids would be there. But swimming lessons didn't start for another week.

Evelyn had agreed to watch one of her students; a little girl named Emily, while her mother attended a doctor's appointment and ran some errands. Evelyn was very fond of Emily. She had been the sweetest child in Evelyn's kindergarten class that year. With her pale, baby soft full cheeks, pink, pouty lips, and large blue eyes, all framed by a thick halo of shimmering blonde curls, Emily looked like a doll baby right off the top shelf of the finest toy store. Her angelic looks coupled with her naturally sweet disposition made Evelyn feel certain she had been sent straight from heaven. When Emily's mother, Dorris, with whom Evelyn had become friendly over the course of the school year, had mentioned she had a full day of appointments and errands and was planning to drag Emily with her on her first day of summer, Evelyn didn't hesitate to offer to watch her for the day. Besides, Emily would be a good playmate for Katherine and William.

Evelyn slid the fried eggs she had been cooking onto three separate plates – three for Edward and one for each of the kids. She added a side of fried ham and buttered toast with a touch of homemade jam made from the blackberries that grew wild in the fields out back. The sun streamed through the windows, lending a warm glow to the cozy kitchen. Evelyn wiped her hands on her apron and went to wake the children and hustle Edward out of the bedroom where he was dressing.

After the four of them finished breakfast and five-year-old Katherine had helped clear the table, Evelyn kissed Edward goodbye and busied herself tidying the kitchen. She washed and dried the china plates and stacked them neatly in the pantry. As she wiped down the counters one last time, she glanced out the window at the tall butterfly-filled fields surrounding our Home and thought "How lucky am I to live in this wonderful house on such a beautiful day? Today is going to be glorious." Evelyn's happiness warmed me and I settled in, ready to enjoy the day.

Shortly after nine o'clock, Evelyn heard Emily's mother's Ford Deluxe pull into the driveway. Evelyn smoothed her short wavy hair and went outside to greet little Emily and her mother.

"Good morning, Dorris! Good morning, Emily, dear!" Evelyn said cheerfully as they exited the car.

"Good morning to you, Evelyn," replied Dorris. "How are you? You must be so relieved to be able to spend some time at home after the long school year," Dorris replied, immediately feeling a pang of guilt that she was dumping Emily on Evelyn on her first day of vacation. Evelyn was known throughout Scituate and Cohasset as the best kindergarten teacher in the area. Dorris felt lucky that the two women had become friendly over the past year when Emily was in Evelyn's class. Emily just adored Mrs. Lockhart.

47

Evelyn was young and pretty and had the patience of Job. She was also creative, energetic and fun. Most of all, she recognized that kindergarten, while a child's first introduction to learning, was mostly a time for kids to learn to be kids. When Dorris had expressed concern that Emily couldn't tie her shoes – something that most of the other kids in her class could do – Evelyn had smiled kindly and touched her arm gently and said "so, let's let her wear buckled shoes until she gets there. We will practice in school. She will be tying shoes in no time!" Dorris had immediately liked her.

"Yes, it is so nice not to have to rush out the door on such a beautiful day. God has certainly blessed us with the most perfect weather – as if he is helping us celebrate the end of a wonderful school year." Evelyn waved her arm toward the cloudless blue sky and twirled in a circle. Emily giggled and twirled also.

"Hi Mrs. Lockhart," Emily sang as she twirled on last time and then wrapped her arms around Evelyn's waist, almost knocking her off balance.

"Emily!" cried Dorris. "Please mind yourself! Mrs. Lockhart does not need you tackling her to the ground this morning."

"Oh, it's quite alright," laughed Evelyn as she playfully pulled on one of Emily's bouncy curls. "I'm a tough old girl – you can't knock me down that easily. I'm happy to see you too, honey." She reached around her back and clasped Emily's hands gently pulling them forward and then she knelt so she was eye to eye with Emily. A hint of mischief glinted in her eyes as she said, "If you run on inside you will find that Katherine is desperately awaiting your arrival and she has some fun things planned!" Emily clapped her hands excitedly and then skipped up the kitchen steps into the house without so much as another glance at her mother.

"Be a good girl, Emily. I love you," called Dorris. She then looked at Evelyn with gratitude. "Far from 'tough' or 'old' I think. Nevertheless, I do wish she would be more careful. She just bounds ahead sometimes without a care in the world or any thought as to consequences."

"She is one of the happiest children I have ever known, Dorris," replied Evelyn. "She is full of life and energy and has so much compassion. You know she would never hurt a flea, right? Remember the time she got upset about the boys burying the beetle bug in the dirt at recess and we had to dig him out and set him free after the boys moved on to play kick ball? Ha – she is going to be a wonderful, loving, free-spirited woman some day. You don't have to worry about her, trust me."

"Oh how I wish I had your patience," sighed Dorris. "You are a true gem and I can see why Emily loves you so. Thank you again for offering to watch her today. I must get going or I will be late and Dr. Ward will scold me. You know how scary he is!" Dorris said, winking. Dr. Ward had been Evelyn's family physician for the past several years. He had grown up with Edward and had delivered Katherine. He was one of the gentlest, kindest men Evelyn had ever known and the best doctor on the South Shore.

"Oh yes," Evelyn laughed, "he is a true ogre! You had better go or he is likely to put his stethoscope in the freezer while he waits for you."

"Ha – might be just the jolt I've been needing," teased Dorris. "I'll plan to pick Emily up at two if that is okay with you?"

"Absolutely! No rush. Please take your time. We will be here enjoying this beautiful day."

Dorris kissed Evelyn's cheek and then walked down the grey flagstone path to her car. She drove off with a smile and wave.

The children played in the fields in the back yard for over an hour while Evelyn finished some household chores. They caught ladybugs for Katherine's bug house and explored the woods just on the edge of the yard. William had gathered sticks of all sizes and had built a small teepee over which they draped a white sheet. They then decorated their make-shift abode with wild flowers, branches, and leaves. Evelyn checked on them periodically through the open window, smiling and sometimes laughing out loud as she could hear them, pretending to be grown ups and using phrases they had clearly heard from their parents. She watched William pretending to come home from work and she marveled at how much he was like her own father – a man William hadn't even known except as a baby.

49

As Evelyn brought a basket of linens to hang on the clothesline in the yard, she heard Katherine scream. Her heart leapt and she turned to see Katherine scramble out of the tee pee shaking with anger.

"I HATE you William!" Katherine spat as she brushed her hands frantically through her golden curls. "I really, really hate you! You are the stupidest brother ever!" She ran to Evelyn crying and continuing to slap at her head and brush her hands all over her body.

"Stupidest is not a word, sweetheart," Evelyn said calmly as Katherine crashed into her, sobbing. "What in the world is going on?"

"That dumb-dumb put inchies in my hair, mommy!" Katherine wailed, shivering as she recalled the horror. "Inchies" was the name the kids had for the tiny green inchworms that dripped from silk strands all around the yard this time of year. The kids collected them by the dozens and made shoebox habitats filled with grass, leaves and sticks where the inchies would live until they made cocoons in their cardboard environments. Evelyn ran her hands gently through Katherine's hair.

"But, sweetie, you love inchies. You know they aren't poisonous and they don't bite or sting."

"I KNOW that, Mom, but he put them in my HAIR and they got stuck and I hate him so much. Why does he even want to play with us anyway? He is a boy and too old. Please make him go away! I wish he had never been born!" She began sobbing all over again.

"Hey now, I don't want to hear talk like that. He is your brother and if something were to happen to him you would regret such hateful words," Evelyn scolded softly as William and Emily emerged from the teepee and walked to where Evelyn stood with Katherine's head buried in her side. Evelyn could barely suppress a smirk as she looked over Katherine's head at William. Emily looked very concerned and on the verge of tears.

"William, do you have something to say to your sister?" Evelyn asked, staring him straight in the eye, trying her hardest to look stern.

"Little inchworm small and green – in your hair he'll make you scream!!" William sang and then broke into uncontrollable laughter.

A tiny giggle escaped Evelyn's lips before she could control herself.

"MOM!!!! It's not funny!" cried Katherine as she recoiled from her mother as if she had been slapped. "He is so mean and you think it's funny?" she accused.

Emily stood looking from one Lockhart to the other with wide eyes. Evelyn worked to compose herself and put on a serious face.

"No, it isn't funny, you are right. William, I would like you to apologize to your sister this instant," instructed Evelyn. "And, apologize to Emily for scaring her, too."

William shuffled his feet and looked at the ground, sheepishly. He knew his mother wasn't angry but he also knew to obey her order. "Oh alright. I'm sorry Katherine. It was just a joke. And I'm sorry, Emily. I didn't mean to scare you." He winked at Emily who smiled shyly.

Just as everyone was calming down and Katherine looked like she might accept William's apology, a golden curl flopped in front of Katherine's face and dangling off the end was a tiny little green worm, clinging tightly. Katherine screamed. Emily jumped. William fell on the ground in a fit of laughter.

Katherine instantly became inconsolable. Despite that a part of her thought the whole situation was incredibly funny, Evelyn knew Katherine would not calm down until William was punished. She sent William to his room and ushered Katherine and Emily into the house and gave them both a class of cold lemonade. She sat Katherine down at the kitchen table and brushed Katherine's hair out fully to convince her the inchies were gone. As they sat there, Evelyn saw Emily lean into Katherine and look up at her with giant blue eyes and whisper, "You know, I wish I had a brother as fun as William. You are lucky even though sometimes he makes you mad." Katherine stared into Emily's innocent gaze and, while Katherine wasn't buying it fully, Evelyn saw Katherine's face soften just a bit. Evelyn wanted to kiss their sweet little guest.

"Tell you what, girls," Evelyn jumped up, "how would you like to do a little treasure hunting with me?" Evelyn looked at the girls with her eyebrows raised, her face filled with the promise of adventure. Katherine looked skeptical. Emily's blue eyes sparkled with interest and grew even bigger as she asked, "What kind of treasure?" Evelyn leaned in close, looked right into Emily's eyes and whispered, "the very best kind – the kind that nobody can take from you!"

"Oh yes!" whispered Emily back. "I would like that very much."

Katherine sniffled and looked at her mother curiously. "Just us though, right? No William allowed?"

"No William allowed," confirmed Evelyn. "This treasure hunt is for girls only. Follow me."

The trio walked to the front of the house and Evelyn took Emily's little hand in hers and led her up the steep, creaky stairs to the second floor, which was mostly attic but a small part had been built out to be a small bedroom for William. Evelyn put her ear to William's bedroom door to listen. "Stay right here a second, okay?" she said to Emily and Katherine. Evelyn knocked on the door softly and then turned the glass handle and slowly pushed the door open. William was on his bed, reading a book. He looked up as the old door creaked open.

"Hi, Mother," William said solemnly. He was sad that he was being punished for what he had thought was a harmless prank.

"Hi sweetheart," Evelyn smiled. "I know it doesn't seem fair, but you can't tease your sister like that. It hurts her feelings. Why don't you stay here and read for a bit and then you can go outside and play with your new kickball with Emily for a while after lunch?" Evelyn kissed the top of his head, feeling his silky brown hair on her lips and inhaling his scent. He smelled just like Edward. She stood slowly, careful not to bump her head on the sloped ceiling and backed out of the room, closing the door gently as she stepped back onto the stair landing where Emily and Katherine were whispering about what kind of treasure they would find.

"Okay, girls, ready to hunt for treasure?" Evelyn asked them.

"Yes, please!" replied Emily while Katherine nodded in agreement.

Evelyn opened the only other door at the top of the stairs and the musty smell of warm, stale air tingled their noses. The attic was hot and the air stagnant and dark. Cobwebs decorated the old wooden rafters ad layers of dust covered the plywood floor. Emily took a step backwards out the door and too close to the top of the long stairwell.

"Oh, it's okay sweetheart," said Evelyn carefully, reaching for Emily's hand. "This is where the treasure is. It's a happy place, I promise. It's just a little dark. But that's why I brought this new flashlight that you can hold for me so that we can see where we are going. Look how it makes pretty patterns on the ceiling," Evelyn said as she pulled the flashlight from her pocket and shined it into the attic.

Emily, still a little unsure, but excited to be given some responsibility, smiled and nodded. Katherine peered around, squinting in the dark and said, "Mom, what is up here anyway?"

"You'll see!" exclaimed Evelyn, relieved that Emily was pacified. Evelyn led the girls to a corner of the attic that held a small cedar chest. When she lifted the lid, a cloud of dust erupted and a strong pungent odor assaulted their nostrils.

"Ewwww," said Emily, crinkling her little nose and pursing her lips.

"That's just moth balls," Evelyn explained. "They help keep the moth pirates away so they don't eat the treasure. Now, who wants to see what we can find in here?"

"Meeeeee!" both Katherine and Emily sang in unison.

"Ha ha, okay, okay, one at a time," Evelyn laughed, glad they were excited. "Since Katherine had a bit of a rough day, why don't we let her go first, Emily? Is that okay with you?"

"Yes, Ma'am," Emily said as she lifted the flashlight higher to shine more light on the chest. Evelyn marveled at how sweet and giving Emily was. Most kids in her class would have whined about not being able to go first. Evelyn made a mental note to be sure to tell Dorris how selfless Emily was.

Katherine reached into the chest and pulled out a very old handkerchief, stained yellow but with intricate lace around the edges. The letters EGL were monogrammed with embroidery in a corner.

"What is this old hanky?" Katherine asked as she lifted it between her thumb and forefinger as if it was a smelly sock.

Evelyn laughed at Katherine's expression of intrigue mixed with utter disgust. "That is my father's old handkerchief," she wistfully, remembering how her father carried it everywhere he went.

"Oh Mom, that's gross," Katherine said frowning. "Why would you keep this and how is this considered treasure?" She was clearly growing disappointed with this expedition.

"Well, that handkerchief was made especially for my father, your grandfather, by my mother only shortly after he began courting her. She knew he was the man for her and she sewed all of that lace by hand and embroidered his initials to show him how she felt about him. He kept it in his pocket every day from that day on, but he never used it and would never let anyone use it. He always carried a spare if one became necessary. He made one exception, one time - on my wedding day. As he took my arm to walk me to my groom, my father kissed my cheek and told me he loved me and was proud of me. He wasn't normally the emotional type, and he hadn't initially been happy about my decision to marry your father and move so far from home. So, seeing his eyes filling with tears as he said those words to me sent me into an emotional tailspin and I started to cry. He was afraid that I would ruin my veil and makeup so he reached into his pocket and wiped my tears away with this handkerchief. He didn't even hesitate. So, you see, that handkerchief isn't just an old piece of linen. It has love woven right into it and it holds one of my fondest memories of my father. It is a true, invaluable treasure."

Katherine carefully ran her fingertips along the lacy edge and over the light grey thread of the embroidered monogram. The look of disgust was gone, replaced by a curious wonder.

Emily stood patiently by, smiling and holding the flashlight steady.

"Okay, your turn, Em," said Evelyn taking the flashlight gently so Emily could be free to explore the treasure chest. Emily knelt by the chest, reached a small hand inside and pulled out an old porcelain baby doll with a soft, cloth body and dainty porcelain head. The doll had tiny, pink, bow-shaped lips, green eyes, and soft brown curls that peeked out from beneath a floral bonnet. She wore a matching floral dress and tiny, brown, lace-up boots. She was a little crinkled and her hair slightly flattened, but Emily thought she was beautiful.

"Wooooowwwwwww," Emily whispered as she raised the doll to the light. "She's so pretty!"

"Yes she is, Emily," replied Evelyn softly, looking at the doll with a flood of memories flashing past her eyes. "That is Isabelle. She was my favorite doll when I was a girl just about your age. My father brought her to me when he came home from traveling back to Norway to see his family. I used to carry her everywhere. You can see where I had to glue her foot back together after I dropped her one time. I loved her very much."

"Oh, I love her, too, Mrs. Lockhart!" exclaimed Emily. "Very much." She pulled Isabel to her chest and hugged her tightly. Evelyn was touched at the instant love this little girl felt for her old, musty doll.

"You're an angel, Emily," Evelyn said smiling at the child. "*You* are a treasure." She kissed Emily's chubby cheek. The three stayed in the attic looking through the chest for as long as they could stand the heat. When sweat started dripping down Evelyn's back, Evelyn straightened her stiff knees and stretched. "What do you say we go get William and cut some watermelon?" Evelyn suggested.

"Aw Mom, do we have to?" whined Katherine. "He's sooooo mean.

"Come on now, Katherine, don't you think he has had time to think about what he did and don't you think it's time to forgive him? He's your brother," answered Evelyn softly but firmly.

"Fine, he can have watermelon," Katherine compromised. But I'm not playing with him."

Evelyn carefully closed the lid on the old chest and ushered the girls carefully out of the hot attic, closing the door behind them.

"Oh no, Mrs. Lockhart!" cried Emily. "Isabelle!" She held up the doll she had been clutching the whole time they had been in the attic.

"Tell you what, Em," Evelyn said with a smile and a playful wink, "bring her with you. It's been years since she had any watermelon!"

After they ate all of the watermelon, they sat on a blanket in the grass on the hill at the side of the house. The breeze blew softly as William sucked on the green rinds and Katherine stared at him in disgust. Emily was pretending to feed Isabel leftover watermelon pieces and Evelyn laid back in the grass to watch the white fluffy clouds sail overhead. She felt peaceful and happy.

"Hey you guys, do you wanna play kickball?" William asked, smacking his lips loudly.

"Not with you," Katherine sneered.

"Be nice, Katherine," Evelyn murmured to the sky, feeling sleepy.

Emily looked at Katherine expectantly and then turned her gaze to William who looked hurt. "I'll play, William," piped up Emily. "I love kickball."

Katherine frowned at Emily accusingly. "I'm sorry," whispered Emily to Katherine. "It's just that he looks so sad and, like your Mom said, it's best to forgive him. You really are lucky to have a brother."

Katherine pursed her lips in consideration and shrugged. "Well, I still don't wanna play, but I guess it's okay if you want to." She smiled down at Emily.

"How can we play with only two people, William?" asked Emily.

"Oh not a problem at all!" replied William. "One of us can kick the ball and the other can catch it and try to throw it at the kicker to get them out before the kicker can run the bases. That's kickball right there! Plus, we have Isabel!" William said as he picked up Isabel's leg and made her kick the ball he had picked up. Emily giggled.

Katherine rolled her eyes. "I'm going inside," she announced as she jumped up and skipped into the house.

Evelyn, who had propped herself up on an elbow watching this exchange, smiled to herself, satisfied that the kids had worked this out themselves, and lay back down to absorb more warm sunshine.

"Come on kiddo," William said to Emily. Bring Isabelle. It's me against you two doll faces!"

Evelyn laughed inwardly, noting that her young son was already becoming quite the charmer. As William and Emily played their two-on-one game of kickball in the side yard, Evelyn struggled to stay awake as the sun warmed her skin. She was tired after the busy end-of-the-school-year activities and multiple parent conferences assuring parents that their child was developing just as a kindergartner should. The warm summer breeze blowing through the yard, with the soft laughter of the kids playing in the background was like a lullaby and Evelyn closed her eyes.

The ear splitting sound of an angry car horn sent Evelyn bolting upright. Shielding her eyes from the bright sunlight, the awful sounds of tires screeching and metal grinding on metal assaulted her ears. William was screaming, "OH MY GOD! NO, NO, NO, Oh God, NO!"

Evelyn's eyes adjusted and she turned toward the screams coming from the front yard. A pickup truck was sideways in the road, the driver frozen in his seat, fear and disbelief contorting his weathered face. She could see William's red kickball lying in the tall weeds across the road. William was running toward the truck still screaming. Evelyn frowned, confused. Why was William so upset? The ball looked undamaged. There was no other car and no crash. What was happen….. Emily!! Where was Emily? Oh God, no! Evelyn jumped to her feet and ran. She reached the road just behind William who was on his knees frantically reaching under the truck. Evelyn dropped beside him and that's when she saw her. Emily's small head of blond curls was visible just behind the left front tire.

Evelyn, fighting back the bile that rose in her throat, choked out, "Go inside and call the emergency number. Hurry!"

Evelyn lay flat on her stomach in the road. As Evelyn's eyes traveled over Emily's body, she could see that her torso was grotesquely misshapen and contorted. Her left arm was at an unnatural angle. The truck had run right over her little body. Just beyond her outstretched fingertips, lay Isabelle. Evelyn could make out tiny shattered porcelain pieces strewn across the pavement.

Evelyn squirmed her body under the truck and pulled Emily to her. Emerging from under the truck, she wrapped Emily's broken body in her arms and felt her labored breath. She was still alive! Evelyn turned toward the house. The truck driver was crouched by the side of the road vomiting profusely and sobbing. "I'm sorry, I can't help you right now," Evelyn sobbed to him as she walked quickly but gently to her front door. Evelyn laid Emily on the sofa in the front room, carefully supporting her neck and head. The little girl's breathing had become shallow and her body felt cold. Evelyn covered her with a blanket and held her, praying as hard as she could. But, as she held her, Evelyn felt the life drain from Emily's broken body. All she could think as she held the sweet little girl who had filled their day with love and kindness was that she had been terribly mistaken earlier when they had started their treasure hunt – any treasure could, in fact, be stolen at any time. Then her thoughts were dimmed by a terrible, suffocating darkness that fell over the room.

✠✠✠✠

I stood firm, but helpless, as the emergency personnel arrived and rushed Emily's lifeless body away. A kind police officer had coaxed Evelyn into a chair and had wrapped her shivering body with a blanket. The truck's driver, who had gone into shock, had been taken to the hospital by ambulance. Edward arrived at some point with Doctor Ward, who gave Evelyn a shot and some pills. Evelyn's sadness and pain radiated so violently from her soul that I felt it in my old plaster walls. I never saw Emily's parents, as they were told to go straight to the hospital. I was thankful for that. I did hear about them over the years that followed, as Evelyn would sob in her room whenever she would see Dorris at the Woolworth's or elsewhere around town. While Dorris didn't publicly blame Evelyn for what had happened, Dorris and Evelyn were never again friends. I guess it is just too hard to repair a heart broken so badly that it never is truly whole again and it is just too painful to look into the eyes of someone who reminds you of the part of your heart that is missing. I don't know, really – I'm "just a house." I do know, however, that I felt every bit of the energy and life that had been so pure and good leave us that day. I also experienced the devastating pain and loss that ushered in the darkness that descended on poor Evelyn, enveloping her and drowning the light in her soul. I didn't know what all of it would mean and I certainly couldn't understand the effect this tragedy would have on my family for years to come. All I knew then was that the pain of what had happened was too great for my walls to swallow and so it rose, like bile, forcing its way out of me, creating a crack in my kitchen wall that throbbed with a pain that I now understand is called "heartbreak."

This was my first experience with heartbreak. But it wouldn't be my last.

Chapter 8

PRESENT DAY

After breakfast and a shower, Caroline calls to check in with her husband, John, who is at their home in Florida. John is a Florida boy through and through. He was born and raised in Orlando in the days before Walt Disney, when citrus groves had bloomed as far as the eye could see. Of course, Orlando is now a concrete jungle, and Caroline has little affection for that part of Florida. But there are other parts of Florida that Caroline adores. The Everglades are pure magic – the great river of grass with its abundant, incredibly diverse wildlife. The crystal clear, cool springs that hide in the tropical forests of central Florida are like little secret havens. The lakes and rivers and, of course, the seas – from the Gulf Coast to the East Coast, to the Caribbean Seas of Key West – all lend their own unique beauty to the ecologically diverse State.

John had grown up playing in the citrus groves and exploring the wonderful nature of "real" Florida. And, as Caroline has learned in her thirty-plus years of marriage, you can't take the Florida out of a Florida boy. God knows she tried. After they met in Orlando when they were in their early twenties, they moved to Birmingham, Alabama where they both attended law school. They stayed in Birmingham for over twenty years. But John had always longed to move back to his home state, so when they had the chance, they relocated with their two daughters to Vero Beach, a small town on the East Coast of Florida, with miles of quiet sandy beaches, acres of citrus and cattle farms and a homegrown feel that made her think of Scituate – only warmer. She was happy to call this gem on the Treasure Coast home. Caroline's motto has always been "Home is where your heart is," and her heart belonged to Vero Beach.

Caroline thinks about this now as she sits on the floor of the upstairs hallway, sifting through the contents of her mother's attic. *What happens when your heart is in more than one place?* Caroline thinks, flipping through her mother's photo albums. The photos in these books depict many different places their family had called home over the years. Because of their father's Navy career, they had moved many times during Caroline's childhood. Caroline had attended five different elementary schools as a kid.

She touches a photo of her mother in a bikini waving out the back door of their small upstairs unit in a quadruplex in Navy housing in Honolulu. Another photo shows Caroline and Thomas riding their bicycles around the circle where their two story Colonial had been in Virginia Beach. Then there was the small ranch in Jacksonville, Florida that their mother had despised, followed by more Navy Housing in Newport, Rhode Island. Caroline is reminded of two-year-old Anna in their duplex in Newport throwing down her Fischer Price vacuum cleaner and stomping her feet as she imitated her mother's common complaint: "Good God I hate this shitty house!" Mom had loved to tell that story.

But between every move to a new house, they had always come back to Scituate and the house on North Hill - at least for a little while. Jim would get his orders from the Navy and Marie would pack up whatever house they had been in, load the kids and the dog in the station wagon, and drive to Scituate, where they would live temporarily while Jim went on ahead to the new town and find a new place for them all to live. Sometimes the process would take several months. As a result, they had lived in this house enough times for Caroline to attend half of kindergarten, part of third grade and part of fifth grade in Scituate public schools. They had moved back permanently when Caroline was thirteen, Marie refusing to make her teenagers move during high school. As Caroline flips through the pictures of all of the houses in which she lived, but never really felt like she belonged, she realizes that this house is, and always has been, their only true Home. *Alden and Thomas are wrong – this place is not just sticks and bricks.*

Caroline thinks back to another time she sat in this exact spot, back when her grandmother still lived here and this hall was nothing but a musty attic filled with spider webs. She used to come up here and snoop through her grandmother's trunks and boxes. She remembers once asking her grandmother to show her the things in the trunks. Nana had looked panicked for a moment, then very sad, and had waved her hand in the air. "Oh there is nothing important in those old trunks," she had said. "Just some old junk." Then she had disappeared into her bedroom and didn't come out for over an hour.

Caroline closes her eyes and swears she can still smell the dampness of the old wooden rafters. But those rafters are now covered in drywall as her parents had renovated the upstairs in the 1980's. Caroline opens her eyes and looks around, dwelling on the fact that her great, great aunt, her grandmother, her aunt Katherine, her mother, herself, and her own daughters had all stood in this spot at some point. Five generations of women of North Hill. Caroline pictures the elders: Aunt Grace in flapper dresses, Nana Lockhart with her fascinator hats and skirt suits of the 1940's, Katherine in her 1960's pencil skirts, and Marie, her mother, in her mid-1980's knickers, argyle socks and feathered hair. But they were all gone now.

Caroline had never met Aunt Grace but she had vivid memories of the others, and she missed them greatly. They had all been strong, independent, intelligent women but each one unique. Nana had possessed a patient, sweet nature and rarely became rattled enough to lose her temper. Although, she did remember that time when she and Thomas had been little and Nana was fixing bowls of ice cream for them. Thomas had been excessively whiny that day and had complained loudly that Caroline's bowl held more ice cream. Nana had tried to make the bowls as even as possible but Thomas kept insisting that it wasn't fair. Finally, Nana had stopped and stared at him and then dipped her bare hand into the ice cream carton, scooped out a fistful of the creamy treat and smeared it across Thomas's mouth, sneering through clenched teeth, "you want more ice cream? There, now you have more ice cream!" Caroline laughs to herself at the memory of her sweet grandmother losing her patience. Even Nana had had her limits. But for the most part, Nana had been a kind and lovely grandmother. She had cooked the most delicious chicken and barley soup Caroline had ever tasted. And her lemon meringue pies made from scratch were famous throughout town. Caroline's eyes fill with tears. She misses her grandmother.

Caroline blinks the tears back and then picks up a photograph of Aunt Katherine. Katherine Lockhart had possessed a quick wit and a wicked sense of humor. She was sarcastic and silly and had a contagious laugh that sent everyone near her into giggles. She had loved to dance and she was incredibly beautiful, with blonde, wavy hair, and mischievous green eyes. She was the kind of aunt every girl should have. On Caroline's eighth birthday, all of her gifts had been dresses and dolls. But Aunt Katherine had given her a baseball bat and glove, telling her she could do anything boys can do – and better! When Caroline was twelve, Katherine taught her to play "You are My Sunshine" on the guitar and introduced her to Carly Simon's music. Caroline smiles, thinking back to when she was a freshman in high school and Katherine had dropped her off at a party on Scituate's West End. She had pressed a $20 bill into Caroline's hand, saying, "you know, in case you need beer money." Caroline had thought Katherine was absolutely the coolest woman in the world.

Then there was her mother, Marie Lockhart Freeman. Caroline picks up a black and white photograph of her mother surrounded by her three toddlers as she sits in the captain's chair of a Navy destroyer in Hawaii. Marie had been only twenty-six years old at the time; living in Hawaii with three babies while Jim was off at war in Vietnam. Caroline stares at the profile of her beautiful young mother wearing a fitted mini dress and oversized sunglasses, holding baby Thomas in her lap while Caroline and Alden, both toddlers, balance on the chair beside her. She had been gorgeous. Tears slide down Caroline's cheeks. She can't believe her beautiful mother is gone. She had seemed indestructible. Caroline had expected her to live forever. She had been the strongest, most giving, selfless woman Caroline had ever known. Sure, she had had a temper and, in true New England style, she never shied away from giving her opinion, but she had always been kind and respectful of others. She had loved Scituate and its people with a deep passion and was immensely proud of her heritage. She had loved this house as if it was a member of the family. She had cried for a week when the 100-year old pine tree in the front yard – the one she, her sister, brother, and all of her children had all stood under waiting for the school bus each morning - became sick and had to be removed. Even as she got older and the cold winters instigated her arthritis into constant flare-ups, Marie couldn't leave New England. She would not dream of leaving Scituate. Even after Jim had died, Marie remained stubborn about staying right here at Home.

Caroline reaches for another photo showing Marie as a little girl sitting on the front porch with her siblings. Until she married, this was the only home Marie had ever known. Caroline tries to imagine what it would feel like to grow up in only one house – to see the same walls every day, walk the same halls year after year, stare at the same ceilings night after night. As hard as she tries, Caroline knows that she would never – could never – fully understand the bond their mother had with her Home. She knew that Marie had desperately wanted the house to stay in the family. But who would take it? At one point it seemed logical that Anna might be the one to inherit the house as she had stayed in Scituate and raised her children right here in the house. But Marie and Jim knew that Anna had stayed only out of necessity and that she had longed to move closer to Caroline. Besides, as a single mother, she didn't have the means to maintain such a big house and property. With no easy answer, their parents had agonized over how to draft their wills so that their assets could be fairly divided between the four siblings. But, other than a couple of retirement accounts, the house and surrounding land was their only true asset of value. And how do you divide a house between four adults, each with their own families and children? After consulting attorneys, tax professionals, and dear friends, Jim had eventually decided that the only fair thing to do was to set up a trust whereby the house would be owned equally by each of the four siblings. They would then need to figure out how to keep the property or liquidate it. When her father had first informed Caroline of this arrangement she had known then that she and her siblings would be sitting right where they are today – unable to reach an agreement, road-blocked by emotion, financial constraints, and family history. Caroline remembers trying to convince her mother to sell the house and take the money and travel the world with Dad. It had been a selfish (and fruitless) endeavor. Of course, Caroline had known then that her mother would never - could never – watch the house be sold to strangers. She had already been through losing her parents and her two siblings. She would never inflict upon herself the heartbreak of losing her Home also.

Caroline leans against the wall with the photo albums spread around her. She thinks about her mother's life, trying to fully understand the depth of her mother's ties to this house. Caroline's thoughts turn to her mother's father, Edward Lockhart. He had died before Caroline was born, when her mother was only twenty-three. She considers what it must have been like to lose a father so young; to raise children who never knew him. Caroline had always felt a void where her grandfather should have been. She wishes she had known him. She flips open her mother's earliest photo books, looking for photographs of her grandfather. There aren't many. But she finds one of him sitting in a chair in the large living room, with Katherine on one side and William on the other. Caroline's mother, Marie, is a toddler in his lap. He is bald and, even though he is seated, Caroline can tell he is very tall. All of her life, her mother had told her stories of her grandfather and Caroline grew up feeling as if she had known him. Caroline's bedroom had been the room where Edward had died. She had always liked to think this fact gave her a special connection with him somehow. As she sits looking at the black and white photograph of the man with the same nose and full cheeks she has – "the Lockhart bulldog face" her mother used to call it – she is hit with a profound sadness and a longing for a connection to him. She starts frantically looking for more photos, hoping to find some of him as a young man.

✚✚✚✚

What Caroline doesn't realize is that all she needs to know about Edward Lockhart lives within my walls. He is here, with me. His story is here. Let me tell you about him.

Chapter 9

EDWARD
1944

Edward crouched low behind the pile of rubble that was once an ornate church made of stone, carved marble and stained glass. *The French really knew how to design buildings*, thought Edward. Everyone was an artist in this country. But the bombs didn't care. They had destroyed everything in sight. Factories, hospitals, and private homes, places of worship – nothing was spared. The screaming metal cylinders that fell from the German Gotha Bombers didn't discriminate. And now, this once bustling, lively French town that had been built with an artist's touch was nothing but shattered rock, crumbling concrete and dust. So much dust. It was everywhere – caked in every crease in Edward's clothes and skin. It stung his eyes, matted his hair and seared his throat and lungs. Every breath was a struggle between needing air and avoiding the pain. Edward had come here with the American troops, sent to help the European allies defend France against an invasion by the German army. But, as Edward squatted behind the fallen church walls, his chest on fire with each breath, he looked around him and wondered where the rest of his army had gone. He was alone with only the rasp of his own ragged breathing. The silence and absence of human life confused him.

Just moments ago he was with his platoon. How had he become separated? He pulled off his helmet to wipe his sweaty brow and rub his red, burning eyes.

Edward eased his aching, ashen body a little higher so he could peek over the wall of rubble to look for his fellow soldiers. Just as the top of his head crested the wall of fallen rock, Edward felt the whiz of a bullet streak past his right ear. He fell in a heap; face down in the dusty dirt, scrambling to get his helmet back on his head. "Jesus Christ!" Edward muttered, terrified. His brain scrambled to devise a plan. He was alone and had been discovered by the enemy. He was being fired upon!

Edward felt the presence of the other man long before he heard him or saw him. Edward rolled onto his back just in time to see the large German soldier crest the protective rubble wall and loom over him with the barrel of his gun pointed at his chest.

"Nicht Bewegen!" the soldier screamed as he raised the arm of the rifle to shoot.

Instinctively, Edward's right leg shot out and up, striking the German's left elbow just as he pulled the trigger. The force of Edward's kick interfered with the German's aim and a hail of bullets bounced off the rocks, inches from Edward. As the soldier struggled to regain his balance and take new aim, Edward sat up, grabbed the barrel of the gun and yanked as hard as he could. The enemy, his gun, and his supply pack tumbled on top of Edward, temporarily knocking the wind out of him. As he struggled to breathe, he felt the German's fingers wrap around his throat. Edward tasted the sweat dripping from the tip of his attacker's nose as he straddled Edward and pushed him hard against the dusty rock. Again, Edward's right leg shot up. But this time it was his knee that made contact with the German's groin. The man winced in pain but didn't let go. Edward's vision became spotted as his brain was being deprived of oxygen. *This is it*, he thought. *I am going to die.* Mustering all the strength he had left, Edward once again slammed his knee into the now-bruised testicles of the German. This time the soldier cried out and loosened his grip on Edward's throat enough for Edward to steal a gulp of air, which gave him just enough energy to roll to the left. The German's shoulder struck a pointed slab of concrete, sending searing pain through his muscles and robbing his hand of its strength. Edward was able to lift his head and smash his forehead into the flaring nostrils of his enemy. This time both men cried out in pain.

"Scheisse!" cried the German.

"Shit!" muttered Edward.

Searing pain tore through Edward's brain as blood spurted instantly from the German's nose and a tooth fell onto a rock between them. The German's left hand reflexively flew to hold his damaged face. That was all Edward needed to gain the upper hand. Edward used all the strength he had left to wrap his right leg around the German's torso and flip him onto his back. The German's skull slammed into the jagged shards of rock and concrete and his eyes fluttered. Edward's hands flew to the enemy's throat and his long fingers squeezed as hard as he could. The German's eyes flew open and bulged with panic.

"Bitte!" choked the dying man, gasping for air.

Edward squeezed harder. He squeezed until he could feel the thick neck of the German shrinking, becoming thin and frail beneath his fingers.

"Eddie!" The German rasped. "Please! Stop!"

Edward shook his head. *How does he know my name?* Edward thought, confused.

"Edward!" the German said again, but this time his voice was higher and feminine. "Wake up, Eddie! Please! It's me."

The soldier was coughing and crying in a voice that was oddly familiar. Edward closed his eyes. *Why is he calling me Eddie? What kind of trick is this?* He loosened his grip but didn't let go.

"EDWARD!"

Edward's eyes flew open, filled with a mixture of anger, hatred, and confusion. But this time when he looked into the face of his enemy, the German had disappeared. Staring back at Edward, with wide, panicked blue eyes, was the face of Edward's mother, Amelia. Her brown hair, a wild tangled mane floating around her face, which was contorted in pain and fear. Edward was hovering over her, his hands gripping her throat. Edward's eyes looked beyond her head. He recognized the red and blue pattern of the Oriental rug that decorated the floor of his mother's bedroom. The rock and concrete were gone. His eyes darted to the right. His mother's bed was a tangle of sheets that spilled onto the floor behind them. A broken lamp lay on the floor and small droplets of blood stained the sheets. As reality became clear, Edward's hands flew from around his terrified mother's throat and covered his own face in shame. Edward crumpled on the floor as sobs wracked his body.

Edward Lockhart had never been to war. He was only fifteen years old. He had never even met a German, let alone tried to kill one with his bare hands. But that didn't save him from his nightmares. Frequently, the demons came to him in his sleep. And when they did, they were as real to him as his own flesh and blood. The night terrors were born of a severe nervous disorder called Saint Vitus Dance. Edward had been diagnosed as a child after suffering a bacterial infection that brought with it a high fever and near death. St Vitus Dance had caused young Edward to twitch and his muscles to jerk uncontrollably. With antibiotics not having been discovered yet, little Edward had been prescribed one teaspoon of arsenic each day to choke out the original infection and resulting nervous disorder. Of course, not only the St Vitus Dance was poisoned by this treatment. Edward's toxic-filled body suffered severe side effects – the main one being intense and realistic night terrors that included talking and walking in his sleep. On one such occasion, ten-year-old Edward, who shared a bedroom with his brother, Chet, screamed for Chet to get up. Chet woke to find Edward standing, perched at the end of his bed, looking over the foot rail at the floor.

"Eddie, what are you doing? Go back to bed," Chet had mumbled sleepily, rolling over and covering his head with his pillow.

"Chet! Chet!" Edward had cried, his eyes wide and wild. "Get up now! The boat is sinking. We must get off before we are sucked under!"

Chet, who had been warm and cozy under his blankets sighed loudly. "Ed, brother, wake up. You are not on a boat. You are in our bedroom. You are dreaming. Go back to bed and let me sleep!"

"No, Chet!" Edward had called, his voice growing panicked and high-pitched. "We must go. Follow me, brother!"

Exasperated and exhausted, Chet had sat up just in time to see Edward put his hands over his head and dive, head first onto the hard wood floor. The crash of Edward's face onto the floor had woken him instantly. He sat up, terrified, wiping blood that gushed from his broken nose.

As he grew from a boy to a young man, Edward's nervous disorder had improved and he no longer took the arsenic. The night terrors had eventually subsided in his late teens, but the damage had been done. His own army rejected Edward when he tried to enlist. "We can't take someone with nervous disorders," he was told many times. He had, instead, attended college in Boston and had married Evelyn at twenty-eight. When the United States entered World War II in 1942, Edward watched while friends and neighbors went off to war. While Edward could not put on a uniform or carry a gun to fight the enemy in the traditional sense, he found a way to serve his country right at home. And the price he would pay would be no less devastating than if a bomb had been dropped directly on his head.

In his adult years, Edward worked for the Hunt-Spiller Iron Works Corporation in Boston. The company produced metals essential to the military for the production of artillery, tanks, ships, and machinery. Edward worked his way through the ranks until he was plant manager. In 1941 when America learned that it was years behind Germany in the technology and production of weaponry, the United States government enlisted Edward's service by looking to the Hunt-Spiller Corporation to help in quickly producing enough metals to build weapons and ships in a hurry. Workers were hired at good wages, which wages were then frozen to ensure stability, and Edward found himself working seven days a week to keep up with the demands of the United States military. Each morning, he rose, ate his breakfast, kissed Evelyn goodbye, and drove to Boston where he worked in the factory all day and well into the evenings. He managed the plant and oversaw hundreds of new workers – men and women – who worked day and night to help the government pull off what would go down in history as a production miracle. "*We pour more to win the war*," was the popular slogan of one of the larger iron foundries and Edward wasn't about to let his plant fall behind.

Each day that Edward worked in the foundry, he breathed in air filled with silica dust and poisons. Each breath ushered thousands of microscopic enemies into Edward's lungs. Even when he covered his nose and mouth, the enemy found a way to infiltrate Edward's body through his pores. There was nowhere to hide. No armor or guns would protect him. When Edward arrived home, most of the time late into the evenings, he would immediately remove his clothes and boots in the back hall before walking through the house to the shower. Evelyn would gather his clothes, which were covered in toxic dust and put them directly into the washer. Over time, the inside of the washing machine turned orange. Then, Edward's urine turned orange. Soon, the orange enemy seeped from his pores when he would sweat and his shirts became tinted at the armpits. Evelyn could clean the washer with bleach. But for Edward's body, it was not so easy.

One unseasonably warm evening in early November, 1944, Edward arrived home from work, well after dinner. Evelyn had just finished bathing six-year-old Katherine when the glow of headlights announced Edward's arrival home. "Quick, go put your nightgown on while I warm up your father's dinner," Evelyn said, kissing the top of Katherine's wet, blonde head. "Then maybe he will read you a story before you have to go to bed." Katherine, wrapped in a fluffy bath towel, made her way to her bedroom while Evelyn went to the kitchen to reheat the plate of corned beef and hash she had saved for her husband's dinner. But as Evelyn entered the kitchen, the sight of Edward coming in the back door stopped her cold.

"My Lord, Ed!" Evelyn exclaimed. "You look like death warmed over!" She rushed to her husband, who stood swaying in the doorway, skin pale and glistening with sweat. Her hand flew to his forehead, which was furrowed in pain. His eyes were glassy and blood shot. "Oh my! You are burning up with fever," Evelyn diagnosed as Edward started to shiver.

"I'm freezing," Edward mumbled, tongue thick and dry in his mouth.

"We need to get you into a cool bath right away," Evelyn ordered as she started pulling off Edward's jacket and sweat-soaked shirt. "Here, sit on this bench and don't move." Evelyn unlaced Edward's brown boots caked with orange dust. She then helped him out of his trousers and left the orange-stained clothes in a heap on the floor as she took Edward's arm and helped him to the claw foot tub in the small bathroom. She gently guided her 180-pound husband into the tub and turned on the faucet so that lukewarm, clear water soon swirled around him. Edward, usually one who did not like to be manhandled or fussed over, simply surrendered to her care. He was terribly weak and far too tired to protest as his shivering body filled the cast iron tub. His breathing was ragged and Evelyn could hear the unmistakable wheeze of lungs struggling to find air as they drowned in fluid.

"I'm going to call Dr. Ward," Evelyn stated, growing more worried by the minute.

Twenty minutes later, Clifford Ward arrived with his bag of medical tools and medicines. Evelyn had assisted Edward out of the tub and had lowered him into his large, blue chair, wrapped in warm blankets. The fever had come down a bit and the shivering had subsided. But his breathing remained labored and the burn in his chest was unrelenting.

"Evelyn, I am going to ask that you go in the other room while I examine him," Dr. Ward said.

Evelyn started to protest but stopped as Dr. Ward looked her dead in the eyes, his face stern and eyes filled with warning. Evelyn stepped backward and closed her mouth. Panic rose in her chest.

"But first, please go scrub your hands with soap and water as hot as you can stand it. Do NOT come back into this room."

Dr. Ward held her gaze for a moment longer, making sure she understood, before closing the door to the family room, leaving Evelyn standing alone and confused in the dining room. Evelyn did as she was told and went to the kitchen where she scrubbed her hands until they were raw. She then sat at the kitchen table with a cup of hot tea. Her worry seeped into my walls, making me swell with the weight of her concern. As she sat with her thoughts, I could feel something other than just a worry for Edward's health fill the room. The taste of raw fear hit me then; a fear that was for something unknown. I sagged under the weight of it but didn't yet understand. Was she worried for her children? William and Katherine had both come to see their father and have their nightly story time but Evelyn had shooed them off to bed explaining that Daddy didn't feel well. She watched them go with sadness in her eyes. She knew how important their time with their father was. The kids didn't get much time with Edward these days and when he was home he was often more gruff than usual. Katherine, especially, had grown distant, becoming afraid of her father's short temper and impatient manner. She was only six and she took it personally. This made Evelyn sad.

After what seemed like hours, the hall door opened and Dr. Ward quietly stepped into the dining room, drying his hands with a floral hand towel from the bathroom. Evelyn stood to come toward him but he shook his head and motioned with his hand for her to sit back down at the kitchen table. His eyes cast downward, Cliff Ward wiped his brow and pulled out a chair across from his long-time patient and friend.

"It's pneumonia, Evelyn," Dr. Ward stated. He was not a fan of sugar coating bad news and he respected Evelyn far too much to beat around the bush. "His lungs have taken a beating and they are filled with fluid and severely infected. I'm afraid it is quite serious."

Dr. Ward looked unwaveringly into Evelyn's worried eyes. Evelyn stared back, unblinking and sucked in her breath.

"You can treat him though, Cliff? Right? Of course you can," Evelyn started. "People survive pneumonia all the time. And Edward isn't a baby or an old man. He just needs some rest. He has been working so hard to meet the government's demands for more metal. With some rest and medicine, he will be fine." Evelyn's voice remained steady and emotionless as she worked her words to convince both of them.

Cliff, for the first time, looked away. In that moment, a deep sadness and terrible conflict was palpable. I shivered at its sudden intrusion.

"He needs to go to the hospital, Evelyn," Dr. Ward said as he turned his eyes back to Evelyn. "Edward is a very sick man. He is not old, but his lungs have been filled with iron dust for so long that they are weak and severely damaged. I am afraid there is not much I can do to help him here. He needs to be on a breathing machine."

Evelyn was shaking her head slowly in protest. "No, Cliff. He can't go to the hospital. He hates hospitals. You and I both know what a terrible patient he will be. The doctors and nurses will likely kick him out after one day of his grumbling and short temper. Can't I get a machine and take care of him here?"

Dr. Ward sighed deeply. "No, Evelyn," he said softly as he took her hands in his across the pine table. "You cannot. It is not safe. Not for him or for you...or anyone else."

"Oh Cliff," scoffed Evelyn, "you know I am not worried about myself. I am as healthy as a horse. I will be careful and will wear a mask and gloves and will disinfect everything daily. I will keep the children away from him. We will be fine."

But now it was Dr. Ward who was shaking his head. "Evelyn, listen to me carefully. Edward's pneumonia is severe. His infection is highly contagious. Also, you came to see me the other day because you were feeling dizzy. Do you remember? You asked if you were starting your change. I sent your blood in to be tested."

"Oh please, Cliff," Evelyn interrupted. "Who cares about that right now? You are sitting here telling me that my husband has severe pneumonia and needs to be in the hospital. I couldn't give a squat about whether I am a little dizzy. I am fine – just a little hormones, that's all. I am perfectly capable of caring for my husband."

"You don't understand, Evelyn, please let me finish," Cliff said patiently. "Edward might die. The hospital has the best breathing machines and around-the-clock care. They can administer sulfa drugs and the new penicillin drugs, which need to be monitored carefully. But even with that, he might not recover." Evelyn stared blankly at Dr. Ward. Her head swirled his words around, trying to find a place for them to settle that didn't make her want to throw up. What would she do if Edward didn't recover? How would she manage? What would life be like without her strong, handsome husband by her side? Suddenly she felt terribly dizzy and her stomach filled with nausea. Evelyn dropped her head into her hands and began to cry.

"But that's not all," Dr. Ward continued. "Your blood work came back late this afternoon. I was going to call you in the morning."

Evelyn raised her head, her eyes searching Cliff's face for more information. But somehow she already knew. She had known for weeks but had refused to acknowledge the truth. The bile rose in her throat as she ran for the bathroom.

"Evelyn, you are pregnant." She heard his words through the bathroom door as she vomited into the toilet.

I thought my kitchen walls would cave in from the explosion of conflicting emotions that swirled under my roof like a gathering storm.

✝✝✝✝

We, as a family, healed Edward that long, cold winter of 1944. After learning she was pregnant, Evelyn had agreed to send Edward to the hospital where they treated his pneumonia and slowly coaxed his lungs back to relative health. I say "relative" because Edward's lungs would never be healthy again. The damage from years of breathing toxic dust was irreversible. The high quantity of sulfa drugs required to treat the pneumonia caused Edward to lose all of his hair, which never grew back. He came home from the hospital an old man. While bombs and bullets had killed the men fighting overseas in the war, microscopic armies had waged war inside Edward's body. It was a war Edward would ultimately lose. But not just yet. He had a baby on the way and it was simply not his time to die.

After two weeks at South Weymouth Hospital, Edward had been allowed to come back Home to finish his recovery. William and Katherine helped out when they weren't in school by bringing their father tea and honey, helping with extra chores, and trying not to argue. They knew their Daddy was gravely ill. But they didn't yet know they would soon have another sibling. Evelyn had wanted to wait to tell them until Edward was stronger and they could celebrate as a family. She had given Edward the news when he was in the hospital as she hoped it would motivate him to fight to survive. I did my best that winter to keep our Home warm and comfortable. The New England winter winds assaulted every inch of me, as they always did, trying their hardest to penetrate my wood siding and glass paned windows. But I worked diligently to keep my family healthy, squeezing with all my might to keep out the icy drafts. My hearths nurtured the fires longer. My radiators clanked and groaned when I pushed them to work to ensure my family stayed warm. Edward slowly grew stronger. And Evelyn's stomach swelled with new life.

On Christmas Eve, Evelyn felt the time was right to tell the kids about the baby. Edward was feeling strong enough to join the family in the dining room. I was full of love and excitement as our family gathered around the long mahogany table that Katherine and Evelyn had set with blue and gold china, sterling utensils, and cobalt glasses with cut crystal stems. These dishes had not been used in years, as it just hadn't felt right to enjoy such fineries while the world suffered in war. But it was time. Edward was on the mend and it was Christmas. Besides, news of a new baby called for a true celebration. The family feasted on the traditional honey-drizzled baked ham, mashed potatoes, and green beans. Evelyn announced the joyous news as she served homemade lemon meringue pie for dessert. "Oh, Mrs. Lockhart, I'm going to be a big brother again?" William asked, excitedly. He was in school where Evelyn was a teacher and had become accustomed to calling his own mother Mrs. Lockhart, even at home. Evelyn chuckled and stroked his cheek. "Yes, William. You are going to be the best big brother ever. Again!" Katherine threw her hands above her head and clapped and squealed. "I just know it will be a girl! I can't wait to have a baby sister!"

Edward smiled at Evelyn across the table and said a silent prayer of thanks. It was truly a Christmas miracle that he was sitting here, still weak but no longer at risk of dying, celebrating another new life God had blessed them with.

Spring arrived hesitantly, as was usual for coastal Massachusetts. A warm April day would have Evelyn opening all of my windows to harness some fresh air. Then spring would become shy and flee again, allowing winter to barge back in. The yellow daffodils and pink tulips would be coaxed open by a warm spring sun, only to be sprinkled with winter's snow the next day when spring once again retreated. We were used to spring's fickle ways though and we were patient. In May we received the news that Germany had surrendered and

World War II would finally be over. People all over town celebrated. The world could finally begin healing.

By June, the cherry trees and the wisteria vines at the entrance to the side courtyard were in full, fragrant bloom. On the morning of June 14, 1945, Evelyn woke Edward early in the morning and said, smiling, "It's time." Edward drove his wife to South Weymouth Hospital while William and Katherine stayed home with Edward's sister, Aunt Fran. Purple and pink blossoms all over town exploded in celebration as Helen Marie Lockhart made her way into the world.

I tried to be patient while Evelyn delivered the new baby at the same hospital where Edward had cheated death only months prior. But, I admit, I was bursting at the seams. I sighed heavily with impatience so often that I heard Aunt Fran ask William if he knew whether my pipes had been checked recently. That had made me chuckle.

Finally, the morning of June 20, Evelyn walked through the kitchen door carrying a carefully wrapped pink bundle. Of course I could not see the child, as a house has no eyes. But I could feel her tiny eyes sweep over my walls and rooms, taking me in and making me hers. Little Marie (Edward refused to call his beautiful new baby girl "Helen." "It's a name for an old hag," he had complained to Evelyn who insisted on the name) drank me in and an instant bond was formed. I knew immediately that I would forever be hers. And she would be mine. I let out one big sigh, not of frustration or impatience this time, but of immense relief and pure happiness.

"We might need to get the pipes checked," Edward said to Evelyn as he took his baby girl into his arms to give her the grand tour of her Home.

Chapter 10

THE SAVING GRACE
1952

The years following Marie's birth were good years. The wars were over and the 1950's ushered in a time of prosperity and happiness. The Lockhart family of five thrived and our home was filled with joy and laughter. Edward continued with the Hunt Spiller Corporation, but was transferred to an administrative position as he had been diagnosed with severe emphysema of the lungs and could no longer work in the factory. Evelyn loved her job at the preschool. The children attended school, went to church and grew like weeds. In the summers, wet towels full of sand from Minot Beach were strewn across the lawn where the kids dropped them before they rinsed off in the cold hose. In the winters, snow crusted hats and gloves were laid atop the radiators in the kitchen to dry and rubber snow boots left big puddles in the back hall. On the weekends, Evelyn and Edward threw lavish parties for their friends. Cars lined the street and young couples streamed into our house, which they laughingly referred to as "North Hill Club" to eat, drink, and celebrate life. Music filled our Home and Edward watched his wife blossom in the laughter and joy that surrounded her. Life was good.

Evelyn had grown to love the small seaside town and she made our Home an inviting, happy one. She had insisted that the fields around the property be allowed to grow tall with grass, weeds and wildflowers, through which the children loved to run and play hide-and-seek. Evelyn liked the fields tall and wild because it allowed her to have a much smaller area for a lawn that she could keep neatly cut and manicured. She only wished she could take down the big barn in the back. The old, white barn reminded Evelyn of life on the farms in Minnesota – a life she had been happy to leave. She hated looking at the barn every day. But, because Aunt Grace and Uncle Frank owned the property, she could not ask that it be removed. Young Marie, who loved the outdoors and was always barefoot from April through late October when the freezing temperatures demanded she cover her feet or suffer the consequences of frostbite, was quite adept at hiding in the overgrown fields for hours. She would crouch low while playing hide and seek with William and Katherine until they gave up trying to find her and would move on to another game. Marie would then stay hidden in the tall grass for hours, making up fairytales and imaginary friends, sometimes foraging a path to the woods where she would climb trees, make forts with sticks, and play alone until she heard Evelyn calling for her to come inside. Then, she would run, full speed, cutting a sharp path through the fields, and would emerge from her fairy-tale forest, covered in dirt and pollen, with leaves, and bugs tangled in her golden curls. Evelyn would scowl and shake her head, feigning disapproval. But, as she sent Marie off to the bathroom to wash and change for dinner, she would chuckle quietly to herself, admiring her youngest child's free spirit and love of nature.

One cold and blustery evening in November, 1952, Edward pulled into the driveway after a long commute home from Boston to find Cliff Ward's black sedan in the driveway. Edward's heart jumped into his throat. Cliff wasn't one to make unscheduled social visits. There was only one reason he would be at the house – someone was ill. Edward hurried into the house. As he entered the small kitchen, he saw Dr. Ward sitting at the small kitchen table, a cup of coffee in front of him. Evelyn was at the stove preparing dinner. Confused, Edward closed the door behind him with a bang, causing both Dr. Ward and Evelyn to look in his direction.

"Well, hello there, Cliff," Edward said, his voice deep and filled with concerned curiosity.

"Good evening, Edward," Cliff said as he stood to shake Edward's hand. Cliff smiled at Edward, but his eyes were sad.

Shrugging off his dark wool coat and hanging it on a hook in the back hall, Edward asked "To what do we owe the pleasure of your visit this evening? Did you smell Evelyn burning dinner all the way down at your house and think the house on fire?" Evelyn shot Edward a dirty look.

"Ha, ha, not quite, Edward," Dr. Ward laughed. "Everyone in town knows what a great cook your lovely wife is. I'm surprised you don't have a line of visitors every night just waiting to be invited for dinner."

"True, true," replied Edward as he greeted Evelyn with a kiss on the cheek. "But, something tells me that's not why you are here – just to sample Evelyn's fine cuisine – though you are more than welcome to stay for dinner."

"Well thank you, Ed, that's kind. But no, that isn't why I'm here. Unfortunately, I have some bad news about your Aunt Grace."

Edward sat down slowly across from Dr. Ward, his eyes searching his old friend's face for more information. He grew very still. Auntie Grace, who had never had children of her own, had been like a mother to Edward. She had taken care of him when his own parents could or would not. She let him move in with her and Frank when his own mother, Grace's sister, couldn't handle Edward's teenaged outbursts, saying only that she "didn't have what it takes to be a mother." Grace had shown patience and understanding when Edward had rebelled and had been kicked out of high school. She had been there to help him find his way back and then had paid for him to attend Northeastern University. She was the reason that he and Evelyn lived in such a beautiful home. She charged him rent equal to one week's worth of his salary even though Edward knew she could get much more from another family.

Frank had passed away in 1950 leaving Grace to live in the big white house just down the street with a full time caregiver. Grace had been in good health, although she had developed a nagging cough in the last month that she had dismissed as allergies from working in her garden. "You know I must keep busy now that Frank is not around, Edward," Grace had told Edward on her seventy-eighth birthday. "Gardening keeps me feeling young. I just love feeling all that dirt between my fingers. It makes me feel connected to this gorgeous Earth." Edward had taken her word for it that her cough was due to allergies and had not pushed her about it. But now, looking at Dr. Ward's solemn expression, Edward regretted that he had not insisted she see a doctor.

At hearing Grace's name, Evelyn, who had been mashing potatoes at the kitchen counter, stopped and wiped her hands on her apron that hung loosely over a yellow, flowered dress. Fourteen-year-old Katherine was busily walking to and from the small kitchen and the dining room, where she was setting the table for dinner. "Edward, let's move this discussion into the living room," she suggested, nodding her head toward Katherine. She wanted to give Edward some privacy for what she anticipated would be very sad news about a woman he loved dearly. "I'll get you your whiskey and you can sit in your chair and talk with Dr. Ward privately. Would you like a drink, Cliff?"

"Oh, thank you but no, Evelyn. I'm fine. Well, maybe just a water," Dr. Ward smiled warmly at Evelyn. He was very fond of her and her sweet family. Nobody in town who knew Edward as a rebellious teenager, including Cliff, had expected that he would settle down with a girl as classy and kind as Evelyn. But they had all been proven wrong when it became clear that Evelyn adored Edward. And, Edward had proved to be a good husband and father to their three beautiful children. He had made a good life for himself. Dr. Ward knew that this lovely family rented their home from Aunt Grace. He also knew that, but for Grace's kind generosity, the Lockhart family would have had a difficult time affording a house in Scituate big enough for the five of them. And now…well, Cliff worried for them.

The men made their way to the cozy living room off of the dining room. Edward settled into his chair and Dr. Ward sat beside him on an antique settee. "Okay, Evelyn, we are out of your hair now, are you going to let the good doctor tell me what he came to say now or are we going to play musical chairs all night?" Ignoring her husband, she carefully handed the men their drinks, then smoothed her skirt and sat in the wing-back chair to Dr. Ward's right.

"Katherine is watching the dinner for me," she said in answer to the stares from the men who had clearly expected her to leave them alone to talk. But Evelyn loved Grace and owed her so much. She wasn't leaving. "Now, Cliff, please tell us what is going on with Grace. We saw her the other day and she had a bit of a cough. Please don't tell me she has pneumonia? This family has dealt with enough of that dreadful sickness!" Evelyn reached over to pat Edward's knee as she addressed Dr. Ward.

Cliff shuddered at the memory of Edward's terrible bout with pneumonia. Cliff had sat with Edward almost every day at the hospital, keeping him hydrated, monitoring his fever and caring for him. Cliff had saved Edward's life. Unfortunately, he knew he could not be the savior this time.

"I'm afraid it's worse than pneumonia, Evelyn," Cliff answered looking from Evelyn to Edward. "The cough was just allergies. But Grace had a heart attack this afternoon. Her caregiver called me right away but I'm afraid it was a bad one. There was nothing I could do. She is gone. I am so very sorry."

Evelyn's hand flew to cover her mouth as she gasped and then let out a small sob. Tears immediately spilled from her green eyes onto her cheeks. Edward stared at Cliff as if trying to make sense of his words. He slowly blinked, took a deep breath, then let out a long, slow sigh. "Well, dammit all," Edward murmured. "Christ. She sure was one to do something half-asked." Dr. Ward smiled and nodded in agreement. "Thank you for coming to tell us in person, Cliff. You are a good man. Where is she now? What do we need to do?" Edward appeared calm but inside he was in turmoil. *Why didn't I see this coming?* He thought. *Could I have helped her? Was she alone when she died? Why didn't I go visit her yesterday?* His heart was broken.

"Well, Ed, she died in my arms so there was no need to call an ambulance or spend money sending her to the hospital. I already called Richard Gaffey at the funeral home and he is taking her. Of course, as you are her only next of kin here in town, you will need to make whatever arrangements the family deems necessary. I'm so sorry. Grace was a wonderful woman. She certainly lived up to her name. She will be greatly missed."

"Yes. Yes, she will," replied Edward solemnly as he thought about the aunt who had given him so much.

Evelyn, who had been silently weeping, dabbed her eyes with the corner of her apron. "Why don't you stay for supper, Cliff?" she asked reaching for Dr. Ward's hand. "This must have been a very long day for you. You must be tired and hungry. We have plenty of food. Then, after supper, Edward can call Mr. Gaffey and make arrangements?" Evelyn looked to Edward for confirmation and he nodded distractedly.

"Yes, Cliff, please do stay." Edward mumbled, but his thoughts were far away.

"Oh, you are so kind to ask, Evelyn, and normally I would never decline an invitation to share in your wonderful cooking," Dr. Ward smiled as his left hand covered Evelyn's. "But I must be going. My wife has dinner for me and you two need some privacy to talk to the children and be together as a family tonight. This isn't going to be easy on any of you."

"Well, we think of you as family you know," Evelyn smiled warmly at their good friend as she stood. "Thank you again for coming over like this. And thank you for all that you did for Grace."

"Yes, thank you doc," Edward added, still sitting but coming out of his trance long enough to look up at Dr. Ward and nod.

As Evelyn hugged Dr. Ward and escorted him to the front door, Edward let his head fall heavily into his right hand and he silently sobbed. His shoulders shook as grief wracked his body and tears spilled down his nose. Grace was gone. Edward's own parents had passed away years ago. And now the woman who had loved and treated him like a son had also gone home to the Lord. Edward sat in his chair and allowed himself to grieve in the privacy of his living room. After several minutes, he said a silent prayer, wiped his eyes with his handkerchief, blew his nose and stood. "Children!" he bellowed so that his voice could be heard from every corner of the old farmhouse. "Come for dinner! Your mother has made a wonderful meal and it's about damn time we ate it!"

After dinner, Edward and Evelyn told the children the news. Each of them cried openly as they had loved their great aunt dearly. Later, as Edward and Evelyn lay in bed, they whispered to each other their fondest memories of Aunt Grace and they wept softly, holding and comforting each other until they drifted off to sleep.

Edward and Evelyn slept soundly that night, emotionally exhausted by their grief. But I could not rest. I was nervous. While Grace had seemed wonderful, I had never really had the chance to know her. She "owned" me (whatever that meant in the physical world), but she had never lived within my walls. She came to visit, but she had never slept under my roof. She had never walked barefoot on my floors on hot summer days. She hadn't cried into the pillows in my rooms or danced down my halls when nobody was watching. I couldn't feel her. So, while I was sad that my family was sad, I was more worried about what would happen to them and to me now that Grace was gone. Who would own me? I knew Grace had relatives somewhere in Florida. Would they own me now? I had no knowledge of how these things worked. I just knew that when events like this happened, things usually changed. Would my story with this family be over so soon?

Edward took the rest of the week off from work so that he could make all the arrangements for Aunt Grace's funeral. After calling Richard Gaffey and being assured that all details would be expertly handled by the funeral home, Edward went to Grace's home to see if he could find information about a will or some guidance on how to handle her estate. He couldn't believe that in all the years he had lived so close to her that he had never thought to ask her what she wanted him to do with her things when she died. He had thought he had plenty of time to talk with her about such things. He didn't even know if she had a lawyer or if she had made any arrangements. He would need to contact Frank's nephew in Florida.

As Edward sat in the well-decorated sunroom of Grace's home, pondering where to begin, he heard a soft knock at the door. When Edward answered, a short man with dark hair and thick black glasses reached out to shake Edward's hand.

"You must be Edward Lockhart," the man said, smiling as he removed his hat. "I've heard a lot about you. May I come in?"

"Who are you?" Edward asked, rather gruffly. He sure didn't want to deal with a door-to-door salesman right now. Grace wouldn't need any more encyclopedias, that's for sure.

"Oh, I apologize! Of course, I should have identified myself," the man replied, still smiling. "I am Mr. Patrick Murphy. I am Grace's attorney. I have her will with me here and I need to discuss some urgent matters with you." Mr. Murphy patted a thin, black briefcase.

Edward eyed the case and then turned his gaze back to Mr. Murphy, who was still smiling. Edward didn't smile in return, as he stepped aside and pulled the door open wider so the man could step inside.

"We can talk in here," Edward said, gesturing to the formal dining room. "Can I get you a glass of water? Sorry, but I don't think Grace kept anything stronger in the house."

"Oh, no thank you, I'm fine," replied Mr. Murphy as he gently placed his briefcase on the shiny mahogany dining table. He flipped the locks on the briefcase and pulled out a thin manila folder. He held it in front of him as he sat down in the shield-back mahogany chair with ivory damask upholstery. Edward sat across from him, hands folded, waiting.

"Well, Mr. Lockhart, as I said, I am, er, was… uh, well, I have served as Mrs. Williams's attorney for several years. As you know, she is…was…a woman of substantial means." Edward nodded once in reply.

"Yes, well, she owns…owned…lots of property here in Scituate, including this house and the house where you and your family are currently residing, along with several acres of land. This land is quite valuable, as you might be aware. And I understand that you are renting the house at North Hill at a rental rate quite a bit lower than the market would demand…"

Here we go, thought Edward, bracing himself. He just stared at the lawyer, neither agreeing nor disagreeing with his assessment of Grace's wealth or generosity.

"Right…. Uh, well, it appears that Grace has a nephew in Florida and some other out of town relatives…" Mr. Murphy continued.

It's over, thought Edward.

"She had me draw up this will here to provide for how she wanted her estate divided," Mr. Murphy said, tapping the cover page with large typed words that read "Grace Vinal Williams, Last Will and Testament, Commonwealth of Massachusetts." He flipped open to a tabbed page. "I came here to let you know that here on page fifteen of her will, your Aunt Grace has left you and Mrs. Lockhart the house on North Hill along with several additional acres behind the property. She also left you a substantial sum of money with which she wanted you to renovate the house to ensure it is a suitable home for your family."

Mr. Murphy had been making circles on the typed pages with the butt of his pen and now looked up at Edward whose mouth was agape and eyes wide. Edward was stunned.

"Mr. Lockhart? Did you hear me?" Mr. Murphy asked, grinning. He had seen relatives shocked by will provisions before but he had never seen a tall, gruff man become so mute with emotion. "She left you the house, Mr. Lockhart. North Hill belongs to you. Congratulations! … Although, I am very sorry for the loss of your Aunt."

Edward, still in shock, remained silent. Mr. Murphy cleared his throat loudly and let out a slight chuckle. Edward shook his head to clear his brain.

"Uh, yes, yes, I heard you, sir. I'm just…well, I don't know what to say. That damn woman never ceased to amaze me," Edward said mostly to himself, shaking his head. His blue eyes were damp with emotion as he looked at Mr. Murphy with intense gratitude. "Thank you for this. Thank you for letting me know. She was…well, she was…my family."

"She was a kind, generous woman. Please accept the house, the land, and the money and honor her by making it a beautiful, loving home. I must go now. I will be working to finalize the details of the estate but just wanted you to know that you and your family have been taken care of."

Mr. Murphy closed his file, snapped his briefcase shut and lifted it off the table without leaving so much as a scuff. "I will let myself out. Good day, Mr. Lockhart."

As Mr. Murphy let himself out, he turned to look back at Edward who was still seated at the dining table. "She loved you like a son, Mr. Lockhart."

The door closed and Edward was alone. He dropped his head into his hands and wept tears of gratitude and love.

Edward told Evelyn the news that evening. A plethora of emotions swirled in my rooms – grief over the loss of beloved Grace - who had truly been the "saving grace"- sagged against my floors, heavy and sad, while gratitude over what she had done climbed my walls like a giant vine, hugging me tightly. The excitement – theirs and mine – that I would forever be Home for this loving family threatened to burst my roof and blow out my windows. William was a senior in high school and planned on leaving Scituate after graduation to attend college so he knew he wouldn't be around to see the renovations, but he was thrilled for his parents. Katherine and Marie, who had been sharing a room since Marie was born, were ecstatic that they would finally have their own rooms and they wanted to know exactly when the renovations would begin and how long they would take. Edward laughed at them as they danced around the kitchen singing, in unison "I get my own roooooooommmmm," but he warned them that things might not happen quite as fast as they hoped.

Because I had heard Evelyn and Edward whispering in their room late at night, I knew Edward was worried about the economy. America was at war in Korea and, as always during times of war, money was tight. Edward was not a healthy man and could no longer work as much as he used to. He was concerned about paying for William's college tuition. Grace had left them a good chunk of money but the renovations would have to be thought through and budgeted carefully. Edward wasn't one to rush things and he was conservative with spending.

When he and Evelyn went to bed that night, Evelyn was still wiping random tears that sprung up when she thought of Grace and the incredible gift she had given them – the gift of a secure future. She held Edward close as his weary body lay next to hers and she put her head on his shoulder. Once again I was reminded at how lucky I was to be a part of such a loving family. I was almost asleep when I heard Evelyn finally say, softly "so, can we at least get rid of that God-awful barn now?" To which Edward replied with a roaring laugh that shook my walls, almost waking his sleeping daughters in the next room.

One week later, the barn was removed – sold to a neighbor. Edward and his good friend, Mike Litchfield, the grandson of the man who built me, took the old barn down by hand, piece by piece, and slowly rebuilt it on Mike's property, where it stood for many years until a lightning strike caused a fire in the old dry wood and it burned to the ground.

Chapter 11

PRESENT DAY

Caroline is roused from her thoughts as she hears the back door open and her brothers' deep voices carry from the kitchen to her spot in the narrow hall upstairs. She glances at her phone and is shocked to see that it is already dinnertime. Anna will be getting off of work soon and Caroline has done nothing about grocery shopping or planning anything for them to eat. She feels guilty for just sitting in the house all day, nursing a hangover and crying over old photos. Caroline wipes her eyes with the bottom of her white t-shirt, staining it with yesterday's mascara. She grabs a box full of old photos that Marie had never gotten around to putting in an album and makes her way downstairs. Maybe looking through them with her siblings, over a glass of wine and takeout from Jamie's Pub, will make her laugh and keep her from blubbering all over them.

"Hey guys. How'd you make out at Home Depot?" Caroline asks as she enters the kitchen. Eyeing the bags scattered on the floor, she answers herself, "Guess you found what you were looking for."

"That place is a nightmare!" Alden replies, shrugging off his jacket.

Thomas looks at their oldest brother and rolls his eyes. "Puh-lease! Home Depot is freaking awesome. They have everything you could ever want, all under one roof."

Thomas had worked at Home Depot while training to be a police officer in Georgia and he loved anything to do with tools, machinery, gadgets and home renovations. In high school, he had been nicknamed "McGuyver" after the popular 80's show about a guy who could fix anything with whatever was laying around. After Thomas had gotten married and started fixing things in his own home and doing remodeling and renovations of his home, Caroline had thought that Thomas's true calling and talent lied in carpentry. He built the most beautiful furniture and custom cabinetry, paying strict attention to the tiniest details. He was truly an artist. Caroline always wondered why he didn't start his own carpentry business rather than spend all of his time dressed in business suits, traveling constantly, and climbing a corporate ladder.

"Okay, brother, if you say so. In any event, to answer your question Cee, yes, we got everything we needed and more. I think we could build a whole new house with the stuff we bought today."

Thomas opens the refrigerator and grabs two beers. He tosses one to Alden and then pops the top on another, asking "So what did you do today, CeeCee?" as he takes a long swig.

Caroline puts the box of photos on the kitchen table and replies, "Well, I'll show you in a minute. But first, let me call Jamie's and order some food. How about you open that bottle of Cabernet on the counter while I make the call? Do y'all want a pizza or a pasta dinner?"

"Pizza's good with me," replies Alden.

"Yeah, that's fine with me," Thomas agrees. "I never get good pizza anymore. My wife the health nut won't allow real pizza in our house – it's always some gluten free crap. Also, they just don't know how to make decent pizza in Colorado. I think it's the altitude. Good pizza is one thing I miss about this place."

"Okay, I'll get two large ones and also a couple of salads so you can at least tell Mindy you ate something green," Caroline offers as she pulls her phone from her pocket.

She likes the fact that she has to actually call the restaurant and speak to a live person to place her order. Jamie's is still a small-town joint and doesn't have an app for instant ordering. Caroline orders a large meat lovers pizza, a large veggie pizza, and two large

Greek salads for delivery and then sits down at the kitchen table next to the box of photos. Thomas hands her a glass of red wine. The smell of the wine reminds her stomach of last night's vodka and she sets it down next to the open box full of their mother's memories. *Maybe after the food arrives*, she thinks.

"Come look at this stuff I found today, guys," Caroline says.

"Should we wait for Anna?" Alden asks, glancing at his watch.

"She just texted me that she is on her way. She's gonna pick up the pizza. She has seen most of this already. I wanted to show you guys though."

Thomas and Alden pull out a couple chairs and sit down. Caroline opens a photo album and sets a stack of loose photographs on the table.

"Wow, look at Aunt Katherine," Thomas says wistfully, holding up a color photo depicting their beautiful aunt with shoulder length blonde hair and a wide, bright smile, laughing and waving at the camera. "She was such a cool lady."

Caroline smiles at the image. "I know. I miss her so much," she said quietly. "She was hysterical and her laugh was contagious. You couldn't help but have fun when she was around."

"Yeah, cousin Mary is just like her. I wish we could all get together sometime," Thomas replies. Aunt Katherine had four children – Stephen Jr., Katie, Mary, and Bill. Although they were a few years older, the cousins had been close.

"Oh my God, look at Nana in this photo," Alden laughs, holding up a formal black and white portrait of Evelyn sitting in a chair. She must have been in her early twenties. "She looks exactly like Laura!" Anna's oldest child, Laura was the spitting image of the great grandmother she never knew.

"Oh I know!" Caroline exclaims, smiling at the portrait of their grandmother. "Mom always said that Laura reminded her of Nana – even her mannerisms are the same, which is so weird because Laura never met her, of course. Mom always commented that it was as if Nana was reincarnated. Kind of creepy, but also interesting how strong family genes can be!"

The three of them sit, sifting through the old photos – some they have seen before while others are new to them. There is a group of photos bound by a rubber band – each depicting a different child sitting on the front steps of the house, on their first day of school, waiting for the school bus. There are black and whites of their mother, Uncle William, and Aunt Katherine from the '40's and '50's. There is a photo of Alden, on the same stoop, standing with plaid, wide bottom pants and a bowl haircut, holding a Star Wars lunch box, clearly taken in the mid 1970's. Another photo shows Anna, in 1984 heading off to first grade, dressed in a floral dress with two vertical ruffles down the front and long curly hair. Behind that are photos of each of Anna's children during the 90's, each on their first day of kindergarten. In each photo, the child sits or stands in the same spot. And, other than the color of the front door, which changed from black to green to purple, the House looks the same in each image. The three siblings shuffle through each photo in silence, each deep in his and her thoughts and memories. Their silence is broken by the sound of the breezeway door slamming and footsteps on the back stairs. Alden jumps up to open the door for Anna who walks in weighed down with pizza boxes and grocery sacks.

"Jeez, Anna, we could have helped you carry that stuff from the car," Caroline says marveling at her sister's ability to carry so many items at once without dropping anything.

"I've got it," Anna answers slinging everything up onto the counter. "Doesn't make sense to make everyone go out there when I can do it one trip."

Caroline immediately begins unloading the grocery bags and putting things away. Thomas grabs some plates and napkins and sets the pizza boxes on the table. Within seconds, they are each munching on cheesy pizza and salad.

"We were just looking through this box of old photos that I found in Mom's closet upstairs," Caroline says through a mouthful of food.

"I see that," Anna replies. "I've seen all of those before. Before Mom died she used to like to look through those and tell me stories about the people in the photos. She would even tell me stories about my own kids as if I hadn't been here to experience them for myself," Anna laughed. "You know how Mom could be. She loved to talk. I know everything there is to know about those photos."

It strikes Caroline then how much she has missed by living so far away. Of course Anna knows everything about their ancestors in the photographs. She had spent numerous hours with Mom over the years, living in Scituate her whole life – most of it right in this house. A mixture of admiration and sympathy rushes over Caroline as she watches her sister pick some photos from the box. This whole situation has to be exponentially harder on her than it is for the rest of them.

"There aren't many pictures of Papa Lockhart in here," Alden remarks.

"Well, that's because he died so young," Anna answered. "And not everyone had a camera back then. But there are a few in here." She pulls out an old photo album with a blue leather cover and starts flipping the pages until she finds what she is looking for. "Here he is," she says, pointing to a photo of a stern-looking man with the signature Lockhart pug nose, sitting in an armchair by a fireplace. "This was taken in Caroline's bedroom, which was his sitting room back then."

"Dang, look at that face," Caroline says. "I've seen that look before." Caroline turns the edges of her mouth down and lowers her jaw.

"Haha, the classic Lockhart bulldog face!" Thomas laughs. "Nana's genes clearly weren't the only strong ones in the family."

"Yeah, you look a lot like him, too, brother," Caroline retorts. "Look at that bald head and long face!"

"Whoooaaaa, ouch! Okay, then…"

"He was a good looking guy and you've got nothing to worry about." Caroline assures her younger brother, knowing she hit a soft spot.

"I don't know what you guys are talking about," Alden says, running his hand through his thick hair in an exaggerated manner.

"Aw man, shut up," Thomas scowls at Alden. "I don't know where you got that mop – so not fair, bro!" Alden laughs.

"Well, Alden may not have Papa Lockhart's bald head, but he did inherit his gruff demeanor," Anna chimes in, winking at her older brother.

"Well, we wouldn't know much about that since he died when Alden was only one and before the rest of us were born," Caroline says. "Mom told stories over the years but I sure wish we could have known him."

They all nod in solemn agreement. They get quiet again as they turn the pages of the photo album, taking in the images of the grandfather they never knew. As Caroline flips the pages, the siblings are treated to a glimpse into life at North Hill during the 1950's. The images depict a lovely family of five living right here under this roof.

"What was this mangy dog's name again?" Alden asks picking up a black and white of their mother, young and smiling, hugging a big, shaggy, white and brown dog.

"That's Whiskers," Anna answers. "His full name was Whiskers Walrus Heinz 57 Sneak Fats Domino Lockhart."

"Of course it was," Alden replies shaking his head. "Man, our mother was weird. What happened to something simple, like 'Spot' or even just 'Whiskers'?"

"Have you ever known Mom to keep things simple, brother?" Thomas asks.

"Good point."

✟✟✟✟

The mood is lighthearted and my soul is warmed to see the Freeman kids traveling down memory lane. I, of course, can't flip through old boxes of photographs to trigger my memories. But I don't need to. My memories are still alive, secure within my walls. I hold the sounds of this family's laughter, the energy of their love, the spirit of each member, and I can still feel them every day. While the siblings flip through images of the 1950's and 1960's, the memories of those years come flooding forward.

Chapter 12

WILLIAM
1954

Evelyn stood at the kitchen stove, stirring with her wooden spoon in an attempt to keep the spaghetti sauce from burning. But it was difficult to concentrate while she strained to hear the exchange between her husband and her oldest child in the next room. She could hear their voices rise and then fall again. The curiosity of what was being said was overwhelming. She knew it couldn't be good.

Just moments ago, William had appeared at the back door unexpectedly. He had arrived in North Scituate on the six-thirty bus and then walked to North Hill and through the kitchen door, surprising them all. It was early November, and William was a freshman at Norwich University in Vermont. He had left for college in September and wasn't expected home until Thanksgiving. Yet here he was. He was currently seated defiantly at the dining room table, involved in an intense discussion with Edward, while two suitcases and a duffle bag with his belongings sat in a heap in the tiny hall by the back door. He clearly wasn't home just for a long weekend and Evelyn was concerned. She turned the burner to simmer and silently inched closer to the door to the dining room to hear better.

"Well, son, I can respect that," Evelyn heard Edward say, his voice slow with patient self-restraint. "You are a man and a man makes his own decisions. But a man also doesn't live with his parents and do nothing, especially when other men are serving their country. So, be ready at dawn and I will take you to see John O'Connor."

Evelyn's hand flew to her mouth and her heart sank. John O'Connor was the local army recruiter in the Harbor. He had sent many young men from Scituate off to fight that God-awful war in Korea. Surely Edward didn't intend for William to sign up with the Army! He was a college student. Evelyn couldn't imagine that the Selective Service was drafting kids out of college. So why would Edward be taking William to see John O'Connor? A nauseating feeling of dread crept up Evelyn's spine. She shivered and walked back toward the stove to check on her sauce. She wasn't sure how long she had been standing there, mechanically pushing the wooden spoon through the thick tomatoes while her worried mind raced, when she felt Edward's hand on her shoulder. Evelyn whipped around to face him.

"What is going on?" she whispered, looking deep into her husband's eyes that were heavy with worry.

"He left school," Edward replied, gravely.

"What? Why? For good?" Evelyn blinked and glanced at the bags piled in the back hall.

"Yes, for good. Or, at least for now – I don't know. He says he couldn't do it. He was miserable. He said he wasn't cut out for it and he just packed his bags and bought a bus ticket home. He is very upset."

Evelyn frowned and shook her head. "I don't understand. He never indicated that he was unhappy. Why would he just leave without telling us first? What is he going to do now?"

Edward took both of her hands in his and looked down at her, his eyes serious and firm. Evelyn's brow, furrowed in confusion, slowly softened as she gazed into her husband's eyes, and then knitted together again with deep worry as she began to understand what he was trying to tell her.

"Oh no, no, no," she whimpered, shaking her head back and forth. "Ed, he can't go. He just can't. He is only seventeen for God's sake. He is our only son! What are you thinking?"

"He can. And he will," Edward said, sternly. "He has quit college and has no other plan. He will get drafted anyway as soon as he turns eighteen and they find out he isn't enrolled in school. No son of mine is going to just sit around this house and wait for them to force him to go. If he doesn't want to be in college right now, I can accept that. But I cannot accept him living here, doing nothing. He will go see John in the morning and will be on the train to Boston by lunchtime. He understands that this is what he has to do."

Evelyn yanked her hands out of Edward's grasp and turned away from him, covering her face as she began to sob. She was scared. The war in Korea had officially ended only weeks ago, but U.S. troops remained, helping to establish the demilitarized zone. Fighting still broke out regularly and it was still very dangerous. Even if he somehow escaped being sent to Korea, Evelyn knew that he would still go somewhere far away for training camp. She wasn't ready for her oldest child, her only son, to be gone, engaging in risky activities where she couldn't visit him. He was still her baby.

But deep down Evelyn knew Edward was right. Scituate offered no opportunities for a seventeen-year-old boy just out of high school. And, although the war had technically ended, the Army was still drafting young men who weren't enrolled in college. It was only a matter of time before he would be sent away. Evelyn tried to imagine her son marching with an army.

Her thoughts took her back to that day in April 1936 when she gave birth to William right here in this house. She and Edward had been married less than a month when she had started feeling nauseated in the mornings. Dr. Ward had said she was six weeks along. Evelyn hadn't needed to do the math to know that she had conceived William the night she and Edward had snuck into their new house as it was being renovated prior to their wedding. They had laid together right here, where she was standing now. William had been a beautiful, easy baby and Evelyn loved being a mother.

Only two years after William was born, baby Katherine had arrived. A boy and a girl. The family had felt complete.

William had grown to be a precocious, intelligent child. She loved how he had called her "Mrs. Lockhart" even at home and long after he graduated from her kindergarten class at the Cohasset Baptist Church. He was strong and independent and his grade school teachers had all loved him. The year that little Emily had been hit by the truck had been a particularly difficult year for all of them and William had never really recovered from the trauma of it all. After all, he had been the one who kicked the ball that Emily had chased into the road. William had become somewhat quiet and sullen after that event and, unfortunately, Evelyn hadn't been able to comfort him as she suffered with her own demons from that tragedy. At only nine years old, William had been Evelyn's rock the following year when Edward had almost died from pneumonia. And then, nine months later, when Marie had been born, Evelyn had been relieved and happy to see the glimmer of light in William's eyes return. He had loved his baby sister and he grew to be a protective, loving big brother. But he also had a bit of a wild side and, throughout his four years in high school he had tested Evelyn and Edward's patience to the breaking point.

William was smart and had a quick wit. And he loved teasing other people just to get a reaction. As a young teen he was forever playing practical jokes on his teachers, friends, and family. This resulted in Evelyn being called in for many teacher conferences to discuss "William's energetic sense of humor." In his junior and senior years of high school, his "energy" resulted in many days of skipping school and partying down by the beach with his friends. Many nights Evelyn and Edward had sat up waiting to hear the car pull into the driveway so they could finally sleep knowing he was home safely. This had caused many arguments between William and his father and a rift had developed between them, as the two men were each very stubborn. Evelyn, however, could see that William was much like his father and gently reminded Edward on occasion that he hadn't exactly been an easy teen, to which Edward always scoffed and replied, "the kids these days!" Evelyn would then turn away and roll her eyes toward heaven and ask God for the patience required to deal with them both.

God, or someone, had listened to her prayers because, by some miracle of faith, William Lockhart had graduated from Scituate High School at the age of seventeen and had been accepted to Norwich College. Evelyn had worried that he was young and perhaps a bit immature for college. But, she had proudly driven to Vermont with Edward to drop William off at campus in September. Now, only two months later, her fears were confirmed. William had quit college and had come home. And now he would be enlisting in the Army!

Her heart was heavy as she laid in the dark of her bedroom that night, listening to my pipes creak as the radiators turned on. Edward lay snoring softly next to her and she turned her back to him. Although she knew her husband was only doing what he believed to be right, she was nonetheless angry with him. She knew her anger was irrational but she didn't care. This was their son - her little boy. She closed her eyes and prayed silently until sleep finally came.

Edward drove William to the recruiter early the next morning and a mere three hours later Edward was on the train to Boston where he would then board another train to Texas. Evelyn had hugged her only son tightly and cried silently as she said good-bye. When he had gone, she sat alone at the small kitchen table, put her head in her hands and sobbed until her shoulders shook and she could barely breathe. Katherine and Marie had watched from front porch as their father had driven up the hill with William sitting in the passenger seat, staring straight ahead. Their big brother was going to be a soldier. Katherine was a junior in high school and knew boys who had gone off to war. They were the older brothers of her friends or boys from church. She was worried. Marie, who was only eight years old, didn't fully understand why everyone was so upset. To her, William leaving was not much different than when he had left for college. She didn't know about "war" or understand fully what it meant. She only knew that she was proud of her big brother and that she would miss him.

After Edward returned home from the train station, he was solemn and short tempered. He poured himself a scotch and water and sat in his favorite blue chair in the living room. He didn't turn on the radio or the television. He just sat, looking thoughtfully around the room, taking in my plaster walls with the patterned wallpaper.

That winter, perhaps as a way to get the family's mind off of the fact that their boy was off serving his country, or maybe as an apology to Evelyn, or both, Edward had a new, grand living room built to the left of the front door, complete with large plate glass window facing the street and a full-sized fireplace with mantle on the side wall with built in bookshelves on either side. Hardwood floors were installed to match the rest of the house and beautiful french doors led to the dining room. This allowed the old front parlor to be converted to a bedroom, now making three bedrooms downstairs. And, for his bride, Edward had the kitchen renovated with new cabinets, a bigger pantry, and new appliances. A new refrigerator boasted an icemaker, which was considered quite a luxury. Evelyn picked out a matching electric oven and range. I was so proud of my new modern kitchen.

As the old barn had been removed, Edward decided he needed a space for his car and tools. He had a garage built at the end of the driveway, big enough for two cars. He connected the garage to the house via a long breezeway that led from the side of the garage to the kitchen door. Now, they could park the car inside a garage and access it without ever having to go out in the rain or snow. The breezeway was essentially a wide hallway with windows for walls. In the summer, the windows would hold screens to allow the warm summer breezes to flow through. In the winter, glass windows would be installed to protect against the elements while still allowing light to shine in. The hill sloped down from the kitchen so the back steps remained and then another step down led from the breezeway to the garage and a side door was installed that stepped down onto a flag stone walkway that sloped down to the driveway. Evelyn furnished the breezeway with wicker furniture and a glass top dining table with iron chairs, to allow the family a lovely summer dining area. I had never felt so fancy. But all the lovely improvements couldn't fill the void left by William's enlisting and, although Evelyn smiled and often and went about her days normally, I could feel her worry for her only son.

It was the beginning of a lot of changes for our family.

Chapter 13

KATHERINE
1957

During the late 1950's, Katherine Lockhart was a teenage beauty. To nine-year-old Marie, Katherine was the picture of sophistication. Marie watched her big sister's every move, idolizing everything about her from her stylish bobbed haircut to the way she held her cigarette and blew smoke rings high in the air. In Katherine's senior year of high school, she began dating Stephen Scott, a local boy who had grown up on third cliff and was as charming as he was handsome. He was two years older than Katherine and was enlisted in the Marines. To Katherine, he was mature and worldly and she was absolutely smitten. Marie would sit at the kitchen table, watching Katherine and Stephen breeze through the back door, hand in hand. Marie loved to watch them, marveling at how romantic it seemed to be so young, so beautiful, and so much in love.

Stephen always made a big show about how much he adored Katherine. He was always touching her, holding her in his arms and spinning her around the room. Her blonde curls would fall in front of her face and then she would throw her head back laughing, her eyes sparkling with total adoration. When he went away for active duty, Stephen wrote love poems and sent flowers. When he was able to get leave and come home, a dozen red roses would appear at our house prior to his arrival. Katherine would receive the roses and her entire face would light up. She would spend the next twenty-four hours ironing her best dresses, fixing her hair, and getting her makeup just right. She never knew exactly when he would show up. It was his style to simply send the roses and then surprise her with great romantic fanfare, arriving with an armful of more roses and champagne. He would swoop her into his arms and spin her around the room, then set her down to kiss her long and gentle before pulling away, looking deep into her blue eyes and saying "Hello, Princess!" Katherine would visibly swoon. She was captivated by his looks, his charm, and his obvious infatuation with her. Watching them was like watching a fairy tale playing out right there in the living room. Marie had thought they were the most wonderfully perfect couple she had ever seen.

The summer after Katherine's high school graduation, Stephen was based in South Carolina and Katherine missed him terribly. She had enrolled in the Katherine Gibbs secretarial school in Boston to keep busy. One afternoon, Katherine arrived home from her classes in Boston to find one dozen red roses on the kitchen table.

"He's coming!" she sighed as she pressed a single flower to her nose and inhaled deeply.

Marie dreamily watched her sister as she twirled around the kitchen, eyes closed with the rose held tightly to her chest. Katherine then danced down the hall to begin her flurry of preparing for Stephen's arrival. Evelyn was preparing dinner. Edward entered the kitchen and was almost knocked over by Katherine twirling through the doorway with a faraway look in her eyes.

"Jesus Christ, is that asshole coming again?" Edward gruffed. "I swear, they don't run the military like they used to. That son of a bitch has more leave time in one month than most of my friends had their entire time in the military. And what's with all the roses every time he comes to visit? Hasn't the kid heard of a telephone to let her know he is coming?"

"Oh, Ed, it's romantic," Evelyn replied shaking her head as she sliced potatoes for the pot roast.

"You call that romance? I call it nonsense!" Edward grumbled. "I hope you aren't buying this, Marie." Edward ruffled the curls on top of his youngest child's head. Marie looked up at her father who soared above her, looking gruff with his bald head and scowled brow. "Oh Daddy, but it *is* romantic! I want to be in love someday just like Katherine. And Stephen is so handsome. He's dreamy!"

"*Dreamy??*" Edward roared, throwing his head back laughing. "Well, now! If that skinny, smooth-talking greaser is dreamy, I don't want to ever fall asleep! Come over here, Stink Britches. I'll show you Dreamy!" He sat in one of the ladder back chairs and patted his right knee.

Marie loved sitting on her father's lap, even at age twelve, and she didn't care that he called her "stink britches." She knew he meant it with love. She climbed up and put her head on his strong shoulder, inhaling the scent of his spicy aftershave mixed with whiskey and old cigars.

"She really loves him, Daddy. And he loves her. Just look at all the roses he sends, and the love poems. And the way he is so happy to see her that he spins her around so fast her dress flies out like a ballerina."

"Hmmmppfff" Edward grumbled, clearly not as charmed by young Stephen Scott as the females in his family. "A man who truly loves a woman doesn't need such fanfare. It feels phony to me."

Marie looked up at her father, her eyebrows knitted together. "Don't you think he loves her, Daddy?"

"Oh, your father is just being grumpy," Evelyn chimed in, shooting Edward a look of warning over Marie's head. "He just doesn't have a romantic bone in his body, that's all. I think he might even be a little jealous." Evelyn teased.

Again, Edward threw his head back and laughed a big, deep laugh that always made Marie giggle. "Why would you be jealous, Daddy? You can't marry Katherine, she's your daughter, silly!" Edward's laughter roared louder.

"Not jealous in that way, sweetie," Evelyn explained, laughing softly. "He is jealous because he wishes he could be as romantic and charming as Stephen."

Edward let out a loud gaffaw. "You want romance, Piano Legs? I'll show you romance!" He stood abruptly, placing Marie in the chair next to him. He grabbed his wife around the waist and spun her around to face him, holding her close.

"Edward! I am holding a very large, very sharp knife!" Evelyn said slowly.

Edward covered her right hand with his and slowly eased the knife out of her fingers and placed it on the counter behind her.

"Well I hope you weren't planning to use it," he whispered in her ear as he started swaying back and forth in a close, slow dance in the middle of the kitchen. Marie giggled. She wasn't used to seeing her father act like this. He was obviously in a very good mood.

"Edward, I have to finish the dinner." Evelyn said, staring up at her husband, but making no move to free herself from his embrace. Edward just pulled his wife closer, holding her right hand firmly, with his left arm encircling her waist. He bent his head to her left ear and whispered something Marie couldn't hear. At that, she saw her mother close her eyes and lean into her husband, seemingly forgetting where she was, forgetting all about cooking dinner, and forgetting anyone else was in the room. The moment was fleeting before Edward gave Evelyn's hand a squeeze and released her from his grip.

"You wanted romance, you got your romance. Now, I'm hungry!"

He was back to his normal self. But in the brief moment when her parents stood, eyes closed, dancing in the kitchen, twelve year old Marie knew she had just witnessed something special.

Stephen and Katherine continued dating while he finished his tour in South Carolina. Stephen proposed to Katherine the following summer and the lovebirds were married in a small, but lovely outdoor ceremony at Stephen's parents' house on third cliff. On a grassy lawn high above the Atlantic ocean, with the waves crashing below, thirteen-year-old Marie stood by her older sister as a bridesmaid. She didn't care what their father had said, Marie was sure that she was witnessing true love. Anybody could see how in love the young couple was. Marie watched the newlyweds dance that afternoon and fantasized about what her own wedding would be like one day.

After the wedding, Stephen surprised everyone with the announcement that he was leaving the marines and had enrolled in flight school in Florida. Katherine was the most surprised of all.

✟✟✟✟

And with that, our golden girl moved away to Fort Lauderdale.

None of it felt right to me. But nobody asked my opinion and life moved on.

Chapter 14

MARIE AND JIM
1965

Evelyn stood in the attic staring at the blue-gray Lady Baltimore suitcase and matching makeup case she had purchased for Marie for her high school graduation gift two years ago. The tags were still on them. Evelyn couldn't believe two years had passed since Marie's graduation dinner when she had given Marie the luggage along with a plane ticket to London and Marie had burst into tears. Evelyn remembered how excited she had been to be able to offer her youngest daughter a trip of a lifetime - a two-week, mother and daughter tour of Europe! She had wrapped the luggage carefully in bright blue and white striped wrapping paper. The tickets had been safely tucked inside a pocket of the makeup case. Evelyn would have died of happiness if her parents had given her such a gift on her own high school graduation and she couldn't wait to see Marie's face when she opened it. But it hadn't gone quite the way Evelyn had planned. *With daughters, does it ever?* Evelyn thought, as she remembered that day.

"Mom, I'm sorry. I just can't possibly go. I know you planned this and spent so much money on this gorgeous luggage and the plane tickets and everything, but can't you see why I can't go? Please don't make me go!"

Marie and Evelyn had stood in the formal living room, torn bits of blue and white wrapping paper strewn across the floor. A "Congratulations" banner hung in the wide opening between the living room and the dining room. Remnants of a half-eaten double layer carrot cake sat on the dining room table, its edges hardening in the evening air. Edward still sat at the head of the table watching the exchange between his youngest child and his wife. Evelyn had been ecstatic to give Marie her graduation gift. But then Marie had opened it and had immediately begun to cry. Edward had sat very still, not sure how, or if, he should intervene.

"Marie, don't be silly," Evelyn had replied, clearly irritated. "This is a trip of a lifetime. Most girls would kill for a chance like this. I know you love Jim and that you don't want to be away from him, but for heaven's sake, it's only two weeks. You just graduated from high school. You are young! I'm giving you an opportunity to see a different part of the world. With me. We may not get this chance again. Please don't be crazy and pass this up just to spend your summer following Jim Freeman around town."

"Oh my God, Mom! You just don't get it, do you?" Marie had cried. "This is the last summer I have with him. He is leaving in August to go to college in Pennsylvania. I need to be with him as much as possible before he leaves me. How am I supposed to be away from him for two whole weeks in Europe? That is *sooo long* and *sooo far away*. I would rather die!"

Evelyn had turned away from her daughter, her feelings hurt and her patience wearing thin. She had looked at Edward who had raised his eyebrows, silently asking her if she wanted him to step in. Part of Evelyn wanted him to. He could be gruff and authoritative and order Marie to stop being so dramatic and ungrateful and take the trip with her mother, no more discussion. But Evelyn had taken a deep breath and shook her head. She turned back to her eighteen-year-old daughter. Evelyn sighed, her heart a bit broken but her eyes conveyed a deep understanding of what it was like to be eighteen and want something very different than what your parents wanted for you. Ironic that her daughter wanted for herself exactly what Evelyn's parents had wanted for Evelyn at the same age – to settle down with a nice local boy. But all Evelyn had wanted was to travel and see new things, experience new places and meet new people - the very thing her daughter was now rejecting. Evelyn marveled at how different she and Marie were. Evelyn realized, however, that if she hadn't followed her own heart, she would have stayed in Minnesota and married the dentist and she would have never met Edward. And what would happen if she didn't permit Marie to follow her own heart? Funny how the lessons we learn when we are young shape the decisions and the things we want for our own children; but then our children want what is opposite. Evelyn let out a heavy sigh.

"I will return the luggage and cancel the tickets. I just hope you know what you are doing."

Marie and Jim had met during their sophomore year of high school when Jim moved to Anne Vinal Road in Scituate Harbor with his parents and four younger siblings. Prior to moving to Scituate, the Freeman family had lived in the Philippines where Jim's father had been stationed with the U.S. Navy. The fact that Jim had lived overseas had automatically made him somewhat of an exotic newcomer in the small, predominantly Irish town. All the kids in town had wanted to know the new boy from the Philippines. The boys sized him up. The girls swooned. Marie, born of stubborn Lockhart stock and never one to follow the pack, initially pegged this new boy as conceited and a show-off and she made a conscious effort to pay him no attention – and to make sure he knew it. Whether she had known then that such behavior was the fastest way to get a boy's attention, I still wonder. Either way, Marie's deliberate indifference was like a magnet that attracted fifteen-year-old Jim with a force even he didn't understand. After several months of flirting, Jim persuaded Marie to go on a date. Of course, as they were only fifteen, their "first date" consisted of meeting after school with a group of friends at Ronnie Shone's, the local convenience store that was within walking distance of the high school. There, Jim bought Marie a Coca Cola. It didn't take long for the meetings at Ronnie Shone's to become a weekly thing – sometimes twice a week. One warm, sunny afternoon in June of their sophomore year, just before school let out for the summer,

Jim got up the nerve to kiss Marie behind the store when nobody was around. As Marie would later tell her children and grandchildren: "I didn't much care for your grandfather when I first met him, but after he kissed me, well, I knew right then that I would marry him one day."

Throughout the summer after sophomore year, the two were inseparable and by junior year they had officially become boyfriend and girlfriend. One hot, muggy August evening just before the start of senior year, Jim had arrived at our Home to pick up Marie for a date at the movies. Edward and Evelyn were out to dinner and the house was quiet. Jim knocked on the back door to the kitchen and waited. Even though he had been in the house a million times, he still waited for Marie to invite him in. Marie, dressed in a light pink summer dress and sandals, opened the door, kissed him on the cheek and motioned for him to come inside.

"I'm almost ready. I just need to find my purse and my lipstick," she said over her shoulder as she ran back down the hall toward her room.

Jim stood, waiting in the kitchen, looking at the familiar walls and furnishings. He had been dating Marie for a year and a half and he felt very comfortable in this house. Even though Marie's father liked to give him a hard time, Jim knew Mr. and Mrs. Lockhart liked him. He had spent many evenings dining with the family. He liked how they always ate in the formal dining room and that meals were a time for quiet, adult conversation. Unlike Marie, who was the youngest and the only sibling left at home, Jim was the oldest of four siblings; the youngest still in elementary school. Suppertime at his house was fairly chaotic. It was impossible to hold a meaningful conversation over the chatter about sports, homework, and the latest playground fistfight. Jim enjoyed the peacefulness of dinner with the Lockhart's, despite that Edward always started the evening with some sort of dig at Jim. A favorite insult that he used quite often went something like: "Jesus, Son, your ears are so big you look like a taxi cab coming down Tremont Street with both doors wide open." Jim, always polite, would laugh and nod his head. He had come to understand that Edward only insulted those he could trust to handle it, and it was his way of showing acceptance.

110

Jim had grown to love this family, and he was madly in love with Marie. He had never met anyone like her. She was beautiful, smart, and sophisticated, with just enough of a wild side to keep things fun and interesting. While Jim was serious and reserved, Marie was a free spirit and she made him feel light and happy when they were together. Plus, she was the most beautiful girl at Scituate High, with her small, sloped nose and hazel eyes peering at him over high cheekbones. She had a pretty mouth that turned down naturally, giving her a haughty look when she wasn't smiling. She would chew on the inside of her cheeks and scowl when she was worried or thinking hard about something, which Jim thought was adorable. She was not exactly athletic but, wow, the girl could dance. At parties or even just on the sidewalk down at Nantasket Beach, where the bands played on the weekends, she would grab Jim's hand and pull him to her and beg him to dance. Jim, who was much more reserved, would initially shake his head, no, but then she would start swinging her hips and shaking her body to the music, filling him with longing and laughter that was contagious until there was nothing else to do but join her. She was impossible to resist. Marie was a good girl and, while they had certainly done their share of kissing and messing around in Jim's car while they parked at Peggotty Beach, or by the water tower in the woods, they had always been careful to stop when things got too heated. After all, they had both just turned seventeen and everyone knew what happened to a girl's reputation if she went all the way. Not that Jim didn't want to …

"Jimmy, can you help me, please?" Marie's voice roused him from his thoughts. She had changed her dress and was standing before him in a knee-length, lavender dress with a full skirt that made her hazel eyes look like the swirled marbles he collected as a child. He liked this one that showed off her sculpted collarbone and her tiny waist. She turned her back to him and eyed him over her bare shoulder. "Can you zip me? I can't reach the last bit myself," Marie had asked motioning her eyes toward her zipper. Jim's eyes roamed over her exposed back as he placed one hand on her hip and gently guided the zipper up. She turned toward him, staring up into his deep blue eyes, that were filled with a desire no seventeen-year-old could resist, and whispered, "thank you." God, she loved him. She loved the way he smelled, the way his hands felt on her waist and her shoulders. She could feel the warmth radiating from him and she longed to melt into him. But Marie's eyes suddenly filled with tears and she looked away abruptly, stepping to the side. Surprised by the sudden shift in her mood, Jim had frowned.

"What is it? What's wrong?"

Marie had stared out the kitchen window at the lush green yard and the setting sun's rays filtering through the trees. She shook her head, slowly, trying to regain her composure. Her emotions had come out of nowhere.

"I'm sorry," she muttered, still not turning around. "I just suddenly felt like…like I was losing you."

Jim had stepped toward her and gently laid is hand on her arm, pulling her around to face him. "Marie, why would you ever think you are losing me?"

"I don't know. It just came out of nowhere. I was looking at you and then it just hit me. We are seniors. We are going to be making plans for college. Your Dad has already said you will be going to Penn on an ROTC scholarship. It's just so far away." Giant tears had spilled from Marie's eyes.

"Hey. Hey, now. Slow down. That's not for a whole year. We don't have to think about that now." Jim had pulled her to him and wrapped his arms tightly around her as she pushed her tear-filled cheek into his chest.

She nodded as she silently cried in his arms. Jim acted strong but inside his heart was breaking also. He knew he was expected to go to Penn. He had worked so hard in his ROTC program throughout high school and was rewarded with a full-ride scholarship at the ivy-league university. It was an opportunity of a lifetime. He wanted to go, but he didn't want to leave Marie. But what choice did he have? He just held her, both of them feeling like their future was not within their control.

Jim and Marie went to the movie theater that night and sat in silence watching *Mutiny on the Bounty*, each of them lost in thought. After the movie, Jim had driven to their favorite spot up in the rocky cliffs of The Glades, a secluded area in North Scituate overlooking Minot's lighthouse. With the windows down, the soft summer breeze was cool and Marie had snuggled into Jim who pulled her close as they stared out over the Atlantic Ocean. Minot's light was blinking to warn passing ships of the submerged ledge. They watched the light blink once, then four times, then three – 1-4-3 -- a sequence locals have, for years, ascribed to meaning "I love you."

"There is a storm coming," Jim had whispered, looking up at the starless black sky. "That's why it's blinking tonight."

"And here I am thinking it is blinking just for us," Marie had replied. "I thought you ordered it to blink like that just for me." She lifted her head from Jim's shoulder to look at him.

"I do love you, you know," Jim had said, looking intently into Marie's eyes, which immediately filled again with tears.

"I love you, too."

"Then no more tears," Jim had whispered, wiping at her eye with his thumb and cradling her face in his hands.

He leaned his face down and his lips met hers. Her breath caught as she leaned into his kiss, feeling a desperation born of great love and uncertainty for their future. Her kiss deepened as she melted her body to his. She couldn't get close enough to him, this boy she loved more than she had ever loved anything. Lightning lit up the sky, startling them both so that they pulled apart, laughing.

"One..two…three…" Jim counted before thunder boomed and rolled over them so they could feel it in their chests.

"Wow, that's pretty close." Marie scooted closer again.

Just then the rain began, pelting the car with big, fat drops, slowly at first and then a downpour that matched the intensity of the lightning and thunder. They laughed and raced to roll up the windows. As the storm moved on-shore and wrapped the teenagers in its building fury, the electricity inside the car sparked a need that could no longer be denied and Jim and Marie comforted each other in the only way that seemed natural. Finally, after the storm had begun to wane, the young first-time lovers held tightly, clinging to each other for their lives and staring down an uncertain future. They didn't know what would happen in the coming year. They only knew that the love they felt was as real and as powerful as anything God had ever created.

Senior year went by all too quickly. Marie and Jim were voted "cutest couple" for the class of 1963 and were faced daily with questions about their plans after graduation. "Are you going to get married?" their friends would inquire. "When does Jim leave for Penn?" the adults would ask. "How will you possibly survive without him?" teen girls looking for drama would throw out there. It had become almost unbearable. Jim had talked at length with his mother and father about his options but they all knew he could not pass up the scholarship. He and Marie would just have to be patient. After several discussions with her parents and school advisors, Marie decided that she would remain at home in Scituate and would attend a teacher's college in Boston. Jim promised to marry her after college and she vowed to wait for him.

In September, the young couple said a tearful goodbye and the plans others had set for them were set into motion. Jim left for Pennsylvania and Marie started classes in Boston and worked as a model for Priscilla's of Boston bridal shop. Every morning she rode the P&B Bus from North Scituate to South Station and returned home late in the evening. Every day, she stared out the bus window, watching the traffic go by, and dreamed of when Jim would come back. They kept in touch through letters and occasional phone calls. But Jim lived in a dorm where the only long distance line was in a crowded hallway, most days with a long line of other boys waiting to steal a few minutes to talk to their families or girlfriends. And, Jim was at ROTC early every morning and late into the evenings. There wasn't much time for calls. When he did call he sounded distant, exhausted, and unhappy. He told Marie stories of other students crumbling under the pressure of the elite education and vigorous ROTC training they had signed up for. Many were dropping out and returning home to disappointed families. Marie was worried for Jim's health, both mentally and physically.

The Freeman family had sold their house in Scituate and had moved to Cincinnati where Jim's father had been hired by Proctor & Gamble. Jim didn't even have family in Scituate any longer. The young couple could feel their future slipping through their grasps. Jim became depressed and withdrawn. Marie felt uncertain and lonely. And at nineteen and in love, the months felt like years, and desperation descended over them like a thick blanket, suffocating them until the only thing left to do was something drastic and unplanned.

On a cold, clear evening in November, 1963, Marie exited the 7:05p.m. bus in North Scituate. With her head down, watching where she stepped in case of ice, she headed for the parking lot on Gannet Road where she had parked her car that morning. In the summer and early fall she would have walked the mile from North Hill to the bus stop, but this time of year when it got dark early and the air was frigid, driving made much more sense. As she approached the lot, she sensed she was being watched and the hairs on the back of her neck tingled with adrenaline. She had been the only commuter to get off at this stop tonight and, while Scituate was a very safe little town, there were some local characters who liked to walk this route after leaving the local bars. If they were drunk and wanted to cause trouble, a single girl alone at night might have a problem. Marie looked up, scanning the parking lot, expecting to see Jigger Jenkins, the infamous townie known for his drunken escapades. But, as Maries eyes focused in the dark, her heart jumped into her throat and she momentarily froze. It was not old Jigger. Her mouth gaped open and her feet propelled her forward into a full run.

"JIMMY!" She gasped as she barreled into him, where he stood leaning against her car with a half-grin and a duffle bag at his feet. He wrapped his arms around her and held her to him as tightly as he could.

"What are you doing here?" Marie whispered into his neck as his hand caressed the back of her head, holding her to him.

"I left," Jim answered softly, loosening his grip just enough so that she could look at him but still able to feel her body against his. "I left school. I'm not going back. I'm done." Marie's eyes widened in shock and confusion but not before Jim saw the initial happy relief that passed across her face.

"Oh my gosh. But what will you do? Your parents will flip out. Where will you stay? Your family is in Ohio! Did you tell them?"

Jim had laughed nervously. "Well, I was hoping we could go talk to your parents first."

Standing in the attic now, dusting off the old luggage, Evelyn recalled that evening over one year ago when Marie had come home after work with Jim in tow. A college dropout. They had sat in the dining room and ate a late dinner and then talked over tea until midnight. Jim had explained that he hated the University and that he just couldn't stay. He had explained to his ROTC recruiter that he understood he would be giving up his scholarship but that he simply had to go home. Evelyn still remembers Edward's face when Jim asked if he could live with them while he found a job and got back on his feet. Evelyn had seen the judgment and initial rejection on Edward's face and had quickly shushed him with a stern look before he had the chance to explode and kick the poor boy out into the cold night. Evelyn had told the kids to go to sleep (Jim could have William's room), and they would discuss it tomorrow after everyone had rested a bit. It took almost a full week to convince Edward not to march Jim to the train station with a one-way ticket back to Pennsylvania or to Ohio or to "any goddam place he wants to go as long as it's not in this house playing kissy face with my daughter!"

Jim's father had been furious. His mother had cried. They couldn't believe that Jim had just dropped out of college after only a few months and had voluntarily given up his full scholarship to Penn. There were harsh words over the telephone about wasted opportunities and bad decisions. When Jim's father had said, "Boy, you are throwing away your future for a pretty face!" Jim had told his parents simply that he was sorry but his mind was made up.

As Evelyn looked at the beautiful, unused luggage she realized that sometimes life throws you for a loop. But, if you were lucky, that loop may just bring you full circle and make a whole lot of sense someday. Evelyn had told Marie that she would return the luggage, cancel the ticket to London, and give Marie the refunded money for her graduation gift. Evelyn had obtained a refund on the plane tickets, but she never could bring herself to return the beautiful luggage that seemed to Evelyn to be a ticket to a life she would have killed for as a young woman. She had hoped that Marie might change her mind and want to take the trip at a later date. Evelyn had hidden the luggage in the attic, where it had been sitting for the last two years collecting dust and providing a place for spiders to attach silky strings supporting their webs. Now, Evelyn blew the dust off of the large suitcase and swatted away the cobwebs. She picked up the blue-gray hard case with brass closures that snapped open when the buttons next to them were pushed. The price tags, still attached, had yellowed but Evelyn could make out the amount of money she had splurged on this gorgeous luggage. She had been determined that she and her daughter would travel in style. Now, she decided that these cases would still make a nice present. This time, however, it was not a graduation they would be celebrating. It was a wedding! Six months after returning home, Jim had proposed to Marie. Evelyn smiled to herself and thought of her words to her daughter that day at her graduation dinner: *I hope you know what you are doing.*

As it turned out, Marie had known exactly what she was doing. Jim and Marie married on September 11, 1965 at St. Mary's Catholic Church in Scituate Harbor. Despite threats not to attend, Jim's parents and siblings traveled from Ohio to Scituate for the occasion. Katherine was a bridesmaid along with Marie's best friend, Cheryl. All of Jim and Marie's high school friends were there. The ceremony was beautiful and Marie looked exquisite with her cropped curls framing her face beneath a fashionable shoulder length veil. Nobody who attended the wedding could deny the love that radiated from the young couple.

After the wedding, Jim and Marie moved into an apartment in an old house less than one mile away. Mark and Patty Litchfield, a robust, loud, Italian couple with three young children lived on one side of the antique yellow house and Jim and Marie rented the other side. They had one bedroom, a living room, a kitchen and one bathroom. It was small and simple but it was theirs. Jim continued to work as a door-to-door salesman, selling brushes and encyclopedias. Marie continued modeling and worked at the local preschool where Evelyn taught. It was a far cry from the hallowed halls of the University of Pennsylvania and not what had been expected of them. But Jim and Marie had forged their own path - one that was lined with hope and love.

✞✞✞✞

Life was strange at Home with Edward and Evelyn being empty nesters. All of the kids had grown and moved on. We had come full circle. Unfortunately, Edward's health had continued to deteriorate to the point he was no longer able to work. After Marie moved out, he had converted the front bedroom back into a sitting room, and he spent most of his days sitting in his chair, watching television and struggling to breathe. Evelyn was worried sick. But she stayed busy working at the school and doing anything possible to make Edward comfortable. We were blessed with wonderful news when Marie announced in early 1967 that she was pregnant. The joy and anticipation over the birth of Marie's first baby and another grandchild for Edward and Evelyn distracted everybody from the stress of Edward's failing health. Marie was, of course, thrilled. She just knew that she would have this baby and her father would rally and everything would be perfect. Sure enough, Alden Lockhart Freeman was born in October, 1967, and was perfect and healthy. The Lockhart and Freeman families rejoiced!

But Edward did not rally and an unexpected heartbreak soon eclipsed our joy.

Chapter 15

GOODBYE
1968

In April 1968, Edward's emphysema finally announced last call on his lungs. Evelyn, who had been by his side night and day, summoned her children Home. Dr. Ward had been at the house all day and was doing everything he could to make Edward comfortable as his labored breathing slowed to a barely detectable level. William sat quietly talking to Evelyn in the dining room. Marie had rushed up the hill from her apartment to be with her father in his final hours. She came out of the front sitting room where Edward lay struggling to breathe and falling in and out of consciousness. Her eyes were puffy and red and her shoulders slumped with sadness and exhaustion. She walked to the kitchen to get a glass of water and found Katherine standing alone at the sink, staring out the window. Stephen, who had initially come to the house with her, was nowhere to be seen.

"Hi," Marie said as she reached for a water glass in the pantry cabinet. Katherine did not respond. "Dad isn't doing so well," Marie whispered, sniffling. "You might want to go in there soon." Katherine's head dropped but she did not turn around.

"Where is Stephen?" Marie asked. "Did he leave?"

Katherine drew in a sharp breath and raised her chin. She turned to face her younger sister. Her eyes were red and she looked ten years older. Marie was initially taken aback but then realized she probably didn't look any better. They were all heartbroken and had

119

been crying all evening. Katherine just stared blankly at Marie. A shiver went through Marie as she realized Katherine's countenance wasn't due solely to their father dying. She narrowed her eyes and cocked her head. "Where is Stephen?" she asked again, slowly.

Katherine blinked once and looked at the floor. "He left me," she whispered so softly that Marie was sure she had misheard.

"What? What do you mean? Where did he go? This isn't the time to be running out for cigarettes or whatever. Dad is dying. When will he be back?"

Katherine shook her head slowly. "He won't be back. He *left* me," she emphasized to avoid confusion. Katherine's face sagged with the weight of a sorrow so great that it threatened to pull her entire body to the floor. "He just told me he bought a house in New Hampshire and that he was going to move there. And that I am to stay here."

Marie stared at her older sister, her red, tear-filled eyes wide with disbelief. "Are you sure he meant permanently? We knew he was looking at places in New Hampshire. For all of you. Maybe he just means you should stay here while he gets things settled?"

Katherine shook her head slowly and raised shaking fingers to her temples, making large circles on her hairline. "No. He is moving there without me. He said he couldn't be a husband or a father anymore. He's gone. He just told me and left."

"That son-of-a-bitch!" Marie spat, fuming. "How can he do this to you and the kids? And to lay this on you right now - as our father lay dying? What kind of person does that?"

Katherine just stared at her fingers and fiddled with her wedding ring. A single tear ran down her face. "I guess a person who doesn't love me," she whispered as fresh tears spilled from her eyes.

Marie went to Katherine and wrapped her older sister in her arms. Marie suddenly felt dizzy with exhaustion. She sat down in the caned bottom, ladder-back chair, her brain swirling with thoughts and emotions. Her beloved father was dying in the next room. Her mother, Evelyn, a pillar of strength dealing with her husband's imminent death, would be devastated by the news that her oldest daughter and her four children were abandoned by the man who had sworn to take care of them. How could all of this be

120

happening at the same time? This Home, which had been filled with so much joy, was now blanketed in tragedy and sadness.

Marie looked around the kitchen and recalled the day she watched Katherine dance in circles right here, holding roses to her nose. She had been filled with such love and hope. Now she was shattered and filled with despair; she was heartbroken. Suddenly, their father's words filled her mind: *A man who is truly in love doesn't need all that fanfare.* Marie, who had been so young and impressed with Stephen's romantic ways, had scoffed at her father's words as those of a cynical old man. But now she knew there had been truth in his suspicions of Stephen.

Stephen had shocked them all after the wedding by announcing his enrollment in flight school and the move to Florida. Edward had been furious. "What kind of man keeps that information to himself and doesn't even tell his own bride-to-be or her family?" Edward had railed. But Katherine had assured him that she was fine with the plans and had left for Florida willingly and very much in love. After the move, Katherine had immediately become pregnant and had returned home to Scituate nine months later to have her baby while Stephen stayed in Florida for flight training. She had gone back to Florida with their new baby, Stephen Jr. But her husband was never home. Katherine was alone for weeks at a time while Stephen flew to far away towns. When she became pregnant with her second child, Katie, two years later, Katherine again returned to Scituate. This time, she informed Stephen she would not return to Florida. By then, Stephen had secured a job with American Airlines and he was able to obtain assignment to Logan Airport in Boston. They moved into his family home on Third Cliff, where Katherine had two more babies – Mary and Bill. But no matter how many of his children Katherine birthed – four kids in five years -- nothing could keep Stephen at home. He was always flying, even on his time off. *"To keep my skills sharp,"* he would claim. Katherine had been lonely for quite some time and Marie had begun to doubt Stephen's loyalty.

Turning her attention to her broken-hearted sister, Marie asked, "What about the kids? Did he just walk out on them too?"

Katherine, suddenly let out a sob. "He said that we should move in here with Mom. He said that he was sorry about Dad dying but that it was perfect timing." She shook her head in disgusted disbelief. "Can you believe that? Who says something like that?"

Another sob escaped her as Marie hugged her sister tighter. Katherine shook with grief over losing the only two men she had ever loved. But what nobody knew, perhaps not even Katherine herself, was that she was also suffering from the pain of believing that neither of them had fully loved her back. Clearly Stephen would not be doing this if he had ever loved her. That much was obvious. As for Edward, Katherine knew that her father had loved her, but something had always been missing from their relationship and it left her feeling a bit empty. His gruff demeanor had caused her to be guarded around him and she had never learned how to break through his tough exterior. Like any daughter, she had yearned for her father's love and acceptance. But Edward had never been a man who wore his heart on his sleeve. He wasn't outwardly affectionate or verbal about how much he loved his children and Katherine had taken this as rejection. As such, she had kept her distance, emotionally. She had always wished she could be like Marie who didn't seem affected by Edward's stern countenance. Marie would climb in Edward's lap and smother him with kisses even while he pushed her away, grumbling about her being a "stink pot" or "smell britches." His name-calling would only make Marie giggle and climb all over him until he would break down laughing and give in. Katherine, however, was much more reserved, fearful of rejection, and would have never dreamed of demanding her father's affection so boldly. Unfortunately, because neither father nor daughter knew how to reach each other, Katherine had never truly understood the depth of her father's love for her. Even Edward's nickname for Katherine -- "Queenie"-- had left her feeling spoiled, chastised, and insecure. What she didn't know – couldn't know – was that Edward had given her the nickname when she was born because he had been so in love with her and taken by her beauty that she had reminded him of royalty. She hadn't known how much he had adored her. And shame on Edward for not knowing how to show his oldest daughter the true extent of his love! But, it was too late now. Edward was dying and neither of them could repair the mistakes of the past.

Suddenly, Edward's presence filled my room as his oldest daughter cried on the shoulder of his youngest. Of course they couldn't see him or feel him but I saw him clearly standing tall and strong in my kitchen. He ached to reach out to both of them and tell them how cherished they were to him. But, of course, his time had passed. He was now only a soul, without a body or a voice to use as tools to express what he felt. He could only hope that maturity and time would help Katherine understand the kind of man he had been and that she would one day know how much he had loved her.

Unfortunately, as I know now, after having lived with this family for many generations, sometimes a daughter's true knowledge and understanding of her father's affections becomes clear only after many years of searching for acceptance in other places and scavenging for a love that she has had all along. Katherine would accept her father's shortcomings and accept herself one day – but not before some serious damage would be done.

After consoling her mother and her sister, Marie went home that night with a crushing weight on her heart. Edward was dead. Her big, strong father who had seemed invincible was gone. Marie had adored him. She was devastated. And, as if the death of her father wasn't enough, Stephen had walked out on Katherine. What had he been thinking? Marie's heart broke for her older sister and her four children. What would happen now? Where will they all live? Could she just expect to move her family into their mother's house? Was that fair to Mother? Marie was worried for their mother as well. Her husband, the man she had left everything for when she was a young woman, was gone. Edward had been the love of Evelyn's life. Everyone who knew them could see it. Sure, he had been gruff and not what most women would call "romantic," but he and Evelyn had shared a unique bond. Marie knew how much they had loved each other. As Marie lay her exhausted body down next to Jim that night, she felt as if her whole world had just shifted on it axis and that the events of the day had redirected everyone she held dear onto a new path – one that would be long and difficult to navigate. Tears spilled down her face onto the pillow. Jim silently pulled her into his arms. She was grateful for the warmth of his body and she allowed herself to relax into him, the love of her husband a lullaby, coaxing her to sleep. At least they were secure in their little home with their beautiful baby boy. And she would be there to help her sister and her mother.

Just as she was slipping into sleep, Jim whispered, "I've been accepted into University of Miami in Ohio. Classes start in September."

Her eyes flew open. Sleep would not be comforting her that night.

✟✟✟✟

Katherine, having little other choice, moved Home and my rooms were filled with the busy lives of children once again. Evelyn resigned from her teaching job after Edward's death and seemed glad for the distraction. She busied herself preparing meals and being a second mother to her grandchildren. Katherine got a job working as a bank teller in Scituate Harbor. Stephen moved to his new house in New Hampshire and word on the street was that he had a young flight attendant living with him. Heartbroken, angry, and wanting nothing to do with him, Katherine agreed to a quick divorce and didn't ask him for anything more than the bare minimum the law granted her to help with the expenses for their four children. She worked every weekday and went out most evenings with friends. She wasn't Home much during the months following Edward's death. When she was here, she was either quiet and melancholy or impatient and angry. On the rare nights she was Home for dinner, Evelyn would watch her across the dining table, worrying. But she let Katherine be. Evelyn was a patient woman. She believed that Katherine simply needed to heal and that, in time, she would grow strong again and would be the woman and mother she needed to be.

Marie and Jim moved with baby Alden to Ohio in August. About a month after the move, Marie called with news that she was pregnant again. Upon hearing that she would have another grandchild, Evelyn was both elated and heartbroken. It would be bittersweet to welcome a new grandchild without Edward there to share in her joy. She missed him terribly. Evelyn talked to

124

Edward every night when she would lay her head on his pillow and breathe in the fading scent of his aftershave. I don't know if she could feel it or not, but Edward heard every word she said, for he had refused to leave. He knew he was supposed to move on to wherever human souls go after their bodies die, but he, stubborn as ever, would not go. He would lie next to Evelyn at night, tortured that he could not stroke her hair or smell her skin. I tried to assure him that he could go and that I would watch over his bride, but he refused, choosing instead to remain and continue loving Evelyn with every inch of his soul.

I could feel that Edward was anxious about Katherine, though he never told me. He would follow her through the house, moving around her in an agitated manner, stirring up the air. It was as if he was trying to wrap her up, to protect her from something. Or, perhaps he was trying to wake her from the downward spiral of self-doubt she seemed to be caught in. I didn't really know. He seemed propelled by a desperate guilt and painful regret that he had never found a way to convey his love to his oldest daughter.

One afternoon in late Autumn, Katherine announced to Evelyn that she had eloped with a young man she had been dating for a short while and that she was going away for a two-week honeymoon. Shocked and confused, but unable to do much about it, Evelyn agreed to watch the children while Katherine was gone. Edward paced my rooms continuously. Ten days after Katherine left, she returned. Alone. She was somber and agitated and she and Evelyn went outside to talk. I couldn't hear what they were saying but I could feel an unnerving mixture of grief, fear, and disappointment emanating from them both. After an hour, both women returned inside, their eyes red and puffy. Something was very wrong.

Two days later, Katherine walked into the kitchen with a suitcase in her hand, kissed each of her children good-bye, and left in a taxicab. Evelyn stared silently out the window long after the cab had disappeared over the hill. After several minutes she breathed in deeply, shook her head, and began busying herself with getting the children ready for school. There was no changing what her daughter had already set into motion. No use dwelling on what she couldn't change.

After Katherine's departure, Evelyn filled her days with work, meals, school, and housework. She put on a smile for the children but the light within her did not shine. Only at night would she sob herself to sleep. Edward stopped his pacing and just sat in the corner, watching Evelyn closely. He never said a word to me but I could feel the despair that hung over both of them like a dense fog. I

125

didn't really know what was happening. I only knew none of us would ever be the same. My core ached. I felt the old crack in my wall shift and grow deeper.

One month after Katherine left, Evelyn came home with one of those new clock radios that she put by her bedside.

Chapter 16

PRESENT DAY

Dinner had been nice. The siblings had sat in the kitchen eating their pizza and sorting through the box of old photographs. They had genuinely enjoyed each other's company and, based on their laugher as they reminisced, they all clearly had fond memories of their time living under my roof. I feel warm and content seeing them all like this and I let myself feel hopeful that they will come together to figure out a way to preserve their heritage. But that hope is short lived.

"Mom and Dad's lawyer called me today," Anna says as she nibbles on the leftover pieces of pizza crust. "He wants to know if we can come into his office tomorrow afternoon to discuss Mom's will and the trust she and Dad made. Since you guys are only here for a few more days, I thought we should go ahead and get it over with. I told him we would be at his office at two-thirty if that works for you guys."

The air, that had been light and breathable just moments before, suddenly feels thick with tension. I stiffen. Caroline sighs. Alden and Thomas look at each other and Thomas gives Alden a barely perceptible nod. Caroline turns her gaze toward her younger brother. She narrows her eyes, looking from Thomas to Alden and back again.

"What? What was that look for?" she asks, accusingly.

"Relax, CeeCee," Alden says, holding up a hand.

"Don't tell me to relax, Alden. Clearly you two have been talking and have something up your sleeves."

"Whoa, Caroline," replies Thomas, "we aren't hiding anything in our sleeves or anywhere else. It's just that Alden and I talked today and the two of us feel the same way about what we should do with the house. We were going to talk with you and Anna. But it's no secret how we feel about trying to keep it."

"Well, it certainly has been clear how *you* feel, Mr. I-hate-Scituate, but I didn't know Alden felt as strongly. Obviously you have convinced him to sell and the two of you have decided how this is going to go down."

Anna stands quickly, jostling the table. She begins grabbing empty glasses and plates, busying herself clearing the remnants of dinner. Her movements are short and forceful, her rising frustration seeming to drive her momentum. Thomas watches her warily.

"Caroline, Thomas hasn't convinced me of anything," Alden responds, calmly. "I have always had my reservations about trying to hold onto this house. You know that. I just don't think it makes sense, given that none of us wants to live here."

Across the kitchen, Anna slams a glass down hard into the sink, shattering it. Her frustration sends negative energy through the small room, rattling my windows.

"So, what you saying then, Alden?" Anna turns and glares at him and then at Thomas. "Are we supposed to just agree to wipe out one hundred years of our family history and let some strangers take this place? Mom was born here. Mom died in that room over there." She pointed a shaking finger toward the pink bedroom. "Nana and Papa Lockhart both died in this house. My children were raised here. It is the only Home they know. Mom loved this house like it was a member of the family. It holds all of our memories; and you just want to throw it all away so you can take your share and leave and pretend that you don't belong here? Like

128

all of this is meaningless?" Tears stream down Anna's face. Caroline listens to her sister's rant and wipes at her eyes but remains quiet. Alden shakes his head sadly but does not respond. Thomas stands and walks to Anna. He takes her shaking hands in his. She tries to pull away but he holds firm.

"Anna, nobody wants to throw away our past. Or our heritage. Of course it's not meaningless. But what are we supposed to do here? Mom and Dad left us in this position because even *they* couldn't figure out what to do. Mom knew we would probably have to sell. She even talked about selling at one point herself. She just couldn't bring herself to do it. But she is gone now and we have to figure something out. We all know what it would cost to keep this place. You know none of us can afford it. Even if we could rent it and use the rent to cover the expenses, we would barely be breaking even. And for what? It's not a typical investment property that we would be looking to sell for a profit one day. If we can't sell it now because it's part of our family, then we will never sell it. And then what do we do when we are gone? Who are we going to pass it down to? All of our kids, so they can be in the same situation we are in right now but with ten of them fighting over it? That wouldn't be fair to them. And, frankly this isn't fair to us. Mom should have never put us in this position."

Thomas lets out a deep sigh and dips his head trying to look at Anna whose face is now pointed at the floor where a puddle of tears collect by her feet. Anna knows that what she is asking of her siblings is a lot. But this house is a part of them. Anna feels it in her bones. Thomas and Alden want to treat it like it is just sticks and bricks – something cold and meaningless, that could be discarded and forgotten. Part of her wants to lash out in anger over their callousness. *How can they be so blasé?* She thinks. *Because they didn't grow up here, they just don't understand. But Caroline does.* She knows Caroline does. She suddenly feels an overwhelming need to talk to her sister - alone. She raises her eyes to Thomas who still holds her hands and she sniffles.

"I need to take a drive," Anna says, evenly, working hard to keep her voice from shaking. "Caroline, do you want to go grab a coffee and drive down to Minot Beach with me?"

Thomas sighs and lets his grip on Anna's hands go. "I love you Anna. I love this family. I hope you know that." Anna nods but doesn't reply. Caroline stands slowly, looking from Alden to Thomas and then at her baby sister. She is torn. She understands her brother's point but her heart breaks for Anna. It also breaks for her mother, and Aunt Katherine, and Nana. The bonds this house holds between the women who have lived here, loved here, raised children here, and suffered broken hearts here, are strong. Caroline feels the bonds holding her, as if the house itself holds her in a tight embrace. Suddenly, she has a strange feeling that maybe the ties holding her are born not only of a desire to keep the family here but because there may be something more – something unfinished. Something that needs to be resolved. Caroline looks toward the wall with the crack and blinks. It suddenly reminds her of a wound that has been opened and then closed again, but never truly healed.

"Caroline, you ok?" Alden is looking at her, his brows knit together in concern. The strange feeling vanishes instantly. *What was that about?* She looks at Alden and nods. "Yeah, I'm fine. Maybe a coffee and a drive would be a good idea."

Twenty minutes later, Caroline and Anna are sitting in Anna's car sipping large coffees from MaryLou's Coffee Shop and staring out at Well Rock on Minot Beach. The full moon sparkles off the soft waves and the smell of saltwater and seaweed fills their nostrils. "This place never changes," Caroline says. "It even smells the same. People laugh at me when I tell them I love the smell of low tide. But I guess when you grow up in a harbor town, it just smells like home – stinky, but where I belong."

Anna laughs. "Yeah, that's about right. We are just old stinkers now, I guess."

"Some of us older than others," Caroline replies patting her younger sister's leg.

"I'm feeling pretty damn old right now. This whole business with the house is making me so stressed out and sad."

"I know, Anna. I feel the same way, although I know it has to be worse for you. That house was your family home for so many years. You grew up there and you raised your kids there. Dang, if those walls could talk!"

"Oh God, let's all be glad that they can't! You don't even want to know what's all gone on in there. After dealing with my dysfunction, that poor house is probably more than ready to see us all get the hell out."

"I have a feeling that house has witnessed some pretty crazy stuff even before you lived there," Caroline replies. "Speaking of the house, what's with that crack in the kitchen wall? It has been there since as long as I can remember and has been wallpapered over, but has anyone ever tried to repair it?"

"That old crack? Mom said it was there for as long as she could remember also. Dad repaired it a few times but it just opens back up again. It hasn't gotten any bigger and no new cracks have shown up, so we just leave it. Why? You don't buy that nonsense about there being possible structural issues, do you? You know the foundation of the house is a boulder that isn't going anywhere, right?"

"Yeah, I know. I'm not worried about the structure of the house. It's as solid as it was the day it was built. Something is weird about that crack though. For some reason it has really drawn my attention lately and I can't figure out why."

The sisters sit staring out at the ocean for several minutes, each deep in thought. Finally, Caroline clears her throat and looks at Anna. "Do you think everything was okay with Aunt Katherine? I mean, I know she went through a hard time after Stephen left her and all, but do you think there was more there? I always felt like even though Mom was seven years younger, that she was the one who was the big sister and not the other way around."

"Mom never said anything to me. But you know that house holds so many secrets that we will probably never know. I sure do miss Aunt Katherine though."

"Yeah, so do I."

Later that night, Caroline stands in the moonlit kitchen and stares at the crack in the wall, feeling the same unsettling sense she had felt earlier. There is definitely an energy here telling her that something is not right. But, what? Caroline runs her hand along the crack, asking the House to tell her what it knows. *Why are you broken?* Caroline asks silently.

✟✟✟

As Caroline stands in my kitchen asking me for my stories, I allow myself to remember things that I had buried deep in my walls for many years. Of course these events have always been a part of me. After all, despite that humans believe a house is built of wood, stone, bricks, and plaster, a Home is built on the love, the dreams, the heartache, and the memories of all that happens between its walls. But there are some things that a Home can't control, such as the decisions its humans make about their own lives. And when those decisions turn out to have terrible consequences, all a Home can do is try to provide comfort to the hearts and souls that are left shattered. Then, when lives are rebuilt and time moves on, a Home buries the bad things; pushes them deeper into the walls, so that the love can heal and the Home can once again be a happy place. But the loss is still there. And when it is kept hidden and not fully dealt with, the sadness finds its way to the surface again. I was, for the most part, a very happy Home. My family shared an enormous amount of love and laughter under my roof. But, like all families, mine has had its secrets. The crack in my kitchen is where a terrible, untreated wound still lies. And I don't know how to heal it. All I know is that the wound that opened the day little Emily died in my rooms had healed to a scar that reopened when Katherine left that day after Edward's death, and it is still a place where deep sadness seeps out again and again.

Let me tell you about the 1970's.

THE LONELY YEARS
1970's

The years following Edward's death were hard and lonely for Evelyn. William, who had married and had two boys, moved to Maine where William began working for LL Bean. Marie and Jim were in Ohio where Jim attended University of Miami at Ohio in the Navy ROTC program and worked as a police officer. Marie gave birth to a baby girl she named Caroline in April of 1969. Only two short years later, Thomas was born. Marie and Jim took three small children to Jim's college graduation in June, 1972. Evelyn missed her youngest daughter terribly and she often wondered at how so much could have changed so quickly.

Katherine had returned Home almost a full year after she had left in the taxi that summer morning. She didn't say much about where she had been. I heard only bits and pieces of hushed conversations between her and Evelyn: " … marriage was annulled … I'm fine…good care…no information on who …" She packed up her belongings and moved out of our Home almost immediately after she had returned, taking the kids with her. Evelyn didn't see much of her oldest daughter after that. Katherine rented a house near the Harbor, worked at the bank, and bounced around from boyfriend to boyfriend. Stephen had sold his house in New Hampshire and had moved back to Scituate, alone. He and Katherine fought constantly about money and their children and sometimes they split the family so that the boys lived with Stephen and the girls lived with Katherine. Evelyn's heart broke for all of them but there wasn't much she could do. There was a distance between Evelyn and Katherine that hadn't been there before the day the taxi drove Katherine away. I felt the tension between them when Katherine came over but mostly I felt a great disappointment and helplessness from Evelyn after her visits with Katherine. I couldn't put my finger on it but I knew that some obstacle bigger than all of us was present and it seemed insurmountable. After Katherine's visits, Evelyn would sit by the window for hours, staring silently out into the yard. Then one day, Katherine stopped by to inform Evelyn that she was moving to Vermont to live on a farm with a man she had met at the bank only two months earlier. Once again, Katherine was off chasing love in all the wrong places. Evelyn knew that she couldn't stop her so she just let her go, praying that her oldest daughter would somehow learn to fill the hole in her heart.

Edward was still around, as he stubbornly refused to leave. The great part about having him here was that I could talk to him. Now that he was dead, he could hear me, or feel me, or whatever – I'm not quite sure how we communicated exactly, but we did. I spent years telling him he needed to go, and that it wasn't healthy for anyone for him to be haunting my halls like he was doing. But he would simply let me know that he could not leave his bride and he ignored my pleas to move on. So I stopped trying and instead began to enjoy having him there, although at times it was heartbreaking. Evelyn, who slept with talk radio on all night, was still fighting demons – some old, some more recent – and she was doing it alone. She was a strong woman, but some nights I would feel her loneliness, heavy and suffocating, and I would hear her crying softly in her room. On those nights, Edward ached to be able to hold her and comfort her. He tried and I do believe that at times she felt his presence, which seemed to calm her. I longed for the days when we were a busy little family with kids running everywhere; the smells from Evelyn's famous cooking permeating my walls. Instead, Evelyn rose early every morning and ate most of her meals outside of the house. She was a regular at Brooks' drugstore counter in North Scituate Center, where she had black coffee and rye toast every morning and a grilled tuna melt in the afternoons.

She hadn't worked since Edward's death and she would sometimes spend all day baking and then donate the delicious creations to the Baptist church near the Town Common. Her lemon meringue and banana crème pies were the talk of the town. She became quite active in politics and devoted much of her time to fundraisers for the Republican party and its efforts to repair the damage after Nixon's scandalous Watergate fiasco. Even in her mid-sixties, Evelyn was still a beautiful, energetic woman. As such, she had many suitors. She dated now and then but every time a man became too serious she would politely let him know that she was not interested in becoming anybody's wife. She had several proposals during the 1970's. I guess the men in town assumed that a widow her age would be anxious to remarry. But not Evelyn. "I already have a husband," Evelyn would reply, matter of factly when a boyfriend was brave enough to hint about a future together. "I am Mrs. Edward Lockhart and I will always be Mrs. Edward Lockhart. Just because he isn't here right now doesn't change that." This usually sent her suitors sulking off to find another less independent prospect. Some, however, stuck around for a while despite her rejection of marriage.

In the summer of 1975, Evelyn's phone rang one day while she was pruning the large, pink hydrangea bush by the side door. She ran inside to answer, wiping her hands on her pants. "Hello?" Evelyn said, panting into the receiver.

"Hi Mum. Are you okay? You sound winded." It was Marie. She was calling from Virginia Beach, where Jim had recently been transferred. After graduating from Miami at Ohio, the family had lived in Hawaii where Marie had raised the children while Jim was deployed in Vietnam. Two years later, the Navy had moved them to Newport, Rhode Island where Jim attended the war college. They had stayed in navy housing in Newport for less than a year before the navy transferred them to Virginia. Evelyn could barely

135

keep up with where her daughter was living. All she knew was that Jim was deployed again, this time for nine months, and Marie was essentially a single mother, raising three elementary-aged children in a rented, two-story colonial on a cul-de-sac in Norfolk. She marveled at how Marie, who had lived in one house her entire life, could just pack up and move to a new home with very little notice.

"Oh yes, Honey, I'm fine. I was just out in the yard, trimming the hydrangeas. The bush is in full bloom and I wanted to put a few bunches around the house. How are you?"

"Well, I'm a bit freaked out right now, actually," replied Marie. "Have you talked with Katherine?" Evelyn's heart sank. *What now?*

"I spoke with her last week," replied Evelyn. "You know she's living up in Vermont with that new man of hers. I think they may have eloped, but I'm not sure. The kids have been living with Stephen. I visit them once a week and take them for lunch at Brooks' lunch counter. Why? What's wrong?"

"Well, apparently Stephen has a new girlfriend or something and he has decided he doesn't have room to keep all of the kids anymore. So he kicked Katie and Mary out. They got off the school bus today to find that he had thrown all of their belongings onto the front yard. He wouldn't even let them in the house. He told them to go live with their mother. Katie was hysterical and went to a neighbor who got ahold of Katherine. Katherine then called me. Apparently, she can't take the girls because she is living on some farm in rural Vermont and the schools aren't good or they don't even have any schools or something. She has asked me if I can take the girls."

"But you are in Virginia!" exclaimed Evelyn, her voice rising with emotion. "What does she expect you to do? You have three little children of your own to care for and a husband who is overseas! How are you supposed to handle two teenaged girls on top of that? This is insane. I will go get those girls right now and bring them here. Why wouldn't she call me?"

"I'm not really sure, except that, well, you know... after everything that happened before I think she is embarrassed and maybe afraid of disappointing you again," Marie replied, her tone gentle. Evelyn involuntarily cringed. "Plus, she needs someone to keep the girls for a while. She doesn't want to put you out. She wants them to come live with me. But I obviously can't get there for a few days and they are stranded at the neighbor's house. Can you go get them and their things and I will figure out how to come up and get them?"

"That bastard, Stephen!" Evelyn muttered. "He is such an arse! Those poor girls, being tossed out like garbage by their own father. I have half a mind to call the police and have him arrested."

"I know, Mum, believe me. I've thought about it many times. But what would that do? It would only hurt the children more and all that would happen is that he would lose all custody rights and we would be in this same situation anyway. Apparently he is letting the boys stay. He just wants the girls out. It's better for them if they can just come live with me. Jim is overseas and I could use the help anyway. Katie can help drive the kids to activities and it will be good to have them here. We have a good high school and they will make tons of friends. It will be okay. Really."

Evelyn sighed deeply into the receiver, her heart aching for her granddaughters and for Katherine. Evelyn felt equal parts frustration and sympathy for her oldest daughter -- a mother unable to care for her own children. Part of Evelyn wanted to go find her in the woods of Vermont and scream, *"what kind of mother abandons her own kids and disappears into the wilderness?"* The other part knew how damaged Katherine was and felt tremendous sadness for her. And guilt. How had her smart, sophisticated daughter become so broken? How had they not seen the true man that Stephen was? Evelyn remembered what Edward had said so many years ago – something about a man who uses so much fanfare is a phony. Edward had never liked Stephen. Evelyn had brushed off Edward's feelings as those of a father who would never approve of anyone who dated his baby girl. But now, as she hung up the phone with Marie and went to wash up to go pick up her granddaughters, she whispered, "Oh Ed, you were so right. I'm just glad you aren't here now to see what a mess that phony bastard has made of our daughter's life."

But, of course, Edward was there, seeing it all and feeling every bit of the concern, the sadness, and the guilt his wife was struggling with. There had to be a way to fix what had been done so that Katherine could heal, - so that they all could heal.

✟✟✟✟

Marie upheld her promise and loaded Alden, Caroline, Thomas, and their giant English Sheep dog into her station wagon and drove six hundred miles to Scituate to pick up her nieces. She stayed almost a week before driving home again; the car loaded with five kids and a giant dog. After they left, things at Home seemed quieter than ever and Evelyn once again busied herself with her daily routine. Our Home had never felt so lonely.

Then one day in mid-March the phone rang again. This time, Marie was calling to inform her that Jim, who had returned from deployment, was being transferred again, this time to Jacksonville, Florida. She also had big news — she was pregnant! And she wanted to have the baby at Home. Jim requested shore duty in Newport, Rhode Island before he had to report to Jacksonville and the Navy had agreed. In the summer of 1977 the Freeman family, along with Katherine's daughters, moved Home. Katie and Mary re-enrolled in Scituate High School and moved back in with their father who had broken up with his girlfriend. Alden, Caroline, and Thomas enrolled in fifth, third, and first grades at Cushing Elementary.

In December, just three days before Christmas, Anna Katherine Freeman was born. She was the best Christmas present we had ever received. After almost ten years of living without my family, I was once again full of love and laughter as we celebrated the holiday season with the miracle and blessings of new life. Edward watched over the celebrations with pride.

Unfortunately, it was all only temporary. The Navy needed Jim in Jacksonville. So, in January, Jim, Marie, and the children moved out again, headed for Florida.

Evelyn was once again alone.

Chapter 18

THE BLIZZARD
1978

I n February of 1978 a ferocious Nor'easter bore down on our little seaside town. Marie and her family had left just in time. A tropical cyclone from the South merged with an arctic cold front and then took aim at New England, ravaging the coastline with hurricane-force winds and record-breaking snowfall. The Boston area saw over twenty-seven inches of snow in three days as the storm raged. But, in Scituate, the snow was the least of our problems. The winds whipped over the great Atlantic, stirring the deep, dark ocean and making it angry. Waves fifteen feet high crashed ashore, tearing apart sea walls and throwing rocks and boulders onto streets and lawns. Down at Sand Hills Beach, near Scituate's lighthouse, the monster waves ripped homes off of their foundations and tossed them on top of other homes. Some homes were simply lifted whole by the giant swells and swept out to sea, leaving no trace.

The people of Scituate had little warning about the true power of the storm and, as such, we were all unprepared. Evelyn had been watching the falling snow up on North Hill, a safe distance from the coastline, thinking that it would be pretty to have a fresh blanket of white snow on the lawn. But several hours later, when the winds began to howl, she knew this was not a normal snowstorm. With wind gusts over 100mph, it wasn't long before the electricity went out. The storm's fury whipped at my roof and walls, trying to find its way in. The winds tugged at my shingles relentlessly and I had to use all of my strength to hold them steady. But, thankfully, I had been built strong and the storm's efforts to break me were fruitless. Evelyn sat for hours, huddled in blankets in the dark hall, with candles and flashlights, hugging her knees to her chest. The wind forced its way down my chimneys, blowing snow into my living room and making it impossible to light a fire for warmth. The howling outside sounded like hell-trapped demons screaming for revenge. Evelyn shivered. Edward stayed beside his wife all night while the storm ravaged the town.

The snow fell for more than thirty hours. When it was over, more than five hundred homes in Scituate were damaged; one hundred of them completely destroyed. After a full day of shoveling snow from her driveway and struggling to clear her car of the towering snowdrifts, Evelyn ventured out to survey the damage. As she drove past the beaches, she couldn't believe the devastation she saw. Cars floated down flooded streets, toilets sat atop the roofs of houses, clothes and personal items littered snow banks that stood over seven feet high. Minot Beach was unrecognizable. Surfside Road was completely under water. Glades Road was piled with rocks, sand, and snow and was impassable. But nothing could have prepared her for the scene over on Rebecca Road.

It was a beautiful day, with cloudless blue skies and bright sunshine that sparkled off the white blanket of snow, making Evelyn squint. If it weren't for the devastation surrounding her, she would have had a hard time believing that ravenous winds and water had assaulted this area only 24 hours ago. But the evidence was everywhere. The little peninsula of land at the end of Sand Hills beach looked like a war zone. Evelyn parked her car on the hill by the Barker Tavern and walked to Lighthouse Road. Almost every house on Rebecca Road was missing; gaping, empty lots where they once stood. And those that had survived were severely damaged. In one house, the entire back of the home was missing and sand and large rocks filled the rooms. Another was cut in half so perfectly it was as if God had sliced it with a sword, the contents in the remaining half still in place. It reminded her of the dollhouse Edward had made for Marie when she was a child.

Evelyn climbed carefully over rocks and snow banks, collecting personal items that she thought might be salvageable. She picked up a doll that lay in the snow, wiping sand from its pink satin dress. Somewhere, a little girl was missing this doll. Evelyn tucked it inside her jacket along with several pieces of jewelry, a pretty china teacup that had miraculously survived, and several photographs that she had collected. These people had lost everything. Maybe she could help by returning some of their precious belongings to them. Evelyn tread carefully over the debris-strewn road until she came to the lighthouse at the point. She was relieved to see that Scituate Light, the guardian of Scituate Harbor, still stood tall and strong - a beacon of hope, flashing its promise that the ravaged town would recover.

Evelyn came home that afternoon heartbroken for her community. She set the items she had collected on the dining room table and carefully cleaned and dried them. She picked up the doll, inspecting her from head to toe. She rinsed and washed the brown hair and then gently combed it out. She peeled off the pink dress so it could be washed. When she turned the doll over she noticed that someone had written the name "Amy" on the doll's cloth torso. Amy! It wouldn't be too difficult to find the doll's owner now. She smiled, anticipating a little girl named Amy being very happy to have her beloved doll back.

Over the next several days, the community of Scituate came together to help each other and begin what would be a long cleanup. Evelyn volunteered at the shelter that had been set up at Scituate High School and she cooked meals to be delivered to people who were still without power. People all over town were cold and hungry. Evelyn was happy to be useful. She brought the items she had collected to the shelter in hopes that their owners would claim them. The teacup and several photographs had been claimed but, so far nobody had claimed the doll. On the third day after the storm, Evelyn was delivering a pot of chicken barley soup to the shelter when she ran into Elmer Prouty, the town's

141

Harbormaster. Elmer's daughter, Cheryl had been Marie's best friend since childhood. When Elmer saw Evelyn he greeted her with a hug.

"Evelyn! It is good to see you," Elmer said, smiling kindly. "I heard you have been busy helping provide food for those who still don't have power. Scituate is lucky to have such a good cook who is willing to help out."

Evelyn waved her hand, dismissively. "Oh, stop, Elmer. It's the least I can do. These poor people. Some of them lost everything in that dreadful storm! So tragic."

"Well, you are a gem," Elmer replied. "I just stopped by to deliver some coats and clothes my wife collected. I need to get back to the Harbor. There is just so much to clean up. Many of the docks were destroyed. And then there is the investigation into the drowning. I have to interview a couple more people and finish the paperwork on that. Such a tragedy!" Elmer shook his head, tears watering his eyes.

Evelyn frowned. She hadn't heard anything about a drowning. She had been so busy cooking and helping with the cleanup that she hadn't paid much attention to the news and hadn't had much time to socialize. "Who drowned, Elmer? I haven't heard anything about that."

"Oh, I'm sorry," Elmer said. "I assumed you knew. A little girl who was being evacuated from her house on First Cliff drowned when the boat she was in capsized in a rogue wave. Two firemen were also injured - hypothermia. Her parents survived. It's heartbreaking."

Evelyn's hand fluttered over her chest. "A little girl?" Evelyn asked. "Who? How old was she?" Evelyn thought of her past kindergarten students.

"She was five," Elmer replied, shaking his head. "Her name was Amy."

After pressing the doll gently into Elmer's hand and quietly asking him to give the doll to Amy's mother, Evelyn drove home feeling the old, familiar, cold darkness engulf her. She closed herself in her bedroom. She did not turn on the clock radio. She could not distract herself from this. She allowed her thoughts and feelings to rush in and take over. She sobbed for the little girl who had lost her life to the terrible storm. She cried for the girl's parents. She cried for the firemen who had tried hard to save her only to have failed while the child was in their care. She knew that pain all too well. She shed tears for sweet Emily as all of the past pain came flooding in. It had been over thirty years since the day little Emily had died here. But the pain, while not in the forefront each day, was like the little sugar ants that marched through her kitchen on occasion – not enough to warrant drastic measures, but nonetheless an ever-present disturbance. Evelyn knew now that the pain was simply a symptom of the greater injury – her broken heart that would never fully heal. And, while time had dulled the pain, nothing could fill the loss. On that day, when Evelyn learned of the little girl taken by the angry sea, the raw wound was laid bare and the pain was as searing as the day, thirty years ago, on which the terrible darkness had fallen.

Chapter 19

COMING HOME
1982

Just after the Great Blizzard of 1978, the Navy transferred Jim to Newport, Rhode Island where he was granted shore duty. Marie had been ecstatic to be living only an hour and a half from Scituate. Evelyn was thrilled to have the family so close. Shore duty never lasted for long though, and after only eighteen months Jim found himself facing some big decisions. He had been quite successful in his naval career and was rewarded with an offer to serve as the Chief Officer of a ship based out of Hawaii. It would mean a big promotion. But it would also mean another big move for the family. And Jim would be out to sea for months at a time. Jim was also coming up on his twenty-year mark in the Navy, which meant he could retire in one year with full retirement income and benefits. After long discussions and careful consideration, Jim and Marie decided that the kids, three of whom were now teenagers, didn't need to face more moving and months without their father home. Jim would turn down the CO position and he would retire the next year. Because Alden was already in high school, Marie insisted that she and the children go ahead and move back to Scituate. Until he retired, Jim would stay in Newport during the week and would come Home on the weekends.

Evelyn could barely contain her excitement. Marie was coming Home to stay! But the family needed a place to live. Evelyn knew immediately what she would do. At age seventy-four, she didn't need a big two-story house anymore. It was simply too much for her to manage on her own. She would give Marie her inheritance now. The house would be hers – a permanent Home for the next generation.

Evelyn found a lovely apartment to rent in a pretty, antique house on Country Way. She was neither old nor feeble and she liked her independence. Also, she had a steady relationship with a wonderful widower and retired judge named Charlie and she wanted a place where they could still visit in private. After over 40 years of living under my roof, Evelyn moved out. But our Home was not big enough for Marie's family of six. Some changes needed to be made.

They started with my attic. Marie needed bedrooms and the big, empty attic was the perfect spot for them. Jim and Marie got to work quickly, gutting the attic - the place where Evelyn had stored her memories; the place where Emily had searched among those memories for hidden treasure; the place Marie used to hide away with her dolls so her older siblings wouldn't bother her; the place where Caroline and Thomas used to scare each other half to death after watching afternoon episodes of "Creature Double Feature." The pitched roof was pushed out to create more room. Windows were installed. A large master bedroom was created on the north side, with a tiny half-bath, tucked in the back. A hallway and another bedroom and full bath were framed out and sheet rocked. Plumbing was installed, some new windows were put in and a new hardwood floor laid, and, VOILA! – the old attic was transformed into a welcoming second story. Jim had done much of the work himself and, while it wasn't master carpentry, it was functional and pretty and they were proud of his handiwork. Marie, not one to shy away from manual labor, and certainly not one to give up control of a project like this, had helped. She planned it all out. She sanded and stained the floors. She hung wallpaper on every wall. She even found the perfect antique dresser that she had Jim turn into a beautiful vanity for the full bathroom. They watched while five men almost broke their backs installing the heavy claw-foot bathtub that she insisted was better than the modern, plastic ones. Of course, this also caused them to have to reinforce the old attic floor to withstand the weight of the old tub. Marie was proud and excited about the new Home. But, when it was all complete and she and Jim stood in the old doorway of their beautiful new bedroom that was once a musty old attic, Marie burst into tears.

"Oh for Christ's sake, Marie, what is the matter?" Jim asked, a bit exasperated at her emotional outburst after he had done everything she had asked.

"I'm sorry. It's wonderful and just what we need. It's just so strange to see this attic with brightly walled rooms and running water," explained Marie, softly. "There are no more dusty rafters dripping with spider webs, no more creaky boards that you have to tiptoe over so you don't fall into the insulation. There is no more swinging bare-bulb with a dirty string you have to fumble in the dark to find; no more chests waiting for a curious child to open and discover someone else's treasure. There is no more musty old attic smell." Marie crinkled her nose. "Okay, well, maybe there is still a little bit of a musty smell, but you get my point. I feel like part of me has been removed somehow." She wiped at her eyes.

"Well," said Jim, putting his arm around his wife and drawing her close. "It is still the same house, only better. And now it is ours. It's yours. And we will make more great memories up here with our kids. And I'm sure the spiders will be back. After all, there are cracks in these floors everywhere!" he said surveying his DIY handiwork.

Marie laughed and put her head on Jim's shoulder. "I know. You're right." She sighed.

"Of course I'm right," Jim teased. "I'm always right. Now let's go find our youngest daughter and show her this new room of hers. And we can make sure our new bedroom doesn't creak too loudly later," he winked and kissed her forehead.

"Oh, Jim, be serious!" Marie rolled her eyes.

"I am being serious. We aren't that old. Yet."

The attic wasn't the only part of me that got a makeover that year. The kitchen, too, was redesigned to accommodate this modern family. The butler's pantry was opened to create a larger kitchen space. A new sink was installed at an angle in the south corner and tile countertops extended along both walls with cabinets below. Jim cut a hole in the wall to the left of the sink and installed a large oval decorative window that Marie had found at a flea market. With the existing windows to the right of the sink, Marie now had lots of natural light and a beautiful view of the large backyard. Jim sanded and re-stained my hardwood floors. And, of course, Marie hung new wallpaper. For the kitchen, she had chosen a small, simple print with blue and burgundy flowers. Jim built a floor to ceiling wooden cabinet in the entry where the back door of the kitchen led to the breezeway and this became the new pantry area. The small half-bath was converted into a laundry closet that housed a washer and dryer and shelving. The structural wall between the kitchen and formal dining room remained and a small breakfast table was pushed up against it. The old hot water radiator still stood below the south-facing window and a new stove/oven was installed just to the right of it.

It was like a growth spurt for me – these changes that catapulted me from a small, three-bedroom, one-bathroom house to a five-bedroom, three-bathroom Home. I felt like a castle! The renovations were done lovingly by Jim to make sure that my character and charm were preserved. He poured his heart into making our Home perfect for his wife and family and I became part of them with every board that was nailed in. I was now as much a Freeman as I was a Lockhart.

Marie remained true to her love of antiques and all things old and had chosen a large antique wooden cabinet with leaded class doors and crystal pulls for the wall in the pantry. An old dresser was installed in the pantry and a bead-board under-counter cabinet was built next to it on the back wall, crating an L-shape with a slab of marble placed on top for the counter. Two more antique cabinets were hung – one over the sink area and one on the wall between the kitchen and dining room. Aside from the appliances, which were new and modern and the new double stainless steel sink with modern faucet, there wasn't much that looked "new" among the kitchen renovations. It was rustic but it was charming. And it was Marie's.

When they hung the wallpaper, Marie covered the old crack in my wall. But, while some things can be covered, they are not easily forgotten. I still felt a *nagging ache in my wall where the crack was, but I chalked it up to the remnants of old scars. Life moves on and I was happy to be a family Home again.*

Edward grew quite restless after Evelyn moved out. While he was happy to have Marie Home, he couldn't understand why Evelyn had to leave. Couldn't they all just live together? He had been accustomed to resting his tired soul next to his wife as she slept. But without her Home, he began to roam at night. His favorite room was the front room — his old sitting room -- the room where he had died. This room was now Caroline's bedroom and had been transformed into a pretty sanctuary for a teenaged girl. Blue wallpaper with tiny white flowers adorned the walls and Caroline had hung pictures and girly decorations around the room. But it was still Edward's favorite room in the house. He would enter the room after midnight and his soul would try to rest there. His presence almost always woke Caroline, spooking her and sending her running upstairs to sleep with her baby sister, Anna. I, again, tried to encourage Edward to move on and let Marie's family be. But he remained, stubbornly determined to wait for Evelyn.

"Princess Caroline will get used to me," he insisted.

Chapter 20

FULL CIRCLE
1985

J im stood on the hard, frozen earth, shovel in hand, wondering how in the hell he was going to put the first break in the rock-hard ground, let alone dig a hole big enough to plant the six-foot live fir tree that had been the family Christmas tree that season. Marie had never permitted a fake Christmas tree in their house. In the past, when they were moving around with the Navy, the trees had been cut trees that they simply discarded after the new year. But, after they had moved into her family Home and Jim had finally retired, Marie had insisted on getting live trees, which they planted in the yard after the new year. This was the fourth one that would be planted. Of the other three, one had died and the other two were growing strong and full in the back yard. This one she wanted in the side yard, right in the middle of the old field. She wanted to string it with tiny white lights so that they could enjoy it all winter. As he did every year, Jim had scoffed at Marie's request and complained loudly. "Jesus Christ, Marie, why can't we just get a cut tree this year?"

"Jim, I am planting this tree." Marie always replied with the same answer. "If you don't want to help, that's okay. I can find someone else to help me. But it's getting planted."

So, there he stood, bundled in his flannel-lined jeans and winter work jacket, clutching a shovel and pick in his gloved hands. Frost was beginning to form on his mustache. He was cold and annoyed, but he knew this needed to be done. It was 1985 and was the last Christmas with all of the kids living at home. And Evelyn would be moving in with them in March.

Evelyn was now seventy-seven years old and had suffered two strokes. Fortunately, the strokes had not been too bad and Evelyn had recovered nicely, but Marie wasn't comfortable with her living on her own any longer. She would move into the same little bedroom she and Edward had shared for so many years. This year would be a year of big changes for the family. Jim knew this year's tree would be symbolic and he had to plant it correctly so that it wouldn't die. But when Jim swung the pick down hard, the frozen ground rejected it, sending it bouncing back at him. He sighed. None of this would be easy for any of them.

Marie stood at the window in the little bedroom downstairs, that was now Alden's room, and watched Jim's losing battle with the frozen earth. She exhaled and sat on the edge of the walnut, spool poster bed. This year was going to bring challenges. She couldn't believe Alden would be leaving for college in the Fall. And, not just any college - the U.S. Naval Academy. He would have to endure plebe summer, which was the equivalent of basic training on steroids. This was when the Academy weeded out the kids who weren't cut out for a military school experience. They purposely made it difficult, physically and mentally, so that the plebes would be brought to their breaking point. Alden had always dreamed of attending the Naval Academy. He had not even applied to other colleges. He was extremely intelligent and had worked hard to earn the grades and test scores necessary for admission. But, he was very tall and skinny – to the point of being scrawny. He was far from athletic and wasn't what one would call "tough." Marie worried about the demands the rigorous program would put on him.

Her thoughts then turned to her mother. Evelyn had always been independent and had lived alone since Edward had died over seventeen years ago. She had always been so healthy. But after the strokes, she now became easily confused and was frail enough that Dr. Ward had called Marie and Jim to his office to talk about his concerns about Evelyn continuing to drive. Marie had been thankful for Dr. Ward's sincere compassion. Having been the family doctor for over forty years, he was likely the only person who could have convinced Evelyn to voluntarily relinquish her car keys. Evelyn had cried at first, but then smiled through her tears as she handed her keys to Jim, saying simply, "Well, I've always imagined I would have a chauffer named James, and I guess now I do!" After that, they all decided that it made more sense for Evelyn to move Home where Jim and Marie could be close to help her. They planned to create a little apartment of sorts for her using Alden's bedroom, the adjacent living room, and downstairs bathroom. They would close off the center hallway to ensure she had her privacy and some independence while allowing Marie to keep an eye on her.

Marie worried about the effect all of this would have on her marriage and the children. Jim had agreed, without question, that moving Evelyn Home was the right thing to do. After all, he loved Evelyn like his own mother and, if it weren't for her generosity, they wouldn't have the Home at all. But Marie knew that caring for an elderly, live-in parent would be stressful; their privacy would be sacrificed, and the arrangement would inevitably put a strain on the family. Alden would be losing his bedroom, which meant that he would have to move into the small sun porch off of the dining room until he left for college. The only downstairs bathroom would now be a part of Evelyn's space, so Caroline, who occupied the only other downstairs bedroom, would have to share the upstairs bathroom with the rest of the family. This wasn't a big deal, but it would be an issue getting ready for school in the mornings. And Caroline was sixteen – you never knew what would set her off these days.

Marie wasn't too concerned about Thomas and Anna. They would adjust easily to having Nana around. Thomas was fourteen and a freshman in high school, busy with classes and sports. When he was home, he was closed off in his bedroom with his boom box. Anna was still young enough to be excited that her Nana would be around to bake her famous pies.

There was also the physical transformation of the House to consider. Marie took a deep breath as she looked around the tiny bedroom that Alden had occupied for the last three years. The walls were painted royal blue and KISS and AC/DC posters were randomly hung with thumbtacks. The smell of stale pizza and onions filled her nostrils. Alden had been working at Maria's sub and pizza shop for the past year and everything in his room smelled like a month-old Italian sub. But Marie knew that once they moved Alden's belongings out of the room, she could clean the old wood floors, put up some fresh wallpaper and the room would be instantly transformed back into the pretty bedroom Evelyn and Edward had shared so many years ago. *You've come full circle, Mum,* Marie thought as she turned her gaze back to the frosty window. Jim was now walking toward the House with the pick and shovel in his hands and a frown on his face. There was no pile of earth to evidence that the hole-digging endeavor had been successful.

Marie met Jim as he entered the kitchen from the breezeway, where he propped the pick and shovel by the back steps. He pulled off his wool cap, revealing a red, sweaty forehead. "No luck, huh?" Marie said as she helped him shrug his army green jacket off and hung it on the low hooks by the back door.

"Christ, Marie, that ground is as hard as a rock today," Jim exclaimed. "The pick just bounced back, almost taking out my face every time I tried to break the ground. There is no way we can plant that damn tree until it warms up a bit."

Marie handed her frustrated husband a cup of black coffee. "Well, I'm sure the tree will keep for a while longer if we wrap the roots and keep it watered. Let's just put it in a bucket in the garage and hope the ground thaws soon. I think the forecast calls for some sunny days next week."

"Hell, we probably won't see the sun until June," Jim grumbled, wiping frozen moisture from his mustache. He sipped his coffee and looked at his wife. She was stubborn, he knew. He had no doubt that she would get that tree planted come hell or high water. "Tell you what," Jim spoke up, "Harry Litchfield's kid, Joey, has a landscape business. I'll ask Harry when we have coffee at the Flounder Inn tomorrow if Joey can come over with his Bobcat and get a hole dug for us. Harry owes me anyway. The cheap son-of-a-bitch never has cash to pay for his breakfast and the Flounder doesn't take credit cards. I don't know why that asshole can't remember that. But I've paid for his breakfast many times – he can get his kid over here to scoop one measly hole for me."

"Jim, Joey has a business to run and doesn't owe you anything. Now stop that nonsense!" Marie admonished. "I will be happy to pay Joey to dig the hole. I'll call him this afternoon."

"Well, do it your way then," Jim answered knowing better than to argue with his wife – the Lockhart's were as stubborn as they come. "But that cheapskate Harry still owes me a breakfast or two!"

Marie laughed. Jim loved his mornings with the guys. There were six of them who met regularly for coffee. They called themselves the Marching Chowdah Club. Most of them were old townies, who had been friends since high school. Marie knew how fond Jim was of Harry and the boys. She patted his shoulder as she took a seat beside him at the table. "Can you believe Alden is leaving for the Naval Academy in just a few months?" She asked changing the subject.

"Yeah. Time has flown by, that's for sure," Jim replied. "I sure hope he knows what he's getting into."

"I still see our fat little babies when I look at the kids," Marie said, her eyes glistening with nostalgia. "It's crazy how fast they've grown. And it feels like only yesterday that we moved Home. I can't believe it's been three years already."

"Well, three years isn't such a long time and kids do grow up, you know," Jim replied, always the logical one. He noticed the sharp look Marie shot at him over her coffee cup. "But, yeah, I know what you mean. It seems like a lot has happened in those three short years," Jim said trying to redeem himself.

"That's what I mean," Marie said. "Alden was a small little ninth grader when we moved here – barely over five-foot-seven and a math geek. He grew six inches just last year and is now on his way to becoming a midshipman at the Naval Academy! You have to be proud of that!" Marie exclaimed, touching Jim's arm. "He wants to be like his father."

Jim nodded. "Well, I never went to the Academy," he said, eyebrows raised in admiration for his son but his eyes also expressed concern. "I hear it's a pretty rigorous program. Plebe summer can be pretty damn tough on those kids. I hope Alden has it in him."

Jim was always cautious and somewhat skeptical. People accused him of being a downright pessimist. But, it was in his nature to prepare for the worst while hoping for the best. He was extremely proud of his eldest son. The boy had genius-level intelligence. He had been in gifted classes since second grade when his IQ test revealed his brilliance. Sure, he had grown very fast and had some awkward years as a teenager, but he was nearing the end of the awkward phase. Jim knew Alden was a good kid, with a big heart and even bigger dreams. He was confident that his son would accomplish what he set out to do. He was also flattered that his son's dreams were to be a naval officer like himself and his own father. Three generations of Navy!

"He has it in him – just like his father and his grandfather," Marie stated confidently, echoing Jim's thoughts. "We did something right with that one. When he and Caroline were little I thought that I was the best mother in the world. I had two perfect babies who were so well behaved and sweet. I had just assumed that it was because we were doing everything right."

"Yeah, and then Thomas came along and shattered that theory!" Jim exclaimed, shaking his head and laughing.

"Oh my God!" Marie exclaimed, laughing with him. "Remember in Hawaii how he used to escape from his crib and would leave the apartment in the middle of the night and toddle down the street? He gave me heart attacks on a regular basis!"

"I even put deadbolts up high so he couldn't reach them. But he would pull chairs and tables to the door, climb them and unlock the doors," Jim said, recalling what a wild-child their youngest son had been. "Jesus. It's a miracle he survived."

"It's a miracle that the neighbors didn't murder him!" Marie agreed. "What about that time Kathy Nesbit had that beautiful olive green shag carpet installed in her living room and Thomas decided that it looked like grass and needed to be watered? I can still hear her screaming my name as she came out of her bedroom and got blasted in the face from the sprinkler Thomas had dragged into her house. Everything she owned had been soaked!"

Jim laughed and shook his head. Marie wiped a tear that had formed from laughing so hard. Thomas had certainly made their lives interesting over the years. He was the class clown at school and, despite having to constantly reprimand him to get him to focus, every teacher he had ever had had loved him. After all, he was adorable with his light blonde hair and giant hazel eyes. And, he was always happy and kind. Sure, he was high energy and loved to talk and joke but it was always in good-natured fun. He stole the hearts of everyone who met him.

"So, what's the story with Caroline?" Jim asked, changing the focus of the conversation to their second born. "Is she still all ga-ga over that preppy kid from Cohasset?"

Caroline was a junior in high school. Only eighteen months younger than Alden and two years older than Thomas, Caroline had always been the typical middle child. She was the peacemaker and the pleaser. She always did what was expected of her and did well in school but she was not the straight-A student Alden was. She dabbled in various sports – a couple years of soccer, a season of basketball, a season of track – but nothing that stuck. She wasn't good enough or interested enough in athletics to put in much effort. Caroline didn't fit squarely into any of the cliques at school. She was as "middle of the road" as a middle child could get, able to hang with any crowd but standing out in none. She had recently begun dating a boy she had met through friends in Cohasset, with whom she was quite enamored. Marie knew she had to keep a close eye on that situation. After all, Marie had met Jim at the same age and she recognized the look on her oldest daughter's face when she talked about this boy. Marie knew in her gut that this was going to be more than a casual fling.

"Yes, she is still seeing Cory," Marie replied. "She seems to really like him."

"What is with that kid, anyway," Jim asked. "He looks like a ninny."

Marie didn't know what a "ninny" was and she laughed at her husband's protective instincts. Of course, Jim knew nothing about Cory as he had only met him once when he had come to pick Caroline up for their first date. Cory had pulled up in his father's jaguar and had been dressed in jeans and an argyle sweater. He was a preppy kid from Cohasset, a town known for its expensive real estate and residents with big names and deep pockets. Cory was smart and good looking. He played football and seemed like a nice boy. But, of course, nobody would be good enough in Jim's eyes to date his daughter.

"Oh Jim, stop it, you are being silly," Marie scolded. "Cory is a perfectly nice boy from a lovely family. He seems sweet."

"Yeah, I'll bet he just wants to be 'sweet' to her," Jim retorted. Marie laughed out loud.

"You know, we were actually a bit younger than Caroline when you started being 'sweet' to me," Marie reminded him.

"That's not making me feel any better," Jim grumbled.

"Ha ha. Well, don't worry. Caroline is a good girl with a good head on her shoulders. She will be just fine," Marie attempted to reassure him, patting his arm as she stood to unload the dishwasher.

"You know she is applying to only southern colleges," Marie informed her husband, changing the subject from young love.

"What? Why?" Jim asked. "How does she think she is going to afford that? And why would she want to go so far away?"

"She says she is used to moving around and that she is going stir crazy. She says we have stayed here too long and she is ready to move. Plus, she hates the cold winters. She really wants to be someplace warmer. She has her eye on some schools that have good journalism programs. University of Maryland is her top choice. You know, the news broadcaster Connie Chung graduated from there? Anyway, she is also looking at University of North Carolina, a couple schools in Virginia and the University of Central Florida."

156

"Jesus Christ, Marie, how does she expect to pay for those out-of-state, big schools?" Jim asked, sounding slightly panicked.

"Well, she has decent grades so hopefully she will get some financial aid. Plus, we don't have to pay for the Naval Academy, so we should be able to help her a bit." Marie replied, testing the waters. Marie was conflicted. On one hand, she wanted her daughter to follow her dreams, leave home, and pursue a career in journalism. On the other, she wasn't ready to lose her baby girl to the world. " I am still going to talk to her about applying to a state school here just to be safe."

"How is she going to play kissy face with Cohasset Cory if she goes that far away to college?" Jim asked. "Maybe he can convince her to stay in state."

"Oh, I see how you are, James Freeman," Marie laughed. "You are suddenly fine with your daughter dating the boy so long as your wallet is safe!" Marie swatted at him with a floral dishtowel. Jim smirked just as the back door burst open and Caroline and Anna came through the door, followed by Caroline's friends, Nancy and Kristy, who lived down the street. The girls were all giggling as they unwrapped their scarves revealing red, wind-chapped cheeks.

"Well hello girls! How was the ice skating?" Marie asked as they crowded into the small kitchen. "Leave your skates on the breezeway and put your wet gloves and scarves on the radiator to dry."

Jim stood and greeted the girls. "Did you all master your Olympic ice skating skills out there today?" Jim asked playfully. While most of Caroline's friends were terrified of Jim and his gruff manner, Nancy and Kristy, who had been Caroline's friends since she had lived in Scituate briefly in kindergarten and had remained close throughout all of Caroline's moves, knew him well enough to be comfortable around him.

"Ha ha, oh yeah, we are going for the gold, Mr. Freeman," Kristy replied, always one to play back with him.

"I will be rooting for you, Marylou Retton!" Jim replied, winking at the girls as he exited the kitchen for the family room.

"Hot chocolate girls?" Marie asked

157

"Maybe later, Mom," Caroline answered for all of them. "We are going to hang out I my room for a bit. We need to find outfits for the party tonight. Come on guys, I have some ideas."

"Okay then! Bye, girls. Go make yourselves beautiful," Marie called after them as they filed through the dining room and down the hall to Caroline's bedroom. Marie turned to Anna who was left standing in the kitchen. "How about you Beanie?" Marie turned to her youngest child, using the nickname Jim had given her as a baby because she was "squishy like a Beanie Baby" he would say. "Hot chocolate for my cutie pie?"

"Yay!" Anna exclaimed as she climbed into a chair. "Can I have mini marshmallows in it?"

"Of course you can," replied Marie, kissing her eight-year old baby girl on her chubby cheek. "Tell you what – I'll make some popcorn too and we can snuggle on the couch and watch the Care Bear movie on the VCR."

An hour later, the mugs and popcorn bowl sat empty on the coffee table and Anna lay asleep with her head in Marie's lap. The movie had ended and Marie sat running her fingers through Anna's blonde hair, wishing she would never grow up. Jim was reclined in his Lazy Boy chair, reading a book.

"You know, there are going to be a lot of changes this year and in the next few years," Marie said softly. "But it's all going to be okay. We have a lot to be thankful for."

"That we do," replied Jim, looking fondly at his wife and sleeping daughter. "That, we do."

✝✝✝✝

Joey Litchfield successfully planted the fir tree the following week after the sun had come out and thawed the frozen ground. While he offered to do it for free, Jim paid him a fair wage. Evelyn moved Home in late January and, as planned, Jim and Marie converted the north side of our Home into an apartment. The small living room was closed off and a kitchenette, complete with a sink, small oven, a two-burner stove, and microwave was installed to the left of the fireplace. Evelyn had her own private entrance so she and her guests could come and go without traipsing through the main part of the house. Marie cleaned out Alden's bedroom and hung pink wallpaper with tiny flowers, transforming the tiny room into a pretty antique bedroom ready once again to welcome its original occupant. Evelyn had come full circle. She was Home.

Alden graduated from high school in the top of his class and left for the Naval Academy in late June. Marie had cried and fretted all summer, wondering how he was doing. After what seemed like an eternity, family weekend arrived and Jim and Marie drove to Annapolis to see him. He had made it through plebe summer and, other than having lost weight he couldn't really afford to lose and being exhausted, he was doing great. We were all very proud.

In August, Jim and Marie decided that I would undergo a major change. With Evelyn's area closed off, there was no longer a separate living space where the kids could hang out with their friends. Jim and Marie felt strongly that their home be place where the kids wanted to spend time. So they decided to blow out the exterior kitchen wall and demolish the small sun porch off of the dining room. In its place, they built a large, bright great room with honey-colored oak floors and tall floor to ceiling windows and skylights. Large sliding doors led to a large deck in the back yard. Jim hand-crafted a beautiful, built-in television cabinet with cabinets and shelving. Marie furnished the room with a comfortable green chenille sofa, two chairs, and a large pastel oriental rug. The space allowed Jim and Marie a comfortable place to entertain and gave the kids more space to have their friends over. I felt at peace with my family and was happy to have Evelyn once again living under my roof, where she belonged. Edward was happy to have his bride back and he finally stopped roaming at night, allowing Caroline to sleep through the night in her own bed.

Chapter 21

PRESENT DAY

Caroline awakens after a fretful night of little sleep. Images of her mother, grandmother and aunt ran through her head all night. She dreamt her mother was alive and was pregnant and was begging Caroline to take the baby because she was too old to care for it. She dreamt her grandfather was trying to patch the crack in the kitchen wall but every time he would finish, the crack would reopen, black birds would fly out of it, and he would have to start all over. Visions of her Aunt Katherine and Uncle William swirled in her mind all night.

As the darkness finally begins to yield to the blue light of early morning, Caroline is relieved.

She slips out of bed, wraps her terrycloth robe around her, and pads out to the kitchen to make coffee. The first morning rays are weaving ribbons of gold and pink through the dense woods behind the house. It is just after five o'clock. Nobody else is awake. Caroline was always amazed at how early the sun comes up in Eastern Massachusetts. It always takes her some getting used to when she comes Home. In Florida, when she wakes, usually between six and seven, the sun is just barely peeking over the horizon. Most mornings, she is able to wake, grab a coffee and head to the beach to watch the sunrise. But here in Massachusetts, when she wakes, the sun is already high in a bright, sunny sky and she panics that she has overslept. Normally, she would take advantage of being up this early and would grab her camera to go photograph the marsh as the sun bathes the green grass and dark waters in its golden glow. Scituate has always been such a beautiful town, offering an abundance of photographic opportunities, from the rocky beaches, to the antique lighthouses, to the river winding through the marshes, thick with mud. But this morning, Caroline has no desire to go anywhere. She simply wants to enjoy her morning right here in her family Home.

Caroline fixes herself a large mug of strong coffee with cream and a touch of honey and quietly exits the back door onto the breezeway where she curls up on the white wicker sofa with floral cushions. She listens to the birds sing their greetings to the day as she sips her steaming coffee. Caroline glances around the long, narrow room that connects the kitchen to the garage and the memories come flooding in. She remembers being a kid, running up the driveway and flagstone walkway after a long road trip from Jacksonville or Virginia Beach, or wherever they had been living. Nana would be standing on this breezeway, her curly hair cut to just above her chin, a big smile on her face, and arms wide open to greet Caroline and her brothers with big hugs. The smells and feelings just come flooding in as if forty years hadn't passed. Caroline is instantly that ten-year old girl who pushed the screen door open for her brother, leaned out too far over the walkway, and fell onto the flagstones, breaking her hand. She remembers being even younger than that, standing in the very spot where she now sits, when a violent thunderstorm rolled in. She had been listening to her mother and grandmother talking when lighting struck the house. The jolt of electrical energy had sent Caroline jumping what felt like ten feet in the air, her heart thumping out of her chest. Her mother had laughed about that one for years. Caroline glances out the screened windows and can almost see the family of raccoons that came by every night at dinner, waiting for Evelyn to throw them some corn on the cob or leftover casserole. Even the cobwebs that hang in the dark brown rafters above her head seem to be the same ones that have always been there. As she relives these old memories, Caroline knows that every room in this house can provide enough memories to carry her down memory lane for days.

As the sun chases away the last remnants of night and climbs higher above the trees, the yard becomes bright and sunny. The light is no longer dappled and every inch of the vast property is illuminated - the woods, the vast fields, the ancient rock walls, the family Christmas trees planted over the years. Some new family probably won't even know that those trees are special. Just then, Caroline hears someone moving about in the kitchen. Suddenly, her sister's beautiful face, a halo of messy blond waves falling softly past her shoulders, peeks around the corner.

"Oh, you're up," Anna says. "I thought I heard someone. You got up early, huh?"

"Yes, I couldn't sleep," Caroline replies. "I'm surprised to see *you* up so early though. You are even less of a morning person than I am."

"Yeah, well, stuff, ya know. My mind is too full." Anna walks down the kitchen steps onto the breezeway holding a large mug of coffee.

"I know what you mean. This is tough, huh?"

Anna ignores the question and clears her throat. She lets out a raspy cough as she sits down, wrapping a blanket tightly around her. Caroline wishes silently that her sister would stop smoking, but knows this is not the time for a lecture.

Anna drinks her coffee and stares silently out the back windows. Caroline struggles for conversation. Anna has always been reserved, forthcoming with her feelings only after much poking and prodding. *She is so much like Dad*, thinks Caroline as she finally gives up searching for the right words or question and decides to just embrace the silence. She turns her face in the direction Anna is staring and the sisters, together, watch the light dance in the woods, each woman lost in her own thoughts. After several minutes, Anna sighs and clears her throat again.

"Well, we are going to meet with Mom and Dad's lawyer today so I guess he can answer all of our questions about selling this place." Anna's tone is impatient and she shakes her head back and

162

forth as she speaks as if to negate her own words. Caroline wonders if she even knows she is doing this.

"I think we just need to talk a little more," Caroline says softly. "Let's ask questions about selling but also maybe get some ideas about how to keep it?"

Anna snorts disgustedly. "Whatever, Caroline. You heard Alden and Thomas. They aren't going to make any effort to help keep it and you know I can't afford to buy them out so I don't really see what "ideas" the lawyer is going to have. We are going to have to sell. It's probably for the best. I need to get out of this town once and for all anyway."

The anger and frustration in her voice is palpable. She looks into her coffee mug. She feels helpless. She wishes she could swoop in and save the day but her finances can't support a buyout of her siblings either. Suddenly Caroline feels chilled and exhausted.

"What was it like here after we all left?" Caroline asks, wanting to change the subject. "I mean, Alden left and then I did and then Thomas right after me. You were so young and lived here with Mom and Dad alone. You were like an only child. I was so caught up in my own world that I never really stopped to think about what your life was like in this house with all of us gone."

Anna snorts and looks sharply at Caroline. "How do you *think* it was? Dad was retired and home full time by then. He worked at the elevator company and mom had her antique shop but other than that, I was their only focus. They were on top of my every move. It was pretty suffocating. Shit, they sent me to an all-girl, private Catholic school for Christ's sake. You guys ALL went to Scituate High. *They* even went to Scituate High. But all of a sudden Scituate High wasn't good enough for their youngest daughter?"

"Yeah, I remember when Mom told me she was sending you to Notre Dame. I told her not to but she said Scituate High had changed and that you would do better at an all girl's school. I disagreed with her but she wouldn't listen. Was it really that bad?"

"HA! You know what happened. Do you think it was any better than SHS? What a joke! But no, the school itself was fine. I didn't hate it. It just didn't "save" me from anything, including myself."

"Hmm. No, I guess not. But I'd say you turned out okay in the long run." Caroline winks at her sister and smiles. Her love for Anna wraps itself around her heart and her eyes fill with tears. Caroline has always regretted that she missed a big chunk of Anna's life at a time when Anna was the most impressionable and vulnerable. She feels the sharp pain of guilt, like a knife in her gut, over not being there when her sister really needed someone to stand up for her and guide her.

Caroline and Anna have always been very close. With nine years separating them, Caroline had always viewed her baby sister sort of like her own child. When Anna was a newborn and Caroline only ten, they had shared a bedroom at their house in Jacksonville. Anna's crib had been pushed against the wall at the end of Caroline's full bed. Marie had put her old rocking chair in the corner of the room. When Anna woke up crying at night, Caroline, not wanting to wake her mother, was the one who would comfort her and rock her back to sleep. And when Anna got older, Caroline and Anna shared a bed in their townhome in Rhode Island. Even after they had moved back to Scituate when Caroline was a teenager, the sisters slept together often, tickling each other's arms while Caroline sang Anna to sleep.

"You know, Anna, when I left Home, it didn't have anything to do with you. You understand that, right? You knew that then, didn't you?"

Anna takes a deep breath and lets it out slowly. "I know it now. I don't know that I knew it then. I was a kid. I mean, I guess I knew. You were older and had to do your thing and all. But, to be honest, it hurt me. A lot."

A tear escapes Anna's eyes as she is suddenly unable to hide the decades-old pain. Caroline looks at her sadly and wishes she could go back in time. But would she do it any differently? She had been so desperate to get out of Scituate and pursue her own life. She had been twenty. She had just finished her second year as an early education major at the local college, a school she had had no desire to attend, but had decided to enroll at the last minute so that she could stay closer to Cory who was attending college in Boston. She had given up her dreams to study journalism at a southern college because she had been in love. But after two years, Caroline had felt stifled and frustrated. She realized that the decisions she had made had been wrong for her. It was not what she had truly wanted. And so, Caroline had quit school, bought a car, told Cory she was leaving, and made plans to drive to Florida.

"I will never forget the day we left to take you to Florida," Anna says softly. "You slept in my bed the night before. Do you remember that?"

Caroline didn't remember, but she is not surprised that she had spent her last night at home in her sister's room. She had loved to sleep with her little sister's warm body cuddled up next to hers. She is suddenly sad to realize that that night must have been the last time they did that. And she doesn't even remember. How could she not have remembered that? She looks at Anna sadly.

"Huh. You don't remember," Anna says matter of factly. "Well, I'm not surprised, actually. You had a lot going on then. You were saying good-bye to Cory the next morning and moving a thousand miles away. You had a lot on your mind."

Caroline nods, remembering that morning like it was yesterday. Cory had come over before the sun came up to say good-bye. He had handed her a stack of envelopes with the names of each state she would drive through scrawled on the front. "Open one at each state line," he had said as he kissed her good-bye. He promised to visit during winter break and then he had driven up the hill as Caroline sobbed.

"Yeah, I remember. I was crying so hard Mom had to drive for the first five hours of the trip because I was such a mess," Caroline replies.

"Yeah, and then every time we crossed a state line you opened one and started crying all over again! I thought Mom was going to throw all those cards out the window."

Caroline laughs and shakes her head. "I'm just so glad you and Mom drove with me. I was way more scared than I even knew. I don't know if I could have done it if you hadn't come with me and helped me find a place to live and get settled," Caroline looks lovingly at Anna.

"Well, there were many times I wished Mom had just told you no," Anna admits. "I wanted her to make you come back home. I felt like I lost my best friend. When Mom and I got on that plane to head home without you, I cried so hard I threw up. Twice."

"Oh my God, what? You did? I had no idea."

"No, Mom never would have told you. She didn't want you to feel guilty or sad. She told me that you needed to live your life and she tried to make me understand. And I did. Sort of. But I was only eleven and I missed you so much."

Now both sisters were crying openly.

"I'm so sorry, Anna. I should have stayed."

"No, no you shouldn't have. It was what you needed to do. And if you hadn't have gone, you would never have met John or had your beautiful daughters. It was meant to be."

"I guess so. But it still makes me sad. I should have done more for you, somehow. You were so young."

"Yes, I was. And it certainly wasn't easy. Especially since things seemed to change so fast after you moved. It was like you left and we all entered some weird time warp."

Caroline thinks back and realizes her sister is right. After her move to Florida, the changes to our family and our Home came fast and furious.

The first event that had affected all of them came only three months after Caroline's move. It had been one that had brought her running right back to a Home that would never be the same again.

Chapter 22

EVELYN
1989

M arie woke early. It was still dark outside and she could tell it was bitter cold. The attic-turned-master bedroom lacked heat and the icy winter weather seeped through the windows and cracks in the wood floors. Marie sunk deeper under the covers and put her warm hand over her cold nose. But she knew she couldn't hibernate for long. She had a lot to do today. It was Thanksgiving Day. And, like she had done every year since moving Home, Marie was hosting Thanksgiving Dinner. She was expecting somewhere between fifteen and thirty close friends and family for a traditional buffet-style dinner, with all of the trimmings.

With a deep breath, Marie summoned the courage to throw off the blankets, brave the cold and get her day started. Jim lay snoring, warm and blissfully ignorant of all that had to be done before dinner. *Men have it made sometimes*, thought Marie as she wrapped her dark blue, merino wool robe over her flannel nightgown and slid her feet into her fuzzy slippers. Jim would be free of any cleaning or cooking obligations today, with his only task being in charge of the adult beverages and firewood. Jim always accused her of making too much of a fuss over preparing the house and food for holiday meals. But, how else would she be able to invite everyone over to give thanks and celebrate? The house had to be presentable and the food prepared. Men just didn't have to worry about such things. Caroline often scolded her for "allowing" Jim's chauvinistic behavior but Marie didn't complain – it was how things were in her generation and it worked for them. Jim worked hard and had sacrificed so much for both his country and his family and it was Marie's job to take care of the house and the children. Plus, Marie knew how difficult her life would be if Jim, God forbid, actually wanted to help out. Marie liked to have things just right and she had learned after twenty years as a navy wife – who spent months at a time with no husband around - how to handle things on her own. If Jim was to get involved, he would want to do things a certain way and there would be arguments and frustration. No, it was much better to just keep him out of it. *Caroline will one day learn this the hard way*, Marie chuckled to herself as she padded downstairs.

As Marie passed through the hall toward the kitchen, she could hear the soft chatter from Evelyn's radio and she knew her mother was not yet up. Evelyn had been living back at Home for a few years. Her boyfriend Charlie visited most days and took her out to eat at the Gannett Grill at least four times each week. Charlie was a loyal, loving companion and friend. Marie chuckled to herself thinking about how many times poor Charlie had begged Evelyn to marry him. She had to hand it to him – he wasn't afraid of rejection and he must really love her because he kept coming around. Of course, he would be Evelyn's date for Thanksgiving dinner.

Marie filled her percolator with cold water and poured fresh grounds into the tin filter. While all of her friends raved about their new Mr. Coffee electric brewer, Marie preferred the old percolator. But she was like that; preferring old things over new. She still had an old rotary dial phone on the kitchen wall with a cord that reached into the dining room. The new cordless phones sounded tinny and fake to her. She always said she had been born in the wrong decade.

While the coffee brewed, Marie washed and peeled potatoes and prepared the ingredients for the stuffing. She had made the breads and muffins the day before and they sat on the pantry counter, covered in tin foil. She pulled the 20-pound turkey from where it had been thawing the refrigerator and began removing the gizzards and rubbing it with herbs and butter. People would begin arriving at three o'clock and the turkey would take about four hours to cook fully. Just as she stood with her right hand buried deep into the cavity of the big bird, Jim sauntered into the kitchen.

"Where's my coffee, woman?" Jim demanded with a wink. She knew he was kidding but she couldn't help but wonder what he would do if she hadn't made his coffee for him. Would he even know how to use the percolator? She made a mental note to purchase a Mr. Coffee to just keep in a cupboard just in case something were to happen to her and he needed to make his own coffee. Caroline would be so disappointed in her. Jim poured his own mug and put an English muffin in the toaster.

"Do you want more than an English muffin?" Marie asked, happy to make him something more substantial.

"Nah – there will be so much eating to do later that I had better take it easy right now," Jim answered patting his belly.

Jim had always been thin. Early in his twenties and even into his thirties he had been almost too thin. His six-foot frame had been long and lanky throughout their marriage. And he hadn't needed to exercise to keep it that way. He had been blessed with a fast metabolism. But now, as he entered his mid forties, things were starting to change. His once trim belly now showed signs of softening and protruded slightly when he sat down. He was still slim and quite handsome but the signs of aging were starting to appear. He had silver at his temples and his brown, wavy hair was starting to recede. Marie thought it make him look distinguished. She had always admired Jim's physical appearance and now was no different.

"You're still a looker in my book" Marie said as she stuffed the last of her homemade stuffing into the bird. "But look at me! I know how irresistible I must look at the moment." She joked as she wiped her forehead with the sleeve of her robe, leaving a streak of food in its wake. Her hair was still messy from sleeping and her robe hung half open revealing her favorite old, tattered nightgown.

"Damn you old hag, who are you and what have done with my hot bride?" Jim laughed as he swept her into his arms and planted a kiss on her lips. He reached around to grab a handful of Marie's ample bottom. "Oh, it IS you after all," he growled into her ear.

"Good Lord, Jim, you're a pig," Marie laughed as she gently pushed him away. "I have lots to do here so either make yourself useful or be gone!"

"Okay, okay," Jim said, resignation in his voice. "I'll go check the fire wood. It's gonna be a cold one today." Jim exited the kitchen door into the breezeway, coffee in his hand. Marie smiled to herself. They had been together since they were fifteen years old. How was it possible that she still loved that man as much as she did? Sure, they had experienced their rough patches and there were times when she thought she might kill him. But she still loved him and could not imagine going through life with anyone else.

Marie pulled her robe tightly around her as the icy air rushed in through the open door. She glanced at the clock on the stove. Eight-thirty already! She had to get a move-on. The house needed to be picked up, dusted, vacuumed, the bathrooms cleaned, and the china and crystal would have to be pulled out of the old, built in china cabinet, rinsed, and dried. But first, she had to check on Evelyn and get some clothes on. Marie carefully placed the turkey in the oven and left the kitchen filling with the promising aroma of a delicious Thanksgiving meal.

As Marie entered the dining room, she could hear the bath running in Evelyn's apartment. She turned the glass doorknob on the heavy wooden door and called softly, "Mum, are you awake?" she asked, cracking the door slightly.

"Oh, good morning, Honey." Evelyn smiled as she came out of her bedroom wearing a pink flannel robe and matching slippers. Her short, grey hair was mussed and she wasn't wearing her glasses, which Marie thought made her look older.

"Good morning, Mum," Marie said gently as she took in the thin, frail figure standing before her. "I just wanted to check on you. I heard the water running. Are you about to take a bath?" Marie had a knack for asking the obvious – a trait for which her family teased her incessantly.

"No, Dear, I thought I might make some moonshine in the tub this morning." Evelyn joked sarcastically.

"Ha. Ha. Ha." Marie deadpanned and rolled her eyes, only a little hurt by the teasing. "Well, I'll leave you to it then, you smart Alec. Yell up if you need any help. I'm heading upstairs to get dressed and then I'm going to clean. I'll shower later, before everyone arrives. Don't forget, I told people to come around three. The food is mostly prepared and the turkey is in the oven. Jim is collecting firewood and will be getting the drinks together. Anna and Thomas and Alden are still sleeping but should be up soon and …."

"Thank you for the news hour dear," Evelyn said interrupting her but laughing kindly. Marie had a way of going on and on and Evelyn's bath was in danger of overflowing.

"Just trying to keep you in the loop," Marie said. But she kissed her mother's soft cheek, feeling the thin, fragile skin against her lips and whispered, "I love you, Mom. See you in a bit." She then backed out into the dining room, pushing the door closed behind her.

After throwing on a pair of blue slacks and a wool argyle sweater, Marie woke Anna first. Thomas and Alden were both home on school break and she decided to let them sleep a little longer.

Marie set Anna up in the dining room, dusting off and organizing the china and gave her a list of other chores. She spent the next few hours cooking, cleaning, polishing, dusting, and getting everything just right for their holiday feast and party. She had popped in to check on Evelyn a couple of times and found her watching the news, making her favorite deviled eggs in her small kitchenette, and doing crossword puzzles.

"What can I do to help, you, Dear?" Evelyn asked when Marie poked her head around the corner for the third time. "You know I hate to just sit in here when there is so much to be done."

She put down her crossword and started to rise from her light blue sofa.

"Well, actually, I could use a hand with the silverware," Marie responded. "I have some cloth napkins that I would like to roll the silverware in. If I bring you the napkins and the silver, could you make some roll-ups for me?"

"Oh my goodness, that's *all* you need? Well of course I would be happy to do that for you."

Marie glanced at Evelyn's hands, veins enlarged and joints swollen and deformed by arthritis and said "Thanks, Mom. That would actually be a huge help. Just do as many as you can and I'll send Anna in to help you."

"Oh, that would be lovely," replied Evelyn. "She is such a good girl."

By one o'clock most everything had been done and the house looked beautiful. The blue and gold china was arranged neatly atop the ivory damask tablecloth draped over the dining table. The cobalt crystal goblets that Evelyn had received as a wedding gift and had passed down to Marie were sparkling and beautifully arranged. The silver had been polished and the serving pieces were displayed near the china. Evelyn and Anna had expertly rolled the eating utensils in cloth napkins that matched the tablecloth. Pies of every variety sat on cooling racks on the kitchen counters and the house was filled with the mouth-watering aromas of a complete Thanksgiving Day feast. Marie stood in the dining room, surveying the spread and recalling the many Thanksgivings she had celebrated in this room, at this very table, with the same china and crystal. She recalled the story of the year before her birth when her father had sat at the head of the table, thin and frail after barely surviving a long battle with pneumonia. Her family had learned that year what it was like to be truly thankful. She remembered the years when extra places were set as the family grew – first for William's wife, Carol, and then Katherine's husband, Stephen, and then for Jim when Marie fell in love as a teenager. She smiled to herself as she pictured her father teasing seventeen-year old Jim about his ears during dinner. Of course she had been horrified at the time, but she knew that it was her father's way of showing he accepted Jim. It had been the people Edward didn't make fun of who had to worry! *Oh, if these walls could talk*, Marie thought as she shook away the memories and headed upstairs to shower and dress for dinner.

Forty-five minutes later, Marie made her way back down the creaky front staircase, wearing a plaid, wool skirt, a blue, silk blouse with a tie at the neck, pantyhose, and simple, navy blue flats with bows on the top. Her medium length brown hair had been hot-rolled and the curls bounced around her shoulders as she walked down the old staircase. She wore very little makeup – just some foundation to even out her skin tone, mascara, and mauve lipstick. Despite that she was forty-four years old, she looked young and beautiful. When she reached the bottom of the steep stairs, she could see that Jim had started a fire in the fireplace in the formal living room and Anna was lying in front of it, on the Persian rug, coloring with colored pencils in a giant coloring book. Jim and the boys were in the new family room watching football.

"Hey guys, you all need to get dressed soon," Marie said entering the family room and planting herself directly in front of the television. "People will be arriving in about an hour."

"What do you mean, 'get dressed,'?" Jim asked, straining to his right to see past Marie. "I am dressed. Do I look naked?"

"Don't be ridiculous, Jim," Marie scolded. It is Thanksgiving. You can't wear those dungarees and that dirty flannel shirt. You will need to put on some slacks and maybe your blue cashmere sweater. Something presentable please. We have guests coming."

Despite that it was 1989 and the entire modern world considered jeans a wardrobe staple and acceptable in almost any situation, save for maybe a wedding or a funeral, Marie stubbornly insisted that denim was not appropriate attire outside of the farm. She referred to jeans as "dungarees" because, as she said, "they were made to wear while shoveling cow dung." Her family teased her about her archaic fashion ideas, but she held firm and, as Caroline could attest, she would not allow her children to wear jeans to school until they were old enough to get a job and pay for their own clothes. And nobody was allowed to wear their "dungarees" to holiday dinners, no matter who bought them.

"That goes for you too, Missy." Marie said, walking toward Anna, who was dressed in her favorite Guess jeans with the fold-down pockets on the knees that she had inherited from Caroline. "I want you to put on your pretty red sweater dress please."

"Oh my God, Mom, why??" Anna whined, looking up from her coloring book. "We aren't going anywhere and nobody cares if I'm dressed up. Plus, I don't have any tights that aren't ripped. Please don't make me wear that awful dress."

Marie looked at her youngest child and wondered how it was possible that she was already at the age that she would talk back and argue about things like what she should wear. The years just seemed to be flying by. Marie had mellowed a bit in her middle age and had learned the hard way that, with teens, you had to pick your battles. She acquiesced with a heavy sigh. "Fine, Anna, you don't have to wear the dress. But you do need to wear nice slacks or a skirt and not those *dungarees* you live in. Now, please go put on something pretty and brush your hair. Then you can sit with Nana until the guests arrive."

"Okay, okay, I'm going," Anna sighed, relieved that she was off the hook with the sweater dress. She gathered the colored pencils that were strewn across the rug and hurried upstairs to change. Anna loved spending time with her grandmother. Nana was funny and she always gave Anna sour, hard candies that came in beautiful little round tins. And she always let Anna sit right up against her on the sofa and rest her head on her shoulder while they watched TV together. Nana loved to make fun of the people on the television programs and she never failed to make Anna laugh.

"Alright boys, you need to go change also. Please don't make me ask again," Marie said, looking pointedly at Jim as she walked out of the living room. She then knocked lightly on the door to Evelyn's apartment before pushing it open.

"Mum, you probably ought to go ahead and get dressed for dinner. You know Charlie will be coming soon and I'm sure you want to be ready," Marie called as she walked into the tiny hall by the bedroom. "Can I help you with your dress or your jewelry?"

Evelyn opened the bedroom door and stood before Marie, already dressed in a navy blue, silk dress with a white tie at the neck. The dress had another tie at the waist and fell just below the knee. Evelyn wore nude panty hose on her thin legs and navy pumps

174

with a low heel. Her short grey hair was curled and parted neatly on the side. She wore simple pearl earrings and her wedding rings. She looked refined, classy, and beautiful.

"Well, you certainly look lovely Mother," Marie smiled looking at Evelyn whose eyes were downcast. As Evelyn raised her eyes to meet Marie's gaze, Marie's smile faded instantly. Something was wrong.

"Mum? Are you okay?" Marie asked, taking Evelyn's bony elbow into her hand and guiding her through the doorway into Evelyn's small living room. Evelyn's steps were shaky.

"I – I don't think I feel very well," Evelyn replied, her voice shaky.

Marie eased her mother onto the pale blue sofa. "Are you dizzy? Do you have any pain?"

Evelyn took a deep breath and stared at her youngest daughter. One look into Evelyn's eyes told Marie all she needed to know. There would be no Thanksgiving celebration. Marie began to panic and moved to call 9-1-1 immediately. But as she reached for the phone, a sudden wave of peace and love washed over the room, easing her panic and she withdrew her hand. She felt a familiar presence – one that made Marie catch her breath and slow down.

"Oh Mom," Marie sighed, "It's okay. It's all right. I'm here. I've got you." She gently pulled Evelyn to her and felt the weight of Evelyn's frail body relax into her. "Let's just sit together a minute. You are fine and I've got you. Dad's here, too. He's right here with us."

Evelyn slowly nodded. "I know he is, dear. He has always been here. He has been waiting for me."

Tears filled Marie's eyes as she thought back to all the times she had felt her father's presence in the old Home. She had always known deep down that her father had never left.

"Are you in pain Mum? Are you going to be sick? Maybe I should get you some water? I could call Dr. Ward if you …"

"Sssshhhh, Marie," Evelyn soothed, patting her daughter's hand. "Just shush and sit with me. I'm not in pain. I'm not thirsty. I just feel very tired and a bit numb, actually. Everything will be fine in just a few moments. Just stay with me. You can call Cliff soon."

The smooth calmness of Evelyn's voice settled Marie and she again felt an overwhelming sense of peace, which gave her the strength to do as her mother was asking. She inhaled deeply and leaned back into the couch cushions holding Evelyn in her arms like a child. She felt Evelyn smile and then heard her whisper, "I love you, Marie. You are a good girl. Tell the others I love them, too."

"They know, Mom. We all know. We love you, too," Marie whispered back, voice breaking.

Then, suddenly Evelyn lifted her head and looked at Marie with intense clarity. "You must find him. Don't forget. Tell him about me – about us. He deserves to know." Shocked and confused at this sudden outburst, but concerned that Evelyn was becoming agitated, Marie covered her mother's hands with her own.

"Ssshhhh, it's okay. It will all be okay."

Mother and daughter sat together quietly for several minutes, Evelyn feeling the soft beating of Marie's heart as her head rested on Marie's chest, and Marie listening to the shallow breathing of the woman who had loved and supported her her entire life. Marie didn't cry. She just held her mother firmly until she felt the increased weight of Evelyn's body as Evelyn took a series of rapid, raspy breaths and then finally exhaled one long, last breath.

Marie's tears came then, flowing freely as she stroked her mother's soft, gray hair. "Take care of her, Daddy. Take good care of her," she sobbed.

✝✝✝✝

I felt Edward and Evelyn leave even before Marie got up from the sofa to call Dr. Ward. My room filled with love as Edward greeted his bride and took her hand in his. Finally, together again, they walked toward the light to enter that place that human souls go when they have lived a good life full of love. Edward had been waiting so long to be with his bride again. He had lovingly haunted my rooms for so many years that, when he left, I felt like part of me went missing. But, it was a part that needed to go, and my walls and foundation felt lighter with his departure.

Marie was strong and held herself together as she called Dr. Ward, who came immediately with Frank Gaffey, the local coroner. She then called friends and family to let them know. Those she couldn't reach by phone were told in person as they arrived for Thanksgiving Dinner. Some stayed to comfort Marie and the family. They helped put the food out and they ate and cried and spoke of their fond memories of Evelyn. There was laughter and tears and giving thanks for the love Evelyn had brought into all of their lives.

Charlie was devastated. He cried on the telephone when Marie called and he did not come over despite Marie strongly encouraging him to be with them. Sadly, we didn't see much of Charlie after the funeral although Marie was good to call him every so often to check in. I felt sorry for him and I wondered if Evelyn had agreed to marry him whether things would have been different.

Everyone came Home for the funeral. William and his family arrived. Katherine and all four of her grown children were there. Caroline came Home from Florida. Cousins, second cousins, and scores of friends filled the Episcopalian church by Lawson Tower to celebrate Evelyn's life and say good-bye. Marie was a pillar of strength through it all. Of course, she invited everyone to our house for food and drinks after the service and the celebration of life lasted well into the evening. Evelyn would have loved the party.

After Evelyn's funeral, I was restless. It was hard to believe Edward and Evelyn were now both gone. Left in their wake were two more generations of children and grandchildren - some living within my walls but most of them having moved on with their lives elsewhere. It was a lot for me to grasp and, for the first time in my existence, I began to worry what might happen to me. What if Jim and Marie decided they wanted to live somewhere else — somewhere warmer near Caroline? Or maybe they would decide to get a smaller place — something less difficult to maintain? But, life moved on and Marie seemed determined to keep me as her Home.

Now that the apartment was no longer needed, Marie and Jim removed the efficiency kitchen from the small living room and opened the hallway between the front door and the dining room again so that people could pass through without having to go through the larger den area. Evelyn's small, pink bedroom became a pretty guest room and our Home was open and bright. As always, I adapted to the changing needs of our family.

That winter passed uneventfully. The boys went back to college and Anna was alone with Jim and Marie. Jim became involved with town politics and

Marie worked in her antique shop. Everyone settled into routines and the days passed uneventfully. I learned that humans have a way of dealing with loss of loved ones and moving on and so I decided I must do the same. My first chapter as "Home" ended with Evelyn's death. But I realized that I was already well into my second and even third chapters with the lives they created and left behind; lives that still thrived within my walls and under my roof. And I would remain strong and steady to provide them a safe and secure Home. But I wondered at Evelyn's last words. Who had she been talking about? Who needed to know about us? The crack in my wall throbbed and I suddenly realized that my walls might hold secrets of which even I was not aware.

Chapter 23

CAROLINE
1992

Marie stared at her mother's antique, silk wedding gown and wondered how the three years since Evelyn's death had managed to fly by so quickly. In many ways it felt like yesterday. But, as Marie examined the dress, trying to figure out how to modify it while still being true to its original style, she felt that it had been ages ago. After all, so many things had happened in the past three years. Life was on fast-forward and Marie could barely catch her breath.

She looked at the beautiful silk gown and tried to focus on the task at hand. The sleek gown had been her mother's. She didn't want to ruin it, but somehow she needed to make it somewhat contemporary. It was a gorgeous gown, with tiny silk covered buttons up the back, a high neck and tiny bodice that was meant to skim the body before draping at the hips into a long gown reaching the floor, flaring out into a modest train. When Evelyn had worn it at her wedding in 1935 it had been the epitome of bridal fashion. Marie had kept the gown stored carefully in the attic in hopes that, one day, one of her girls would want to wear it. And now, Caroline was getting married!

Of course, it was 1992 and the styles were different – the wedding dresses all had puffy sleeves and gobs of lace, satin, and pearls – all a far cry from this simple yet elegant gown before her. Caroline had already picked out her wedding dress and it was lovely, even with the puffy sleeves and all the lace. Marie knew better than to try to insist she be married wearing her grandmother's gown. Instead, however, Marie planned to give Caroline a modified version of the gown to wear on her wedding night, as a nightgown. Caroline had tiny bones and a slender figure like Evelyn and Marie just knew that the expensive silk would hug her waist and the few curves she had and would be a sophisticated and lovely nightgown. It was to be her gift of "something old" for her first born daughter and she wanted it to be perfect. She ran her hands down the length of the dress, feeling the luxurious silk kiss her fingertips. She touched each tiny button that ran up the back. She let long, silk strands that were meant to be tied at the low back, slip through her fingers. She tried to picture her mother as a young woman standing before her father, her eyes filled with love and excitement. That image was easy to conjure. What was more difficult was picturing her own daughter as a bride, standing before a man Marie barely knew, promising to spend her life with him far away from her Home.

Marie sucked in her breath and exhaled loudly as she tried to reconcile how so much had changed in such a short time. Only three years ago Marie had driven Caroline, who had been sobbing over leaving her high school sweetheart, to Florida to chase her dreams. Never did it occur to Marie that Caroline would not be returning Home. Now, here she was planning a wedding for that same daughter who, after only two short years in Florida, had shown up in Scituate with a blonde Florida boy and announced that they were moving to Alabama together. They had gotten engaged only four months later and were planning an August wedding in Scituate. In addition, Alden had graduated from the Naval Academy in 1990 and had gotten married the following January, and immediately moved to Texas where he attended flight training. And they were expecting a baby in August! Marie would be throwing a wedding and becoming a grandmother all in the same month. Marie was somewhat in shock at all the changes that seemed to be coming way too fast. But isn't this what life was about? Changing as children grew, growing as life changed?

Had it really only been a little over two years since she buried her own mother? She glanced toward the old pink bedroom and could almost convince herself that if she went in the room she would find her mother listening to the AM radio. While Marie knew Evelyn was gone, she could still feel her mother in every inch of the house. Her body and spirit were gone – she hadn't stayed around the way her father had after his death – but her soul would forever be imprinted in these walls. Evelyn had loved this house. It was as much a part of her as her own heart had been. And Marie was grateful for its comforting warmth. Marie stood and put her left ear to the wall that separated the dining room and the kitchen. She pressed her whole cheek against the ivory wallpaper and then pressed her chest and body to the wall, palms pressed on either side of her, fingers splayed. She knew she looked insane, but she wanted to feel the heart of the house. She wanted its energy to merge with her own heartbeat and she breathed deeply, slowly. Her eyes closed.

"I miss you, Mom. I wish you were going to be here to see Caroline get married and meet your great-grandbaby." Marie whispered as a single tear spilled down her right cheek.

"They're heeerrrre." A male voice sang, imitating the famous line from the paranormal horror movie, Poltergeists. Marie jumped away from the wall, cheeks flushed with embarrassment. "Jesus Jim! Could you sneak up on someone any creepier?"

"Hey, I'm not the one hugging a wall and talking to ghosts. What in God's name are you doing, anyway?"

"Oh never mind," Marie waved her hand dismissively and walked back to the dining table where the gown still lay. "I'm trying to figure out how to alter Mom's old wedding dress so Caroline can wear it on her wedding night."

"And the answer is in the wall?" Jim asked, looking at his wife as if she had lost her mind.

"Actually, yes, I believe these walls hold many answers if we are just willing to listen," Marie replied in a tone that let him know not to challenge her further.

"Well, I don't know about the dress stuff," Jim said, wisely changing the subject, "but I do know that if we are going to have a bunch of people coming to town for this wedding, this house

181

needs some sprucing. We've got windows that need repair, painting that needs to be done, a hot water tank that could use updating and several other things. I'm heading up to Home Depot. Do you want to go with me and grab some lunch while we are out?"

Scituate was still a small town that didn't allow for much commercial growth. No chain stores existed in the town and the closest Home Depot was about twenty minutes away in Hanover. Marie knew that Jim's idea of "grabbing lunch" was swinging through a Burger King drive thru. Not that she had anything against a big juicy Whopper every now and then, but she wasn't in the mood today. And she didn't like the big home improvement stores, with their giant ceilings and aisles filled with far too many things that people didn't really need.

"What could you possibly need at that God-awful Home Depot store that you can't find right here at the local hardware store?" Marie asked. "Do you really need to go all the way to Hanover? Why don't we go to the harbor, grab a sub from Maria's and watch the boats for a while and then you can get what you need at the hardware store right there on Front Street?"

Jim sighed. It was just like Marie to always have a better way to approach a task. But, he had to admit that a Maria's sub sounded a lot better than an over-processed, re-heated burger. Maria's had been a Scituate staple since 1964. Jim remembered when it first opened – in the exact location where it still operated. They sold subs with only four toppings – tomatoes, pickles, onions, and "hots" – all finely chopped and heaped across the top of piles of meat and cheese layered across the softest open faced sub rolls you've ever tasted. No green peppers, no cucumbers or avocadoes, and all the locals knew not to *ever* request lettuce. Of course the no-lettuce rule drove the out-of-towners crazy. Nonetheless, the line was out the door every afternoon. Just thinking about a tender roast beef sub from Maria's set Jim's mouth watering and, as much as he didn't want to admit his wife might actually have a better idea, he gave in.

"Okay, fine. I'm not sure the hardware store in the harbor will have everything I need and it will be more expensive, but I guess I won't have to spend the gas money to get to Hanover."

"Great!" Marie said smugly. "While we are out we can swing by the Barker Tavern so I can talk to them about the menu for the wedding reception. They sent it over and it's all meat and potatoes. I need them to come up with a lighter menu more appropriate for an August afternoon."

Jim sighed. His trip to Home Depot and Burger King had just been expertly hijacked.

The morning of August 15, 1992, Marie's emotions were all over the place. She had been awake since five o'clock, unable to sleep. It was wedding day! Her oldest daughter was getting married. Marie was happy that Caroline had found a man she clearly loved and who loved her. But it also made her feel a bit old and, if she was being honest, a little sad. Caroline was marrying a man from Florida. Marie had a sinking feeling she may never live near home again. The conflicting emotions swirled inside her and she had been a bit teary eyed since she got up. Caroline had come home the week before the wedding to help with final preparations. She had been staying in Evelyn's old bedroom, as her old room was occupied by other family members who were in town for the wedding.

Marie tip-toed to the room and quietly pushed the door open to peek in on her daughter. Caroline lay peacefully under the off-white, crocheted bedspread, her long hair spread across the pillow in a mass of brunette curls. The ceremony, which Marie had planned very carefully, was scheduled to start at eleven with a luncheon reception to follow. Caroline had a hair appointment at nine and Marie knew Caroline was not a morning person. She would need time to have a cup of coffee and wake up slowly before heading to the hair salon. Marie eased herself onto the edge of the antique bed, which creaked softly under her weight. She gazed at her grown daughter who she still thought of as a little girl. Caroline looked so young lying there with her full cheeks, small, turned up nose, and thick dark eyebrows. She had always looked much younger than her age. It didn't help that she had small bones and no curves. When they had gone dress shopping, everything she had tried on had made her look like a little girl playing dress up, rather than the twenty-three-year-old bride-to-be that she was. But Caroline had picked out a beautiful gown with a form fitted lace bodice that accentuated her tiny waist, pillowy white sleeves to add some volume to her small frame and a gorgeous full, silk skirt that skimmed the ground.

Marie glanced at the stunning dress hanging on the closet door, waiting to be worn. Next to it, in a garment bag, hung Evelyn's silk wedding dress that Marie had tastefully modified to be the perfect wedding nightgown. Suddenly Marie's watery eyes overflowed and the tears spilled silently down her cheeks. Seeing the two dresses – one worn by her mother almost 60 years ago and the other to be worn by her daughter on this day - triggered a tsunami of unexpected emotion that washed over her and rendered her momentarily lachrymose. She closed her eyes and breathed in deeply to compose herself. Yes, things were changing far too quickly. But this was a big day – a happy day. And Caroline needed to wake up and greet it. Marie said a silent prayer to her mother then opened her eyes. She reached out to stroke Caroline's bare arm.

"Good morning!" she sang softly. "It's your wedding day! Time to rise and shine, my dear."

She knew that her kids hated when she woke them this way and that they had long outgrown the need or desire of their mother's soft touch. But a mother's natural instincts to touch and hold her babies doesn't diminish when those babies are grown and, frankly, she needed the touch for her own comfort in that moment. Caroline opened her eyes with a slight scowl, initially pulling away from her mother. But as she woke fully and realized what day it was, she softened and sat up, allowing Marie to pull her into her arms.

"Good morning, Mom."

"Good morning, baby girl. It's your wedding day!"

"Oh my God, I know. Wow. What time is it?"

"Just after seven. I know it's early but you have a hair appointment and I know you will want to eat a little something and get some coffee before you head to the salon. I will put a pot on. Why don't you jump in the shower to wake up and come on out and let me feed you your last breakfast as a single woman."

Caroline stretched and rubbed a hand across her still-puffy eyes. "Okay, sure. Just something super light though, Mum. I don't want a poochy stomach on my wedding day. I do need some good, strong coffee for sure though. I can't believe I'm going to be Mrs. King in just a few hours." Caroline wrinkled her nose and pulled a face that made Marie laugh. "That makes me sound so old."

"I always used to say that Mrs. Freeman was my mother in law until one day it seemed to fit me. But that wasn't until my kids were old enough to have friends and having them call me 'Marie' just wasn't appropriate. You'll get used it to, love."

"Caroline King, it has a nice ring!" Caroline sang, laughing at her rhyme and making Marie laugh also. Marie kissed her daughter's forehead and left Caroline to prepare for her big day.

As Marie pulled the percolator out of the cabinet and spooned the coffee grounds into the metal filter basket, her head was filled with conflicting emotions. Mrs. King? Really? Despite what she had said earlier, she couldn't make the name fit. Why was it so hard on the ears to hear the name you gave your baby changed to something new? It wasn't that King was a bad name; it just sounded like, well, like it belonged to someone else. But isn't that what Caroline was now? Someone else? Only three short years ago she had been the naïve local girl intent on marrying her high school love. Even when Caroline had up and left for Florida, the plan had been that her boyfriend, Cory would join her after he graduated. But in June, as Cory was graduating, Caroline had shown up in Scituate with John King and had informed Jim and Marie that she was in love and moving to Birmingham. Marie had been shocked and upset.

"What are you thinking?" Marie had asked, worried and indignant.

"I'm thinking I love him, Mom." Caroline had replied, looking evenly into her mother's worried face.

"How do you know that?" Marie had implored. "You haven't known him even six months! And now you are suddenly moving to a new state with him and giving up the freedom and independence

185

you just worked so hard to obtain? And what about Cory? I thought he was planning to move to Florida to be with you?"

Caroline had snorted. "Well, Mom, which is it? Are you worried about my 'freedom' and 'independence' or are you worried about me not being with Cory? No, don't answer – it doesn't matter anyway. Cory doesn't want me. He made that clear when he called to tell me he wasn't coming to Florida after graduation after all. He asked me to move to Michigan with him instead. Michigan! I moved from Boston because I can't live in this cold weather and he wanted me to go to Michigan? Bottom line is that was never the plan and he knew it. He made his decision without regard to me or any future with me. It was his way of breaking up for good. I told him about John and it didn't change anything for him. And, to be honest, I was actually a little relieved. We just aren't meant to be together. I knew it the moment I met John. I love him, Mom. I really do. He's sweet, smart, and funny. And he wants the same things I want. Give him a chance."

Marie had noticed a tiny flicker of sadness cross Caroline's face as she talked about Cory, but she had watched the sadness immediately replaced by something else as Caroline spoke about this new man in her life; she saw love reflected in the green, pleading eyes, along with a resolve and confidence that helped to erase the worry of a concerned mother. Marie had sighed and nodded her head, acknowledging that she would not argue Caroline's love for John. The "he wants the same things I want" part worried her though. Marie knew that it didn't involve living anywhere near Scituate, Massachusetts.

"Okay, so you love him. I get it. I do. But – Birmingham? Really? After all you have worked for in Florida? You just got your residency. What about school?" These were legitimate questions.

"We have talked about all of it, Mom. Birmingham is only temporary. He will go to law school. And I will finally finish college. We will both be students and will have to take out some student loans. But we will both work in restaurants to pay our living expenses and help keep the loans down as much as possible. We found an inexpensive house near campus."

Marie had narrowed her eyes at her daughter. "So you plan to live together?" she had asked slowly, judgment dripping from every syllable. Caroline sighed. She had known this was going to be the hardest part. Her mother was terribly old fashioned.

"Yes, Mother," Caroline had replied, evenly and with determination. "It is 1991. Couples live together all of the time before marriage." Marie had felt hot tears spring to her eyes. This daughter of hers — so modern and independent and strong willed. This was not how she had raised her. Marie knew that modern couples lived together but she was old fashioned and considered it a sin. It was not what she had hoped for her oldest daughter and it had made her distrust this John person even more.

"This is not how we do things in our family," Marie had scolded. "When your grandmother and grandfather fell in love it was also a whirlwind romance, much like yours. Nana had to move all the way from Minnesota to Massachusetts to be with your grandfather. But they never dreamed of living together unwed. They got married like respectable people." Caroline had sucked in her breath trying to stay patient, as Marie continued. "And when your father and I were twenty and couldn't stand to be apart one more day, we didn't just shack up together. He left college, came home, and married me so that we could be together. That's what men do when they want to live with a woman they love!"

Caroline's patience was nearing its limit. "Yes, Mom, I know all of this. But that was in the 1930's and 1960's. So much has changed since then. It's completely acceptable for a man and woman to live together before marriage nowadays. I'm sorry you don't approve, but this is what we are doing. I don't WANT to get married right now. One minute you are mad at me because you think I'm giving up my independence by moving to Birmingham with him and the next you are mad at me because I'm not marrying him immediately. I don't get you or your generation!" A tear had slipped down Marie's cheek and Caroline softened her tone. "Look, Mom, I'm sorry. I don't mean to get frustrated. Just trust me that I know what I am doing. We really do love each other. He's the one for me. We just need a little more time to get ready. And in the meantime, we will get our education and save some money by living together. It

187

will certainly be a great way to know for sure whether we can make it long term." Caroline had reached over and gently touched her mother's arm.

"You will be living in sin," Marie had said softly but her tone made it clear she had surrendered.

"Well, Mom, I think you already know it's too late to save my soul on that one," Caroline had replied with a laugh.

Marie had shaken her head but smiled at her daughter, so grown up and determined.

And now, it was one year later and everything seemed to have worked out. After moving to Birmingham, where John had started law school and Caroline had enrolled as a full time, undergraduate journalism student, it had only taken five months for John to propose. It is what Marie had wanted for Caroline and she should have been thrilled.

But as Marie listened to the percolator gurgling on her daughter's wedding day, she realized that it sounded a lot like her stomach felt this wedding day morning. Everything had happened so fast and she was second-guessing it all. Had she pushed the kids to take this step before they were truly ready? Caroline was still so young. Could she really be sure that this is what she really wanted? Only one year ago she had insisted she didn't want to get married. Yet, here she was, just in the next room dressing for her wedding day. "Oh God, please let this be the right decision," Marie whispered to the empty kitchen.

Just down the hall, in the downstairs bathroom, Caroline stood, wiping the fog from the vanity mirror, uttering the same words as she stared at her reflection. The girl staring back at her looked like the same girl who had lived in this house only three years prior. Caroline felt as though she had changed significantly since she had left Home. She felt much older and like a different person after being on her own in Florida and then with John in Alabama. But the girl in the mirror with skin still damp from the shower and wet, slicked back hair sure looked like the same girl who, not so long ago, had looked in this same mirror practicing her first name matched with the last name of her high school boyfriend. Suddenly,

Caroline didn't recognize the green eyes in the mirror staring back at her. Who was this person who now lived in the deep South with a man who had been a stranger only two years ago? Tears welled in her eyes as she thought about making a permanent commitment to a life so far from Home. But isn't that what her life had always been? A series of starting over somewhere new; becoming someone new? Suddenly, she wasn't feeling sure about any of her choices.

"Oh God, please let this be the right decision," Caroline said to her reflection. But, as soon as the words left her lips, she felt a wave of clarity wash over her and she laughed at herself. This was probably the only time in her life she had ever made a decision based solely on what *she* wanted and not what was expected of her. As such, this was, indeed, the *perfect* decision. Lifting her chin, she smoothed her wet hair and looked herself in the eye, staring down what she knew were simply wedding day jitters. *Stop being so dramatic, silly,* she told herself. Caroline then saluted her reflection and bid farewell to her past.

✞✞✞✞

As Marie collapsed into bed that night, images of her daughter, looking radiant in her lace and silk wedding gown were fresh on her mind. It had been a long, but lovely day. Love and happiness had shone like a halo over Caroline and John all day. I heard Marie say to Jim that she had never seen Caroline look so happy and so sure of herself. I couldn't help but think about how much Caroline reminded me of Evelyn. The parallels between grandmother and granddaughter were undeniable. Like Evelyn, Caroline had originally planned to marry a boy from her home town. Evelyn's plans had drastically changed when she had traveled to Boston the summer before her wedding and met Edward. Caroline moved to Florida and met John. Evelyn had broken her engagement to the dentist after knowing Edward for less than a month and then had married Edward only one year later. Caroline had broken off her relationship with Cory after knowing John for only four months and, like Evelyn, had married John only one year later. In both cases, everything had happened so fast! But Evelyn had been in love and she and Edward had built a wonderful family and long lasting marriage based on that love. Now,

Evelyn's granddaughter, with her modern ideas and a different way of doing things, seemed to be following in her grandmother's footsteps. Caroline was really the same person she had been all her life — she just needed to discover it for herself. Like her grandmother, Caroline was a confident, independent woman with the strength to change her path to one of her own choosing. As Marie fell asleep we both prayed that Caroline's path would lead her to the blessings, love, and companionship that Evelyn had found on her path.

Chapter 24

PRESENT DAY

After her talk with Anna, Caroline is emotionally drained and her eyes and face are puffy from crying. She steps into the shower, allowing the hot water to scald her skin, relishing the pain as her body turns deep red from the assault. She thinks about what Anna went through in the years after Caroline left Home. She is amazed and somewhat disgusted with herself for not paying more attention to what had transpired during those years. She had been so self absorbed. She reaches back in her mind in an attempt to conjure up any memories of Thomas during those years and she is shocked and sad to realize she has very little memory of him. *God, I'm so selfish*, Caroline thinks to herself. *I was so caught up in my own life that I completely ignored my family.* She recounts the years after she left home: the move to Florida, then to Alabama. She finished college and then went on to law school. She and John had gotten jobs at law firms in Birmingham and had settled there. When Caroline had left home Anna was eleven years old. By the time Anna turned fourteen, Caroline was married. And in the years after that, while Caroline focused on college, law school and married life, Anna had grown up, graduated high school, and had gone to college in Boston for a semester before realizing it wasn't for her. She moved back home and did what? Caroline is ashamed to realize that she doesn't know. As she steps out of the shower and wraps a towel around her aging body, she thinks about the years between 1990 and 1999 and she realizes that she knows very little of what went on at Home during those years. Sure, she had talked with her mother every week and had been filled in on the basics. But she needed someone to fill in the gaps. How could any of them make a decision about what to do with the house without fully understanding its entire history?

Caroline dresses and goes in search of her two younger siblings. But the house is quiet. Nobody is around. Caroline had already rummaged through the boxes in the closets of the main house and, except for some photos of Thomas at graduation and Anna at different high school dances, nothing had really given her any clues about what life at Home had been like during those years. Caroline ventures to the smaller house to see what her mother may have squirreled away that would give her some answers. As she enters through the back porch, adjacent to her mother's large garden, a wave of nostalgia slams into her chest making her catch her breath. The wicker chairs, still upholstered in the colorful floral prints Marie had loved, the glass topped iron table and chairs where her mother had held tea parties with her granddaughters, the clutter of small framed photographs, figurines, and nature-themed knick knacks – all of it throws memories at her that were so vibrant that they might have happened just yesterday. Tears fill Caroline's eyes as she sits in the same white iron café chair her own daughters had occupied many times, dressed in Victorian era dresses and feather plumed hats, enjoying an old fashioned tea party with Neena. *Mom, you were the best grandma in the world*, Caroline thinks as she remembers. *All of your grandchildren adored you.* But Marie had been more than just a grandmother, Caroline realizes. She had been more like a second mother to Anna's children, raising them alongside Anna. Her death would affect that family for years to come. *Selling this house will affect* all *of us deeply,* Caroline thinks as she gazes out at the tall weeds beginning to choke the day lilies that had just begun to bloom. Her mother would have a fit if she could see her beloved garden in this condition. Caroline makes a mental note to pull some weeds before she leaves town.

After rummaging through the downstairs closets and finding only old linens, stored winter clothes, and several boxes of knick-knacks, Caroline climbs the stairs to the room that had been her father's bedroom. She had only been up here a handful of times. Because Jim had had sleep apnea, he was a horrific snorer and eventually had needed a CPAP machine. Marie had insisted he move to his own bedroom so she could get some sleep. They had built out this attic space to contain a small bedroom, full bath and a storage closet. There was one window that looked out over the back woods and the morning sun sent dust-filled rays through the room. Caroline looks around the room and thinks about her father, a man she loved dearly but with whom she had not been particularly close.

Jim had been deployed for much of Caroline's childhood and her memories of him in the early years of her life are thin. When they had lived in Hawaii, he had been deployed off the coast of Vietnam in the war. Caroline's most prevalent memory of her father during those years was talking with him over ship to shore radio: "Hello Daddy... Over... I love you Dad ... Over ..." The conversations were difficult, delayed and full of static and if she didn't remember to say "over" after every sentence her words wouldn't be transmitted. When she was nine and they lived in Jacksonville, Jim had been home more. Caroline remembers body-surfing in the waves with him and hunting for sharks' teeth on Neptune Beach. Those were fun memories. But then she had become a teenager and became caught up in her own little world of friends, clothes, and boys. Jim hadn't had much patience with her during those years.

Being a strict military man who was used to giving orders and having them followed with a salute and a "yes, sir!", Jim hadn't known exactly how to interact with a hormonal teenaged girl who would burst into tears if he raised his voice. So he had left the parenting mostly to Marie and had kept his distance. He did help with things like buying her first car, learning how to change a tire and balance a checkbook, but any issue that required sensitivity or emotional support was simply not his forte. Caroline had loved and respected her father and she knew that he loved her, but sometimes she missed the closeness some of her friends seemed to have with their Dads.

When Jim died of a major heart attack in his sleep, Caroline had been heartbroken. She mourned the loss of her father but she also mourned the fact that she had never been able to completely bridge the gap between them. After Caroline had left home, married, and graduated from law school, her relationship with her father had morphed into one of love and mutual respect. She had known her father was proud of her and she loved seeing him when she would come home to visit. But, the relationship had remained somewhat distant and she had always found discussing any personal issues with her father difficult. When she called home and he answered they would make polite small talk for a few minutes before he would hand the phone to Marie. But they each always said "I love you" before ending their conversation and Caroline had learned to accept her relationship with her father for what it was and not yearn for more. He had been a good man. He had been a great Dad.

Caroline looks around her father's old bedroom. Although her parents had moved back into the main house after Anna moved to her own apartment the year Heather had left for college, this room still holds many of Jim's things. His mahogany highboy dresser with brass pulls stands against the wall. On top is the silver dish where he always placed his steel watch and his car keys. An old silver money clip, engraved with the U.S. Navy insignia lies beside it. Caroline opens the middle dresser drawer. A few of Jim's shirts sill lay neatly folded. Caroline picks up a blue t-shirt and holds it to her nose. She inhales the fading scent of Old Spice aftershave mixed with Tide laundry detergent and the musky smell all the Freeman men had. Caroline remembers how, as a teenager, she would steal her father's sweaters from this very drawer. In the 1980's it was fashionable to wear sweaters five sizes too large and her Dad's drawer had been her favorite "shopping" place. She pulls the old t-shirt over her tank top and closes the drawer.

Caroline moves to the closet, which she finds packed with plastic containers and cardboard boxes. *This could take all day*, she thinks with a sigh. Scanning the boxes for clues as to what is inside, she sees that many of the plastic bins contain her grandmother's old doll collection, along with the many dolls Caroline had collected when she was young. Caroline had almost forgotten about the beautiful dolls her father had brought home to her during his many deployments. She lifts the cover off of one bin and pulls out her favorite – a beautiful and fragile doll with olive skin, black hair, and a red dot in the middle of her forehead. She is dressed in a breathtaking turquoise sari with gold piping and gold threads woven throughout. Her father had brought this doll to her from India when she had been only ten. Caroline had thought she was exotic and beautiful and she had always displayed her front and center in her vast collection. Smiling at the memory, Caroline gently places the doll back in the bin and continues to scan the closet's contents.

A cardboard box with a business card taped to the front catches her eye. Caroline leans closer, recognizing the business card with a drawing of a white duck wearing a flower-adorned straw hat and sporting a wooden leg. It was the logo from her mother's old antique store, The Peg Leg Duck. Caroline had, at the time, laughed at the odd name for an antique shop. But then her mother had told her a story about how she and Aunt Katherine, as children, had fed the ducks on Hunter's Pond near Bound Brook in North Scituate. They had befriended a duck with only one leg. The sisters would bring bread to the pond every day in the Springs and Summers, year after year, until one year the duck did not return. Katherine had moved back to Scituate in the mid '80's, after three failed marriages and years of living in the woods of Vermont. The sisters, happy to be reunited in the same town, had decided to open an antique store. They chose an old, yellow Victorian house in North Scituate Center that sat across from Hunter's Pond. To Marie, it had seemed only fitting that the sisters name their new store after the one-legged duck they had visited here as children.

Caroline pulls and lifts and manages to drag the box to the front of the closet. She remembers how excited her mother had been to be opening the store with her sister. Caroline had been a senior in high school in 1986 when the Peg Leg Duck opened its doors. At the time, she really hadn't known much about her Aunt Katherine other than that she was beautiful, talented, and hysterically funny, with a wide smile and the kind of infectious laugh that could send a even a person in the foulest of moods into a fit of giggles.

195

Caroline knew that Katherine had been married and divorced several times and had dealt with heavy emotional struggles throughout her adult life. She knew that Katherine had eventually returned to Scituate where she had reconnected with an old high school friend and married him. It had been her fourth marriage. After she moved back, Katherine had visited Marie at the house at least once a week and the sisters would drink tea on the breezeway and share stories from their childhood. They never failed to make each other laugh until tears streamed down their faces. Katherine's children had all grown and moved away and, aside from Anna who was still young, Marie's kids were in high school and college. The sister's had time for each other for the first time in many years and they had seemed to relish the chance to reconnect. Opening the store together had seemed like the perfect idea. *Until the duck didn't return*, Caroline thinks sadly as she remembers.

Caroline pulls a photograph from the top of the items in the box and a dull ache fills her chest as she stares at her teenage self, standing in the doorway of the Peg Leg Duck, with Cory by her side. She and Cory used to stop by the store after school just to check in. They looked so young; *almost like a different lifetime*, Caroline thinks as she sets the photograph aside and grabs a stack of others. Flipping through them, she finds several from the day of the grand opening. She gazes at the familiar, smiling faces of the friends who had stopped by to support the Lockhart sister's new venture. Caroline chuckles at the hairstyles and clothes from the late 1980's and wonders silently how so much time had passed so quickly. She stops at a photograph of her mother and aunt – the only one taken of them that day. The sisters have one arm wrapped around the other's shoulders and the other arm outstretched like Vanna White showcasing their grand prize. They were, of course, laughing. Whatever demons had kept Katherine away from Scituate and her family – even her own children - for so long had clearly been defeated and Katherine looked healthy and happy to be Home.

Caroline reaches further into the box and pulls out a large, grey, hardbound book. She opens it and realizes it is a sales ledger. She immediately recognizes her mother's unique handwriting, with its half cursive, half print, and curly tails. Items sold are listed on the left with the price in the right hand column and handwritten notes throughout. *"October, 7, 1989 - Mahogany dresser ….. $500.00… Mrs. Green will pick up on Thursday when her son can come from Boston with his truck to help."* In this ledger Marie had also recorded who worked at the shop each day. Caroline skims the pages. In the beginning of the ledger it looks like Marie and Katherine had both been in the shop every day. As time went on, the entries show Marie at the store in the mornings and Katherine in the afternoons with only an hour or so of overlap. Caroline finds this odd as the whole point of the store had been for the sisters to spend time together.

In the margins of the ledger are some other notations, not in her mother's handwriting: "Anna's school called, please call – 383.6657." Then, a few days later, "Call Notre Dame ASAP." A post-it note is stuck to one page: "Katherine, I closed early. Can't find Anna. Cash still in drawer." Caroline purses her lips as she recalls her mother's weekly phone calls during this time period. She knew Anna had been fairly rebellious, but how bad had it really been? Her mother used to tell her about Anna's constant partying and hanging out until late at night with boys or not coming home at all after the two had had a terrible argument. Caroline had always chalked it up to typical teenage drama – same as they all went through. But Caroline now considers that maybe it had been different for Anna and for her mother. Looking at the ledger and seeing how many days her mother had missed working at the store, she realizes her mother must have been dealing with quite a bit of drama with Anna.

Caroline thinks back to when she and her brothers went through high school. They had had their share of fun and trouble. But there were three of them. They had each other. She now considers that when Anna was in high school she had no siblings to turn to. No sister to confide in. No brothers to watch out for her. Her siblings had all moved away. There had been nobody else for Mom and Dad to focus on other than Anna. She must have been the subject of their full attention, no matter what she did. Caroline remembers her mother calling to tell her that they were sending Anna to Notre Dame private Catholic school rather than allowing Anna to attend Scituate High School.

"That's crazy, Mom," Caroline had laughed. "We ALL went to Scituate High, even you and Dad. We are all perfectly fine. Since when is it not good enough for a member of our family?"

"Since your sister has decided to be a bit more wild than the rest of you," their mother had replied. "She can't handle what goes on socially at Scituate High School. She needs more structure and more discipline. A nice Catholic school is perfect." Caroline, busy with law school in Alabama at the time, had just laughed at her mother but hadn't thought much more about it. She shakes her head now, understanding what Anna had said earlier about Notre Dame not saving her. Clearly she had been quite wild even at the nice Catholic girl's school and she must have found her share of trouble. What all had Caroline missed by moving so far from Home?

Anna had been a sweet eleven year old when Caroline had moved thousands of miles away, wrapped up in her own little world. She hadn't been there when Anna started dating boys. She hadn't been there to give her sister advice about clothes, or driving, or sex. She hadn't been there when Anna met her husband, Ron. She hadn't even been available when nineteen-year old Anna got pregnant. Marie had actually been the one to call and tell Caroline. Nine months later, when Anna had given birth to baby Laura, Caroline was not by her sister's side. She did return home for the wedding when Anna had married Ron a year after Laura was born, but she had to get back to her life in Alabama and she wasn't there for the births of Ron, Jr. or Heather, Anna's youngest. She hadn't been there for morning coffee, or an afternoon walk, or an evening cocktail. She hadn't been there when Anna's marriage started falling apart or that awful day that ended it for good. She certainly hadn't been there to start a business with her sister and reconnect. Sure, she had come home for the summers. But it was always temporary and ended every year with tear-filled goodbye's. Tears sting Caroline's eyes as she realizes a few fun-filled weeks every summer were a poor substitute for having your sister just down the street. Would Anna's life had been any different had Caroline stayed close to Home? Could she have steered her sister from some of the poor decisions she had made and have saved her from some of the heart break? Her mother certainly hadn't been able to keep Aunt Katherine from her mistakes.

Caroline puts the photo of her mother and Aunt Katherine in her pocket. She offers a prayer of thanks that her mother had been given the time to get to know her big sister before it was too late. And it had been close. Will she and Anna have the same kind of opportunity before it's too late? Caroline realizes that of course they won't – not unless one of them makes it happen. She vows to figure out a way to reconnect with her baby sister. Maybe selling the Home would encourage Anna to go ahead and make the move to Florida where they could live near each other again. Or, maybe keeping the Home is just what they need to make sure they always have a place to go to be together. She closes the box knowing that there really isn't more she needs to understand about her years away. She knows all she needs to know, which is that she must find some way to be a better sister.

✝ ✝ ✝ ✝

I think back to the years the Lockhart sisters spent re-connecting and sharing their lives as adults. They had filled my rooms with much laughter in those days. I remember how Katherine would play Stevie Nicks' music and dance around my kitchen, singing at the top of her lungs. She loved the song 'Landslide' and would cry as she sang the lyrics that seemed to have been written just for her:

Mirror in the sky, what is love?
Can the child in my heart rise above?
Can I sail through the changing ocean tide,
can I handle the seasons of my life?
I don't know..."

Even though Katherine would cry as she sang, she wasn't sad any longer. Or at least she was no longer broken. Age and time had calmed her emotions and she was now married to a man she truly loved and who loved her back. All of her years of searching for love had finally taught her that to truly love someone else, and allow yourself to be truly loved, you must first understand that you are worthy of true love. You must love yourself. Does it seem strange that a house would have theories on love and acceptance? Maybe. But, after all of my years of observing my family, I learned some things about human nature. And I know that, many years ago, on the night Edward had died and Stephen walked out, Katherine had deduced that she wasn't worthy of a man's love. And when she had disappeared for almost a year, something had happened that resulted in her punishing herself. All I know is that she had spent many years trying to prove her worth to herself and to men who were all wrong for her. But at some point she had grown and had somehow learned that she could handle the seasons of her own life, and she had come Home.

Unfortunately, she couldn't stay

Chapter 25

KATHERINE
1995

Marie reached her hand into the colorful cloisonné jar and dug her fingers into the soft ash. She filled her fist and slowly lifted her trembling hand. She raised her eyes to look into the faces of the intimate group of family and friends she loved – those Katherine had loved. She then raised her eyes to look at the bright sun rays filtering through the green and yellow autumn leaves of the giant oak tree that sheltered the group of gathered mourners, its long, thick branches holding them all in a foliage embrace.

"I love you, my sister," Marie whispered.

She extended her arm over a small hole dug into the fertile soil under the great tree. *This location is perfect,* she thought. Katherine had been such a hippie and a nature-lover and she would have loved to sit under the branches of this tree, play her guitar, and watch the birds and squirrels for hours. Marie could hear the soft songs Katherine would have been singing as the gentle breeze played in her blonde hair. Of course, now there would be no singing. And instead of sitting under the branches in the breeze, Katherine would be nestled in the cool ground, among the strong, ancient roots that had anchored this tree in this spot for more than a hundred years.

Marie spread her fingers, letting the fine, grey ash seep through her hands and fall into the hole. As she sunk to her knees and used her hand to gently mix the ash with the rich, brown, New England soil, Marie wondered how it could be possible that she was burying her big sister. Wasn't it only yesterday that they had opened the little antique store together in North Scituate Village – so happy to finally be living close to each other in their hometown? And wasn't it just a few years ago that Marie was raising Katherine's teenaged daughters while Katherine was off "finding herself" in the hills of Vermont, growing her own vegetables, raising pigs and getting high by a camp fire under a blanket of stars? Surely it couldn't have been that long ago that they were little girls, running through the fields behind their house, hiding in the tall grass and giggling as their mother called for them to come in and help with dinner. The sisters had shared a disdain for cooking and they thought it was great fun to hide out together, whispering and laughing, until Evelyn had all but put the meal on the table. That wasn't that long ago, was it? Surely not long enough for Katherine to now be gone. Katherine was too young to be ashes in the ground. But the cancer hadn't cared.

Katherine had been first diagnosed with breast cancer when she was only forty years old. She had been in the shower one morning when she felt a small lump in her right breast. She was scared of the cancer, but more scared of the thought of chemotherapy. Katherine believed in eating healthy and living naturally and the thought of putting that poison into her body terrified her. So she had told the doctors no chemo and opted for a lumpectomy, coupled with a high intensity three-day radiation "pack" that was designed to target the area where the cancer was likely to recur. Only a few weeks later, Katherine was done with the treatment and moving on with her busy life.

Then, seventeen years later, on a hot and sunny day in the summer of 1995, Marie was working in her garden when the phone rang. The knees of her "dungarees" were wet and muddy and her hands were stuffed into gardening gloves, caked with dark soil. She ignored the incessant ringing, allowing the answering machine to take the call. It was a beautiful summer day and the windows to the kitchen and sliding door to the family room were wide open. Marie was just nestling some new daisies into the turned up dirt when she heard the beep of the answering machine, followed by Katherine's husband, Don's grim voice.

"Uh, hi Marie. Give me a call when you get this. Okay, well, yeah, okay, bye now."

Frowning, Marie knew something was up. Don, who had a heart of gold but a gruff exterior, didn't believe in answering machines and he never left messages. His philosophy was that if he called you and you didn't answer, then you really didn't want to talk with him in the first place – never mind that you might not even have been home. That was his reasoning and he stubbornly stuck to it no matter how many times Marie had argued with him that sometimes people simply can't get to the phone. So to hear his voice on her machine was a tad alarming. Marie wiped her forearm across her brow, smearing dirt with sweat, and sat back on her haunches, her brain taking inventory of recent events that might provide a clue as to why Don would be leaving messages on answering machines. Not able to come up with a viable clue, Marie stood, brushing off her knees and headed to the house. Just as she was wiping her muddy shoes on the doormat, the phone began to ring again and something inside her knew immediately that it was Don calling again and that something was very, very wrong.

"Hello?" Marie said tentatively into the phone.

Don audibly sighed with apparent relief that she had answered. He then drew a large, shaky breath and said, very slowly, "It's – it's back, Marie. The cancer; it's back."

Katherine had been enjoying a beautiful, summer day swimming in the pool with her grandchildren when she suddenly felt a tingling in her lower back that quickly spread down her legs. She tried to walk to the ladder to exit the pool, but the pain was excruciating. Don had jumped in and lifted her out of the pool. They headed straight to the hospital, believing that she had somehow strained her back. After enduring several hours of tests, an MRI, and lots of poking and prodding, Katherine, learned that she once again had cancer. And this time it wasn't playing games. She soon learned that the cancer had started in her breast, but instead of producing a lump that could be detected easily like last time, it had hidden in the tissue where, undetected, it spread rapidly. It had invaded her lymph nodes, which had accommodatingly broadcast the aggressive disease throughout her body. The pain in her back and the paralysis in her legs were due to a tumor that had already formed on her spine. She was told the type of cancer she had was called "popcorn cancer," a deceitful name that made one think of carnivals and movies and fun. But there was nothing fun about this. Tumors literally popped up out of nowhere and grew rapidly, climbing her spine like an alien force intent on devouring everything it its path. There wasn't anything the doctors could do. Even with aggressive treatment, she had mere months to live.

Marie had gone with Katherine to all of her appointments and heard the diagnosis first-hand. She had asked all of the right questions: *what about chemo? Aren't there any experimental procedures we can try? How could we have all missed this?* She cried. She raged. She laughed bitterly at the bullshit the doctors fed them about the need for chemo – more poison that would prolong Katherine's life by months, but would make those extra months a living hell. She blamed God. She blamed modern medicine. She even blamed Katherine for not taking better care of herself. She tried to imagine life without her sister. And then, she finally reached the point of acceptance. There wasn't anywhere else to go with this. Katherine would die. But first, she would live. And Marie would be right there with her.

Marie and Katherine spent as much time as they could together. They closed the Peg Leg Duck so they could have more time to do the things they loved. They drove around town to all of the beaches in Marie's big wood-paneled station wagon, listening to oldies on the radio and singing at the top of their lungs. They watched sunrises and sunsets and the fog rolling in off the ocean and the waves crashing against Minot's Ledge in stormy weather. They poked around in other people's antique shops; they ate ice cream from Wilburs ice cream shop in North Scituate almost every day. They spent many days in the library together, researching the cancer and trying to demise ways to beat it. They poured over scientific articles and medical journals until they were asked to leave because Katherine wouldn't stop making inappropriate jokes about the photos in the books and Marie got to laughing so hard the librarian got tired of shushing them.

But by September, the tumors were so numerous and so big that they were pushing against Katherine's spine, robbing her of the use of her legs. She was hospitalized and the station wagon expeditions were over. Marie visited the hospital daily, bringing Katherine food, trinkets, and flowers. One day, as she was talking with Katherine, Marie watched a small lump on Katherine's neck form and grow to the size of a tennis ball in a matter of hours. The sparkle in Katherine's eyes began to dim as she realized she was dying. But she was still tall, blonde, and beautiful and, other than the fact that she was laying in a hospital bed with tubes connected everywhere, her body was filled out and healthy looking. Marie had always pictured someone who was dying of cancer as a skinny, frail, old person who looked sick and miserable. It was surreal and made no sense.

"Marie, I need you to do something for me," Katherine asked her one afternoon when Marie was visiting. They were alone in Katherine's hospital room. It was early evening and the sun was low, sending golden rays through the window and casting long shadows. Katherine had been staring silently out the window, the sunlight glistening off of her blonde hair. She turned her porcelain face toward Marie who had been reorganizing the flower arrangements, getting rid of wilted flowers, and consolidating the ones that still had some life left.

"Of course," Marie replied, placing a white daisy next to a beautiful blue hydrangea, "what do you need?"

"I want you to go to the department store and buy me a few pairs of pretty pajamas. Something silky and fancy, not flannel or frumpy. I'll be damned if I'm going to sit in this bed and die looking like an old hag in sweatpants."

"You could never look like an old hag," Marie replied, smiling. "You are our Queenie, remember?" Katherine smiled hearing the nickname her father had given her as a child. She had finally come to understand how much he had loved her. "I'll swing by Marshalls tomorrow and if they don't have anything I'll go to Filene's at the mall."

"You and your Marshalls," Katherine laughed, shaking her head. "You always love to find that bargain. Thank you." She started to say something else, then hesitated. Marie set the flower arrangement aside and sat on the edge of Katherine's bed, taking Katherine's long, beautiful fingers in her own small hand.

"What is it, Katherine? What are you thinking about?" Marie dipped her head, inviting Katherine to raise her face to meet Marie's gaze.

"I need something else from you," Katherine whispered. "Something only you can do." Her blue-grey eyes bore into Marie's hazel ones, pleading with a sadness and desperation that made Marie catch her breath.

"I will do anything for you, Katherine. Anything at all. Just tell me what you need," Marie assured.

Katherine stared at Marie for what felt like a long time, her eyes conveying the importance of what she was about to ask. Then she transferred her gaze back to the waning light in the window and spoke, softly. "I'm going to die soon. I know this. Before I was admitted to the hospital, I tried to organize everything. I talked to Don about my possessions. I made my will. I cleaned the house. I organized and cleaned out my closets and drawers. And I cleaned out the closets of my life." Her eyes moved back to Marie's as she said this. "I made peace with Stephen and all of my ex-husbands. I made peace with my children, after all the years of behaving like everything but a wife and mother. I made peace with myself and with God. But there is one closet I can't clean. You know what it is. You are the only one left who knows. I am out of time and can't fix it. I need you to care for that closet for me. I need you to help. Promise me you will be there to help with the mess I made."

Tears filled Marie's eyes as she squeezed her older sister's hand and looked into her pleading face with determination. Marie recalled Evelyn's last words as she died: *Please tell him about me...* She knew she would do as they asked. "I will, Katherine. I promise. I will take care of it. You know I will."

Katherine sucked in a deep breath of air and let out a deep sigh laden with regret and sadness, but also with relief, as if Marie was lifting a giant burden off of her chest. She then laid her head back and slept.

Four days later, on September 7th, 1995, Katherine's cancer found her brain. During those days researching cancer and treatment in the library, the sisters had also researched death and dying. Katherine had been intent on not lingering and suffering. On a Thursday, she informed the doctors that she wanted to be discharged so she could die in her own home. Once out of the reach of the nurses and doctors, Katherine refused all food, water, and medications. She knew she wouldn't last long without nourishment. She told Marie she was prepared to take the "fast train."

On Saturday evening, Katherine was in and out of consciousness with Don, Marie, and Katie by her side. When she was awake, she insisted that she was not in pain – just very tired – and she refused to take any of the morphine that the doctors had sent home with her, even when Marie tried to coax her into taking some "just in case." Marie had been with her since she left the hospital and was exhausted. Katherine told her to go home and get some rest. Marie didn't want to leave, but Don assured her that he would call if anything changed. She lived only two miles down the road - she could be back in an instant. Reluctantly, Marie left Don and Katie to stay with Katherine while she went home to check on Anna and Jim and get a few hours of sleep.

Marie laid her tired body in bed that night and cried and prayed. She prayed hard. She talked to her mother and her father. She told them Katherine was coming to be with them. She prayed herself to sleep and dreamed. She dreamed of Easter egg hunts in the backyard, of Christmas mornings and family dinners in the dining room. She dreamed of cold nights, laying in bed with her sister, staring at the stars out of the bedroom window while they tickled each other's arms and whispered about boys. She dreamed of millions of roses filling the kitchen and of soldiers dancing with girls with pretty dresses that swished around their knees when they twirled. She dreamed of weddings and children and grandchildren. She dreamed of a small boy wandering a field, lost. A bright ball of light barreled toward the boy and he turned to run. But it caught up to him and enveloped him into a burst of hot white, glowing light. Marie heard her sister's voice call her name as the bright light filled her brain. Marie woke with a start, her heart pounding. She was sweaty. She reached for her water glass by the clock radio that glowed: 2:32 am. She had the alarm set for five thirty so she could be with Katherine to watch the sunrise. Marie laid her head back down, trying to still her nerves after the strange dream. Just as she began to doze off again, the phone rang. Marie grabbed it, suddenly wide awake.

"Don?"

"She's gone, Marie," Don sobbed. "She's gone."

"When?" Marie whispered, voice hoarse and low.

"About ten minutes ago. 2:32. Please come."

Marie stayed with Katherine's body while Don called the hospice nurse and then the coroner. She had stared at her sister's beautiful, peaceful face, free of lines and wrinkles, haloed by her thick, blonde waves. She was dressed in her fancy pajamas. "Queenie," Marie whispered as she put her cheek down on Katherine's cool, smooth cheek. "You will always be young and beautiful."

When the hospice nurse arrived, she asked Marie to step out of the room so she could clean Katherine and dress her. But Marie refused, insisting instead that she and Katie be the ones to do it. Katherine would not have wanted a stranger performing this task. As the two women, who were like mother and daughter, sponged and dried Katherine's porcelain skin, Marie looked up at her niece.

"How did she go? Was she in pain?"

Katie shifted her eyes to the floor and then back up to meet her aunt's gaze. She then turned slowly and walked to the dresser where she picked up a medicine bottle. It was the morphine prescription that Katherine had refused to touch. It was now empty.

Katie's face twisted in agony and her tear-filled eyes begged for forgiveness. But forgiveness wasn't necessary. Katherine had orchestrated her death perfectly. She had known what she was doing when she had insisted she wasn't in pain when she so clearly had been. Marie pulled Katie into a tight embrace and the women cried in each other's arms until the tears would no longer come.

Now, as Marie dug her fingers into the rich New England soil, mixing it with the soft gray ash, she squeezed a fistful of the mixture. She squeezed as hard as she could until her hand ached. Tears slid down her nose as she closed her eyes and silently asked God and her mother and father to greet Katherine and welcome her home. She then turned to Anna who handed her a pot of white daisies, Katherine's favorite flower. Marie carefully coaxed the roots of the flowers out of their pot, placed them in the ashy dirt, and covered them gently with the soil.

"I love you," she whispered again. "And I will take care of what you asked me to." Then she stood and, without looking at anyone else, turned to go home.

✝✝✝✝

When Marie came Home from burying Katherine, she first went to the garden where she sat quietly, directly in the dirt, among the autumn mums and buzzing bees. After a long while, she came inside and walked through my rooms, stopping in each one to stare into the past, recreating her memories of her family, all together, talking, eating, watching television, laughing, dancing - living. Together. At Home. I made everything as still as possible while she remembered, trying my hardest to squeeze forward all the love and memories that were imbedded in my walls to help her see. Together, we watched the memories of years gone by like a movie — a story of a family and a story of love. When we were done and Marie's eyes were heavy with sadness and sleep, she made her way to the tiny pink bedroom where she stretched out on her mother's bed and, there, all alone, she finally fell apart.

Chapter 26

PRESENT DAY

Caroline walks back to the main house, the photograph of her mother and aunt tucked into her back pocket. Her emotions are all over the place. Why had she never stopped to really think about what it meant to have a sister and what she was missing by having moved so far away from her own? Had she been that self-centered? Had growing up a military brat made her cold and too accustomed to saying goodbye to people she cared about? Was she immune to the need to be close to the ones she loved, including her own sister? Or had it been simply a matter of taking for granted that her baby sister would always be around and that they had time? All of these scenarios are suddenly entirely unacceptable to her. Anna is her only sister. She realizes now how much she needs her, needs to be close to her. She also realizes she isn't getting any younger. Katherine had been only fifty-seven, very close to Caroline's age, when she died.

She is almost in a panic as she enters the kitchen. Alden and Thomas are seated at the kitchen table, eating breakfast while staring at their iPads. Anna is doing dishes. Caroline watches her for a minute, noticing how young and pretty she looks with her long blonde waves and her beautiful, smooth skin. Anna always had amazing skin that felt like velvet. She tanned easily but somehow never developed all of the freckles and moles that

Caroline had from years of too much sun exposure. Even in her late forties, Anna still has a youthful appearance.

"Good morning, guys," Caroline says to her brothers who mutter greetings, barely looking up from their electronics. "Anna, what time do we need to be at the attorney's office?"

"Not until two. Why, what's up?" Anna replies, drying her hands on a dishtowel.

"I need some exercise. I was thinking of going for a walk at the Norris Reservation. Want to join me? We can bring Lucy and let her run a bit."

"Sure. That would be great. She could use some exercise also and it's beautiful outside today. Do you guys want to come?" Anna asks Thomas and Alden.

Alden looks up, appearing surprised that the girls are even in the room. "Oh, uh, no, thanks. I have some work to do, so I'll just stay here."

Thomas is already on a work call and motions for them to go ahead without him. The sisters load Anna's black lab, Lucy, into Anna's car and drive to Norwell to walk in the wooded trails along the North River and marshes. The Norris Reservation had always been their mother's favorite place to walk and talk.

They walk quietly along the winding paths, enjoying the beauty of the woods, the smell of the tall pine trees, the sounds of the birds in the trees, and the feel of the rocks and grass under their feet. Lucy runs ahead, knowing the way to her favorite spot along the river to swim. Each sister is lost in memories of being here with their mother. The path winds along through the woods until a small boathouse appears before them. It is an old, wooden structure, on stilts, jutting out above the clear river. The current is strong and Anna calls to Lucy so she won't swim out too deep. They walk through the old, wooden boathouse to the back porch where they sit on wooden benches and watch Lucy play in the cold, dark rushing water. The green marsh grasses bend with the current and the thick trees catch the soft breeze as it rustles their dark green leaves. Two houses are visible down river, each with lush, green lawns and long, wooden docks that boast kayaks and Boston Whalers. The sky is blue and clear with white, puffy clouds and the air is crisp and clean. There is none of the Florida heat or humidity and Caroline feels invigorated. The entire scene reminds Caroline why she loves New England and she wishes she could stay longer. She understands why her mother loved it here so much. She wonders if she gave New England another chance, could she live here year 'round? Right now, sitting here in the warm sunshine, the answer would be *absolutely*! *If only the nice weather wasn't so short lived,* she thinks.

"You know that photograph you took of Mom sitting on this bench with all of the kids?" Anna asks, breaking Caroline's thoughts.

"Of course. I love that picture. Mum was only seventy then and our girls were so young. I love how they all surrounded her with their blonde hair and big smiles. She looked like a kid herself in that picture." Caroline pictures her mother's face and how her features had given her a youthful appearance even in old age. She had been a beautiful woman.

"I wish I could have been half the mother she was," Anna says sadly.

"Anna, you were – *are* – a great mother!" Caroline responds, frowning at her sister. "You did the best job you could given your circumstances and your kids all turned out great!"

"Well, there were some rough patches when I wasn't so sure what would become of them and sometimes I was sure that I had scarred them forever." Caroline thinks back to the years during Anna's divorce and the following years when her son, Ron, Jr. rebelled so badly the police had to be called on several occasions. But he had ultimately calmed down and currently worked a full time job and had a steady girlfriend.

"Look, all mothers scar their kids at some point," Caroline says, putting her arm around Anna's shoulders. "Even Mom, who was a wonderful mother, left us with some scars."

"Huh. Yes, I guess she did."

"But we turned out fine. Right?"

"I guess," Anna sighs, looking down the river as if peering into her past, a tear escaping her right eye.

"Hey, now," Caroline says softly. "You ok?"

"Yeah, I'm fine," Anna sniffles and draws a deep breath. "I just miss her. And I wish I could go back and fix some of the mistakes I made. And tell her I'm sorry."

"I hear you. I'm sorry, too."

"What do you have to be sorry for? You were the perfect daughter."

"Ha! Well that certainly isn't true, but I was actually talking about you. I wish I could fix the mistakes I made with you. With us. At least I can still tell you I'm sorry. And I am."

"What do you mean?" Anna says. "Why are you apologizing to *me*?"

"Because I left you. I know we have already talked about it and you say you understood why I moved away when I was young, but what about as you got older and I wasn't there for you? Not just physically, but emotionally. I wasn't available to you. I was caught up in my own life, living worlds away. I didn't make sure that you knew I was still there for you. You grew into a teenager and didn't have a big sister to talk to. I don't remember you ever coming to me for advice or anything. Hell, I found out you were pregnant from Mom! You were nineteen. You clearly didn't feel like you could talk to me. What was it like for you?"

"Oh God, that was so long ago," Anna replies. She whistles for Lucy who has strayed too far down river, traipsing through the muddy banks. When Lucy comes bounding back and plops under a bush to rest, Anna turns back toward Caroline.

"Well, it was hard, I guess. I just remember leaving college after the first semester because I didn't care anything about school and my grades were awful. I didn't even go to class. I just drank and smoked pot and partied. Mom and Dad cut me off after they learned what was going on and I had to move Home. After that, I started working at Jamie's and I met Ron. We only dated for about a month before I found out I was pregnant."

Caroline watches a blue heron glide over the water and then land on the opposite bank, eyeing them, cautiously. She remembers their mother calling her in Birmingham to tell her that Anna was pregnant. Caroline had been married for several years by then and she and John had been trying for a baby without success. When she

213

got the call, she had felt a rush of conflicting emotions. She had been immediately worried and fearful for Anna, wondering what she would do being pregnant so young and not married. But she had also been jealous. Why was her baby sister pregnant when she, who was married with a stable career, was not? The jealousy had given way to anger. Anna hadn't bothered to tell her. How could her own sister have kept this from her? But the anger had been short lived and it quickly morphed into sadness when it sank in just how distant she and Anna were. And in the days that followed, Anna hadn't confided in her or asked her advice about what she should do about the pregnancy – even after Caroline had called her and offered to help in any way she could. Caroline remembers begging her sister to let her know if she wanted to talk. But Anna had been distant and not forthcoming with either her feelings or her plans. Again, Caroline had learned in a phone call with their mother that Anna had struggled with whether to keep the baby and had ultimately decided that she would. Mom had also broken the news that Anna and Ron would be moving in together – in Mom's house.

"I couldn't believe it when Mom told me that Ron Dickerson was the father," Caroline says. "I remember him from high school. He was a few years younger than I was. He was trouble even back then."

"Ha! That's an understatement," Anna snorts. "He was a mess. But he was wicked cute and I was young and dumb and I fell for him quickly. What a mistake that was!"

"You know, though, sis, it wasn't a mistake, really. Sure, Ron didn't turn out to be a lifetime partner, or even a friend. But you got three beautiful babies out of that relationship and you certainly learned a lot about yourself and marriage – even it was mainly what you *don't* want out of a man!" Caroline laughs half-heartedly. "What was it like though, telling Mom and Dad that you were pregnant? And then moving into their house with your boyfriend, unmarried? I cannot even imagine! They would have never allowed me to do that. Hell, when I moved with John to Birmingham, Mom was apoplectic that we were living together 'in sin.' But then she invites

214

Ron to live in her house with her pregnant nineteen year old daughter? What kind of spell did you put on her?"

Anna laughs and shakes her head. "I don't really know, Cee. It was so bizarre and surreal at the time. I remember saying that I was going to have an abortion and Mom just flipped out, saying that she would never be able to forgive me if I did that. I was forced to talk with Dad about taking me to have it done and paying for it. God, that was mortifying. But then I thought that maybe I would have the baby and give it up for adoption, thinking Mom would be okay with that. But I swear she freaked out even more about that! I was so confused. She kept saying 'not again' when we would talk about it. At first I thought she meant that she didn't want me to ever do this again and I was like 'yeah, duh' but she kept saying it and looking at the sky. Then she would cry. I didn't know what to do. I thought she was losing it."

"Yeah, that's weird," Caroline says. "I wonder what that was all about? Anyway, you were under a lot of pressure for a nineteen year old girl. I sure wish you had called me to talk about it."

"I should have. But I was so embarrassed and scared. You had this perfect life with the perfect husband and new job as a lawyer in a fancy law firm. I didn't want to worry you. Plus, I knew how badly you wanted a baby. I felt so irresponsible getting pregnant so young. I also worried that you would be angry and disappointed in me and I felt so guilty that I was pregnant instead of you. It just seemed so unfair."

Caroline cringes at all the "perfect" characterizations. Her life had certainly not been perfect. She recalls the long hours at work; the stress and the strain it had placed on her marriage. And all of the months trying to conceive with no luck. That heartbreak and frustration had been difficult. It had ultimately taken two years and several fertility treatments before she finally became pregnant with Gracee.

"I would have helped you anyway," Caroline replies, taking Anna's hand. "I can't imagine what that was like, not having your big sister around to confide in. I am so so sorry!" Caroline chokes on the last word.

Anna looks up at Caroline, her face twisted with emotion. "Don't be sorry! And please don't cry. It turned out fine. I had the baby and it all worked out. Laura is the best thing that ever happened to me. The day she was born, I knew I had made the right choice and I was so happy!"

"And I wasn't there for that either," Caroline says, her voice low with guilt.

"You couldn't be, silly!" Anna replied. "You were six months pregnant yourself by then. And hey, I wasn't there for Gracee's birth either, so we are even!" Anna pushes Caroline's arm, trying to lighten the mood. "And you did come for her christening and then you came for the wedding. And by that time, we were both mothers! You were there for me, Caroline."

It was true, Caroline did serve as Anna's maid of honor at the wedding. But she had felt out of place and like she should have been a regular bridesmaid and let Anna's best friend, Tammy, be the maid of honor. Caroline remembers not knowing anybody at the wedding other than family. Anna's friends were all strangers. She didn't know any of Ron's family or friends. Hell, she didn't even know Ron. She cringes remembering helping Anna into the limousine on the way to the church. The limo had pulled up in the grass by the front door of their Home. Caroline had a glass of white wine in her hand. She was still nursing Gracie at the time and wasn't used to drinking much. The wine had gone to her head and made her a bit dizzy. As she was helping Anna into the car, she had slipped and spilled her wine down the front of Anna's wedding gown. She looked down, mortified, as the wet stain spread down the front of the dress. Their father had turned to Caroline with anger in his eyes and yelled, "What in the hell are you doing with that wine?" as Anna burst into tears. Caroline had felt so stupid and clumsy and small in that moment. She had grabbed a towel and dried Anna's dress until the stain started to dissipate. Luckily the wine had been a light sauvignon blanc and the satin had dried quickly. By the time Anna got to the church, thankfully the stain was invisible.

"I almost ruined your wedding," Caroline said, an eyebrow raised asking Anna if she remembered.

Anna laughed. "Ha ha. What? That wine incident? Thankfully it was white wine and it all worked out fine. Dad was pretty upset with you, though."

"Yeah he was. I felt about an inch tall that day."

"But nothing was ruined and hey, the drunk girl who wanted to beat me up in the bathroom made the wine incident look like a walk in the park."

"Oh my God, yes that was crazy!" Caroline laughs out loud. "Good old Scituate. It was like something off of the Jerry Springer Show."

The sisters are both laughing now. "Why were we all so dumb back then?" Anna asks.

"Well, at least you had the excuse of being very young. What was my excuse?" Caroline laughs. "I can't believe you got married at twenty. You weren't even legally allowed to drink."

"I know. And yet, I had a one-year-old."

"Yes, you did." Caroline smiles remembering her sweet little niece in the white dress and flowered crown on her head, holding her hand as Caroline helped her toddle down the aisle.

After the wedding, Ron and Anna had moved out of Jim and Marie's house and rented a house in Marshfield. Anna had immediately gotten pregnant again and in November, 2000 she had her son, Ron, Jr. Caroline hadn't been there for his birth either. *What was wrong with me back then?* she thinks, sadly. *Why didn't I make an effort to be there for my sister on the most important days of her life?*

Caroline had been such a workaholic at the time. Gracee was only one and a half and Caroline had been working long hours. Again, she had been too consumed with her own life to be the sister she should have been. Caroline looks at Anna and feels and overwhelming sense of regret and sadness. She pulls the photograph out of her back pocket and stares at it.

"What is that?" Anna asks, looking over Caroline's shoulder. They are still sitting on the bench of the boat house, but the sun has gone behind some ominous looking clouds. Lucy lays sleeping inside the boathouse with her paws stretched out the door onto the deck.

"It's a photo of Mom and Katherine. I found it today when I was going through the closet upstairs in the small house." She passes the photograph to Anna.

"Aw, look at them. This is at the opening of their shop," Anna states, instantly recognizing the image. "They were so happy that day."

Caroline nods. "Of course they were. They were finally back together after all those years of being away from each other. Katherine had come home from wandering Vermont and Mom was done following Dad around in the Navy. They were given a chance to be together before..." Caroline can't continue. Her throat is thick and she knows if she says one more word it will come out as one giant sob.

"They were lucky," Anna says simply.

The sisters sit in silence, each lost in her own thoughts, each searching for a way to bridge a gap that had opened up decades ago and now seemed impossibly deep. Caroline wonders if selling the house will make things worse. She worries Anna may resent her and their brothers for not working harder to keep it. After all, Anna raised her children there. She has lived in that Home for all of her life. She and Ron didn't live in Marshfield for long. Marie had made certain of that. Caroline remembers the day their mother had called with big news – news that, once again, Caroline heard from Mom and not from Anna

Chapter 27

GROWING PAINS
2002

"Hi Mom," Caroline sighed into the phone after staring at the caller ID for about three rings, contemplating whether to pick up. Caroline enjoyed her conversations with her mother and sometimes stayed on the phone for well over an hour talking about everything from kids to politics. But she wasn't in the mood today. It was a beautiful Spring day in Alabama and Caroline, who worked six days a week, was hoping to spend some quiet time playing with her four year old daughter and then go outside to get some gardening done before it got too hot.

"Oh, hi Honey, how is my girl this morning?" her mother's voice gushed into her ear, a little too sweetly, triggering Caroline's instincts that something was going on.

"I'm good, Mom. Just hanging out. It's been a crazy week at work and I'm just chilling with Gracee right now getting ready to head outside to plant some flowers." She hoped her mother would pick up on the subtle hint.

"Am I catching you getting ready for church or did you go earlier?" Marie asked.

Caroline wondered if her mother just hadn't heard her or if she was deliberately ignoring her. Marie knew full well that Caroline

219

and her family didn't attend church and Caroline knew how much this bothered her mother, so she suspected the latter.

Patiently, Caroline replied, "Mom, you know we don't go to church. And you know why. After six-day work weeks and Gracie attending school and day care, I don't think God minds if we choose to celebrate his love in the privacy of our home. I promise, I will say a prayer with each flower I plant in God's earth today." Caroline rolled her eyes to an empty kitchen.

"Haha, okay, okay, no need to get testy," Marie laughed. "Well, your father and I just got home from a *wonderful* service where your darling niece sang in the children's choir making Peepa and I the proudest grandparents in town. You could hear her sing louder than all of the other children – such a beautiful voice!"

"That's sweet. Laura is adorable. I wish I could have been there to hear her sing." Caroline threw Marie a bone. She loved her niece and was sincere. It was difficult being so far away sometimes and she hated that she missed out on so much of her sister's life.

"Yes, I do, too. You would have loved it," Marie replied seemingly satisfied.

Caroline and Marie talked for a bit sharing news about their lives. Most of Marie's news concerned Anna and her family. Ron worked seven days a week at his plumbing business and Anna was a stay at home mom to four-year-old Laura and two-year-old son, Ron, Jr.; and she was pregnant with her third. Caroline envied Anna's ability to become pregnant so easily, as it seemed to require an act of Congress for Caroline to conceive. Caroline and John had been trying for another baby for almost a year, with no results.

"So what else is new, Mom?" Caroline was anxious to conclude the phone call. She didn't really want to hear about Anna's latest pregnancy and she really needed to get this gardening done.

"Well, actually, Honey, I want to run something by you." Her mother answered hesitantly.

"Okaaaay...?" Caroline urged.

"Well, your father and I have been talking. About Anna, and the kids. You know they are renting that tiny two bedroom house in Marshfield. And you know Anna is pregnant again..." Marie paused.

"Yes, Mother, I know...." Caroline answered, impatiently wondering where her mother was going with this.

"Well, it's just that they can't possibly stay in that small house. Plus, it's all the way in Marshfield and she is going to need my help with three little ones at home."

"Mom, Marshfield is only 15 minutes down the road," Caroline interrupted. "And Anna is a grown, married woman. What do you think? That she should live with you or something?" Caroline laughed. But she didn't hear Marie laugh with her. Instead, a long silence ensued. "Mom? Are you still there?"

"Yes. I'm still here." Another pause.

Caroline raised her eyebrows and her green eyes grew wide. "Wait a second, Mom. Are you really calling me to tell me that Anna and her family are *moving in* with you and Dad?"

"Well, not exactly." Marie answered slowly. "We are talking about letting Anna and Ron rent our house and we would build a separate house attached to the other side of the garage for me and your father. Like an in-law wing sort of."

"Oh, an in-law wing. Of course. Because we are people who have homes with 'wings' now," Caroline snorts.

So many thoughts swirled through her head. She couldn't believe that her parents were actually going to build an entire house onto the other side of the garage of the existing house. She couldn't believe that her sister would be given the use of the beautiful, antique five-bedroom home. She couldn't believe her mother would be living right next door to Anna and intended to help raise her children. She couldn't believe Anna would agree to that. *Am I jealous?* Caroline wondered. Maybe a little, but she was also concerned. Anna would be living next door to Mom. In Mom's house. Caroline knew how strong willed and stubborn both Marie and Anna were and she knew this arrangement wouldn't be all rainbows and butterflies. But, Marie was right – Anna did need a bigger place and she would need some help with three babies. Living at Home could provide Anna and Ron a place to raise the kids until they could afford a home of their own. But it could also be a disaster in ways nobody had thought about yet. Her head began to ache.

"Well, what do you think?" Marie asked through the phone.

"Um, well, I'm not sure yet, Mom. I guess I need more information like can you and Dad afford to build this 'wing?' And how much will Anna's rent be? What will you do if she can't pay? Will you have an actual lease with terms you all agree to? What are Ron's occupancy rights if something happens with them? What about utility costs? What if Anna changes her mind and doesn't want to live in your house with you that close but you have already spent your money and irrevocably altered the house in a way that can't easily be undone?" Caroline had a million questions and at least a hundred worst case scenarios.

"Whoa, okay honey, slow down. I know you are a lawyer and all of these concerns are valid and need to be discussed," Marie sighed. "But I want to know what YOU think - you, being my daughter and Anna's sister, not you the lawyer-you. Take off the legal hat and just talk to me, mother to daughter."

Caroline took a long, deep breath in and paused while she thought about how to express her concerns without hurting feelings or causing her mother to be defensive. "Mom, does it really matter what I think? You seem to have made up your mind and I know you – once you have decided something like this, you are going to do what you want, no matter what I think." As soon as the words were out of her mouth, Caroline knew this was the wrong thing to say.

"That is NOT true," Marie replied defensively. "What you think matters to me. This house is your inheritance. And your brothers'. Someday it will belong to all of you."

"Yeah, with Anna and her kids living in it," Caroline shot back, a little more harshly than intended. "What are we supposed to do? Kick her out when the time comes so we can have our 'inheritance?' I'm afraid you are going to create a situation that will just be impossible for us to handle in the future."

"Your father and I have talked to a lawyer and we will have provisions for how to deal with the living arrangements if something happens to us and Anna is still living here. Hopefully that won't happen anytime soon. If it does, she will have the right to keep living there until the kids are grown, but she will have to pay rent of course." *So she was fully expecting this to be a long-term arrangement and not "just until they can afford their own place",* Caroline thought.

Caroline didn't want to think about that scenario and all the things that could go wrong. "Look, Mom, it's your house. You and Dad need to do what you feel is right. I'm not worried about my inheritance or even if I will have an inheritance. That's your business. But have you carefully thought through what it will be like having Anna and her family basically living with you and Dad in what should be your retirement years?"

"Your father and I will have our own separate house in the back with a separate entrance altogether. They won't be living with us. They will simply be living next door," Marie reasoned.

"Uh-huh. And what happens when you don't agree with something Anna or Ron or the kids do? When they aren't living the way you would like? You know you will be over there every day, looking in on them, seeing everything they do. And you are going to end up being a live-in babysitter. What about your own life? And Dad's? You will be sacrificing your retirement years. I just worry this might be a bad idea." Caroline tread cautiously, shuddering at the thought of her mother just popping by unannounced, seeing the days when she didn't feel like cleaning or cooking or even parenting. Caroline could just hear the judgmental tone and guilt trips that would be inevitable.

"I will *not* be checking on her every day. I don't even *want* to be checking in on her that much. I have a life, too, you know. Look, I just wanted to share the idea with you and I hoped you would be supportive of your sister who is soon to be saddled with three babies. You know she isn't a lawyer and is struggling financially. She can't afford day care or nannies." Caroline cringed at the subtle jab. "So, your father and I thought it would be a way we can help her until she and Ron can afford a place of their own."

The guilt trip was being laid on thick and Caroline knew she had said too much. Her mother was now defensive and frustrated. Caroline knew from years of experience that further conversation that was anything less than acquiescence would degrade the conversation even further. Her mother's mind was made up. That was clear. And, really, why should Caroline care? If this is what her sister wanted and Mom and Dad were willing to take such drastic steps to help her have a stable place to call home, why shouldn't they do it? Caroline pushed aside her nagging, uneasy feeling.

"Mom, okay. Okay. I get it. It sounds like you really want to do this and your mind is made up. Anna is very lucky that she has you and Dad to help her out like this. I would have killed to live in that gorgeous house when I was just starting out. And to have free help with the kids? Shit, I would have killed a whole village for that!"

Caroline was trying to lighten the mood. It was clear that her mother had called to get her blessing, not her true opinion. Caroline wanted more than ever to get off the phone and get on with her day.

"Well, it's not as if we will be letting her live here for free, you know," Marie answered still feeling the need to justify her decision. "They will have to pay rent and maintain the house. And, while I will obviously be more than happy to be with my grandchildren when I can, it's not like I am going to volunteer to be her nanny."

"Good, Mom. I'm glad you have it all figured out. Let me know if I can help at all," Caroline muttered into the phone that now rested between her cheek and shoulder as she began gathering gardening tools from the mud room.

"Well, it sounds like you are now distracted," accused Marie. "I will let you go do whatever it is that you have to do today."

Oh my God, I can't win!! Caroline thought to herself.

"Not distracted, Mom. I just have a lot to do today and this is my only day off. And I think we have exhausted this topic. I'm all for it. I'm on your side. Do whatever you think is right. But I really do need to go now."

"Yes, I know it is your only day off. You work too much," Marie replied.

After Caroline said good-bye to her mother, she sat down, feeling emotionally drained. Why did she feel so exasperated after talking with her mother sometimes? She wondered if her own sweet daughter would feel the same way about her someday. She hoped not. But she smiled to herself, knowing that it was inevitable and part of what made it possible to leave home. It was nature's way of pushing grown children out of the nest so they could spread your wings and fly.

Then she sighed as she feared that her sister's wings were about to be permanently clipped.

✝✝✝✝

Over the next several months, construction on my new addition commenced. The plans were drawn, the foundation for the new wing was poured, the walls went up and the roof went on. I was no longer a single family home. I wasn't sure how I felt about being a two-family structure. Was I now a duplex?? Ugh – how very modern. At least they didn't make me a condominium. The new house was attached to the back of the garage and was architecturally consistent so it blended nicely with my original structure. The addition was a two-bedroom, one bath home with an open floor plan and pitched roof. A large living area contained both living room and dining area with a bar countertop separating the small kitchen area. The front door faced the driveway, which they reconfigured so that the entrance was a bit farther down the hill and the drive snaked along the front of the addition, with a small parking pad installed for Jim and Marie, then it connected with the existing parking/drive area in front of the old garage. Fill dirt and sod were installed where the old, straight driveway previously connected to the street.

A small front stoop with three steps and a portico led to the front door, which opened directly into the living area. A coat closet with folding doors was built to the right of the door and, to the left, stairs went straight up to an attic that had room for plenty of storage and expansion should the need arise. A laundry closet was built off of the living area. The kitchen was small and cozy with a window over the sink, looking out over the backyard. At the back of the house, a master bedroom connected to the living area and another small bedroom connected to the dining area. A full bathroom with tub and stand-alone shower was built between the bedrooms and connected to both the living area and the master bedroom. Pretty honey-colored hardwood floors were installed throughout. The kitchen boasted oak cabinets, simple formica countertops and modest, functional appliances. It was not a large kitchen, which Marie said was by design as she always claimed her "dream house" would have no kitchen at all. Marie lovingly decorated the 1500 square foot structure with beautiful oriental rugs and antique furniture with her signature knick-knacks on shelves and curio cabinets placed strategically to maximize space.

My original Home remained in-tact and Anna's family moved in during the Spring of 2003. Heather Dickerson had been born the previous October. I had grown to accommodate my family's needs and was now Home to three generations. From a small two-room farmhouse with an outhouse, to a sprawling seven bedroom family compound, I hardly recognized myself.

But it wasn't long before I learned that some families just aren't meant to be.

Chapter 28

ANNA
2006

Life at our Home was busy after Anna and her family moved in. Ron worked long hours, seven days a week at his plumbing business and was barely around. Anna was solely responsible for keeping the house and raising the kids. She rose early every morning to get their breakfasts and lunches made and get them out the door to school. She then had a few hours to grocery shop, run errands, wash multiple loads of laundry and other chores before they all came barreling back through the door when the bus dropped them off at three o'clock. Then came the taxi driver portion of her day, shuttling them to and from dance class, soccer practice, football practice and other activities, then finally rushing home to throw some sort of dinner together so they could eat in time to still do homework and get into bed at a decent hour.

Despite his business being so busy, Ron never seemed to have enough money to go out to eat or to hire babysitters. Anna never knew how much money they really had. Ron refused to share any financial information with her. She had no idea how much the business made. She didn't know what his expenses were. And if she asked, he would look at her sharply and say "that's none of your business. This is my business. I will run it. Stay out of it." He dealt mainly in cash and she would find wads of cash in his jeans when he would just discard them on the bathroom floor, obviously forgetting the money was there. When she would ask about it, he would snatch it from her and say it was payment from a client and she would never see the money again. He handled all of the finances for the family and kept the bank accounts solely in his name. He gave Anna a cash allowance each week for food and gas and made it clear that she was not to question him or ask for more.

Jim and Marie lived quietly next door, each working and keeping a watchful eye on the busy family sharing their property. Marie tried her best to give the young family space, but she helped out where she could, making extra food at dinnertime, offering to drive the kids around, and being a sounding board for Anna.

Ron was never home. On the weekdays he typically rolled in, dirty and tired, well past dinner. He would re-heat whatever plate Anna left out for him, shower (leaving his dirty clothes in a pile on the bathroom floor) and go straight to bed. Anna, still young and very much a night owl, would stay up, late into the evening, drinking wine and watching television. Over time she realized her marriage was not a partnership. She grew resentful, exhausted and lonely. The loneliness was the worst in the winters, when the weather was icy cold and the dark descended at four in the afternoon. Summers were a bit easier as the days were longer and the nice weather allowed for more outside activities. Anna spent her days with the kids at the beach or at the neighbor's pool. But she rarely had time with her husband. She had a few friends who came over regularly. They would sit on the breezeway after the kids went to bed and they would drink and smoke and laugh until they were all quite drunk. On the nights Ron came home to find Anna's friends still there, he would become annoyed and sometimes they would argue loudly and the friends would slowly leave.

Marie and Jim watched their youngest daughter's life from their side of the property and they steadily grew concerned. Marie, despite her promises to let Anna live her life without maternal interference, couldn't help but to step in when she thought it was necessary. And she thought it was necessary quite often. Meaning well, but failing to acknowledge the intrusion, she offered Anna constant advice – what food to buy, what clothes the kids should be wearing, when the kids should be going to bed, how much Anna should be drinking – nothing was off limits. Of course, it was never done in an overt manner – more like suggestions, or even offers, such as "why don't I take Heather upstairs and give her a bath and get her into bed so you can clean up the kitchen?" when it was past eight o'clock on a school night and Marie had popped over to drop off the mail. Or, "Well, I have to go to the store tomorrow, so I will pick you up some more fruit!" after opening the cabinets and seeing chips and cookies. And regarding Anna's personal choices: after opening the trash can and seeing two empty bottles of wine, "oh boy, you must have had a little party last night. Do you know how many calories are in red wine?" None of it was done with mean intentions but the intrusion on Anna's lifestyle and choices left Anna feeling judged and incompetent - and angry.

Over time she grew angry with Ron for not helping her more. She grew angry with Marie for interfering too much. She even grew angry with her own children for their constant demands. And she grew most angry with herself for not knowing how to please everyone. Of course, she could never have pleased everyone. But she couldn't see that and so it became a vicious cycle. She spent her days trying to please her children – by trying to keep them entertained and fulfilled with outings, activities, crafts, food, and toys. She spent her evenings trying to please her husband by making sure his dinner was warm, cleaning up after him, having sex when he wanted, and not asking too many questions. When she did get time to herself, she simply wanted to escape the responsibility of pleasing everyone and she found that escape in wine and friends. Her friends began coming over more frequently. The more they came, the more Anna and Ron fought. The more they fought, the more Marie "dropped by." The more Marie dropped by, the more Anna felt resentful and frustrated. The more Anna felt resentful and frustrated, the more she became angry and would pick fights. And the more they fought, the more Anna tried to escape with wine and time with her friends; and so on, in a never-ending cycle of destructive behavior that no marriage could survive. The snowball of resentment and anger slowly grew over the years until it sat upon all of us, suffocating my rooms, making it difficult to find relief, until I felt like a shaken up soda bottle ready to explode at the tiniest opening. Then one the day, the pressure became too much.

"What the FUCK, Anna?" bellowed Ron, red-faced and seething with anger. "What the fuck is your fucking problem?"

Anna walked swiftly from room to room, trying to escape the verbal onslaught. But Ron was right on her heels, his burgundy face contorted in rage. Their three children were perched on the sofa in the family room where they had been quietly watching American Idol. Ron had come home late, surly from something that had happened at work. Anna was in a sour mood and had already had two glasses of wine. It didn't take long before they were bickering with each other. To tell you the truth, I can't even remember what they were fighting about. The two of them fought about anything and everything. The kids were used to it. They knew to stay out of it and so they sat, very still and quiet on the couch, while their parents screamed at each other.

"Stop fucking following me!" Anna screeched, turning to come face to face with Ron's anger.

Anna was no wallflower and she was not one to shrink from conflict, especially when it came to her relationship with her husband of eleven years. Their relationship had started when she was merely nineteen and he was twenty-four. She had just finished high school and was working as a waitress at Jamie's Pub in North Scituate when Ron had walked in with a group of local boys grabbing a beer after work. Ron had gone to high school in Hull, two towns North of Scituate. He had been a wild teenager, having been arrested more than once for DUI's and public drunkenness. He had gone through rehab twice and was in AA. While he was loud and had his issues, he was a hard working kid with his own plumbing company and he was committed to his sobriety. Plus, he was easy on the eyes. With thick, dark, wavy hair and a long, lean build, he caught Anna's attention as she served buffalo chicken fingers and fries to him and his friends. He had flirted with her unabashedly and it didn't take long for them to start dating. They were both highly attracted to each other, emotional, and young and their relationship was fueled by a passion that was undeniable.

Eleven years later, Anna and Ron's passion that had resulted in a baby, a wedding, and two more babies (in that order), revealed another side that was akin to pure hatred when they argued. The old saying that there is a fine line between love and hate proved true and Anna had been balancing on that line for at least five of the last eleven years. The frequency of their arguments had increased steadily as their family grew and the stress built. There were financial issues, jealousy issues, control issues – all the things a young marriage works through but, like with everything with Ron and Anna, the intensity was triple that of other couples. Anna resented Ron for working such long hours while she was home with the children every day. Ron resented Anna because she didn't work. He resented her constant need for money to pay for food, clothes, and everything else a growing family needs. Anna resented Ron for spending money on motorcycles when they could barely afford the rent or food. Ron resented that Anna had any say in how he spent his money. It went on and on and built up until every discussion deteriorated into a heated argument complete with name-calling and, sometimes, physical altercations. Lamps had been thrown, mirrors shattered, plates and glasses obliterated as one or the other took their frustrations out on household items. For a while, passionate make-ups followed the clashes and things would settle down for a while. But as the years went by the making up occurred less and less until it gave way altogether to silent fuming. An undercurrent of anger, like boiling lava waiting to surface, tainted every interaction. On this night, the volcano of rage built as the two paced under my roof.

"I'll walk wherever I damn well please!" Ron shot back. "I live here, too you stupid bitch!" Ron spit the last word inches from Anna's face, splattering her in the eye with spittle.

"Oh yeah? This is my fucking house!" Anna snarled, wiping her eye with the back of her right hand.

"Wrong! This is your parents' house which they rent to me," Ron shot back. "I pay the rent here, not you. I can do whatever the hell I want here and nobody can do anything about it."

Anna pushed past him and went into the kitchen trying to escape. She glanced into the family room and could see the kids, still on the sofa, staring at her. *Calm down*, she thought to herself. She opened the refrigerator and took out a half empty bottle of pino grigio. When she stood up and turned around to get a wine glass from the cabinet, Ron was standing so close to her that she bumped into him, sending the wine bottle crashing to the floor.

"Jesus Christ, Ron! What the fuck?" Anna exclaimed, as the liquid and shattered glass spread across the floor.

"Oh, okay, Anna, now it's my fault that you dropped your beloved wine? Maybe you should be more careful where you are going!" Ron spat, not moving. "Or maybe you are already so drunk you can't even see where you are going."

"Are you kidding me?" Anna asked, her voice high and loud with frustration and growing anger. "You did that on purpose, you asshole!" She pushed past him to grab a rag to sop up the spilled wine.

"*I'm* the asshole? *I'm the asshole*?" Ron repeated, indignant. "You sit here all day and do nothing but play with the kids. You go to the beach. You play at the park. I go to work every goddamn day of my life and I give you money for food and shopping and everything else you need and yet I'm the asshole? You are a spoiled bitch, you know that? You sit here in your parents' house like you are entitled to everything and you don't appreciate a damn thing I do for this family!"

Anna saw red. Her frustration and resentment clouded any rational thought and I felt the lava bubble to the surface. "You have GOT to be kidding me right now," Anna screamed, her own face turning crimson with rage. "You think it's a day in the park watching three little kids all day with no help? I do everything around here. Every. Single. Thing. And you want to talk about money for food and shopping? You give me barely enough to get what we need. You don't tell me how much you make, you don't put me on a joint bank account, you give me a fucking allowance and I have to get everything this family needs within that allowance. I'm not a wife, Ron. I am your servant – doing everything for you so that you can be gone from sunrise to sunset seven days a week, never spending time with your kids or with me. Where does all of your money go? You say we can't afford to a buy a house so my parents were kind enough to let us rent this house for cheaper than we could get anywhere else. And some months, you don't even pay them on time and I am stuck having to explain to my father why the rent is late. But yet you can go out and spend over $10,000.00 on a fucking Harley? We can't even afford to have health insurance for the kids but, 'hey, look at Ron Dickerson riding around town on his shiny new Harley! Because hey, he deserves it. He works so hard!' You know what, Ron? Fuck you! I'm done. Get the fuck out!"

Anna let it all come out. The anger erupted and spewed in a dialogue of built up resentment she had been harboring for years. She knew the kids were listening to every word but she felt herself crossing the line to the electrically charged emotional place where one doesn't care who is watching. She felt crazed as she let it all go like a rush of toxic sludge flowing from her body. Ron stood, hearing her screeching but not listening. His anger clogged his ears and his self-righteousness rejected her words so that they didn't even enter his thought process. Until her last sentence: *You know what, Ron? Fuck you. I'm done. Get the fuck out!* Those words registered. And they enraged him.

Ron stepped forward and grabbed Anna hard by her upper arm, his mouth set in a thin, hard line and his eyes blazing. Anna instinctively yanked her arm upward to free herself from his grasp. When she did, her hand connected hard with Ron's nose, sending his head snapping backward. He grabbed his face. Anna's eyes widened when she realized she had hit him.

"Oh God, I'm Sorry! That was an accident. I didn't mean to…." Anna started but was silenced as Ron regained his composure and lunged at her. Anna pivoted on her left foot and ran toward the dining room. She had made it to the doorway when she felt Ron grab her right wrist. He yanked hard, spinning her back toward him. Anna lost her balance and fell into him, her forehead smashing into

Ron's chin with a sickening thud. The searing pain Ron felt was like gasoline on a raging fire.

"God DAMMIT! Jesus Fucking Christ!" was all Anna heard as she felt Ron's hand around her throat, pushing her into the wall between the dining room and the pink bedroom. Her head slammed backward against the ivory wallpaper. Anna's vision blurred as her gaze shifted over Ron's shoulder to the three little faces watching in helpless disbelief. Never had one of their arguments gotten this out of control. Before she could tell Ron his children were watching, his fist flew through the air, aimed directly at Anna's face. But her world had already gone black.

The instant Anna's head hit my wall I was filled with protective rage. If I had fists I would have gladly used them to give Ron a taste of his own medicine. I was strong, but I lacked the ability to move. I willed my ceiling to crumble on his head. I strained to collapse my floors so the ground would swallow him whole. But I was capable of neither. Instead, I gathered every memory and every ounce of love that had seeped into my walls and I harnessed every bit of energy that the members of this family had left behind and which had become part of my soul. Their energy gave me life and I used to it to summon them. Evelyn, come! Katherine, come! Edward, help! Come Home!

"Let go of her!" roared a voice as deep and as loud as I had ever heard.

Ron simultaneously turned toward the sound and loosened his grip on Anna's throat allowing the blood to rush back to her brain. She blinked the room into focus, registering a man's figure looming in the kitchen doorway. It was her father. He was rigid and composed. But his face was twisted in anger, his fists clenched at his sides. His whole body radiated warning as his anger flooded the room. Ron released Anna and she squirmed away. Bits of plaster and dust fell from her hair as she skittered toward her father who tucked her behind his body into the safety of the kitchen. A fist-sized hole gaped in the wall next to where her head had been. Ron was rubbing his bloodied and swelling knuckles, cursing under his breath.

"Get. Out. I want you out of my house immediately," Jim's words were even and steady and loaded with authoritative warning.

"Your daughter is fucking crazy," Ron replied. "She is the one who hit me. Look at my nose! And my forehead! I didn't even hit her. Look, I hit the wall."

"I will say it one more time and then I will call the police and put you out myself," Jim responded, ignoring Ron's babbling. "Get the Hell out of my house. Now!"

Ron's eyes flashed with anger but even he could feel that the forces in the room were unsettled and dangerous and he checked himself.

"I'll leave this time," Ron spat. "But your daughter isn't going to get away with making this all my fault. I didn't touch that bitch!"

"GO!!!" roared Jim, finally losing his cool.

And with that, the whole room swelled and the air filled an all-consuming energy that left no space for a physical being. Ron felt himself moving, being ejected against his will, albeit his own legs were moving him toward the door. Jim felt the presence, too. It was powerful and strong and filled Jim with a sense of authority and confidence that someone, something, had his back. He breathed in deeply, letting the static air fill his lungs and push out his chest. He felt four feet taller. As Ron passed him, Jim's whispered words rained down on Ron's shoulders: "Don't you ever – and I mean EVER - step foot on my property again."

Ron cut his narrowed eyes at Jim but words uncharacteristically failed him. Before he could stop himself, he was out the door. Jim slammed the door so hard every floorboard shook. The pressure inside was immediately relieved. The dense, energy-filled air released with a whoosh and my rooms were instantly light again – as if someone had popped the top off a pressure filled soda bottle.

Anna sat at the kitchen table, shaking and crying. Jim sat down heavily and reached across the small square table to take her hands in his.

"Ron, Jr. ran across the yard," Jim said slowly. "He said he thought his father was going to kill his mother. The kids are all over there now with your mother." Anna let out a sob as she realized what her kids just witnessed. "What the hell happened here tonight, Anna? Did he hit you? Are you hurt?"

"I'm not hurt, Dad. I'm ok. He came home from work angry about some bullshit someone told him that wasn't true. I was already in a bad mood that he was late again without even bothering to call and I guess I egged him on. We got into it and it got out of control fast. I lost my temper and then he lost his worse. He had me by the throat. I couldn't breathe. He tried to hit me. I saw his fist coming but I must have blacked out for a second. I honestly don't know how he missed. He didn't miss on purpose."

Anna glanced at the hole in the plaster wall and frowned.

"Well, this can't happen," Jim said softly but firmly. "I won't stand for this. The kids are constantly witnessing your arguments and now this. He isn't going to be allowed back into this house. You have to get your shit together and do what's right for your children."

Jim had always been a strict father, not letting his kids off the hook for their own shortcomings, even if they were hurting, and he wasn't about to let Anna play the victim in this situation. He had been watching the fighting in this house for several years and had been trying to stay out of it, to give Anna and Ron space to work out their own marriage. Marie had been telling him for months that she was concerned Ron was abusive. But Anna always poo-pooed it when they asked her and made excuses for her husband. And they knew she wasn't entirely innocent. She instigated him at times – picking fights instead of discussing issues. As Jim sat looking at his beaten-down daughter, he wondered if he and Marie had played a role in stunting Anna's emotional growth when they let her move into their house. Should they have let her figure all of this out on her own like they had to when they were newly married? He and Marie had argued often in the early days. Once, Marie had gotten so angry she had emptied a dirty diaper pail over Jim's head. They had been living in Ohio at the time with no parents to come over and intervene. They had figured things out and had eventually learned how to behave like adults. But times were different then and other than the diaper pail on the head, their arguments never turned physical. Jim shuddered to think of what might have happened if he and Marie hadn't been next door tonight. Nonetheless, it was time for Anna to grow up and take charge of her life and her family.

Anna looked into her father's eyes and she knew he was right. But what could she do? Ron was her husband. He was the father of her three children. She didn't have a job beyond occasionally picking up a shift at Jamie's Pub. How could she support herself if they divorced? She closed her eyes and took a deep breath. She saw Ron's closed fist coming straight for her face.

That fist should not have missed.

Anna recalled the look in his eyes. He hadn't been just trying to scare her. He had truly wanted to hurt her. She was sure of it. So, how did he instead end up hitting the wall beside her head? Suddenly, as she considered this, Anna was filled with a sense of strength that built not from deep in her own resolve but somewhere in the air around her. She felt it rise and grow until it enveloped her. She sucked in her breath and felt the sensation fill her body, nurturing her lungs, her heart and her muscles until she felt so strong that she was sure she could do anything. She opened her eyes and looked deep into her father's sad eyes. "Don't worry, Dad. I'm okay. I'm going to fix this. It will all be okay."

Of course Anna had no idea what caused Ron's angry fist to veer off course and miss her. Nor did she have any clue where her sudden strength and resolve had come from. She likely credited God, or luck, or her love for her kids, or even herself. But I knew exactly what - or should I say who - helped her that day. For I know that some souls belong to the homes where they lived and that some souls forever stay connected with still-living souls they loved. That day, Anna had both. I had summoned the two souls who would always belong with me and would have never allowed such nastiness to occur in their home. I had also summoned another who identified with Anna and would forever help her find the strength she wished she had possessed when she was Anna's age. They say Home is Where the Heart is. That is true. I am the keeper of the hearts of this family. I am also the keeper of their souls. The souls of the past generations protect and strengthen those that come after them and that is exactly what

happened this fateful day. Evelyn, Edward and Katherine had come Home.
And Ron never called me Home again.

Chapter 29

PRESENT DAY

The siblings ride to the attorney's office together in silence, each lost in his and her private thoughts. Each of them feels a little sad, a bit angry, and a lot tired. They haven't reached any sort of agreement over the past few days, although each has been slowly realizing the inevitable. I nervously watched them drive away to this meeting that would decide my fate. What would happen to me? Would they ever truly understand the importance of a Home? Were they even capable of understanding? After all, they were nomads of sorts – finding their "homes" wherever they landed. Except for Anna, each had bought and sold many houses through their adult lives, moving from place to place – even across the globe in some instances -- like it was the most natural thing to do. They had no more roots than the small, brightly colored annuals that lined their manicured flower-beds each spring and died each winter. But I had real roots. Like the Christmas trees that Jim and Marie had planted around my yard, I was invested. My roots ran deep. Would these siblings be the generation that yanked those roots up?

Caroline rides in the back seat going over all of the legal issues in her head. She has read through the trust documents and wills and she is quite familiar with the legalities involved. All of the land and the houses had been placed into the trust, of which each sibling would inherit equal shares. But this arrangement works only

239

if they can all agree on what to do with the property. As a lawyer, Caroline knows that if they can't agree, one sibling could simply ask the court to order a sale and distribute the proceeds. She expects their parents' lawyer simply wanted to go over the documents and make sure that they all understand them. She isn't looking forward to sitting through a long meeting and certainly does not want everyone to start arguing about selling the house in front of the attorney. She is hoping this meeting is just a formality and they can all just say that they understand their rights and that they are still discussing the matter and be done with it for today. She isn't ready for a final decision. She needs more time.

Caroline had always felt like her mother would live forever and this whole thing just doesn't seem real. Marie had been the glue that held the whole family together – not just their immediate family but also the cousins, the second cousins, and even beyond. "Auntie Marie" was the one everyone turned to for advice, for comfort, for … mothering.

Caroline watches the familiar trees and houses go by as Alden drives toward the harbor where the attorney's office is located. They pass the house that had belonged to Uncle Frank and Aunt Grace. They turn onto Country Way where they pass the brand new house that stands where the Litchfield's house had been – where their newly wed parents had lived when Alden was born. A little further down, they pass the graveyard where Frank and Grace are buried, Edward and Evelyn's graves just a few rows over, and now Jim and Marie's next to theirs. Suddenly Caroline's skin prickles with heat and her ears start ringing. She feels a panic rising in her chest. "Stop, Alden!" she says softly.

"What?" Alden asks, meeting her eyes in the rearview mirror.

"Stop!" she says a little too loudly. Then, softly, "Please. I need to go to the cemetery for a minute."

"Caroline, the attorney is expecting us in ten minutes," Anna reminds her.

"I know. But…I know. Can you just call him and tell him we are running a bit late? I need a few minutes. I have to talk to Mom. Just a few minutes." A tear rolls down her cheek and Anna nods and motions for Alden to turn around.

240

Alden parks the car on the gravel path inside the cemetery and they get out. Caroline takes a deep breath, inhaling the scent of the maple trees, the overgrown grass, and the rich New England soil. Of all the places she has lived, nowhere else smells quite like Massachusetts in the summer. It's a raw, earthy smell that is new and alive. She thinks it is because the ground is frozen over the long, cold winters and the naked trees hibernate for so long that when Spring finally arrives and the earth again becomes alive, and the trees thrust their leaves out into the world with such desperation and exuberance that the smells are amplified threefold. Whatever it is, it smells like Home. Caroline inhales deeply as the memories of her childhood race through her mind. She remembers running through the fields around their house when Nana used to let the grass grow tall. She would have to strip off all of her clothes afterward and check carefully for ticks, but Mom hadn't cared. She remembers setting up plastic kiddie pools and splashing away on hot summer days – the pool quickly becoming full of grass clippings from her and her sibling's wet feet as they ran through the yard, belly flopping into the icy cold hose water. She remembers throwing balls for their dogs – Benji the English Sheep/St Bernard mix, then Sneakers, the crazy black lab, then Cosby, the fluffy black newfoundland – Mom had always loved great big dogs complete with slobbery jowls and thick, unmanageable fur. All of these memories flash through her mind, conjured up simply by the smell of the pungent grass. Caroline opens her eyes and looks at her siblings.

"I'm sorry, guys. I don't know what I was thinking. I guess I have been running on autopilot since Mom's death. It has all been such a shock to me. I need to say goodbye to her, to feel her, before I can talk to anyone outside of the family about what to do with the house."

"Cee, you were here for the funeral," Thomas says patiently, a concerned scowl on his brow. "We all said goodbye then. That was months ago. You okay? That was you who was here, right?"

Caroline laughs and nods. "Of course that was me. But, it wasn't real somehow. I don't know. I guess it was just so fast and maybe I was still in shock. And all the people that were there – so many cousins, aunts, uncles, nieces, nephews. And boy, all the friends and townspeople. It was such a wonderful tribute to have such a giant crowd of people come to pay respects and share their love and memories. But it was all so overwhelming and I was on autopilot. I guess I just don't feel like I got to say a proper good-bye. Just us, you know? This probably makes no sense, but I need to feel it all again before I can talk about any possibility of letting it all go."

"It makes perfect sense, sis," Alden says rubbing Caroline's back. "We all dispersed to our homes in different states after the funeral and I also sometimes have to remind myself that it even happened and that it's real. I find myself picking up the phone to call her only to put it back down when I remember that she is gone."

"Not me," Anna says. "I am reminded every day that she is gone. I see people around town who stop me and want to talk to me about her. Some just want to reminisce about high school. Others want to thank me for all the conservation work she did in town, among other things. You know she was very instrumental in saving the Ellis Property from development, and also the old Gates School. She made some enemies along the way – boy, those in favor of new development weren't happy with her at all – but most of the people in town think of her as a small-town hero."

"She was a hero," Thomas chokes out, tears stinging his eyes. Caroline wraps her arms around her little brother. "She was. She was a true Mother – to everyone and to this town," Caroline whispers. "Let's just remember her and celebrate her for a few moments before we talk to an attorney about … well, about … moving on."

✝✝✝✝

After the siblings left for the attorney's office, I was left alone, to just sit helpless and await whatever fate they decided for me. Oh how I wanted to be with them – to tell this attorney person what I wanted, what the right thing to do is. How do people just decide to throw away their history? How do they simply move away and leave everything behind? After everything we have been through, from the deaths to the births, from the heartbreaks to the healing, you don't just turn your back and walk away. Of course, I have no understanding of this thing they call "money" or how it affects their decisions. But whatever it is, is it really bigger than our family and our legacy? I think about Evelyn and Edward and how they loved me. They would have never dreamed of leaving me, let alone selling me to some strangers. They had three kids and had to figure out this inheritance thing, whatever that means. They managed to find a way to make sure I stayed in the family. Evelyn certainly had her opportunities to live in bigger and nicer houses. Frank and Grace's house just down the street is fancier than I am. And Grace's brother, Alden's house on Booth Hill Road, with the widows walk and circular wrap around porches was certainly far more grand. Evelyn had inherited them all. Evelyn could have kept any of those houses to make as her home. But instead, she sold both of those and stayed right here, with me — the little old farmhouse where she had created her family and where her memories lived. Marie shared Evelyn's strong ties to family history and allowed me to provide a wonderful home to her and her children. I guess, though, that the military way of life, with all of its uprooting and moving, prevented her oldest children from feeling the strong bonds of "Home." To them, I guess I am just another house that sheltered them for a short while before they spread their wings and left on their own — keeping with the transient lifestyle they had grown up with.

But, Anna! She belongs here. She knows every single inch of me the way Evelyn and Marie did. She feels the souls of those that came before her still present in my rooms. She has struggled here and loved here. She has lived here. Anna's roots are firmly planted within me and I know that, despite her claims of wanting to move to Florida, she belongs here. She may have to leave for a while to find out who she is without Marie or her children influencing her decision, but she will be back. And I should be here waiting for her with open doors to welcome her Home.

But how? I am powerless to ensure that happens. The decision is in the hands of the four siblings and I am at their mercy. The worry overwhelms me and I begin to groan under the weight of my helplessness. Suddenly, I feel a calmness enter me, soothing me, telling me not to worry. I settle instantly as I realize Marie is here. And she is surrounded by Katherine who seems to encase her like a giant hug. They are letting me know that things are going to be okay. They are laughing and filled with joy and light and sisterly love. They implore

me to remember. They want to celebrate the day that they were reunited, forever
– the day that Marie came Home.

Chapter 30

THE END OF AN ERA

Marie woke early – long before the sun. Despite the early hour, she felt strangely energetic. Her joints, which had become quite achy over the years, didn't hurt. She felt rested and wide-awake as she looked around the small, pink bedroom. Marie liked being in this room. It was one of the original rooms in the house and it was comforting to be here. She had left the pink wallpaper with the small floral print that she hung long ago and she surveyed it now, remembering the day she hung it after Alden had left for college. It was surprisingly still in good shape. She and Jim had planned to renovate the house a bit after Anna's kids left, but Jim's health had deteriorated and he hadn't the energy to tackle most of the projects. They had updated the kitchen with new appliances and countertops and had brought back the antique furniture, including her mother's old dining room set. But then Jim had died in his sleep and she hadn't gotten around to re-doing the wallpaper in the kitchen and dining room like she wanted. She was planning to tackle that project during the winter when it was too cold to go outside and do much of anything else. But today was going to be a beautiful Fall day – Marie's favorite time of year – and she was feeling too good to stay inside. She got up and shuffled to the kitchen to put on a pot of coffee.

As Marie stood by the sliding doors in the living room, wrapped in her favorite terrycloth robe and sipping her black coffee, she looked out over the still dark back yard and thought of her family. Her very first memories are right here, with her mother, father, brother, and sister. Sure, she had moved around and had enjoyed the adventures and made wonderful friends who felt like family. But no place had ever felt like home to her other than right here, under this roof. Even the years she spent living in the "new" house next door while Anna raised her family here in the original house, Marie hadn't felt quite at home. Jim had questioned why she wanted to move into the main house after Anna left. "Why do we want that big space now? And to move all of our things is such a hassle when we are settled in nicely right here," he had said. He had had a point but she had insisted. She wanted to be Home – in her childhood house.

But now, there were no kids to run around that big yard and leave sandy bathing suits strewn in the summer grass; nobody to make snowmen or ice skate on the back pond in the winter; nobody to check for ticks after playing in the back woods. Things were quiet. After the drama and endless activities of Anna's family, the calmness was welcomed. But Marie missed the kids and the energy they brought to the house. This house was meant to be a Home. It was perfectly suited for a big family, with its sprawling yard, many rooms, and its lived-in warmth.

As Marie stared into the darkness, she wondered what would happen. Her own kids were scattered across the country and didn't want to live here. Even if they did, their kids were already grown. And none of them were ready to settle down here – they were still out finding themselves, finishing college, getting jobs, and figuring out who they wanted to be. Everyone it seemed had either grown out of the Home or didn't quite fit into it yet. Jim had agonized over how to handle the disposition of the house. It had driven him crazy that there was no perfect solution, nobody to neatly step into the role as master of the Home. He had once, years ago, begged Marie to sell it and suggested they could take the money and travel the world. Marie had laughed. She had no desire to travel to foreign lands where she didn't speak the language and the culture wasn't familiar and Jim had already seen the world in his career with the Navy. Marie and Jim had both liked where they were and they ultimately agreed that they wanted to stay put, right here, in the town she adored. Marie was done leaving. It was time to stay.

After the sun rose and brightened the morning into the type of perfect, crisp autumn day that endeared New England to Marie's heart, she dressed in a pair of khaki slacks and a soft, pink cashmere sweater. She pulled on her favorite Merrell's, and wrapped a blue paisley scarf around her neck. She was going for a walk in her favorite place to explore – the Ellis property that abutted her own. Marie had grown up exploring the large tract of land that had been owned by the elderly Ellis sisters. The sisters had lived together in a beautiful, antique, Victorian home and owned thirty acres of some of the most beautiful wooded property on the South Shore. The land was filled with beautiful pines, oaks, and maples, and was dotted with small ponds and streams. Abundant wildlife called this land home and Marie had never grown tired of searching for deer, owls, fox, raccoons, and many species of beautiful birds. When the Ellis sisters had passed away, they generously donated the land to the town of Scituate for conservation purposes. All of Marie's life those woods had been a haven for the town's people to escape to, walk through, reflect upon, and enjoy.

But sometime in the early 2000's, the town administration had somehow convinced the people that the land should be built upon. After a hotly contested vote, the people approved the town's plan to carve out almost twenty acres, which they clear-cut of the beautiful trees, displaced the animals, and erected a 30,000 square foot structure to house the town's firefighters, police and town administrative offices. Marie had been beside herself. Before they could destroy the remaining acreage, Marie educated herself on land use laws in Massachusetts, contacted the Attorney General, organized a large group of concerned citizens and fought to keep the land as conservation land. Jim had watched his wife in awe as she became somewhat of an expert in conservation rules and spearheaded the arduous effort to save her beloved forest. After much opposition from the town and a year-long battle, Marie finally succeeded in convincing the town administration to confirm the remaining acres as conservation land and record an instrument to that effect that would not be able to be refuted or rescinded. While her efforts had angered some, most people in town hailed

Marie as a hero. But she hadn't done it for accolades or gratitude. She had done it simply because she had loved the town, loved that land, and had loved the Ellis sisters. It had been the right thing to do. As she walked, with the bright sun sparkling through the red and gold autumn leaves, filling her pockets with fallen chestnuts. She breathed in the fresh autumn air and thanked God for all the gifts she had been given and also for the strength to fight to preserve them.

Marie returned from her walk, refreshed and exhilarated. The natural beauty of the woods always filled her with a sense of self and belonging, as if the soles of her feet had been freshly born of the roots of her ancestry that mingled just underground with the those of the trees that lined her path. This was her land. This was her Home. She sang to herself as she fixed a hot cup of tea and sat at the old walnut writing desk that had been her Uncle Alden's. The walk had cleared her mind and had inspired her to do something that she had been contemplating for a while. She wanted to write it down before she forgot or before she reconsidered. She had made a promise to her dying sister many years earlier and she had been slow in keeping it. There had been reasons for that but now was the time to finish it, to fix things. And, ironically, the thing she had promised so long ago to fix might be just the thing to fix something for her. She laughed and shook her head and wondered why she hadn't thought of this before. A sense of completion and fulfillment spread through her as she put her pen to paper and wrote two letters. When she finished writing, she put the letters in an envelope, addressed them to her lawyer, and placed the envelope on the glass table on the breezeway for the mailman to pick up. She felt a sense of closure and peace that was long overdue.

That night as she slept, she dreamed she was walking through the woods. It was dark but she had no trouble finding her way through the paths she had known her entire life. She was searching for something and her heart was racing, but she wasn't scared. She felt excited about what she was looking for but also a bit agitated that she couldn't find it. Suddenly she came out of the woods and stood in her own back yard, staring at the house in which she grew

248

up. She began crossing the grassy field toward the back door but the more she walked, the farther away she was from reaching the door. Her legs felt heavy and became impossible to move. Her heart began to beat faster and she felt panicked. *Wake up!* her mind commanded. *Wake up. It's a dream. Be calm and open your eyes.* Something caught her eye and she turned her head to the right. Three children were playing in an overgrown field. She recognized two as her brother, William, and sister, Katherine. But they were very young. The other child was a lovely young girl whom she did not know, but the girl was staring at her and smiling. A sweetness and light emanated from her and captivated Marie, and she moved toward the girl. Her legs were no longer paralyzed and she walked slowly through the grass toward the threesome. As she got closer, suddenly William and Katherine were no longer children. They were young adults, beautiful and healthy. The other remained a child. They were all smiling at her now and a wave of happiness spread through her, filling her with love.

Suddenly she heard someone calling her name and she turned back toward the house. Her mother, also young and beautiful, was standing in the back door to the kitchen (but where was the breezeway? It had been there a moment ago!). She was calling to Marie to come inside for dinner. Marie heard her mother laugh and suddenly Marie's father was there, pulling her mother her into a hug. Evelyn turned to Edward and then they danced in the doorway, twirling around and around. Evelyn threw her head back and laughed and then Edward leaned down and kissed her.

Marie's heart leapt and she began running to the house calling to them. "Mum! Dad!! I'm coming!"

This time she was able to move freely through the tall grass. In fact, she didn't feel her legs moving at all – she just sort of floated to the kitchen door. The kitchen looked just like it had when she was a child. She stepped through the door and they were all there; Evelyn, Edward, William and Katherine - even Jim, standing by the window in his dress white uniform. "Oh how I've missed you all!" Marie said as they circled around her. Then they were all hugging her at once – a big circle of family and happiness that glowed and filled the room with the brightest light of joy and love that Marie had ever known. At that moment she knew she was truly Home.

Hallelujah!

Chapter 31

PRESENT DAY

Anna parks the car in the Mill Wharf lot, behind the old Welch Company building, and the four siblings walk across the familiar parking lot. Caroline remembers shopping at the Welch Company with her mother and her grandmother when she was a kid. It was one of those local stores that carried everything from shoes and clothes to furniture and home décor. Caroline is fairly certain that they had even sold horse feed back in the day. The store took up the whole building, which was an entire block long. Her family had once maintained an account there, where they could shop on credit without the need for a credit card. But the Welch Company went out of business years ago and now the building is divided into several spaces, occupied by boutiques, clothing stores, a restaurant, and several professional offices.

Attorney, Rich Belsan, a longtime friend of Jim and Marie's, occupies a small office in the back of the building where he operates a general law practice when he isn't out fishing on the small skiff he keeps tied to a dock across the parking lot. Anna simultaneously knocks and opens the door with a small sign saying only, "Rich Belsan, Attorney at Law."

"Come on in," Mr. Belsan welcomes them personally as they enter the tiny office. "Whoa, you shooah look like your mothah," he blurts in a thick Boston accent as he focuses on Caroline.

"So I've been told," Caroline replies, smiling.

Mr. Belsan turns to greet Anna with a kiss on the cheek. "How ya doin' sweet-haht? Hangin' in theyah? How are things ovah at the bah? Still beatin' off the old townies?"

"Yep, beating them off with a stick, Rich. You know how it is." Anna laughs.

Anna turns to Alden and Thomas, "Have you ever met my brothers?"

"Hi, I'm Alden Freeman," Alden's deep voice is very serious as he reaches to shake Rich's hand.

"I remembah when you were boahn," Rich says shaking Alden's firm grip.

"And I'm Thomas," Thomas interjects, stepping forward and reaching his hand out.

"Damn those Lockhaht genes run deep," Rich smiles at Thomas. "You look just like yoah uncle Ed. Well, good to meet you all. Why don't you come on in and have a seat. I have just a few things to talk to you kids about."

Mr. Belsan ushers them over to a small, round conference room table. Caroline notices that he is watching each of them as they take their seats as if trying to size them up. Caroline has an unsettling feeling that he is more than just curious about them or interested in how much they resemble their relatives. He actually seems a bit nervous, which Caroline thinks is odd as he obviously deals with families of dead relatives and estate issues all of the time. Mr. Belsan smiles widely as he takes a seat between Alden and Anna. He places a well-worn, brown legal shuck on the table in front of him. He is suddenly completely composed and at ease, and Caroline laughs at herself for thinking he appeared nervous. After all, what could he possibly be nervous about? This is a straightforward matter and he must know that each of them has already reviewed the trust documents. This meeting should be simply a formality. Still, Caroline can't shake the feeling that this situation is anything but "typical."

"Thank you fah coming today," attorney Belsan says, smiling at them. "As you know, I am Richard Belsan, yoah parents' attorney and long-time friend. I am so very sorry for the loss of your Mothah. She was a damn good woman. I nevah did undahstand why she married yoah fathah though. She was always way too good for that sonofabitch." He winks at Anna and chuckles. Caroline smirks at the thick, dropped-r accent and casual, small-town demeanor. She isn't offended by his words - she knows from her father's Facebook posts that Rich Belsan had been part of an old man's breakfast group her father had met with every morning for years and that their father had been very fond of his old friend.

"Thank you, Mr. Belsan," Caroline responds, looking from him to her siblings. Thomas and Alden look uncomfortable and Caroline wonders if they are simply put off by Mr. Belsan's overly casual manner or if something else is troubling them. "We know how close you were to both of our parents," she added just in case her brothers weren't aware of the friendship.

"Yes, yes, we knew each othah since high school. We were very close." A hint of nostalgia clouds the old attorney's eyes and he looks down at his hands. He suddenly looks old and tired and Caroline feels like they should be consoling him instead of the other way around. After a brief silence, he looks up and says, "Well, I'm shooah you all don't have all day to reminisce with an old man so shall we get down ta business?"

"Please! That would be great," Thomas replies with a barely detectable hint of impatient sarcasm. Caroline shoots him a look that says *be patient!*

Attorney Belsan just smiles and nods and opens his shuck. He passes a folder to each sibling.

"The foldah you are holding contains the wills of each of yoah parents as well as the trust documents they prepared that governs how the houses and propahty on North Hill will be passed down. I know that you have seen these befoah so they should come as no surprise. Basically, all of the real propahty has been put in a trust, in which you each own a quartah share. In othah words, you each inherit a one-foahth interest in the houses and the surrounding real propahty. The separate wills spell out specifics on monetary interests and personal propahty inheritance, such as who gets the jewelry, furnichah, how life insurance proceeds are split, and whatnot. Of coahse, if any of you want to trade things with each othah, you ah free to make those arrangements on yoah own.

253

There are provisions for the grandchildren as well. That paht is pretty simple and I can let you look ovah it all on yoah own. Of coahse, if you have any questions, please feel free to call me." Mr. Belsan then clears his throat and shifts to the right in his seat and then back again.

He IS nervous. Caroline thinks to herself. *What is going on?*

"Now… um… the biggah issue is obviously the real propahty," he continues. "This includes the family home and the smallah house next doah. Have you guys talked about what you want to do with that propahty? I mean, ya don't need a final decision right now or anything but surely you have talked about it. How's that going?" His eyes flit expectantly from one sibling to the other.

"We have discussed it quite a bit, actually," Alden replies in his deep voice that anchors Mr. Belsan's gaze on him. Caroline can't help but be impressed by her older brother's natural ability to command attention just by speaking a few words. "We have not come to any final consensus of what we would like to do yet. We are going to need more time."

"Do we though, Alden?" Thomas interrupts, giving Alden an impatient look. "What for? So we can keep arguing and getting nowhere? I don't want to keep the house. I have no interest in using it or trying to manage and maintain it. And you know you don't either. So, really, we don't need more time. What we need is to know what happens if we can't all agree."

Here it is, Caroline thinks. *This is where he learns that he can ask for immediate liquidation and distribution of proceeds. Anna is going to lose her shit if he demands that today.*

"Whoa, now hold on Thomas," Caroline cuts in. Let's not go there quite yet. We haven't had enough time to research the market and explore all of our options. I wouldn't say we can't agree yet – we don't even really know what we are trying to agree on."

"Seriously, Caroline?" Thomas fires back. "It's not that complicated. We are trying to agree on whether to keep it or sell it. It's irrelevant to me what the market is. I can't, and don't want to, hang on to the house and worry about maintenance costs and taxes. We *have* discussed this exhaustively and I am done talking about it. I don't want to drag this out and, while we are here talking to Mr.

Belsan, I want to know what my options are if you guys won't agree to sell."

"I am interested in the answer to that question also," Alden says.

Caroline sighs. There it is. No getting around it now. "Fine. Of course we should know all of our options. And we should all fully understand the consequences of our decisions." Caroline stares directly at Thomas as she reaches under the table to take Anna's hand. Anna is trembling. Mr. Belsan sits up straight and clears his throat. Caroline squeezes Anna's hand tighter as she braces herself.

"Well, actually, now that you've asked," Mr. Belsan starts, "this is actually why I called you guys in today. I wanted to find out how you all felt about your inheritance and whethah there is any disagreement. Now that I know theyah is, I want to discuss with yahs a last minute change yoah mothah made to the trust documents. She was worried that yahs might not be able to agree on what to do with the propahty and so she made some changes that might help yah. But theyah is... um, well... theyah is something that will come as a surprise. It may upset yas. But then again, it may not. Yoah mothah wasn't shooah how you would react to the news. She was planning to tell yahs herself but she had to wait because, well, you'll see in a minute. She wrote some lettah's in case she died befoah she had a chance to tell yas. And, uh... well, that happened, so I called yah heeyah to show yah the lettahs."

Mr. Belsan reaches into his shuck and pulls out four envelopes, each bearing a sibling's name with their mother's distinct, loopy, cursive handwriting. He puts them neatly in front of him but does not hand them out. He reaches back into the shuck and pulls out another envelope with the name "Jackson Scott" written in the same curly handwriting. Caroline frowns, confused. Who is Jackson Scott? She looks to each of her siblings to see if they know what is going on. Alden shrugs. Thomas shakes his head.

Anna, who hates surprises and is clearly growing impatient, says "Rich, what the hell? Just tell us what's going on. What are these envelopes?"

"I'm about to tell yah, Anna," Rich replies kindly. He points to the four envelopes grouped together. "These envelopes contain a lettah to each of yahs. It's the same lettah in each envelope but she

255

wanted yahs each to read it silently togethah. I will pass them out in a moment. First, howevah, she wanted me to read this lettah aloud. But, because my throat is dry and my accent is horrible, I'm going to have Alden heeyah, with the good speaking voice, read it for me. Alden, do ya mind?"

The room is quiet as Mr. Belsan opens the envelope bearing the stranger's name and smooths out a one-page letter, handwritten by their mother. He hands it to Alden who adjusts his glasses, clears his throat and reads aloud:

"Dear Jackson,

It has been such a pleasure getting to know you over the past several months. You are a wonderful young man and seeing the fine man you have grown into has brought me great joy and peace. If you are reading this, I have passed on to join my sister, your mother, in heaven. I am so thankful that I will be able to meet her in paradise with the wonderful news that I found you and that you are a beautiful person. Please don't be sad – rejoice for me, as I have had an amazing life.

By now my lawyer has called you to explain why I am writing to you. I have thought long and hard about this. When Katherine was dying she asked me to "fix" what she believed to be her greatest mistake: giving you up and never trying to find you even after you had grown. I know her reasons for putting you up for adoption and I know it was not easy for her. I also know she didn't try to look for you after you had grown. But please know that she thought of you every single day for the rest of her life. You and I have discussed all of this already and I won't rehash it here. As I've told you, I believe she had her reasons. She was a deeply emotional person and, frankly, I'm not sure she believed she would have the strength to see you and look into your eyes, seeing all that she missed out on. She obviously regretted her decisions.

I was not sure what she meant for me to do when she looked up at me on her deathbed and asked me to "fix"

256

things. It took me years to even begin the process of looking for you. Even after I found you, I still didn't know what else I could do. Thankfully, you had wonderful adoptive parents and you have had a nice life. There really isn't much for me to "fix" as you are not a broken man. And I don't have a time machine to change the past. But then I thought about her request and I realized that maybe she didn't mean that I needed to fix the past, but that I could somehow try to repair the hole that was created -- in her heart, in our family history, and your heritage -- by your absence.

As I was sitting in my kitchen one evening, drinking a cup of tea, I glanced up and noticed a crack that runs up the wall. The crack has been there my entire life. I don't know when it first occurred. I only know that every attempt to repair it ends up only being temporary and it always seems to return. It's just part of the house. I'm not really sure what the crack has to do with all of this or why I'm telling you about it, other than staring at it got me thinking about the house and our family's history there. The house has been in our family since the early 1900's. It was built in 1847 by the ancestor of our dear family friends. It has been passed down through the generations and its walls hold our family's history. If the house could talk, you would learn about your great grandparents, aunts, uncles, cousins and, of course, about your biological mother. The house has stories to tell and you deserve to know them.

As I've told you, I have four children. They are independent, strong, wonderful people and I hope you will get to know them. They live very spread out – from San Diego to Florida. None of them desires to live in Scituate full-time and I am pretty sure that right about now they are struggling with the idea of selling the house and they are probably arguing over the quandary I have put them in by virtue of their inheritance.

You have told me that you are married and that you have two children, and that you are currently renting a home in western Massachusetts. I would like to give you the option of

257

moving to Scituate and living in our family Home. It is a lovely house but, you should know it will require quite a bit of maintenance that you would need to keep up with. But, you could live there, for free, as long as you like. If you decide to leave, or when you die, the house would revert back to the trust that I have set up and would be left to my children and grandchildren. Basically, you would have what my lawyer has told me is called a "life estate." He can go over the legalities with you.

Jackson, please understand that I do not presume to know what is best for you and I have no idea if you would even want to move from where you are to live in Scituate. If you do not wish to accept this, my children will inherit the home as originally intended. There is no pressure on you one way or the other. This is the only thing I could think to do that might begin to heal the mistakes of the past. And, as I said, I know that nothing I can do will change the past. But this might give you a chance to take your place in this family. Our history lives within those walls. I am inviting you to get to know it if you wish.

Whichever you decide, please know that I am so thankful to have met you. As far as I'm concerned, you are, and always have been, a part of this family. My children are good people and, though they may be upset with my decision, they will accept it and they will welcome you. If they don't, I will haunt them! Ha ha. Good luck, Jackson.

With love,

Your Aunt Marie"

Alden slowly hands the letter back to Mr. Belsan and removes his glasses. The room is silent as confusion and shock register on each face at the conference table. Mr. Belsan stands and places the other envelopes in front of each sibling. He pauses at the conference room door.

"Befoah you all say anything or discuss this, please read what is in the envelope. I am going to step out to give yahs some privacy." He exits, quietly shutting the door behind him.

Alden, Caroline, Thomas and Anna exchange silent glances, too shocked to say a word. Then they each open an envelope and begin to silently read:

"My Dearest Children,

I cannot begin to express to you how much I love each of you. Being your mother has been the greatest privilege of my life. I know my death must be hard on all of you. But please don't be sad for me. Dying is part of living and I would never trade all the living I got to do. I am in a good place now — home in heaven with your father, my family, and our Lord.

Speaking of "home," I know that I left you all with a terribly difficult decision to make. I am sorry about that. Please understand that I simply could not bear to see my family home sold while I was alive. I do not wish to force it on any of you, however. And I certainly don't want it to be a source of contention between the four of you. If you are reading this letter, then I am guessing that is exactly what is happening — you cannot agree on what to do. Please understand that I don't blame you for that. I know that none of you want to live in Scituate forever. I suppose I was hoping that you would all agree to keep our Home as a vacation house for the four of you and your families and that somehow you could all work together to make that happen. But I also know that such an arrangement is likely not practical and the costs of maintaining the old house must be daunting. I anticipated this and that is why Mr. Belsan has called you in today.

By now, Mr. Belsan will have read to you another letter I wrote — a letter to your cousin, Jackson. I am sorry that I didn't tell you about him sooner. I only just found him recently. He asked me not to tell the family about him until he was ready. Unfortunately, if you are learning about him

259

for the first time as you read this, it means that God didn't grant me enough time to allow that to happen.

Jackson is your Aunt Katherine's son. He was born in 1968, one year after Alden, and during a very tough time in Katherine's life. I need you all to understand that Katherine was not a bad person. She was simply in a bad place at the time. We had just lost our father and Stephen had walked out on her. She was hurt and confused and she made some poor choices. She became pregnant by a man who didn't really love her and who did not want children. He refused to support her or the baby, and she felt that she had no choice but to give the baby up. I begged Katherine to let me raise her baby but she refused, feeling that it would not be fair to me and your father (we were young newlyweds with a new baby of our own) and that it would be too emotional for her to watch her sister raise her child. Nana tried to convince her also, but her mind was made up. She left to have the baby at a convent in Western Massachusetts. When he was born, she gave him up for adoption. She never even held him. We never knew what happened to her baby after his birth. The laws at the time prevented the adoption agency from telling us anything about his adoption or his whereabouts. Katherine was terribly ashamed and heartbroken and insisted that nobody know about him – not even her own children. It is a secret that only she, Nana, and I kept all of these years.

The day Katherine died, she gripped my hand and begged me to "fix" her mistake. I knew she was referring to Jackson and I promised her I would try. In honesty, it took me a long time to get started trying to find her child. I don't know why. Perhaps losing my sister was too hard and I needed time to heal. Perhaps I was still angry at her for her decision to give up her baby – something that I could not fathom no matter the circumstances. Perhaps I was afraid of what I would find. I am not sure I could have handled finding out that his story didn't turn out well. Maybe it was all of the above. Regardless, it took me several years to even start looking. When I did, I contacted your cousin Katie and told her about her lost half brother. She helped me search. With the help of the internet, we found him within a year and he agreed to meet with us.

The moment I saw Jackson, I recognized his face immediately. My sister's eyes stared back at me. I was so overcome with emotion that I thought I might scare him off. But he was kind and gracious and wanted to know about our family. Jackson has had a good life. He was adopted by a nice couple and was raised in Western Massachusetts. His adoptive father was a banker and his mother a school teacher. He did not have siblings. He has a wife and two teenaged children. He is a bit shy, but he is a wonderful man.

I hope you four are not upset with me for offering to allow him to live in the family home. I don't expect you to fully understand everything that I have been feeling, but it feels like the right thing to do and I am hopeful that you will all at least try to comprehend my decision. Our home is as much a part of Jackson's heritage as it is yours. Katherine's dying request was that I somehow "fix" the one mistake that caused her so much pain and regret. While I realize that I do not have the power to "fix" the past, and I also realize it is not up to you all to do so or even sacrifice what is rightfully yours, I am hoping each of you will find it in your hearts to respect my wishes and forgive me, forgive your aunt and forgive your grandmother for keeping this deep secret. I have always taught you that it is not healthy to keep secrets from family and I am truly sorry that you have to learn that we kept this one from you and your cousins. It was Katherine's wish that nobody know. By now, Katie has told Stephen, Jr, Mary, and Bill and I hope and pray that they find it in their hearts to forgive their mother and accept Jackson into their lives as their brother. I suspect it won't be easy for them.

I know it may not seem fair that Jackson be permitted to live in our family home. But it gives me peace to be able to offer him a chance to really know his heritage. Of course, one or all of you may still decide that you want to keep the house. His rights only kick in if none of you are willing or able to keep it. In that case, rather than you selling it, Jackson will have a life estate and will have the option to the live in the main house for his lifetime. At his death, or if he vacates the home, the house will revert back to the trust and will be inherited by you and/or your heirs. Of course, he may not want to live there and, in that case, you are back to where you were before you saw these letters. I know it sounds complicated but Rich can walk you through the details.

The remainder of the property, including the side house and the vacant land are unaffected by this arrangement and the four of you are free to do with those as you wish. You will also have the life insurance and your father's retirement accounts. I hope that you will all be satisfied with this arrangement and will honor my wishes.

My beautiful children, please know how much I love you all. Being your mother was everything I ever wanted. I cannot imagine my life without each of you. How Katherine lived out her days not knowing her baby boy, I will never comprehend. But, after years of anger, hurt, and watching her struggle with her demons, I learned it was not my place to judge her. She did what she felt was right at the time. I have been beyond blessed to have you all and your children to love and cherish. Please live your lives in happiness, love, and forgiveness. I will always be with you.

All my Love,

Mom."

The conference room is thick with emotion as each sibling finishes reading the letter. Tears stream down the girls' faces and Alden and Thomas rub at red eyes. Nobody looks up for several minutes. Finally, Alden takes a deep breath. "Wow," he says softly. "I didn't see any of this coming."

Thomas nods his head in agreement. "Anna, did you know anything about this?"

262

Anna clears her throat and sighs heavily. "No. Nothing. I knew Mom had been spending a lot of time with Katie lately, but they have always been close so I didn't think anything of it. I can't believe she didn't tell me."

The room again falls silent, each sibling lost in his and her own thoughts. Caroline reads the letter again and then looks around the room. From each of her siblings' expressions, she has no doubt that, for the first time all week, they are all in agreement.

She puts the letter down, sends up a silent prayer to her mother and her aunt and says, smiling "Well, guys, it looks like we have a cousin to get to know."

EPILOGUE

It has been six months since the siblings learned of their cousin and their mother's decision. Now, they are gathered together in my kitchen, the mood light and joyful. Alden is smiling with his arm around Anna's shoulders as she laughs at one of his jokes. Thomas leans against the counter, a beer in his hand and chimes in with Alden, regurgitating some old movie line, making Anna laugh even harder. Caroline, looking tanned and relaxed, watches the three of them and feels a sense of deep peace. Caroline arrived from Florida two days ago. Her brothers flew in yesterday. This time, they all feel good to be Home. I am like a mother hen with my flock exactly where they belong and I feel incredibly full and satisfied. Marie and Jim are here with me, watching their children and feeling their love. Katherine is here also. This is her chance to take care of some unfinished business. She is the only one whose energy radiates some disturbance. But it is slight.

The sound of car doors slamming catches everyone's attention and they look at each other with raised eyebrows as if to say, in unison, *Here we go!* Caroline stands and pulls open the breezeway door. Cold January air rushes in as two visitors step into the kitchen.

"Well, hello there!" Caroline greets her cousin Katie with a big hug and kiss on the cheek. "I am so glad you could both come today!" She then extends her hand to the stranger next to Katie. "Hi Jackson. I'm Caroline. I am Marie's daughter. Come on in, let's get your coat off and introduce you to everyone."

As the introductions are made with hugs and handshakes, I can barely contain myself. Oh how I wish I had arms! The middle-aged man standing in my kitchen looks just like his mother. As he stands next to Katie, it is clear that the two are related. The physical resemblance is undeniable. I can feel that this man is family. After living with the souls of this family for close to one hundred years, I know their aura, their energy, their nature. And the spirit that emanates from this man is unmistakably part Edward, part Evelyn, and part Katherine and it blends and mixes with those of the other people in my kitchen as if they had been born of the same origin. Which, of course, they have. They are Family.

I feel Katherine move into the kitchen and her spirit glows as she stands next to the son she never knew. The child she had never even held in her arms. Now, she slowly wraps her love around him, bathing him in a light only the non-living can see. I can see it. Or rather, I can feel it. It is bright and warm and filled with a lifetime of grief, longing, guilt, and love. Marie and Jim watch with relief. A sense of healing and forgiveness saturates my walls and I feel myself strengthen.

Anna ushers everyone into the family room and offers drinks. They make small talk for a few minutes and fill Thomas in on who everyone is and a brief history of each of their families. Katie explains that Jackson has met his half-siblings but that none of them could make the trip today due to work schedules and family obligations.

"Well, so tell us…" Caroline begins, directing her gaze at Jackson. "How long had you been in touch with our mother before she died?"

"Not too long, unfortunately," Jackson says looking solemn. "I would have loved the chance to get to know her better. Katie contacted me first about two years ago I guess. I met your mother not long after that. She and Katie came to Westfield together. She was a lovely woman. I am sorry for your loss." The Freeman siblings nod and smile.

"She never said anything to us," Caroline replies. "We didn't know anything about you until the lawyer gave us her letter. Needless to say we were quite surprised." Caroline turns to Katie. "Did you know that your mom had had another baby?"

"I found out several years after my mother died," Katie says. "When she was dying, I heard her ask Aunt Marie to fix something for her. I didn't know what she was talking about then and I chalked it up to her being delirious and not making sense. When your mother first told me, I was obviously stunned and terribly hurt that my mother had never mentioned it. I can't believe she kept that a secret for so long."

"It must have been so hard," Anna says. "She probably had so much guilt and sadness. Our Mom's letter said that Nana knew?"

"Yes. Nana and your mom both knew about it when it happened. Aunt Marie said Nana was distraught and had a very hard time with it. They all did. I guess your mother even offered to take the baby and raise it as her own. I guess your mom was really upset that my mom wouldn't let her. It's kind of ironic that Aunt Marie ended up helping to raise me and Mary anyway," Katie says wistfully.

"Mom was always trying to help other people fix their mistakes," Anna says thinking of her own past.

Caroline coughs and glares at Anna for her word choice.

"Oh my God, I didn't mean to imply you were a mistake, Jackson!" Anna blurts, embarrassed. "That sounded awful. I only meant that, at the time, Katherine felt… Oh God, I'm making it worse. I will shut up now."

But Jackson just laughs and waves his hand dismissively. "No, don't apologize. Don't worry about it. I know what you meant. Whether it was a mistake or an accident or whatever, the pregnancy was not what Katherine wanted or needed at the time. Let's just leave it at that. And, your mother was gracious to offer to raise the baby – er, me – but, look, I was adopted by a wonderful family. I had a good life with parents who love me. It's all good. I am glad that your mom found me though. It's been pretty intense finding out that I have four siblings! I was an only child my whole life so this has been quite a discovery for me."

"For all of us," Katie chimes in. "That's one of the reasons it took so long to take the steps to find Jackson – your mother was quite concerned with how it would affect everyone. Mum's death was hard on me and my sister and brothers. When Aunt Marie told me I had a younger brother out there somewhere, I was shocked and frankly, somewhat upset. I was angry with my mother for not telling us and then I was worried about how everyone would take the news. I decided to keep it to myself for a while and Aunt Marie agreed to give me time to process it all. It took me over a year to tell Stephen, Bill, and Mary. And then, when I did, we didn't all agree on how we should handle it. Mary was adamant that we honor Mom's original decision to keep it a secret and not try to find him. Stephen agreed with her. So we all agreed to wait."

"But our mom had made a promise to her sister," Caroline says.

"Yes. She did. And she talked with me about it often. But life was busy for her and she had her own issues so she didn't push us. A few years ago though, on the anniversary of my mom's death, Aunt Marie called me and said she had to start looking. Even just to satisfy herself. So I told her to go ahead. It was a difficult and long process but I eventually agreed to help her. The internet made the research easier and we finally found him. Then we had to decide whether to disrupt his life with the information."

"Wow," Thomas says, rubbing his beard. "This is so crazy. Our family has always been so close – it's hard to wrap my head around that I have a cousin that I never knew. I can't believe Mom and Aunt Katherine kept this a secret for so long. I mean, Mom was always adamant that we know our relatives – aunts, great uncles, great grandparents, cousins, second cousins, first cousins twice removed, cousins of cousins, even."

Alden laughs and nods in agreement. "Well, man, it's good to get to know you, finally," he says to Jackson. Then he clears his throat, changing the mood from casual to business. "From our discussions with the lawyers, we understand you aren't planning to move here? Is that right?"

Jackson nods and smiles. "No, I'm not. Your mother's letter took me by surprise. I was shocked that she would even think of such a plan. And, while I am appreciative of her generosity, and grateful to all of you for agreeing to go along with it if that's what I chose, it's not the right thing to do. This Home belongs to all of you, not to me. I didn't grow up living here or even visiting here. The love that is present here was apparent to me the second I walked through the door – this house certainly has an energy that seems as if it has a life of its own. But I'm afraid that would be wasted on me. I am in my fifties and very well settled in my own life. I don't need a mother any longer and I don't need to live in this house to feel a sense of belonging. Knowing you all is plenty, and I am hopeful that I can work to establish a relationship with my half siblings. That is enough for me. Besides, I have a good life with a job and a wife in Westfield and my kids wouldn't want to change schools and leave their friends. It wouldn't be practical for me to move to Scituate."

"Understood," Alden replies. "Well, please know that you are welcome to visit and we would like to keep in touch. If you have any questions or anything, you can call any of us anytime."

The six of them sit and talk for a while longer, sharing stories of Katherine, Marie, and Nana and Anna breaks out some of the old photos. After an hour or so, Jackson says he must get on the road and he and Katie say their goodbyes. Caroline and Anna hug Jackson while the men shake hands. Everyone promises to keep in touch, even if just over social media. Katie hugs everyone and thanks them for being so gracious and welcoming.

After they are gone, the four siblings look at each other with expressions of wonder mixed with disbelief. As if to say "did that just happen?" It is then that I realize that Katherine has left. In her place is an aura of peace and resolution. She has forgiven herself.

Marie remains, calmly watching her children as they stand silently in the kitchen. I suddenly feel a touch of anxiety as I realize that if Jackson isn't going to move in, we are back to where we were six months ago. My fate is once again hanging in the balance. But Marie, who can feel my jitters, radiates a calmness that blankets my rooms and puts me at ease. She knows something is about to happen and she is sticking around to watch events unfold.

"Shall we go in the dining room and discuss the rest?" Caroline finally asks.

"Yes, I'll get the champagne," Anna says reaching for a bottle of Dom Perignon chilling in the refrigerator. Thomas raises an eyebrow at the expensive champagne. "Don't worry, Mom bought it." Anna replies with a wink.

Caroline reaches into a leather bag leaning against the wall and pulls out a folder and four pens and they each take a seat around the mahogany dining room table.

"Well, here we go again," Thomas says, but this time there is a lightness in his tone and laughter in his eyes.

Caroline is sitting in her same spot and she looks down at the numbers etched in the wood. *Sometimes it takes a little more than math and numbers to solve a complicated problem,* she thinks, smiling to herself.

Thirty minutes later, there is a stack of documents on the table bearing the signatures of each sibling. The first is an agreement with the town of Scituate for the subdivision of the North Hill property. It carves out the small house and side lot as one parcel, the main house and back acreage as another parcel and a third parcel consists of the property on the south side of the house. It spells out obligations to reconfigure the current driveway to two drives and plans for new septic systems and other concerns.

The second document is a contract for the sale of the small house. The buyers are a young man and his new bride. The man is the grandson of a longtime friend of Jim and Marie's who still lives in Scituate and who is thrilled that his grandson will be staying in town. The contract calls for the existing garage and breezeway to be removed so that the houses are no longer connected. Each property owner can then build a new garage if they desire.

Next to those is another contract for the sale of the half-acre vacant lot on the south side of the North Hill property. The buyers on this contract are a young couple with two elementary school aged children who just moved to Massachusetts from California. The husband is a doctor who just transferred to a practice in Boston and the wife is the newest third grade teacher at Cushing Elementary School. They plan to build a beautiful but modest Cape Cod style home on the property.

269

Another document that is rather lengthy spells out that the proceeds from the two sales will be distributed to Alden and Thomas, evenly, along with provisions regarding distribution of life insurance, retirement account proceeds and other assets to be split among the siblings.

Caroline holds up one last document and looks around the table. This one is not yet signed.

"Last one, guys," she says smiling. She passes a copy to each sibling to read and then sets a signature page in front of Alden. "You go first – you are the oldest."

Alden looks down at the document and reads aloud: "Special Warranty Deed. Grantor does hereby grant, sell, bargain and convey that certain parcel of real property with all improvements thereon, known as North Hill, and as more particularly described herein, to Caroline Freeman King and Anna Freeman ("Grantees") as joint tenants with right of survivorship."

He looks at Caroline and winks. He then turns to Anna, who is openly crying. He reaches across the table and takes her hand. "Congratulations, Little Sis," he says softly as he signs the paper and passes it to Thomas.

"Congratulations to BOTH of our sisters," Thomas says as he scribbles his name and passes the page to Anna.

"I don't know how to thank you," Anna chokes between sobs as she signs her name. She looks at Caroline and stands. She walks around the table and puts the sheet of paper in front of her sister and then pulls her sister into her arms.

Caroline squeezes her baby sister tightly and whispers, "It's our turn now." Then, she gently pulls away. "But don't thank me. thank the house!" Caroline announces as she writes her loopy signature with a flourish and then picks up her champagne flute for a toast. "Here's to our Home!"

"Here's to your book!" Thomas says rubbing his first two fingers against his thumb to represent holding money.

"Yeah," Alden replies. "Why didn't you tell us this was in the works?"

He places a copy of a hardcover book on the table. The cover depicts an old black and white photograph of a farm house with a little girl wearing a white dress, cardigan sweater, and ankle socks sitting on the front step and holding a lunch box. It is titled "The Home on North Hill."

"I guess we all have our secrets," Caroline replies, winking dramatically at them and laughing. "Cheers!"

"Cheers!" the others reply in unison.

I am in shock. Every board, window, and rafter in me stands perfectly still, afraid to move in case this is a dream or a sick joke. Suddenly, Marie, who has been standing in the corner watching her children, begins to laugh and her spirit grows larger and larger until it feels like she has wrapped her arms around my perimeter and is hugging me tightly.

"She published her book!" Marie conveys. "She has been working on it for years. She kept telling me she was struggling with the ending and that's why she didn't finish it sooner. I guess she figured it out," she cries, laughter encircling me like a welcomed storm. "She finished it and got it published! She earned enough in her publishing contract to cover the costs of maintenance and taxes for at least a few years. She and Anna are going to share it as a summer house and rent it out in the winter to cover the remaining costs. They are keeping our Home! Thank you! Thank you for everything!"

My relief at hearing this news is overwhelming. But I am also confused. Why is Marie thanking me? What did I do? Caroline is the one who wrote the book.

"Don't you see?" Marie asks, softly. "The book is about YOU! It is about our family and everyone who lived here, but mostly it is all about you. You have comforted us, protected us, changed for us, and helped heal us. It is *your* story she told, *your* voice she used. You saved us."

That night, after everyone has gone to bed, Caroline stands in the kitchen with a spackle knife in one hand and a jar of drywall compound in the other. "I know this won't be perfect," she whispers to me, softly. "But at least for now, this scar is healed."

As I said in the beginning, I am Home.

ACKNOWLEDGMENTS

My Mother, Andrea Locklin Hunt, deserves so much credit for this book. Her intense love of family, her unwavering dedication to preserving her heritage, and her passion for story-telling were my inspiration. Never stop sharing your stories, Mom. You have great ones! I love you more.

I want to thank my husband, Jack Kowalski, who encouraged me to finally write this. His confidence in me – no matter what crazy thing I try next – still takes me by surprise. I am forever yours.

My beautiful daughters deserve big hugs for their patience and support during the many hours I neglected them while I sat on the beach, scribbling away in my notebook. Johanna – thank you for reading my earliest chapters and helping me to develop my characters a little more. Your advice was incredibly insightful and spot on! Alexandra – I can't tell you how much I appreciate your reading the first draft of my manuscript as quickly as you did and for being so excited about it. You surprised and impressed me with your passion for the story and your thoughtful feedback. You girls are my sunshine.

To my friends who read parts or all of my many drafts and helped me make my life's dream come true - I can't thank you enough. Mickey O'Connell – may you have many days curled up on a couch with a good book!

ABOUT THE AUTHOR

Kirsten Hunt Kowalski was born in 1969 and was raised as a Navy brat. She moved ten times with her family before graduating from Scituate High School in 1987. She received her BA in Photojournalism from Samford University in Birmingham, Alabama in 1993 and her JD from Cumberland Law School in 1996. She and her husband, Jack live in Vero Beach, Florida with their two daughters, Alex and Jojo and their two dogs, Kai and Kona. Kirsten still practices law, is a co-owner of Tiger Lily Art Studios & Gallery where she sells her photography, and writes in her spare time. *Becoming Home* is her first novel.